D0734413

Dangerous Deceptions

A PALACE OF SPIES NOVEL

A PALACE OF SPIES NOVEL

Dangerous Deceptions

BEING THE LATEST VOLUME
IN THE ENTIRELY TRUE AND
WHOLLY REMARKABLE ADVENTURES OF
MARGARET PRESTON FITZROY, MAID OF HONOR,
IMPERSONATOR OF PERSONS OF QUALITY,
CONFIRMED HOUSEBREAKER, APPRENTICE CARDSHARPER,
AND CONFIDENTIAL AGENT AT THE COURT OF
HIS MAJESTY, KING GEORGE I.

SARAH ZETTEL

HOUGHTON MIFFLIN HARCOURT
Boston   New York

www.hmhco.com

Text set in LTC Deepdene
Design by Christine Kettner

LIBRARY OF CONGRESS CATALOGING-IN-PUBLICATION DATA
Zettel, Sarah.
Dangerous deceptions : a Palace of Spies novel : being the latest volume in the
entirely true and wholly remarkable adventures of Margaret Preston Fitzroy,
maid of honor, impersonator of persons of quality, confirmed housebreaker,
apprentice cardsharper, and confidential agent at the court of
His Majesty, King George I / Sarah Zettel.
pages cm. —(Palace of spies ; 2)
Summary: An unwelcome engagement, a mysterious plot that hints at treason,
and a possible murder add even more excitement to sixteen-year-old Peggy Fitzroy's
life as she continues to serve as both a lady in waiting and confidential agent
to King George of England.
ISBN 978-0-544-07409-5
[1. Spies—Fiction. 2. Courts and courtiers—Fiction. 3. Love—Fiction. 4. Orphans—
Fiction. 5. London (England)—History—18th century—Fiction. 6. Great Britain—
History—George I, 1714–1727—Fiction.] I. Title.
PZ7.Z448 Dan 2014
[Fic]—dc23
2013042811

Manufactured in the United States of America
DOC 10 9 8 7 6 5 4 3 2 1
4500497602

This book is dedicated to all those
who refuse to simply stand and wait.

Dangerous Deceptions

A PALACE OF SPIES NOVEL

CHAPTER ONE

London, October 1716

IN WHICH OUR HEROINE PREPARES FOR
BATTLE IN THE LATEST FASHION AND
RECEIVES AN UNWELCOME BLOW.

I begin this newest volume of my memoirs with a frank warning. Soon or late, there comes to the life of every confidential agent and maid of honor an order she wishes with all her heart to refuse.

In my particular case, it involved dinner.

For those as yet unfamiliar with these memoirs, my name is Margaret Preston Fitzroy, though I am more commonly known as Peggy. Until quite recently, I was an orphan girl, living in a state of dependency with my banker uncle, his kind but silly wife, and my dear, dramatic cousin, Olivia. This evening, I sat in my dressing closet at St. James's Palace, trussed up tightly in my corsets and silk mantua, and trying to remember if I'd ordered everything necessary to entertain those same relations in royal style.

"You're certain the kitchen agreed to the partridges?" I asked my maid, Nell Libby.

"Yes, miss," Libby answered through clenched teeth. This was not because I had asked her this same question three or four times in the past hour. At least, not entirely. Rather, it was because she had a mouthful of silver pins and was endeavoring to fix my hair in the latest style.

"What about the jugged hares?" I demanded. My own voice was somewhat muffled from my efforts to keep my teeth from chattering. It had begun to rain outside. Even in the windowless dressing closet of my equally windowless bedchamber, I could hear the steady pounding over the roofs. Each drop carried winter's brutal promise and dragged another icy draft across the wooden floor. My fire was roaring, and I was being positively profligate with the candles, but my rooms remained cold enough that my fingertips had achieved a truly arresting shade of blue. "And the chianti? It's my uncle's favorite wine. Ormand did say he'd have an extra bottle laid by for us?"

I don't believe I had put in as much effort preparing for any court function as I had for this meal. I had spent the better part of the last two weeks arranging for room, food, and drink, all the while assuring the clerks of the household (mostly truthfully) that I could pay for it all and that, upon my sacred honor, my little entertainment would not add extra expense to the royal housekeeping.

Had it been up to me, I would have never laid eyes upon my uncle again. He might have taken me in after my mother died, but we had never warmed to each other. Matters rather came to a head this past spring when he betrothed me to a young man with whom I later shared a mutual misunderstanding. That is to say, I attacked him. To be perfectly fair, though, he did attack me first. This wholly rational argument, however, failed to carry any weight with my uncle, and his response was to throw me out into the street. That the entire unhappy affair ended with my taking up residence in the royal court came as something of a surprise to all concerned. As did the interlude in which I masqueraded as one Lady Francesca, who, it was discovered, had been murdered.

I hasten to add that none of this was actually my own doing or idea. Well, almost none. That is to say, very little.

This admittedly extraordinary run of events had an appropriately extraordinary ending. I now enjoyed a certain amount of royal favor and a post at court. It had not, however, served to mend the rift between myself and my uncle. For my part, I had rather hoped to let that particular matter lie. Unfortunately, my new mistress, Her Royal Highness Princess Caroline, had other ideas.

"Sir Oliver Pierpont is your uncle and legal guardian, Miss Fitzroy," she reminded me, with a hard tap of the royal index finger against the back of my hand. "Whether or not you relish the relationship. You will make peace with him, or trouble will come of it."

She was right. More important, she was Princess of Wales. That fact limited the replies I could make to being lectured or poked. I could not, for example, inform Her Royal

Highness that I would much prefer to be removed to some place of quiet retirement, such as the Tower.

"I've made sure of everything, miss. I promise you." Libby might have been behind me, but the face she pulled showed clearly in the looking glass on my vanity table. "Now, hold still, or I'll have this pin right in your scalp."

"On purpose too."

"Now, miss, would I ever do that?"

"I'm not entirely sure."

"Then you'd better be sure you sit still, hadn't you? Miss."

The perceptive reader will see by this exchange that my luck with maids had not improved since we last communicated. When I first came to court, my maid was a large, raw-boned woman called Mrs. Abbott. We had what might be charitably described as a troubled relationship. The fact that I once accused her of plotting murder did not assist matters. Libby, by contrast, was a tiny girl about my own age. She was so tiny, in fact, that she had to stand on a footstool to properly pin and pomade my hair. Her olive skin and dark eyes might have indicated descent from a Spaniard, or a Roman, or a Gypsy rover. Libby pretended ignorance on the matter, and I pretended to believe her.

I might have tried to find a different, gentler person to whom I could entrust the care of my person but for one grave and overwhelming concern: Libby had mastered the New Art of Hairdressing.

It was a dread and terrible time to be a maid of honor, for we found ourselves in the midst of the storm of revolution. For women, the wig had gone out of fashion.

The wig, or more properly, the *fontange*, had been seen as an indispensable portion of the fashionable lady's toilette since the days of Queen Anne. Its purpose, as far as I could tell, was to ensure woman's rigid adherence to the first two of the Great Rules of Fashion. I will set those down here as a warning to future generations.

Rule 1: Any item of dress for ladies must be both more complicated and less comfortable than the corresponding item for gentlemen.

Rule 2: No woman may show any portion of her personage in public without it being severely, and preferably painfully, altered.

The fontange satisfied both criteria admirably. It was an assemblage of horsehair and wire framework pinned and strapped to the lady's Delicate Head, over which her own hair was then arranged to create sufficient height and approved shape, with the whole topped off by a tall comb or similar adornment. But recently, some daring woman had appeared before the new regent of France with a smooth, sleek head of her own hair on full display. Instead of being shocked beyond endurance, the regent liked it. He liked it, and he said so. Aloud. In public.

Thus are mighty storms generated by the tiniest gust. *En masse*, the ladies of Versailles cast off the fontange to freely and wantonly display their own tresses. Many were scandalized, but where Versailles's ladies led, we lesser mortals were condemned to follow.

For me, this all meant an extra hour in front of the mirror. The fontange might have been consigned to history alongside the neck ruff and the codpiece, but Rules 1 and 2 were not to be altered in any particular. My coarse, dark hair could not be shown in public until it had been cemented into orderly ringlets and lovelocks, then pinned with pearls and flowers and other such maidenly adornments. Libby the Sharp excelled at this feat of fashion, unfortunately.

There was a knock at the door. Libby snorted and jumped off her stool. By then, however, the closet door had opened and Mary Bellenden was sauntering in.

"Hello, Peggy. I've come for that bracelet you said I could borrow." Mary was not a friend to me, or to anyone as far as I could tell. She was, in fact, one of the few genuinely careless people I'd ever met. A diamond and a hen's egg were both the same to the lively Miss Bellenden, as long as they were accompanied by a flattering turn of phrase and the chance to make a good joke.

Without pausing to do more than smile at my reflection, Mary flipped up the lid on the first of the jewel boxes set out on my vanity table and began rooting through the contents. I was not surprised. Mary Bellenden did not believe in pausing for such trifles as permission.

"It's here." I pushed a smaller, sandalwood box toward her, trying not to move my head. Libby had resumed her stool and taken up her pins. She held one up for me to see in the glass. It was a gentle reminder that she was in a position to make my life yet more uncomfortable if I executed any sudden moves.

"Thank you for taking my turn at waiting tonight," I said to Mary, keeping my head rigidly still.

"Not at all." Mary held up the pearl and peridot bracelet. It was a pretty thing, and I rather liked it. However, this loan was understood to be of long duration. Those of us in waiting to the royal family were kept to a strict schedule. We had three months on duty, followed by a month off, during which we might return to our family homes, if we had them. This may not sound terribly onerous, but we were expected to be in attendance between six and seven days each week. If it was a state occasion, a day could stretch to twenty hours out of the twenty-four. Maids of honor, like the other "women of the bedchamber," could take a day off only as long as at least two of us remained in attendance. This resulted in the trading of all sorts of favors and small valuables in return for time.

"But poor Mr. Phelps!" Mary fastened the bracelet onto her slender wrist and turned it around, testing how well the gold and jewels glistened in the candlelight. Mary had the alabaster skin, sloping shoulders, and pale eyes expected of the Maid of Honor Type. She carried the looks, and the style, with an ease I envied. "He will be quite distraught when he sees me wearing his gift instead of you!"

"Well, you'll just have to soothe his spirits, won't you?"

I will not deny that some small ulterior motive guided my choice of which bracelet to "lend" Mary. Mr. Phelps was one of the many court gentlemen I had to tolerate, but not one I wished to encourage.

"Perhaps I will. He certainly has excellent taste." Mary leaned in toward the glass, touching her patches. This blocked Libby's view and caused my maid to eye her last silver pin, and Mary's neck, thoughtfully. "I note you have not yet smoothed things over with our Sophy."

"As a good Christian maid, I know I should turn the other cheek, but both mine are already burned." When Sophy Howe thought I was Lady Francesca, she had done her best to make my life miserable. Now that she knew I was a mere "miss" rather than a titled lady, she seemed to take my continued existence as a personal insult.

"And you will have heard by now that Molly Lepell has returned," Mary went on with a great and obvious show of insouciance.

"Oh? How is she?" I strove to match Mary's unconcern, and failed. First, because no one could match Mary Bellenden when it came to complete and marvelous unconcern for others. Second, because Molly Lepell had been the closest thing to a friend I'd had at court. Unfortunately, that friendship had been formed while she believed I was someone else. When it was revealed just how thoroughly I'd been lying to her, and the rest of the world, Molly did not take it well. She'd left the court for her interlude at home before I'd had a chance to try to mend things.

"I'm sure I couldn't tell how she is." Mary turned a bright eye toward me. "You need to apply to quite a different quarter to find out what little nothings Molly Lepell whispers these days." I might have been the one engaged in spying for the Crown, but when it came to acquiring court gossip, I was a decided amateur compared to Mary.

"What are you talking about?" My patience was stretched dangerously thin. Miss Bellenden might have nothing better to do than flirt and gossip tonight, but I was under orders to make peace out of a private war with a man I detested.

"It seems that while she was at home and out of our tender care, a certain gentleman quite captured Molly's attention."

That stopped all other thoughts dead in their tracks. "Molly Lepell has formed an attachment?" It was Molly who had warned me against losing my heart to any man at court. I found the idea that she might have abandoned her own excellent advice more than a bit disturbing.

"It sounds absurd, doesn't it? I thought her quite impervious." Mary fussed with the fashion-mandated three tiers of lace ruffles trailing from her sleeves, making sure they fell in such a way that they would not obscure her new bracelet. "But I know what I saw, and what I saw was anything but impervious." She tipped me a happy wink. "I fear that with all that's going on, you're going to have to work very hard to recapture anyone's attention, Peggy. I am so looking forward to seeing what invention strikes." She dropped a quick kiss on my cheek and sailed out of my closet under a wind of cheerful anticipation as strong as the one that blew her in.

"Invention," snorted Libby. "She knows too much about invention for her own good, that one."

"She's all right," I answered, somewhat distractedly. Mary Bellenden was indeed all right, simply because she was uncomplicated. She sailed through life as well as doorways. Molly Lepell was another matter. She was beautiful, of course, but she was also deeply intelligent and practical regarding court matters. I wondered who had found her heart. I wondered if he was worthy. I wondered if I'd ever get a chance to explain myself to her and to be her friend again.

"Oh, Peggy!" Mary's voice rang quite unexpectedly from my outer chamber. "You've a visitor."

"What?" I struggled to my feet, ignoring Libby's annoyed exclamations. "Who? The Pierponts aren't due for two hours yet . . ." Could it be Molly?

But the youth I caught in the act of straightening up from the bow he made to Mary Bellenden was no member of my family, much less a maid of honor.

"Heaven defend us," I croaked as the blood drained out of my painted cheeks.

This man was tall and slender with arresting blue eyes set into a hatchet-sharp face. He was the Honorable Mr. Sebastian Sandford. I had met Mr. Sandford last spring, when he attempted unceremoniously to seduce me at a birthday party. When seduction failed, he, with equal lack of ceremony, attempted rape.

He also happened to be my betrothed.

CHAPTER TWO

IN WHICH A MOST UNWELCOME ACQUAINTANCE IS RENEWED.

Miss Fitzroy. How wonderful it is to see you again."

Sebastian presented me with one of his best bows, a feat rendered slightly awkward by the beribboned porcelain jar he carried in both hands. I watched him without moving or even managing to close my mouth. I quite literally could not believe my eyes.

I had last seen Sebastian before I came to court. That also happened to be the same day my uncle threw me out of his house. This was the morning after Sebastian had decided he was going to help himself to my virginity, in a garden shed, without bothering to inquire whether I consented to the act. I did not, as it happened, and was able to make a more forceful argument in that regard than he expected.

As Sebastian straightened from his most recent bow, I struggled to find where I had misplaced my voice. The initial results were not promising.

"I . . . you . . . what are you doing here?"

"Lud, Peggy!" cried Mary, clearly delighted at finding the evening's entertainments had begun so soon. "One might think you had an excess of handsome swains parading in to see you."

"And does she?" Sebastian inquired. For this pretty quip, he was treated to one of Mary's celebrated sparkling laughs.

"If she does, she has kept her secrets very well."

"I am glad to hear it."

These remarks were ornamented by rather overmuch showing of dimples and batting of eyelashes on all sides. I suppressed the urge to slap them both on their noses.

I will say that if one did not know his true character, one could easily make the mistake of considering Sebastian Sandford handsome. He possessed an arresting face, and when it was not covered by a curled and powdered wig, his hair was pale gold. He was tall, a fact emphasized by his high-heeled shoes with their silver bows. The rest of his clothing was as rich as his footwear. Tonight, he dressed in pale mauve silk and white velvet, all decorated with great lashings of lace and silver braid. Mary's mischievous eyes made a thorough and obvious inspection of all these points as she toyed with the lace edging her own low neckline.

"You have not answered my question, Mr. Sandford." I attempted to give Mary a warning glower, but I needn't have bothered. Mary was not paying my discomfort the slightest bit of attention. "What are you doing here?"

Sebastian, in a belated concession to courtesy, moved his gaze from Mary's countenance, and other highly visible attributes, back to me. "I have come for the drawing room, of course," he said. "I was hoping I might see you there, Miss Fitzroy. In fact, I was hoping you'd accept this trifle from me when we did meet." He held out the jar, which was elaborately painted porcelain with a gilded lid.

I did not take it. Mary gave me a look clearly meant to inquire whether I had lost my senses. "Poor Miss Fitzroy, she's quite overcome with seeing you again, Mr. Sandford." She helped herself to the jar and peeked inside. "Oh . . . how wonderful. Look what your admirer's brought you, Peggy."

Curiosity is a slave driver, and as Mary held out the jar to me, I could not help but glance inside, although I made sure to keep an expression of complete indifference on my face. Sebastian was already looking far too satisfied with himself. The jar contained some black, crumbling substance with a strong herbal perfume.

"It's tea," said Sebastian. "Have you tried it?"

"Of course," I answered. This was even true. I'd drunk the stuff once or twice with several grand ladies. I confess I preferred chocolate or coffee, which was just as well. Tea was abominably expensive, and not part of the rations allowed a maid of honor in residence at the palace. When considered in combination with the gilded jar, Sebastian was indeed offering me a costly present. Its value might be best judged by the fact that Mary made no move to hand the jar to me, but did eye Sebastian with fresh interest.

I took the jar out of Mary's hands and set it on the mantel. "You could have sent it up," I said. "That is, after all, the expected form."

"I could," Sebastian admitted with a shrug that I think was supposed to be modest. "But when I arrived, I was told you would not be in attendance at the drawing room. I wanted to assure myself nothing was wrong."

Which meant that either he had been wandering the halls or he had bribed someone to bring him here. I promised myself I would discover who had committed this outrage. He would be turned out. Possibly hanged. Slowly. In chains.

"You might have sent a note."

Seeing that I remained uncharmed by his appearance, his flattery, or his gift, the mirth faded from Sebastian's sharp face, and for a moment he actually looked abashed. "I did not think you would answer."

"You were correct." At this, Mary smothered a laugh, and I felt ready to strangle on my own impatience. Well, I felt ready to strangle something. "Mary, isn't Her Royal Highness expecting you?"

"Not for another hour at least." Mary's tone said she hoped to spare me any undue concern. This was all the acknowledgment she gave me. Her attention remained fixed on Sebastian.

"Tell me, Mr. Sandford, how is it that you know our so-fascinating Peggy?"

"She has not told you?" Sebastian raised his brows, which, I noted, had been plucked as ruthlessly as any girl's.

"Not a word." Mary sidled closer to him and leaned in. "But then, she's a great one for secrets." She nodded vigorously.

Sebastian looked at me over the top of Mary's dark head.

"You wouldn't," I breathed. Which was a mistake, because of course, Mary heard.

"Oh, now I must know." Mary laid her hand on Sebastian's arm. There was this way she had of tipping up her chin and lifting her brows that made her eyes grow to twice their normal size. The effect on gentlemen was extraordinary, and Mary knew it. "Please, Mr. Sandford," she added, sucking in a breath and straightening her shoulders in case Sebastian had failed to take proper note of her finest, snow-white assets.

This once, however, the Bellenden Effect was for naught. Sebastian was not watching her. His gaze remained locked with mine. I have no notion of what he meant to communicate. For my part, I was sorely disappointed to find that, despite rumors to the contrary, looks could not kill. I assure my readers, I did throw heart and soul into the effort.

"I must apologize, Miss Bellenden," said Sebastian slowly. "But this secret is not entirely mine."

"I see." To illustrate this fact, Mary looked ostentatiously from Sebastian to me, then back again. "Well. Isn't this interesting?"

"Mary, it's not what you think," I told her. At the same

time, I did not dare take my gaze from Sebastian. I did not want him to think he had disconcerted me.

"I'm sure it's not, especially if you're involved, Peggy." Mary favored me with a bright smile and a quick pat on my shoulder. "But you're right. I'm wanted downstairs, and you have your dinner to prepare for." She slipped gracefully up to Sebastian, so close her hems all but brushed the tips of his shoes. "How delightful to have met you, Mr. Sandford. I do hope we'll see each other again soon." She curtsied deeply and held the pose.

Sebastian bowed. "I'm sure that we shall, Miss Bellenden."

Mary straightened, presented us both with another knowing glance, trimmed by a fresh, delighted giggle, and skipped off. I let her go. My immediate priority was to quickly dispatch the man in front of me. This, I decided, called for the direct approach.

"Your audience has departed, Mr. Sandford. The farce is over. Why have you really come here?"

Sebastian looked at the door, plainly expecting me to close it. I declined to move and folded my arms to emphasize my stationary status. I would not be so foolish as to shut myself up with this man, even though I knew Libby lurked somewhere in the background.

"I really did come for the drawing room," said Sebastian. "My brother and my father say that as I'm to remain in England, I should make myself better known at court."

"Remain?" The word all but choked me. "I thought the plan was to pack you off back to Barbados."

Sebastian spread his hands, attempting to indicate ignorance and helplessness. "It may have been, but plans have changed."

"Why?"

"It's a long story. May I sit down?" Sebastian added hopefully.

Warning took hold inside me and squeezed several vital organs. "No, you may not sit," I answered. "My maid is waiting to finish my toilette, and then I have my own business to attend to." I stepped back, gesturing to show that the pathway to the door was free of all obstruction. "You have seen me. You can be satisfied that I am entirely well, and you have left your gift. You may now go."

But Sebastian did not turn his footsteps toward the door. Instead, he advanced on me. My first instinct was to retreat, but I caught myself in time and held my ground. I would not let him see me afraid. I touched the jeweled pin that decorated the center of my stomacher—an item I'd requested my patron, Mr. Tinderflint, to commission especially for me—and for a moment silently dared Sebastian to come closer. I had been adding some most unmaidenly skills to my arsenal over the past months, and my carefully manicured fingers were itching for an excuse to unleash them on this particular visitor.

I don't know if he read any of this in my narrowed gaze,

but Sebastian did halt his advance while there was still a good two feet of space between us.

"We need to talk, Peggy," he said in a low, urgent voice.

I looked at the young man in front of me, at his anxious face and melting blue eyes, and I forced myself to remember. I remembered the feeling of his hot, hard fingers as he shoved them under my skirts so he could pinch my thighs. I remembered the leer on his face as he raised himself up above where I lay pinned to the ground. I remembered how he laughed at my screams and my pleading. At least, he laughed until I jammed my fan into his throat. I made myself remember that moment as well.

"I have nothing to say to you, Mr. Sandford."

Sebastian's jaw worked itself back and forth. For a moment, I could have sworn I saw genuine worry in his bright, blue eyes. I told myself not to be ridiculous. There was nothing genuine about this man, and there never would be.

Knowing this as I did, his next words surprised me.

"This is my fault, and I do know it," Sebastian said. "I have begun as badly as possible, again. But you will soon understand that we must talk. Send word for me when you are ready, and I will meet you, where and when you please."

He bowed, this time perfunctorily, and left me standing there.

CHAPTER THREE

IN WHICH, AGAINST ALL EXPECTATIONS, AT
LEAST A FEW PLANS UNFOLD AS HOPED.

Slowly, I closed the door. My heart knocked hard against my ribs. What on earth could Sebastian be playing at? What did he mean, I would understand that we must talk? We had nothing at all to say to each other.

I repeated this to myself and the closed door several times. At the same time, I looked at the porcelain jar on the mantel. It must hold a good pound of tea. My brain, which had been made mercenary by both my public and concealed duties, calculated that to be worth at least forty pounds sterling, not counting the value of the jar itself. As bribes went, it was both respectable and well considered.

"Friend of the family?" inquired Libby from the threshold of my closet. Of course she had stayed in there, where she could listen to every single word without fear of being noticed. I expected no less of her.

"Am I fit to be seen, Libby?" I asked by way of ignoring her far too personal question.

My maid narrowed her dark eyes, inspecting me like a horse at market. "You'll do for tonight."

"Good. Get down to the Color Court and keep watch for my uncle and his family." With that, I snatched up the small purse from my desk and hurried out my apartment door as quickly as my constricting garments would allow.

Had we all still been in residence at Hampton Court Palace, I would have had space enough to host my dinner party in my own apartments. We might even have been warm. But as soon as autumn arrived, the royal family had transplanted themselves to the heart of London and settled beneath the turrets of St. James's Palace. I was told this ungainly brick warren had originally been built by Henry VIII. That gentleman considered it to be a fitting home for his beloved, at the time, Anne Boleyn. If that was true, he thought her fitting home was a cramped, smoky, drafty, bewildering maze of dark corridors and dim, low-ceilinged rooms. The small salon that I had been allotted for my dinner was ten minutes' walk, in fully rigged mantua and high heels, from my apartment, and that was without any wrong turnings.

Even a small court is a good-size village, and I was but one in a stream of richly dressed persons all hurrying to reach their designated places for the evening. I barely noticed who I passed. This neglect would cause me to be accused of snubbery later, but I could not tear my mind away from Sebastian and his abrupt return to my life.

Given the manner in which I'd left my uncle's house and all that had happened since, it simply never occurred to me that anyone would want to enforce the betrothal contract that existed between my uncle and Sebastian's father, Lord Augustus Sandford, Baron of Lynnfield. If I'd thought of it at all, I'd assumed that contract had been broken by my uncle's failure to bring me to church. But now the horrible possibility that I had been wrong descended upon me. The betrothal might still be in effect. As an underage girl, I remained completely under the control of my nearest male relative, no matter where I might temporarily reside. I could, legally and properly, be dragged back to my uncle's house. I could be given into marriage with a street sweeper or sold as an indenture to the Virginia Colony, just as he saw fit.

I will admit, given that my other choice was Sebastian, street sweepers and colonies had a certain appeal.

I told myself I must not panic. I was hardly alone or friendless. It was not possible Her Royal Highness would permit me to be removed from her service by so trivial a person as a lurking bridegroom. Besides, I had planned this evening well. If my personal charms failed to win my uncle over (a very probable outcome), I had laid out a second route by which I might retain my personal place and see my cousin,

Olivia, again. It was admittedly riskier, because it hinged on the whims and generosity of a small girl. I sincerely hoped I would not have to depend on either, but given the way the evening had gone thus far, I felt very glad I'd planned for the contingency.

The farther I went down those dark and busy corridors, the deeper the fear piled around my thoughts. This pessimism readily infected the whole of my mind, causing it to conjure a world of evils waiting for me. Despite Libby's assurances, I was positive the fire had not been lit and the salon was stone cold—or perhaps the fire had been lit but the chimney did not draw, so smoke was filling the room. Perhaps the servants I had been promised had not arrived to lay the table. If those servants had arrived, they might well have stolen the silver spoons and gone to the tavern. If they had not stolen the spoons, it was only because they had stolen the wine and were lounging about on the chairs, drunk as lords, which, I had reason to know, was very drunk indeed.

So it was that by the time I arrived at the correct door, my hand actually trembled as I reached forward to push it open.

The fragrance of tallow and wax laced with an acrid hint of coal wafted out to greet me. I stepped into a plain, warm, well-lit chamber. A tapestry-covered table took up much of the space and was fully laid out. The wine bottles with their silver tags indicating variety and vintage stood in ordered rows on the sideboard. Two youths with serious faces and neat green coats stood sentry on either side.

So powerful was my relief, I failed to notice they were not alone in the room. Then someone cleared his throat.

I jumped. I might have screeched. I definitely turned, poised, perhaps, to run. But then my bewildered eyes made out that it was Matthew Reade who rose from a stool by the fire.

"Hello, Peggy," he said. "I thought you could use the sight of a friendly face."

He spread his arms wide, and I rushed into them.

Matthew's embrace folded around me and I felt, as I always did, that here I had come home at last. Storm wrack, tempest, flood, revolution, all might come crashing down and none of it matter. As long as Matthew held me, I was safe. I tipped my head up so I could feast my gaze on the brilliance of his smile and his shining gray eyes. At that moment, I hated my cosmetics with a fury hot enough to burn the palace down. My face, neck, and any exposed portion of bosom had been slathered with enough paint to cover a good-size canvas and glued with patches of assorted shape, color, and symbolic significance. It might be all well and good to allow the world a peep at one's actual hair, but the Great Rules of Fashion would never be bent enough to permit one to show her actual face. The truth was, I spent most of my glittering evenings surrounded by the powerful and the beautiful, and trying not to expire from the itching.

But far worse than any itch was the fact that while I had my court face on, I couldn't indulge in what had become one of the chief joys of my existence—kissing Matthew. I had to settle for brushing my fingertips along the corners of his mouth and watching his smile broaden.

"Thank you," I breathed. Matthew generally did not wear a wig. One lock of dark copper hair had escaped his short queue to trail along his temple. I fingered that loose tendril of hair and tucked it back behind his ear, slowly, carefully, taking an extra moment to smooth it into place just for the delight of being able to touch him.

In answer, Matthew took up my hand and pressed my knuckles to his mouth. He also moved slowly, allowing us both to savor the gesture. All the while, he bestowed upon me a lingering, welcome, and very warm glance. As little patience as I have for the exaggerations of our more long-winded romantic poets, I can say with complete honesty that lightning shot through me. Matthew knew it too, and he grinned. I grinned in return, not like the sophisticated maid of honor, but like simple, besotted Peggy Fitzroy.

"That's better." Matthew lowered my hand, but did not bother to release his other arm from around my waist. "When you walked in, you looked like there'd been a death."

I truly wished he had not said that, because it brought all my attendant fears crowding back.

"Matthew, this is going to be a disaster."

"It's going to be fine, Peggy Mostly." I kept meaning to inform Matthew that he could not get away with attaching this most undignified cant name to an important person such as myself, but somehow the opportunity never arose. "Even you can play the dutiful for the length of one dinner. When it's over, you'll release your relations into the drawing room, and they'll be so busy making their bows, they won't have time to pester you."

"No, you don't understand, it's more than that. It's—" I froze, the whole tangle of words in my mouth stopped up by a sudden, terrible realization.

I could not tell Matthew what had just happened between myself and Sebastian.

I had shared with Matthew many details about my life. He had even assisted with my spying. But I had somehow entirely failed to mention my status as a betrothed woman. I'm certain there were many excellent reasons for this omission. Given time, I might even have been able to sort through the fear and embarrassment tumbling down upon me to remember what they were.

But I did not have time. Matthew had taken full note of my confusion. He cocked his head in what I'd come to think of as his artistic way—the one that allowed him to break down whatever he saw into its component portions of light and shadow. "Is something wrong?"

I rallied. I could not reveal the existence of Sebastian Sandford with only a few minutes and limited privacy. Explaining the existence of a fiancé to one's paramour required seclusion, time, and a supply of strong drink. Possibly smelling salts as well.

"It's just so strange, meeting my relatives as, well,

equals," I told him, which was true, just not the truth I'd almost let slip. "I'm afraid the moment they walk in I'll turn back into the little orphan I used to be."

Matthew's response to this pretty speech was to frown and step back. "Yes, and there's something more. What is it?"

Becoming infatuated with a keen-eyed artist, it seemed, had distinct drawbacks, especially when one needed to practice some small social deception.

"I can't tell you now." I shot a glance at the waiting men. Both Matthew and I knew they'd talk about anything they heard. I made a note to myself that I must take time later to feel guilty about being glad of their attentive presence. "Matthew, thank you for being here, but you'd best go."

Matthew hesitated, and I watched him try to keep the suspicion from his features. My heart sank. I had deceived Matthew before. I prayed that he had forgiven me, but neither of us had had anything like enough time to forget.

"Peggy, are you in trouble again? Is it . . . Tinderflint business?"

"No. Not this time." We both spoke seriously. Mr. Tinderflint's business was the spying, as Matthew knew full well. "I will tell you everything as soon as I can." *And as soon as I can work out how,* I added to myself. As it was, I was silently thanking my stars that protocol did not allow me to invite Matthew to this family dinner. I had no idea which way the conversation would turn. It was unacceptable that Matthew should learn about my betrothal casually between dinner courses.

"All right." Matthew kissed my hand again. "A promise against later, when you're wearing your own face."

He took his leave then, and one of the servers closed the door behind him. I faced a room grown several degrees colder by Matthew's absence, and far more lonely.

I had believed this dinner would allow me to show both success and contrition to Uncle Pierpont. But with Sebastian's reappearance, everything became much more serious. If I hoped to retain my freedom, I must show Uncle Pierpont that I could be useful to him. I must make it clear that I was not just another hanger-on at court. As maid of honor, I was sought out and cultivated by the wealthy and powerful because of my proximity to our future sovereign. Removing me into a marriage would be a waste of resources.

Tonight, I must look up into the eyes of my flint-hearted uncle and make him change his mind.

CHAPTER FOUR

IN WHICH OUR HEROINE GIVES HER FIRST
PARTY AND DISCOVERS THAT NOT ALL THE
CIRCUMSTANCES OF HER LIFE HAVE CHANGED.

Unfortunately, the small salon offered very few options
to soothe a fluttering of nerves that had ambitions to become
a full-fledged attack. I tried to distract myself by inspecting all aspects of both table and sideboard. The two serving
youths in their green coats watched my every movement from
their posts. I pretended to ignore them. There was a protocol
between the servants and the served for even a small dinner.
As this was my first chance to play hostess at my own table,
I was determined to get it right. I will say that their eyes
lingered a bit more on the leather purse I carried than on any
other detail of the room.

I stopped in front of the servants. The taller of the two
had already begun to turn stout, and his face had been badly

pockmarked, which left him with a sinister appearance, but there was intelligence in his brown eyes.

"And your name is?" I addressed the stout, scarred youth as the senior of the pair.

"Norris, Miss Fitzroy, and Cavey." Stout Norris jerked his spotty chin toward his companion—the smaller, stick-thin youth at the other side, who looked as if he'd as soon bolt as stand and serve. Perspiration trickled down one cheek.

"This is an important gathering," I told Norris, emphasizing my point by dropping a pair of half-crowns into his hand. "It is vital that everything go smoothly."

"Yes, miss. Of course." Norris eyed Cavey and jingled his hand significantly a moment before pocketing the coins. Some of the frightened-rabbit air dispersed from about Cavey's slender person.

"Thank you, and—" I was prevented from finishing that sentence by the door slamming open.

"Peggy!"

I had meant to bestow upon my uncle and aunt my most elegant and dignified curtsy, the one I reserved for the drawing room when everyone was watching. Instead, as Libby pushed open the door, my cousin Olivia exploded into the room, shoved a set of boxes into Libby's hands, and ran forward with a turn of speed that would have impressed even Mary Bellenden. For the second time that evening, I found myself enfolded in a welcome embrace.

"Olivia!" I forgot everything else and hugged her back as hard as I was able.

From the day I arrived at my uncle's house, Olivia had been my most constant companion. Perhaps it would be more accurate to say I was her companion, since she was the star of any social gathering we went to. This was in part because she looked very much the beauteous English rose, with gentle blue eyes and a blooming, creamy complexion that needed only a hint of powder and a single patch to become the envy of half the women at court. She threw off her midnight blue velvet cloak to reveal a gown of ice blue and ivory satin trimmed with silver lace that she wore with an attitude of perfect comfort.

If I had not been the recipient of Olivia's unfailing friendship, I could have dined on my envy. Fortunately, Olivia also had a mind and imagination of diamond clarity and a nerve that could tip from brave to reckless at the least provocation. If our positions had been reversed, she would have taken to this business of court and spying like a duck to water. As it was, she hoarded up descriptions of the adventures we had already shared and stored them in her journals. One day, she swore, she would cobble them all into a play or a dramatic serial for the papers.

If my uncle ever got wind of that plan, he would die of apoplexy.

"Peggy, darling!" My aunt Pierpont glided past her husband to take both my hands. Aunt Pierpont and I had always gotten along well. She was a small, plump housewife now, but she had been a beauty in her youth, and she still remembered how to wear court regalia well. But not even her layers of carefully applied cosmetics could entirely erase the telltale nervousness that was her primary characteristic.

"How good it is to see you again," she bubbled. "And looking so well. I adore your hair in that fashion. It suits you exactly!" Aunt Pierpont still wore a fontange with a tall lace veil to accompany her round gown of figured black velvet and ecru satin. I suspected this styling would change after tonight. "And what a lovely dress! Is our Peggy not looking well, husband?"

My uncle did not glide forward, much less bolt. He stalked, and as he did, he looked down at me from under lowered eyelids. Uncle Pierpont was a tall, thin stork of a man with narrow, calculating eyes. His nose was as pointed as any pen, and his soul matched the sharp severity of his person. His sole concession to palace formality was that he had forsaken his short-queue wig for a great, curling full-bottomed creation with two peaks above his brow that bore an unfortunate resemblance to a bull's horns. Otherwise, he wore the black velvet and white silk that I was used to seeing on him. Even the bows on his shoes were black. All in all, he looked like a demon clergyman with severe indigestion.

I found myself deeply grateful for the past months of practice in deportment and keeping my countenance. I met Uncle Pierpont's narrowed eyes briefly, then sank into a curtsy that, if it did not rise to stateliness, was at least steady and respectful. In acknowledgment of this filial gesture, my uncle grunted and continued his stork-stalking past me to the sideboard, where he set about examining the tags on the wine bottles.

I straightened up and felt my gaze fasten on a spot directly between his sharp shoulder blades that I knew to be a particularly vulnerable point of the human body. It was fortunate for all of us that Olivia recognized the danger signs.

"Come see what I've brought you." Olivia threaded her arm through mine and steered me toward Libby. My maid still held the boxes she'd been so unceremoniously given. She also eyed me from over their tops in a manner both impatient and impudent. My cousin did not seem to notice, however, and took up the entire pile so she could open them and lay out the contents on the table.

"Oh, Olivia!" She had brought me my mother's sandalwood fan, and her sapphire necklace. These were my only legacy from her, and I had not been sure whether I'd ever see them again. Best of all, however, was when Olivia opened the largest box to display Flossie. Flossie was a porcelain doll my cousin had given me. Aside from Olivia, I'd always regarded Flossie as my one true companion. Although I was of course far too old for dolls, the sight of her affected me so, I had to touch the corner of my eye to stop a tear from streaking my cosmetics.

I closed the boxes carefully. "Libby, take these back to the room, please. Thank you, Olivia." I embraced her again. This time I whispered in her ear. "When the time comes, remember to ask about arrangements for Guinevere's confinement."

Before Olivia could stare blankly at me for too long, I turned to my aunt. "And thank you, Aunt, as well, for coming. It is so good to see you again."

Uncle Pierpont had evidently finished his examination of the bottles.

"This one," he grunted to Norris, indicating his choice. "And then this." He turned to me. "I thought we were here to dine."

I trust my reader will fully appreciate the heretofore unplumbed wellsprings of familial feeling and dedication to duty demonstrated by the fact that I here managed to confine my immediate reply to a charming smile. "Indeed we are. You may bring in the first course," I told Norris. "Uncle, won't you please sit here?" I indicated the chair at the foot of the table, the place of second rank. As this was my dinner in what was nominally my home, protocol and etiquette dictated that I sit at the table's head, and there was nothing at all he could do about it.

Uncle Pierpont sat and gulped the wine that Norris poured. I hoped it was the chianti. It might have been vinegar for all that it relaxed his expression. I was not surprised. Indeed everything about him, from his beady-eyed glower to his frozen indifference to all changes in my status, was exactly as I had expected. This was, however, the one contingency I felt entirely prepared for. I called forth my training as maid of honor, fixed on my most winning smile, and started talking.

I talked with Olivia about our mutual acquaintances. I asked who she had seen recently and how they did. I talked with Aunt Pierpont about fashion and asked about her annual summer trip to Bath. I spooned out generous helpings of the tamer court gossip so she could share it with the ladies of her set.

Both Aunt Pierpont and Olivia understood exactly what I was doing, and they were more than ready to keep up their end of the conversation. I heard that my friend Kitty Shaw had recently gotten engaged to Raphael Swinton and was hoping I'd be at the wedding. Lady Clarenda Newbank— another acquaintance, although most definitely not a friend —had apparently been discommoded by the marriage, as she'd been angling for Mr. Swinton herself. I asked Olivia to convey to Lady Clarenda the depth of my sympathies and tell Kitty my direction for the invitation. She could also deliver my promise to invite Kitty and her fiancé to court for a visit as soon as possible. I heard that Mrs. Quint had decided to remain in Bath, probably for good, and taken all her nieces with her. I privately thought those nieces must be the reason for the removal. I did not, however, mention that I'd seen the youngest at a recent masque, without her sisters or any male relative I knew, but most definitely not alone. Instead, I speculated on the latest rumors that the ladies of Versailles had moved on from overturning all accepted hair stylings to adopting a flatter, wider style of skirt hoop. This, naturally, threatened to send as great a shock through our world as the removal of the fontange. The idea of having to acquire a whole new set of fashionable cages for underneath my gowns filled me with horror, but it appeared to delight my aunt.

This conversation and more like it managed to occupy us through the first two courses, with their sole in oyster sauce, the roasted partridges, the ham, the joint of beef, the spinach and ragout of root vegetables, and the savory tarts. As the third course of venison, jugged hares, macaroni in mushroom sauce, and crème Française arrived, I casually turned my conversation to those matters that I had selected especially for my uncle's ears.

I made sure to detail my daily routine, as it brought me into contact with Their Royal Highnesses. I regaled them with the very funny thing the First Lord of the Treasury said, and the excellent question Mr. Robert Walpole had posed, and how I had danced with the Foreign Secretary for the Southern Department. I did not omit to mention how gracious the king himself had been when I first arrived at court, although I glossed over some of the finer points, since he had thought I was Lady Francesca at the time.

My uncle glared quietly through the first course.

He glowered ominously through the second.

By the third, he was silently seething.

It was when the dessert had been achieved and I held out the dish of sugared almonds to invite him to help himself that his hand crashed down on the table.

"Enough! I did not come here to watch you bask in the spoils of your whoring!"

I held my face quite still. I set the almonds down. "Well, then, tell me, Uncle Pierpont. Why did you come here?"

Uncle Pierpont's eyes glittered in anger and challenge. I

met his gaze without fear. Oh, I was reckless. I was doomed. I was throwing away everything I had gained. I did not for a moment forget that I needed to garner Uncle Pierpont's goodwill, but I would not, I could not, back down. Not to this man, and not ever again.

Then, slowly, incredibly, my uncle put a bridle on his temper. He lowered his shoulders and drew his head back. It was something of the effect of a snapping turtle drawing back into its shell. He picked up the wine at his elbow and drained the glass in a single gulp.

"I came," he said slowly, "for the same reason I took you into my house in the first place. Because your aunt insisted."

"That is not entirely fair, you know, husband," said Aunt Pierpont quickly. "You did say you wished to know how Peggy did. You said you were concerned."

"And exactly when, madame, did you hear me say this?" Uncle Pierpont's voice and face were equally icy as he spoke. That cold had its intended effect and set my aunt trembling.

"I can't remember exactly. I—"

"Then you had best say no more about it."

At this, Aunt Pierpont dropped her gaze and began to knot her fingers into her napkin. If I had not already disliked my uncle to the extreme of my ability, that would have done it. I had almost forgotten how infuriating it was to see him so ruthlessly put down my harmless aunt.

This was, may I add, a feat he had never come close to managing with Olivia. "Father, what does staying angry bring you, or any of us?" my cousin inquired. "Having Peggy in favor at court is a stroke of tremendous fortune for the whole family. Any man in the city would envy you."

Before he could answer this, I rallied my wits. "Sir, I recognize that I am indebted to you for the years of my upbringing." The words tasted sour in my mouth, but this was the strongest card I had to play. I would not waste it by appearing reluctant. "It is my hope that I will be able to use my post at court to pay you back, at least in part. You are a clear-eyed and practical man and always have been." The most vital aspect of the flatterer's art is to know how to compliment each person in his own special way. My uncle had always been proud of his hard head. "I am sure you will agree that there are advantages to be gained for your banking house and its business."

"And I'm sure you will agree, miss, that hanging my future on your ability to wheedle and connive among a crowd of jaded sophisticates is hanging it on a weak hook indeed." The languor and disdain with which he spoke chilled me bone deep. Unfortunately, that chill also got hold of my fragile good sense and snapped it in two.

"Then, Uncle, you may write me off. I am no longer your concern and may make my own way in the world." My aunt pressed her fingers to her lips as it sank in that I had just declared my perfect willingness to live without protection. "All I ask is that you allow me to keep some sort of contact with my aunt and cousin. Agree to this, and I shall trouble you no more."

All manner of calculations passed behind my uncle's hard

eyes. He very much wanted to be able to wash his hands of his sister's branch of the family. Despite this, he hesitated, and I read the refusal in his expression before the words left his mouth.

"Olivia is to have nothing to do with you."

"Don't be ridiculous, Father," said Olivia. "I'm to marry into a title and power so I can help advance the family, and we all know it. What could be better than for me to start making friends at court?" Being a banker, my uncle was not happily admitted to the company of the blue-blood aristocrats. My patronage could open that door for Olivia in ways my uncle's could not. I was certain we all felt the irony of this fact most keenly.

Uncle Pierpont did not even look at Olivia. His gaze remained fixed on me. I had looked into a murderer's eyes. I knew when a man had found his own sticking point. This was where the games ended and, even between enemies, there was only honesty left.

"What do you want from me?" I asked him.

My uncle's thin lips twitched. "Honor the contract with your name on it. Marry Sebastian Sandford."

CHAPTER FIVE

IN WHICH A MOST TOUCHING
REUNION IS ACHIEVED.

I had been ready for Uncle Pierpont to issue this command. I could not remain justly proud of my courtier's skills had I missed the signs of it. Especially when one of those signs had been Sebastian Sandford appearing at my door with an expensive gift and consoling manner.

My difficulty lay in the fact that now that the order was laid before me, my outrage obliterated the calm answer I held ready. I blush to report that what replaced it was somewhat less than gracious.

"Uncle, I would not marry Mr. Sandford even if I were dying of the pox and could have the satisfaction of taking him with me."

This drew a startled gasp from Aunt Pierpont and a

salute of appreciation in the form of a pair of abruptly raised eyebrows from Olivia.

My uncle, while less appreciative, was much more demonstrative. He leaned forward and gripped the edges of the table as if he thought to snap them clean off.

"You think I do not know your game? You smile and you simper and you talk of advantages you can give. But what you mean is you will get your hooks in and make me dependent on your largess."

"You don't honestly think—" began Olivia, but her father rounded on her with such an expression of violent fury that even my voluble cousin was shocked into momentary silence.

"I have said you will have nothing to do with her! That is an end to it!"

"Why do you hate me?" I murmured.

Uncle smirked. "I would have thought I'd made myself plain enough. You are the bastard child of my whoring sister."

"Oliver!" cried my aunt.

"My mother served her rightful queen and her native country!" My shout pulled me to my feet so that I was looking down on this small-minded, thin-souled, unutterably foul man who happened to be my nearest living relative. "But you can't be bothered to see that! You prefer to believe your own sister was a whore rather than to learn the truth!"

For a moment, I saw my uncle startled. For a single heartbeat, he looked uncertain, and for that same moment, I thought I might have scored some small victory. But then, a thin smile spread slowly across his face.

"Very well," Uncle Pierpont said. "What is this truth? If you are so filled with loyalty and love for your dearest aunt and cousin, you can surely tell them how you came to receive this most advantageous post in the court of your *rightful* king. The tales the newspapers tell of your uncovering some scheme to defraud the Crown are remarkably short on plausible detail."

"But it's true."

And it was, as far as it went. Of course, the "fraud" was more accurately called "treason." While playing the part of Lady Francesca, I'd found myself in the midst of a grand scheme to overthrow the Royal House of Hanover and to return the House of Stuart from exile in France to take the throne in triumph. The main reason I was still at court was because Their Royal Highnesses wanted me to continue to quietly discover what other traitors might be hiding among the great and glittering.

"If it's true, then tell me, what was the nature of this fraud?" countered my uncle. "What bank, what firm, what titled gentlemen did your action bring to the bar of the king's justice?"

I knew I should find a lie. I was a confidential agent. Surely I had a whole pack of deceptions into which I could delve at will. Uncle Pierpont was waiting. They were all waiting.

"I cannot say," I murmured.

"You will not," Uncle Pierpont replied, that thin, terrible smile still in place. "You certainly did not get here on your own. Someone aided you. Someone placed you here, deliberately, to do his bidding. Who was it? Why did he choose you?"

"I cannot say," I repeated. "I have sworn an oath to remain silent on the subject."

"And there it is. Your loyalty to power is greater than your loyalty to your own flesh and blood. Just like hers."

Had he made some move to leave at that moment, I might have given in. I might have pleaded with him and parted with at least a few of my secrets.

But my uncle did not move. Understanding cleared my mind with an astounding speed, and I was able to look once more into his eyes. In that moment, I saw beyond the oily triumph and his narrow, countinghouse calculations. He was gambling, just as I was. There was something he wanted to win from me, and it wasn't only my agreement to this marriage.

My uncle's thin smile wavered. He turned away, but he did it too quickly. "Wife, Olivia, we are leaving," he said. This time, he did move toward the door. Norris, who had been holding his post by the wine bottles, stepped alertly up, ready to open it for him.

I caught Olivia's eye and made a frantic motion with my hand, indicating she must keep them here. Fortunately, my cousin understood.

"You may be leaving, Father," she said sweetly. "But I most certainly am not." Olivia not only failed to get to her feet, but picked up her wineglass.

"You are impertinent and disobedient, miss!" roared her father.

"Well, Father, as you do not see fit to do your duty in behaving honorably toward your own flesh and blood, as your faithful daughter, I have no choice but to follow your example."

Even I was astounded by this show of bravado. I thought Uncle Pierpont would certainly strike her. So did Aunt Pierpont. I know this because, against all expectations, my little, nervous aunt slipped between her husband and daughter.

"Oliver," she said with a level of decisiveness I seldom heard from her, "you will kindly take me out of here. It is too warm. I am feeling faint."

My uncle reared back. Aunt Pierpont continued to face him, but I saw the terror in her eyes. This finally brought Olivia to her feet, and we closed ranks behind her mother. I had no idea what I would do if Uncle Pierpont raised his hand. I had no idea what Olivia would do. But I would be dead and damned before I let this man strike either of them.

Without warning of any sort, the door opened.

"Her Highness, the Princess Anne," announced a man's voice stiffly.

In the next heartbeat, a living carpet of small, fluffy white dogs surged across the floor, barking at the top of their tiny lungs. The canine mob immediately surrounded

Olivia, leaping up into the air and standing on their hind legs to whine and yip and wag their tails in a show of puppy ecstasy.

This breathtaking onslaught was followed by the far more dignified entrance of a small girl dressed in cream and pink ruffles. She, in turn, was followed by a tall woman in black who looked as if she had eaten a surfeit of pickled cucumbers.

For those who have not experienced it directly, I can hereby attest that the mantle of royalty is a most mystical adornment. It can cause grown men and women to stop whatever they are doing and make their deepest possible reverences to little children. Even a wild pack of fluffy white dogs seeking to gnaw at one's slipper toe will be ignored while this duty is performed. Further, that mantle causes the youngest of children to understand that as long as they can pipe out certain phrases, they wield a great deal of power.

"Peggy, you will introduce us, please," announced the princess, the dignity of the command spoiled only slightly by the royal lisp. Her Highness, the Princess Anne, was six years old, and the first of the three girls George Augustus, the Prince of Wales, had fathered thus far. She was a pretty, sturdy, determined child who was fully aware of her position and power. One of the least expected developments of the previous summer was my becoming Her Tiny Highness's friend. This was in part due to my own merits, but had been much assisted by the fact that I was the one who had arranged for her to be gifted with this flock of obnoxious, spoiled, overfluffed dogs.

"Certainly, Your Highness," I murmured, lowering my curtsy an extra inch, just to show I could. "May I make known to you Sir Oliver Trowbridge Preston Pierpont, my uncle. Lady Trowbridge Preston Pierpont, my aunt." Aunt murmured and bobbled. "And this is their daughter, my cousin, Olivia Amelia Preston Pierpont."

At this, dignity fell away, and the little girl dashed up to Olivia to seize both her hands and squeal, "Oh, I am glad to meet you! You must miss them so much! Don't they look well?" She scooped up two of the fluffy flock and pushed them into Olivia's arms. For a moment, I thought Olivia was going to cry. Until I'd interfered, these creatures had indeed been her beloved pets.

"I've taken most particular care of them," the princess informed Olivia while grabbing her elbow to sit her down in a chair so she could help hold the squirmy dogs on her lap. "And Peggy's helped, haven't you, Peggy?"

"It's been my pleasure, Your Highness." I kept my gaze pointed toward the floor, because Olivia knew full well her dogs and I had never been on speaking terms.

"I cannot thank Your Highness enough for your kindness to them." Olivia hugged the two she held. The princess beamed. I was in no way enamored of the now-royal hounds, but I had to admit, they had taken well to palace life. They were fluffier and fatter than ever, with little blue and pink ribbon bows about their necks and tails. Despite these new ornaments, they remained ready to leap to the defense of whoever had fed them last by growling and lunging at every hemline and ruffle that dared move an inch in their presence.

"As Miss Pierpont misses her dogs so terribly, surely it is time they returned home to her," said the black-clothed governess. Her name was Lady Portland, and she was quite probably the only person in the palace who felt less affection for the dogs than I did. "We spoke about this matter, did we not, Your Highness?"

"Oh, but I could not," said Olivia at once. "I can see how happy they are. It would break their hearts to leave Her Highness now." She made a good show of meaning it too.

The princess was picking up each dog in turn and presenting them to Olivia to be praised and kissed and exclaimed over. I glanced at my uncle, and I confess, I let all my triumph show on my face. Aunt Pierpont reached out and steadied herself against the table. For a moment, I was truly afraid she'd faint. Fortunately, Cavey saw this as well and handed my aunt a glass of wine. I had never seen Aunt Pierpont gulp a drink before, but she did so now.

"I think Miss Pierpont has not yet heard the joyful news, Your Highness," I said.

"You didn't tell her? Peggy, what were you thinking!" I cast my face into the proper lines of regret at this admonishment. "I am sorry, Miss Pierpont," the princess went on to Olivia. "You should have been told. Guinevere's breeding. She's going to have puppies!"

Olivia possessed the ability of all mothers to instantly tell their babies, whether two or four legged, apart. She unerringly picked Guinevere up out of the busy flock and turned her over to see her distended belly and teats. How is it possible for a small dog to look insufferably proud?

"She is! How wonderful, Your Highness!" Olivia rubbed the aforementioned belly, so that Guinevere wriggled and snuggled closer into the crook of her arm.

"She and Arthur are properly married now, of course." The princess gently pulled on Guinevere's ears, so she closed her eyes in puppy bliss. "I am sorry you could not be at the wedding."

Olivia arched her brows at me over the royal curls. I grimaced and indicated with a tilt of my head that I would apprise her of the details later. Princess Anne had decided, quite naturally, that Puppy Arthur must have been the father of Puppy Guinevere's impending offspring and that therefore they must be properly married. Lancelot stood as best dog, and ten of us had been invited to the small private ceremony.

It was another measure of the power of royalty's aura that all those invited did attend and not one dared laugh through the entire marriage, or the wedding breakfast—not even the Prince and Princess of Wales. Should any reader feel inclined to envy this invitation to so intimate an occasion with our future sovereigns, I wish to point out that selecting an appropriate wedding gift for a royal lap dog is no easy task.

I mouthed a reminder at Olivia, and she frowned

impatiently at me. "So, please tell me, Your Highness, what are the arrangements for Guinevere's confinement?"

"Her confinement?" Princess Anne drew back.

I nodded. "You know that when an English lady is ready to be delivered of her baby, she traditionally goes into confinement." I had taken pains previously to explain this was an English custom, because it was most definitely not the one being followed by our German-born Princess of Wales, who was at least as pregnant as Guinevere. "It is for her health, as well as for the baby's. Well, it is the same with puppies. We can't have Guinevere giving birth in a draft, can we?"

"Oh. I hadn't thought." The princess looked decidedly nervous at the idea, and I felt a moment's guilt.

"Olivia is very experienced with puppies," I went on, making sure I caught Olivia's gaze so I could lift my brows in a significant fashion. "And you know there is no one who loves Guinevere more."

The princess, however, was reaching her own conclusions. "You think it will be better because of . . ." Her Highness's eyes shifted sideways toward the Portland.

I nodded, but all I said was, "I think it will be better for Guinevere and her litter."

The princess squinted dubiously up at me, and for a moment, I feared I had gone too far.

"All right. But . . . you'll send me bulletins, won't you?" Princess Anne looked pleadingly into Olivia's eyes.

"Of course you shall have bulletins," Olivia replied. I waggled my eyebrows frantically at her and saw the light dawn. "I can deliver them personally, if Your Highness wishes it."

"Oh, yes!" Princess Anne grabbed the chair arm and jumped up and down. This caused much flapping of curls and ruffles. It also caused Lady Portland to make the most amazing sound, very much like a chicken being throttled. "And when you do, you'll be able to stop and play with all of them, and then you won't miss them so much. Isn't that a good plan?"

"An excellent plan. Of course . . ." Olivia hesitated, and my heart plummeted. If she tried to play this scene out too long, it might still fall to pieces. I risked a glance at my aunt and uncle. I felt I had not until that moment truly understood what it meant to be "staring daggers" at another being, but that is very much what Uncle Pierpont was doing to his own daughter. My aunt, on the other hand, had taken on an expression as close to shrewd as I had ever seen on her.

"What? Are you worried about Mama?" Princess Anne said. "Don't be. I'm sure she'll agree."

"While that is excellent news, I'm afraid I will need my father's permission to visit here on such a regular basis." Olivia's expression of humble piety would have done credit to a cloistered nun.

"Oh." Princess Anne stopped her bouncing, and we were all treated to the sight of that minuscule personage carefully mustering her dignity. Then she folded her hands and scooted up to my uncle, four or five of the dogs traveling with her as a disorderly honor guard.

My uncle watched her approach as one might watch the fall of the headsman's ax.

"Sir Oliver," said Princess Anne, "it is my express wish that your daughter, Olivia, wait on me with updates as to Guinevere's health. Will that be acceptable to you?"

I watched Uncle Pierpont want to refuse. I watched him search frantically for some hint of a way out of this cul-de-sac of etiquette and obedience. I watched Olivia looking down at Guinevere in her arms and saw her face twitch as if she'd contracted some terrible palsy.

Slowly, stiffly, like the most ancient and arthritic of men, my uncle bowed to this miniature specimen of royalty and her attendant puppies.

"It is entirely acceptable, Your Highness."

Princess Anne nodded in stately acknowledgment. "Thank you. I will mention you particularly to Mama as a good friend to me."

Lady Portland, it seemed, could stand this drama no longer. "And now it is time you were in bed, Your Highness," she said.

The sigh with which Princess Anne answered this was long, loud, and gusting. "In a minute. It is too late for Guinevere to travel tonight, don't you think?" she said to Olivia. "There could be rising damps. Or falling."

"Just so, Your Highness," my cousin agreed. "With

permission, I will come for her tomorrow and bring her traveling basket and blanket."

"I'll give orders that you're to be admitted."

"Thank you, Your Highness." Olivia, showing only slight regret, set Guinevere down to make her curtsy.

"And now we must be going, Your Highness." The false sociable gaiety in the Portland's voice barely concealed the warning note.

The princess rolled her eyes and shook her curls. "ArthurLancelotGawainTristanGarethGuinevere, come along." Princess Anne was especially generous in the matter of sharing cakes and cream and such treats. As a result the entire flock yipped at the sound of their names and followed in a tight knot when she trotted out of the room. We all made our respective bows again.

"I'm sorry," I said to my uncle as I straightened up to meet his poisoned glower. "I told Her Highness I would be busy this evening, but you know how it is with little girls, even princesses." I shrugged.

"Spare me your prattle," he snapped. "You have demonstrated your native cunning and your pride in it. Very well. Olivia will visit. But nothing else has changed, Margaret Fitzroy."

He cast a glance back at Olivia and his wife. This time, Olivia made a great show of modesty, with folded hands and lowered eyes, and followed her father as he stalked out the door Norris held open.

It was my aunt who paused and hissed in my ear, "Peggy, you must stop this game. If he gets truly angry, it will not go well for anyone."

I pulled back, startled. But Aunt Pierpont had already turned away to follow husband and daughter.

Norris closed the door behind them all. I stared at the ruins of my dinner and pressed my hand against my stays, suddenly very afraid.

Why would my uncle insist on this marriage? What was it all for? If Uncle did not think I was any good to him when I had the ear of the Princess of Wales, what on earth did he think he would gain if I was married to the second son of a baron from some obscure county in the southeast?

If only . . . I drew up short and had to clap my hand to my mouth to stifle a laugh. For I had been about to think, *If only there were some way I could find out.*

"You seem to be forgetting, Peggy Fitzroy," I murmured. "You not only know people in high places, you have royal permission to spy on them all."

CHAPTER SIX

IN WHICH OUR HEROINE BOLDLY ATTEMPTS,
JUST ONCE, TO BEGIN A NORMAL SORT OF DAY.

That night, Robert Ballantyne returned. It was only in my dreams, of course. At least, I prayed that it was only a dream.

As ever, I heard his approach long before I saw him. The hard heels of his boots clacked against the floorboards, circling my bed and circling it again. When my eyes finally pried themselves open, he stood at the bed's foot, washed in the cold corpse light that always accompanied him. Old blood spread over his shirt and waistcoat, and his head lolled against his shoulder at an unnatural angle that he seemed unable to rectify. In life, Robert had been a handsome young man. Now his shade's lean face was a mottled gray, and his hollow, colorless eyes were sad and staring. His sword dripped black blood as he leveled the blade at me.

I could not move. I could not make a sound. He spoke, but I could not hear. I screamed silently, crying for help, unable to move, unable to even look away.

I woke to unbroken darkness and a throat burning from the force of my screams. It took a long moment for the thunderous beating of my heart to slow. It took a longer moment to understand that I was pressed back on the bolsters. Apparently, in my sleep I'd tried to climb the headboard to escape. I eased myself down, but gingerly, as if I thought the ghost might suddenly return to visit my waking self. May Heaven help me, but that was closer to the truth than I would have wished.

Gradually, I became aware of the night noises of the palace—the creaking of wood, the faint sound of the wind beyond the walls, a patter of entirely earthly footsteps. There were no boot heels, no corpse lights. I laid myself down, as stiff and uneasy as an old dame with rheumatism, and for a long time blinked uselessly at the dark, fighting to stifle my sobs. When my groping hand finally brushed Flossie's ruffled skirts, I curled around my doll like a child and squeezed my eyes shut in a desperate attempt not to see my nightmare return.

No matter how late my nights might be, all mornings were early ones when I was in waiting. Libby was under strict instruction to pull the curtains back, or—in the case of my windowless rooms at St. James's—light the candles, at six of

the clock. This was to be done rain or shine, desperate pleading and bribery attempts notwithstanding.

That Friday morning was no different. Once Libby had
driven me from my bed, a breakfast in the form of chocolate
and a roll was consumed, usually at my writing desk. An increased correspondence was but one of the many changes that
had taken hold in my life since becoming a maid of honor.
Uncle Pierpont might have forbidden me to write Olivia, but
I had other friends whose families were not nearly so fastidi-
ous, to say nothing of the new acquaintances I had made since
my arrival. These were in addition to the letters from my
patron, Mr. Tinderflint.

Mr. Tinderflint was not that gentleman's given name.
That was Hugh Thurlow Flintcross Gainsford, Earl Tierney.
The Earls Tierney were among the oldest peers in England. If
my particular earl was to be believed, they had also been inti-
mately involved in a number of the more, shall we say, abrupt
changes regarding which elevated individual's posterior had
the right to seat itself upon the throne of England. After the
exploits of the summer, I was quite prepared to believe this.

Those exploits, and the Jacobite conspirators they had
helped unmask, led not just to my joining the court, but to
Mr. Tinderflint's hastily arranged exit from the country. The
Prince of Wales had decided it might be prudent if he was
away until the worst of the furor died down. Fortunately, an
excellent and timely excuse to send Mr. Tinderflint to Paris
had arisen.

His Most Christian Majesty, Louis XIV, the Sun King, had finally died.

As almost no one living had ever known any other king of France, the whole of Europe had spent much of the past year in something of a dither. The nature and extent of that dither was among the things Mr. Tinderflint was meant to clarify for the Prince of Wales. But most importantly and urgently, he was to try to discover whether the new regent of France, Philippe, duc d'Orléans, really meant to honor the late king's promise to give aid and comfort to James Edward Stuart.

James E. Stuart was the only legitimate son of James Stuart Sr. (I have never understood this rationing of names among royalty. One would think they'd want to be told apart). J. Stuart Sr., in his turn, had once been King James II and VI of England and Scotland. This was, of course, some years ago, before James Sr. so angered the nobles of our fair isle that they sent him a letter informing him that if he did not surrender the throne to his daughter Mary, her husband, William, and William's army of Dutchmen, they would cut off his head. Those nobles thought this would be a permanent change of power. James Sr. apparently considered it a tempo-rary inconvenience and spent the rest of his life, and a number of other people's lives, trying to reverse his circumstances. Thus the Jacobites were born.

Now, like King Louis, J. Stuart Sr. was dead as any doornail. But rather than a crown, he had bequeathed to his son a court in exile, a crowd of dissatisfied nobles, rebellious

Scots, restless Irishmen, and a burning desire to kick all scions of Hanover off of English soil and restore the British Crown to the storied House of Stuart—meaning himself.

Discerning the extent of the Jacobite support in France was an important assignment. Of course, our king had his ambassadors and ministers working on this very project. There was not, however, any guarantee that those ministers would acquaint the Prince of Wales with the relevant facts, or even tell him the truth. Royals might share names between father and son, but it seemed they did not necessarily share goals. So it was that while King George was away, our prince and princess were creating their own court not simply for entertainment, but also to control politics and power.

Mr. Tinderflint's assignment was a sign that the prince placed a great deal of trust in him. I tried very hard to stop wishing this mark of faith had fallen on somebody else. Which was nothing short of ridiculous. I did not entirely trust Mr. Tinderflint. I had seen firsthand that he was ruthless. I knew for a fact that he was an accomplished liar. But he liked me, and against my better judgment, I liked him.

So it was with a sense of dread and anticipation that I broke the plain seal on his latest letter and unfolded it to decipher as I sipped my chocolate. Mr. Tinderflint wrote his letters in a series of alternating languages, under the guise of giving me lessons. In truth, this was meant to flummox any unauthorized pair of eyes that might catch a glimpse of our correspondence.

My Dear (he wrote, in Latin),

I hope that these few poor lines find you well. The weather keeps me stranded at my inn at Dover, but the captain informs me he expects it will clear tomorrow, so that we may at last be off across the channel. I did receive your letter. Alas, while very pleasant and diverting, it chiefly served to remind me how much I already miss your conversation!

Do not be charmed, I instructed myself. *Do not be flattered.*

The inn is snug and the food is good, but it is very dull and I'm more hungry for news than for the admittedly excellent fish stew my landlady sets in front of me . . .

I snorted. Mr. Tinderflint was as close to a perfect sphere as it was possible for one human being to become, so the delights of the table were of no small moment to him.

I am, of course, particularly anxious to hear how our Jane is doing. You said nothing about her in your previous letter. Before I left, it was being bruited about that she might find herself noticed by some persons of importance. I trust you will exercise your good sense and guide our young friend away from the most reckless of such beaus. I am thinking particularly of Mr. W, but also Mr. T.

"I am delighted you think so much of my powers of

perception, sir," I muttered. "But you could give me more than one letter to work with."

Jane was, of course, myself. Among his other complex rules of correspondence, Mr. Tinderflint forbade me to set down anyone's real name.

For the next paragraph, Mr. Tinderflint switched to being enigmatic in Greek, which he seemed to write with even more flourishes than he did his Latin, let alone his English.

Any letter addressed to M. Gainsford, the Sign of the Little Pig in the street of St. Denis, will find its way to me. Write soon, so I may know you translated this passage properly, and tell me Jane's news.

Remember, my dear, that I remain, as ever,

Yr. Srvt.,

Mr. T

I dropped the letter into my skirt and rubbed my eyes. He wanted all Jane's news. What on earth had Jane to tell him? I'd been too wrapped up in my own affairs to go tiptoeing about looking for Jacobites. Should I tell him about Sebastian's reappearance? Mr. Tinderflint surely knew of my betrothal. It was the sort of thing he kept himself informed of. Perhaps he even knew something of my uncle's business, or better yet, of Sebastian's father, Lord Lynnfield. He might even be able to give me some hint as to why Sir Oliver and Lord Lynnfield between them insisted on this marriage.

I grabbed up a fresh sheet of paper and prepared to muster every Latin verb I possessed.

"Ahem," announced Libby from her post at the closet door.

"Yes, yes, coming," I said, dipping my quill into the ink pot.

"You're not. You're starting another letter, which will make you late for the princess, and then you'll blame me for it."

"Nonsense, Libby," I said as I began to write. "I'd never think of blaming you."

Dear Mr. T (I wrote),

I am glad you are safe arrived at Dover and that the fish stew is to your liking. I hope the salt air does not spoil your blue silk, as you feared it might . . .

In addition to his love of good foods, Mr. Tinderflint had an extraordinary love of fine and elaborate clothing. The collision of these two obsessions had the unfortunate result that in person Mr. Tinderflint looked like nothing so much as a living confection of spun sugar and marzipan.

I regret to say I do not have much news from here to relate. All continue in good health. Guinevere is breeding and will soon be delivered of her children.

Given all my personal worries and the mental shadows remaining from my night visitor, composing this letter was something of a relief. Concentrating on my declensions and on turning accurate phrases to describe the previous night's disastrous dinner party left little space in my thoughts for worry.

Then I bit my lip and slowly, with gritted teeth and clumsy hand, switched over to Greek.

Jane is still in town, and very well. She was asking rather anxiously after Baron L. You know she is acquainted with his younger son, through Sir OP. Of late, however, their business matters seem to have come to a head, and Jane finds herself very confused as to why this matter remains both unsettled and sitting on her doorstep. I told her as you were surely well acquainted with both gentlemen, you would be able to shed some light on the situation.

I underlined the *surely* for emphasis. Was it too obscure? Perhaps I should add a postscript for clarity. But then I thought about the postmaster possibly scanning my lines for any indication of treason and plot, and hesitated again.

There was one other matter of importance to bring up. For this, I switched to German, just to show him I could.

Jane also asks after that jewel you said you might find for her. While I know you will be busy with your Paris friends, I trust you will write soon with any information you have on that score.

Yr. Devoted,
Miss Mostly

That "jewel" was, of course, not a jewel any more than I was a girl named Jane. The jewel was no less a person than my long-absent father, Jonathan Fitzroy.

My father had vanished when I was still a small child. As I grew, I assumed this to be a simple, sordid case of desertion such as men of weak moral underpinnings committed every day. Of course, I remained a pious and dutiful daughter and did not harbor any bitterness toward the man who had never once written or given me any other sign as to whether he still lived. Perhaps in my tender years, I had attempted to blot out the kind memories I held of a smiling father who carried me on his shoulders, let me play with his signet ring, and called me Pretty Peggy-O. However, as a grown woman, I understood such heartfelt resentment was unfilial and unwarranted, especially as I now knew both my parents had been confidential agents to our previous monarch, Queen Anne.

Still, it must be deemed acceptable at all levels of society for a dutiful daughter to provide a delicate reminder of the commonly understood responsibilities belonging to a father. She might also ask a few discreet questions regarding the confluence of events occasioning such a long absence without a word, even after his wife had died alone in her bed.

But before I could impart any such calm and entirely rational communication, someone had to find Jonathan Fitzroy. Mr. Tinderflint had agreed to undertake this task. It was not entirely his idea, and he did not like it, but he owed me a debt. I could, and I would, exact my payment.

"Ahem! Miss," said Libby.

"I said I was coming."

"And is there any indication of the hour when this happy event is likely to occur?" she inquired.

"Yes, yes." I sanded and folded my letter. "Now . . . no, wait."

That Libby rather too visibly bit back a scream was entirely forgivable.

"Those two who waited on table . . . Norris and Cavey. Do you know them?"

"Why? Nothing's missing."

I tucked this statement away in my mental journal for examination later. "I may need someone who can run errands for me, some of which may be long and complex. That person needs to be one I can trust. And yes, since I know it will be asked, I would pay for time and trouble." Between the possibility of arranging clandestine meetings with Sebastian Sandford and the unwelcome reminder from my patron that I had concerns beyond the personal, I was going to need help.

The most extraordinary change came over my maid. A moment ago, Libby had barely been able to spare the patience to listen to me; now she seemed to positively glow with the light of eager expectation. "Norris, I'd say, miss. Cavey, he's . . . more particular. I'm sure you understand."

I did. She meant Cavey was more interested in keeping his post than in taking risks to feather his nest. This made him more intelligent, but less useful.

"Libby, we need to make sure no one knows about this.

If word gets about . . . it will all be no good. Do you understand?"

At this, I saw again that hard intelligence in my maid's eyes, and a respect that was grudging and uncertain. At last, she curtsied. "Leave it to me, miss. I'll see it done." Suiting deeds to words, my maid left me there, presumably to go inform Norris of his new status as assistant to Miss Margaret Fitzroy, spy of honor. We might be late, but what was that now that there were tips to be made?

I fell back into the chair at my desk. I took the key from the chain around my neck, unlocked the drawer, pulled out my purse, and counted my much diminished stack of coins. It was still another week until the Quarter Day. At that point, I could expect fifty pounds of my salary. Before then, however, I had to pay Libby, and now this Norris, enough to keep them quiet and going about my business. What's more, bills from the provisioners of my family's dinner waited among the letters on my desk. Notices had also come from mantua makers, glove makers, milliners, and jewelers. Then there was my upcoming release from waiting to be thought on. Her Royal Highness had so far said nothing about my staying at court all the year round. If this did not change, when the royal family moved back to Hampton Court for the summer, I would be fully expected to quit the palace, or at least stop depending on the royal household for my maintenance.

I looked at my meager supply of coins. I looked at my journal, where I tried to keep notes as to my various outlays, and thought ruefully on all the times I had seen Uncle

Pierpont working at his ledger. I had always wondered what kept him so chained to that book. Now I had begun to learn.

Perhaps I should add a postscript to my letter and ask Mr. Tinderflint for money. As soon as I thought this, pride rebelled. I had been a dependent before. It galled me to think that after scarcely three months on my own, I must become dependent again. But it was not simply pride, or, at least, not only pride. Mr. Tinderflint had come into my life suddenly. He might leave it just as suddenly. I needed to be able to rely on my own resources.

I scooped my coins back into my purse. I could write my patron at any time. There were other means of increasing my income to try first.

CHAPTER SEVEN

IN WHICH OUR HEROINE FINDS HERSELF
ONCE MORE OUT IN THE COLD.

My royal mistress, Caroline, Princess of Wales, is an enlightened woman. She reads much, and argues more. Very little escapes her sharp eyes and clever brain. Included in her extensive studies are the most modern ideas regarding the health of the body. These ideas include, unfortunately, a near fanatical dedication to Fresh Air and Exercise.

Under normal circumstances, nothing short of fire or flood can keep Princess Caroline from walking two or three hours through whatever park might be nearest, or riding out with her husband, who regards time on horseback as one of the greatest felicities known to man.

The current circumstances, however, were not normal. The princess was less than a month from being delivered of her latest child. The physicians and His Royal Highness had all but cornered her and ordered that the daily walks cease for the good of the baby, who might otherwise be tempted to make its entry into this world prematurely. Princess Caroline agreed, reluctantly, but she drew the line absolutely at the kind of close confinement regarded as necessary for English ladies. "Apart from the fact that I will not tolerate being shut up in a dark, smoky room for a month, we shall have no nonsense of warming pans or illegitimacy here."

As there were those who still doubted which side of the blanket the Prince of Wales had been born on, there was sense in this. Still, I was not the only one she made nervous. It was commonly understood that if a breeding woman took in too much fresh air, it might well expose the babe to harmful and noxious vapors. I am no student of medicine, but I can state that if there is one thing that abounds in London, it is noxious vapors.

However, Her Royal Highness had relented exactly as far as she intended. If she could not have exercise, she would, by hook or by crook, have fresh air. So a series of pavilions were daily erected in St. James's singularly plain and symmetrical gardens so that the princess might read, or sew, or argue with the learned gentlemen she frequently invited to visit, all the while imbibing the dubious benefits of the London air.

Blessedly, our mistress regarded these pavilion mornings as casual affairs. Servants waited with pots of coffee, chocolate, and baskets of the French pastries she favored, lest the breeding princess grow faint. But even better was the fact that more than one chair was placed beneath the green canopies, and we waiting maids and ladies were allowed the luxury of sitting down.

I was the last of the maids of honor to arrive in the royal presence. The moment I walked into the pavilion, every eye turned toward me, or almost every eye. Molly Lepell, the person I most wanted to see, sat embroidering a handkerchief and studiously not looking about her. Mary Bellenden, on the other hand, actually smothered a giggle, and Sophy Howe showed her sharp smile. I knew at once I was about to receive the finest sallies of wit that the assembled ladies could muster.

Unfortunately, this appeared to include Her Royal Highness.

"Ah, here you are at last, Margaret," she said, marking with one finger her place in the book she was looking over. Princess Caroline spoke entirely without rancor. When you possess royalty and wit, rancor is seldom required. Not to mention the fact that my mistress would have remained a commanding presence even without the help of her royal status. In appearance, she was a clear-complected, sturdy, and well-curved woman whose poise made her stand out even among the proud and sophisticated ladies who surrounded her. Her advanced state of pregnancy only enhanced these attributes. On this morning, she was clad in a pale green and white sacque gown, rather plainer than her usual style. The Mistress of Robes had been tearing her hair out for months trying to acquire suitable clothing for a woman who could not be tightly corseted and yet refused to hide the fact.

"Tell me, Margaret, do we blame your new maid for your dawdling this morning?"

I felt my cheeks heating. "No, Your Highness," I murmured. "I'm afraid she should be blaming me. I was delayed over my correspondence."

"Ah. Well, that is good." For a moment, I dared hope that I would be let off lightly. Unfortunately, this hope was as false as the smile on Sophy Howe's painted face. "In truth, we were beginning to wonder if you had left us in search of more exciting company."

And thus were the floodgates opened. Unfortunately, Mary Bellenden was the first to leap through.

"Oh, our Peggy's far too organized for that!" She laughed as she took up a dainty from the pastry table.

"What makes you say so, Mary?" inquired Sophy Howe before I could get my mouth open. Sophy was a tall, golden beauty. Among her other noteworthy accomplishments, she had elevated the art of the sly smile to an exact science. The one she turned on me now, for example, was a perfect witch's brew of hollow cheer and sugared poison.

"Why, when she wants excitement, it's brought to her, fresh and piping hot!" Mary doubled over in her laughter as far as corsets and stomacher allowed.

"And does she share?" inquired Sophy.

"Oh, no indeed, greedy thing." Mary licked the crumbs off her finger. "She keeps her hot excitement all to herself."

"Whereas everyone knows there's plenty of Mary Bellenden to go around," I shot back and immediately regretted it. Not only was the princess frowning at me, but Mary's eyes glittered in a dangerously cheerful fashion. Careless she might be, but Mary was proud of her wit and never willingly let anyone else get the last word.

"And what, one wonders, is the flavor of this excitement?" said Sophy. "Is it highly spiced, one wonders?"

"Or exotic?" inquired Mrs. Titchbourne, with an arch look at her friend and companion, Mrs. Claybourne. "Perhaps imported from France?"

The Mistresses T-bourne & C-bourne were determinedly grand ladies who shared a set of fine apartments in whatever palace the court happened to be resident. The princess depended on them a great deal, and invitations to their parties were as sought after as those to any event hosted by the royal family. They did not quite know what to make of me yet. For my part, I respected them the way one should respect any creature with sharp teeth and the willingness to use them.

"France," agreed Mrs. C-bourne. "Or Spain."

"Do you imply Miss Fitzroy has Catholic tastes?" inquired Lady Cowper, with only the briefest glance up from the letter she perused. Part of me wanted to like Lady Cowper. She was possessed of a strong personality and lively wit. She, however, was not inclined to take part in my plan. I knew she had relatives among the Jacobite factions, some of whom had recently been tried and convicted for their treason. Sometimes I caught her looking at me out of the corner of her eye, and wondered just how much she knew about my recent adventures.

"Have you changed your favorites, Miss Fitzroy?" drawled Sophy with pretended surprise. "I believe you previously favored delicacies drawn from the Italian."

"Not everyone has the appetite for such rich and varied dishes as you, Sophy."

"Or such an eye for profitable business as you, Peggy," she replied calmly.

"Miss Fitzroy is much involved in her own business these days," muttered Molly Lepell without looking up from the handkerchief she was pretending to embroider. I winced. I had hoped for a quiet moment alone with Molly, to apologize and explain. That now seemed at the least highly unlikely.

Mary Bellenden did not even give me time to frame a meek reply to Molly's barb. "Perhaps I shall enter into business myself." Mary tossed her head. "It does seem to bring one such *tasty* rewards."

That earned me a fresh round of pursed mouths and wide-eyed looks. But Sophy was not to be deterred. "You sound as if you know something about it."

"Mary knows all about everything," I put in as pleasantly as possible. "I wonder that she doesn't turn to writing verses for the popular press."

"Perhaps I shall." Mary raised her hand and struck a dramatic pose. "*And oh! The blushing dawn does rise above the rooftop. Where she looks in vain for the face she sees not —*"

"*For the fairest maids still lie abed, and for shame of business hide their heads,*" added Sophy.

"*Safe from those with no business to mind, but in minding others' pass their time*," said Mrs. Howard quietly.

A smattering of laughter and applause rippled through the gathering. For my part, I turned and stared.

This was my first look at the famed Henrietta Howard. Mrs. Howard's return to court had been much anticipated in the newspapers, all of which described her as "the loveliest and most charming woman to be found the length and breadth of Britain."

I will pause here to make sure my readers understand that I do not peruse the gutter press looking for my own name, as some of my sister courtiers do. Rather, it is to keep informed as to what those outside the court believe about those of us within it.

Mrs. Howard did not return my overtly curious glance, but concentrated instead on stirring the cup of coffee she was fetching for the princess. I had to agree with the general assessment that she was a beauty. Her long, fine neck broadened into a pair of sloping shoulders and a generous bosom. Her hair was a rich chestnut color, and she wore it simply, which emphasized her oval face and wide-set eyes. Despite her quiet display of wit, I doubted she would prove as interesting a companion as Lady Montagu, who had recently departed for Turkey under something of a cloud. That cloud, incidentally, was caused by a careless verse. Words, in our world, are dangerous things.

As Mrs. Howard turned to carry cup and saucer to Her Royal Highness, I saw that she looked nothing so much as resigned. This I thought strange, especially as the other rumor regarding Mrs. Howard was that she was the current mistress of the Prince of Wales.

"Very witty, Mrs. Howard," said Sophy with just a shade too much enthusiasm. "But then, you were not here to witness what happens when Peggy Fitzroy turns her hand to business. Molly could tell you all about it, I'm sure. Could you not, Molly?"

"Oh, lud, Sophy." Molly Lepell sighed. "If we are to occupy ourselves with telling tales, can they at least be about someone interesting?"

That earned a laugh from the general assembly, but not, I noted, from the princess herself. She eyed me over the rim of her coffee cup, and with the arch of one carefully sculpted royal brow, silently asked me what I intended to do about all this.

"Well, I for one would be glad to be dull for a bit," I began, hoping no one noted my slightly desperate tone. "Too much spice is bad for the digestion and the complexion, as I'm sure Miss Howe could tell us."

Which turned out to be exactly the wrong thing to say. "That's right!" cried Mary, with an air of triumph. "Our Peggy favors good English cooking. Or perhaps I should say English cooking favors her!"

My heart plummeted. She was going to tell them about Sebastian. She was going to tell Sophy Howe about Sebastian, right there, in front of all the ladies and women of the bedchamber. Once she named him, the betrothal would be quickly sniffed out. It would be in the gossip columns by morning. Matthew would read it. Worse, he'd have it read to him. Did the princess know? I hadn't told her. She couldn't find out like this. I'd lose my countenance, and my place.

I had to stop this, now. But panic blanked my wit. For a moment, I wondered if I should actually have to resort to the Faint.

I must have done some good in my life, because at that moment my white knight appeared. He came in the form of a liveried footman who swept open the pavilion door. His stentorian voice rang clearly across all other conversation and killed it stone dead.

"His Royal Highness, George Augustus, Prince of Wales!"

CHAPTER EIGHT

IN WHICH ORDERS ARE GIVEN, AND
ACCEPTED, WITH A CERTAIN AND PERFECTLY
COMPREHENSIBLE AMOUNT OF RELUCTANCE.

The men of Hanover are not a tall breed and are inclined to a certain thickness about the middle. I would not suggest this extends to a certain thickness of skull. I would, in fact, take most special care not to suggest this while still in service.

It may be truthfully acknowledged, however, that our prince is not inclined toward art, or philosophy, or any theater save the opera. Still, he carries his thick frame with a soldier's bearing, and he does possess the art of accurately judging men's characters, especially when it comes to discerning who is actually in agreement with his cause and who is merely flattering. If there is a form of intelligence useful to a future monarch, that is surely it.

As the prince entered, those of us who had been seated

shot at once to our feet and then dropped into deep curtsies, which is not, I assure you, as easy as it might sound, especially on a lumpy carpet covering an uneven lawn. As my gaze lowered, I saw a saucy grin spread across Careless Mary's face and risked tilting my head toward Sophy. Sophy raised hard and glittering eyes from under her low lids, but not toward the prince. Sophy's venom was aimed at Mrs. Howard.

Prince George, for his part, smiled kindly all around and motioned for us to straighten as he strode to the princess.

"And how do you find yourself this morning, my sweet?" Prince George bowed courteously over her hand. He spoke in French, the language of the court here and in Hanover where he had been born.

"I am very well, sir, thank you." At first blush, our hearty, martial prince and his learned wife did not appear to be well matched. But to my eye, there was a mutual understanding in evidence whenever they met. It was partly affection, but there was more to this marriage. This royal couple needed each other, and they were not entirely sorry for it.

I saw this now, even though not ten feet from me stood Mrs. Howard, cloaked in all her rumors.

"It's good, it's good," the prince was saying. "I, unfortunately, find myself dull this morning. I wish you could come riding with me . . ." He shrugged. "But perhaps you could lend me your Mrs. Howard instead?"

The whole air of the gathering became charged with that subtle current created by the formation of fresh gossip. The princess surely felt it, but it caused her not a moment's hesitation. "Of course, sir. I am sure Mrs. Howard can have no objection to riding out with you."

We all now strained our lowered eyes for a glimpse of Mrs. Howard as she made a fresh curtsy.

"I thank Your Highness for the kind invitation," she said. "I fear, however, I would only delay your enjoyment, as I am not dressed to ride."

In response, His Royal Highness smiled benignly but firmly at her. "You could be ready in a trice, I am sure."

I might only be able to see the world in slivers and glimpses, but my ears were wide open, and I clearly heard that resignation in Mrs. Howard I'd taken note of before. "Certainly, sir, if you wish it."

His Royal Highness waved, indicating that he did indeed wish it. Mrs. Howard dropped her curtsy another fraction of an inch and backed out of the pavilion. Careless Mary, in the meantime, trod discreetly on my foot and rolled her eyes. How she could do that from under lowered lids was beyond me, but she managed it most effectively. I could not tell, however, if she meant to indicate her delight at this apparent confirmation of the rumors about Mrs. Howard. It might have also been because Sophy Howe looked ready to expire from jealousy.

I ignored them both and looked to the princess. Her Royal Highness continued to converse smoothly with the prince about who was likely to be present at the next drawing room. I told myself the rumors could not possibly be true. The alternative was to believe that this strong-willed, clever woman was also an ordinary, put-upon wife, and that was too depressing a possibility to entertain.

"It's good, it's good," said the prince again. "Now, I am off. Do not stay out too long, my sweet. The day is chilly." He took his wife's hand and kissed it, looking for all the world as if he were doing anything except going off to ride with another woman.

To say that the silence that followed his departure was awkward would be committing a gross understatement. Glances shifted sharply sideways, and the air was thick as porridge with unspoken words and witticisms about the prince coming for a lady right under his wife's gaze. I personally did not know who to think less of: the prince, for the fact that he had done this, or Sophy Howe, for so plainly wishing it were she he'd come for instead.

My contemplation of this awkward conundrum was cut short by the princess herself. "Come here by me, Margaret Fitzroy. I would speak with you."

"Yes, of course, Your Highness." I did not look back at Mary Bellenden. I was sure she was smirking and mustering her next set of witty remarks. For the moment, however, I did not have to endure them. Protocol dictated that all the other ladies pretend to be doing something else to lend a patina of privacy to the conversation.

I settled on the stool beside Princess Caroline, but she did not begin to speak immediately. Instead, she contemplated me as if I were a particularly complex piece of statuary. I, of course, could not speak until spoken to. I had to stare at my folded hands and work on not fidgeting. Doing this under the gaze of a woman who has the power to send persons who displease her to assorted unpleasant locations is an improving but exhausting exercise. I do not recommend it to the social novice.

"Your dinner last night," she said finally. "It was success-ful?"

Now she spoke in her native German, a language in which I was reasonably fluent, more so at least than those gathered around us.

"It went about as well as could be expected, Your High-ness," I replied, a remark that had the benefit of being polite, noncommittal, and true.

It also earned me a fresh frown, and I blushed. By now I should know better than to try such a maneuver with my mistress.

"It sounds as if you might have had unexpected company as well. Is this so?"

I didn't even consider lying. "Yes, ma'am. I did."

"It was not Mr. Reade?"

"No, ma'am!"

"Someone else, then?"

"Yes."

She sighed, and for the first time that day, I saw her looking tired. Guilt, ever at the ready, stepped up and pre-sented itself. "You have far more important things to do than providing food for gossip, Miss Fitzroy."

"Yes, ma'am. I do know it." *Tell her*, urged some part of

me. *Tell her about Sebastian now.* "I . . . please believe me, this was not my idea."

"Then you will have ideas to spare as to how to finish it."

"Yes, ma'am."

She waited for me to go on. I almost did, but I let the moment fall away. I could not tell her here, not now, when I understood so little and could do even less about it. I owed my living, and my life, to this woman. I could not cause her to regret giving me either.

For her part, my mistress evidently decided I could be allowed my little secrets, for now. Her tone became brisk and far more sympathetic. "Now, I understand you will be visiting Mr. Reade this afternoon in regard to his commission?"

"Yes, ma'am. He writes that it is finished."

"Good. Then you will have time for another commission afterward. There are rumors being put about that the king intends to stay in Hanover permanently. We need these confirmed as soon as may be. You will write your Mr. Tinderflint. Quietly, of course."

There are those among my readers who might find it odd that the princess was resorting to such circumlocutions to obtain this information. If anyone could make an inquiry of the king, it would surely be his daughter-in-law. Unfortunately, the sniping between palace residents neither began nor ended with the maids of honor. The Prince of Wales did not get along with his father the king, and the king did not get along with him. That some members of the cabinet and government actively exploited this rift should not surprise anyone. Like ambassadors, they were ready to tell their own set of lies in answer to any given question. As was King George himself.

"I will write today, ma'am."

"Good." Then Princess Caroline's face softened. "Do not neglect this other matter, either, Miss Fitzroy. I dislike discord for its own sake, but especially where it interferes with necessary business."

"That, Your Highness, is a sentiment I entirely share." I let my eyes drift toward Molly Lepell, knowing full well my mistress would make note of this lapse of attention. That I had succeeded in gaining her attention was signaled by a fresh arching of the royal brows.

I steeled my nerve and hoped my mistress felt up to taking a hint. "But your hands are quite blue, Your Highness," I said, in French, becoming a perfect model of maidenly concern. "May I fetch you a shawl?" I gave several wide-eyed, rapid, and exceedingly innocent blinks for added effect. The tight twist of Her Royal Highness's smiling mouth accused me of overplaying the scene.

But she did let out a guttural "ooof," and massage her rounded belly. "Oh, very well, Margaret. You seem to have designated yourself my duenna for this day. Go. And take Miss Lepell with you."

Molly started. For a moment, it was clear she would have refused if she could. But bounded as we all were by the dictates of service and protocol, she could only lay her handkerchief and needle aside and make her curtsy. "Of course, Your Highness."

I knew a moment of pride as I made my own curtsy and exited the pavilion with Molly Lepell. I had successfully orchestrated that moment alone with her, an event that had seemed highly unlikely. The single flaw in this little plan was that Miss Lepell did not want to be alone with me.

Despite high heels, hoops, and corsets, Molly could achieve a turn of speed that was nothing short of astounding when she chose. She chose this now, and was all but receding into the vasty distance of the gardens before I found a stride that would allow me to catch up.

"Molly," I said, between undignified puffs of breath and silent curses against all mantua makers. "Please, listen."

Molly's response was to increase her pace and keep her heart-shaped face turned determinedly forward. I watched her back and wondered idly if this was what spurned suitors felt like.

Well, if I was to be spurned, I would also be persistent. I hiked up my hems, balanced on the toes of my shoes, and broke into a wobbling trot across the grass, praying that I would not turn an ankle. Given her anger, I was not sure Molly would feel obliged to call for help.

When I caught up again, I had no breath left to be anything but direct. "Molly, I'm a fraud and an impostor, and what I did was appalling, and you have every right to be angry."

"I see that we are in agreement," she snapped.

"But . . ."

Mercifully, we had reached the paved path that ringed the palace, so I no longer had to worry about my heels sinking into the damp lawn. Molly stopped, and she turned. When she spoke, she did so low and quickly. Molly never forgot the court was filled to its gilded brim with listening ears.

"If you are about to say that you never meant to deceive me, I suggest you save your breath."

"Oh, no. I meant to deceive everyone."

In point of fact, I was still deceiving everyone. It was Mr. Tinderflint who had concocted the story of how I came to court. It was almost as fanciful as the reality, but differed in several important details. The story went that Lady Fran-cesca, all innocently, had discovered certain Unscrupulous Personages were attempting to siphon monies from the royal household and line their own pockets. Being a delicate but honest maid, she returned home to consult with her "uncle," Lord Tierney, about what was best to do. While at home, she fell dangerously ill before she could provide the names of those involved in the fraud and theft. I, as a close and loving cousin, was sent back, in disguise, to find who was so callous as to abuse a position of trust within the household—quietly, of course, and without fuss or embarrassment to the king or the prince. Who, after all, wanted such low gossip in the papers?

Unfortunately, Francesca died of her fever. My subsequently taking up her post was both in remembrance of a loyal servant of the Crown and my reward for being Honest and True.

I had no idea whether there was anyone who actually believed a word of this tale, and that included Molly herself. Not that most people really cared. The important thing was that between this story and the princess's favor, they had an excuse to accord me a measure of welcome. Everything else would work itself out in time. But on one point both Their Royal Highnesses were clear. No one was to know my real business of finding Jacobites at court. Firstly, because it would cause a scandal to shake the rooftrees. Secondly, because it might make His Royal Highness look weak and hasten the return of the king from Hanover, something no one among the prince's allies wanted.

Thirdly, because it would effectively ruin my usefulness as a covert agent. Which was something I, at least, did not want.

"I expected I would come here, spend a little time, and vanish again when . . . certain prospects changed," I told Molly. "I did not expect to be offered a post in my own name or to make friends."

The look of surprise this brought to Molly's pretty face was as genuine as it was scornful. "You thought that you and I were friends?"

"I wished that we could be. You were the only one who actually liked Lady Francesca."

Molly winced, and slowly, a new thought occurred to me.

"You did like her, didn't you?"

She turned her face stubbornly away. "What difference would it make whether I liked Fran or not?" she asked bitterly. The line of her jaw hardened as she struggled to hold a flood of harder words in check.

"It makes a difference because I'd like to know whether you are angry at me or at Lady Francesca for deceiving you."

This seemed to give Molly some small pause. Her eyes glittered, and I was almost certain part of that shimmer came from unshed tears. "Well, it would be rather pointless being angry at Francesca," she said with that cold, clipped enunciation that comes from suppressing violent emotion. "She is, after all, dead."

And you just found out, and you've had no chance to mourn. And yet I'm still here to remind you of everything that happened.

"A feeling may be pointless and still monstrously strong," I breathed. "Molly, please hear me. I would like the chance to be your friend, under my own name. You are kind, and you are honest in your friendships. If there is anything . . ."

I meant to say if there was anything I could do, I would. But the look Molly turned on me just then killed that earnest promise. She knew as well as I did that any gesture I made now would be nothing short of a bribe. I was ashamed of myself for even beginning to make such a suggestion, and I think it showed. I also think it might have been the best thing I could do, because Molly looked at me again. This time—and perhaps for the first time—she saw Peggy Fitzroy rather than the poor counterfeit of her deceased, deceitful friend.

"Not yet," she murmured. "Perhaps later. But not yet."

"Then I will ask a favor of you instead."

Molly's expression turned at once suspicious and dangerous. I did my best to ignore it. "I need to sell some jewels, Molly, but I don't know where to go with them. I was hoping you might be able to tell me."

I was prepared for a scathing reply, even for mockery. What I had not expected was the fury that caused her pale skin to flush scarlet from the roots of her hair to the neckline of her gown. "Who have you been talking to? What makes you believe I would know such persons!"

With difficulty I kept my own countenance, and answered as steadily as I could. "Because unlike Mary or Sophy, you actually do know everything that goes on in this place. Ladies sell their jewels to pay their debts every day. I just need to know who they go to, so I can pay my own debts and keep up appearances. That's all, I swear." I paused. "I've nowhere else to turn, Molly."

Whether it was due to my confession or her own understanding of appearances, Molly made a visible effort to rein in her temper. She turned her face away, and for a moment, I thought she must be ashamed. But of what? The answer seemed obvious, as it does after any furious, blushing denial. Despite this, I held my peace. If I pried now, I would break the fragile moment we held between us.

"A Mrs. Egan will be at the next card party," said Molly quietly. "You can speak with her. She is most discreet, or so I've been told."

"Thank you, Molly. I won't trouble you further."

"It was no trouble . . . Peggy."

I nodded, and together we walked the rest of the way in silence, and at a pace I could easily keep. It was not much, but it was a beginning, and for now, it was all I had.

⟡

CHAPTER NINE

IN WHICH OUR HEROINE MAKES
A PERILOUS DESCENT AMONG SOME
UNRULY AND UNKEMPT RUFFIANS.

The morning's diversion made one thing abundantly clear: I had to tell Matthew about my betrothal immediately.

A small, cowardly part of myself tried to reason that I could have my answers and my solutions to the problem Sebastian's existence presented before the week was out, if I moved quickly enough. Once my betrothal was broken, there would be no reason for Matthew to know it had ever been in place and therefore no reason for me to ever have to confess.

Another, more realistic part of myself saw far, far too many ways for this comforting scheme to go horribly wrong, especially since Mary had put no less a hound than Sophy Howe onto the scent of fresh trouble. The best I could do was to make sure that when the thin ice of secrecy broke, I would not be found guilty of lying, at least not to Matthew.

The princess could only send me to the Tower if she caught me deceiving her. Matthew could stop speaking to me.

Whatever my private plans, my errand was nominally royal business, which conferred several advantages. It saved me from having to find a replacement to stand in waiting this afternoon, and I was allowed the use of a small black coach. This conveyance was well sprung, which meant the jouncing passage through the streets was only equal to that of being in a ship on a rough sea, rather than in a rowboat in a tempest. It also meant Libby got to ride with me, rather than having to walk the whole way behind a sedan chair, which improved her outlook slightly. It also gave her an excuse to bring out my traveling cloak and mask.

My mask was a relatively simple affair, being plain white with a bit of diamond-cut onyx in the place of a black patch beside the right eyehole. It was framed with silver ruffles and tied with silver ribbons to match my gray velvet cape with its deep hood. The reasoning I heard for this particular Nuisance of Fashion was that it protected one's delicate skin from accidental contact with the harsher elements, like winter wind or any season's sunlight.

In reality, however, it is to keep the third of the Great Rules: Fashion must make all activity more complicated and open to misinterpretation.

Each woman in court will declare how she shuns gossip and scandal. At the same time, if no one talks about her, she trembles in fear of losing her consequence. If, however, said lady goes out always masked and cloaked, then even if she is not actually on the way to an assignation, someone might at least think she is.

Matthew worked, and lived, at the Academy for the Improvement of Art and Artists in Great Queen Street. His master, James Thornhill, sat on the academy's governing board, but Mr. Thornhill himself was not much there. After a long and bitter fight such as can only occur between rival artists, Mr. Thornhill had been awarded the commission to paint the interior of the new St. Paul's Cathedral. This left him no leisure time to oversee the running of so trivial a thing as an art school. Instead, he consigned that task to his least favorite apprentice.

By this, Mr. Thornhill had meant to disgrace Matthew. What he succeeded in doing, however, was exiling Matthew to Paradise. At last, Matthew was surrounded by art and artists. Despite the errands and being the man-of-all-work, he still managed to sit in on lessons with the academy's masters. He had time to draw and to paint, to read in the library, and to spend hours with men and youths who shared his love and ambition.

For my part, I didn't think he slept enough. Both his shirts were permanently stained with wine and paint, and his hair was usually tousled, which I found terribly endearing. I loved to see the energy and passion blossom in him. But I feared it, too, because that passion must take him away from me. When his apprenticeship ended in three years, Matthew meant to take his status as journeyman literally and travel to Amsterdam and Paris and Rome.

My service, on the other hand, did not end in three years. I did not know when it would end, if ever. Whenever I contemplated this lack of confluence, I suffered a most curious sensation, as if my heart had dried up and begun crumbling within me. I instructed myself firmly, and repeatedly, not to dwell on the future. Anything might happen in the next few months, let alone the next few years. James the Pretender might come from over the water and be successful in his attempt to take back the throne for the Stuarts. Fire and toads might rain from the heavens. Matthew might meet some other girl in the midst of a wholly different set of dramatic adventures and become madly infatuated with her instead.

As this last thought crossed my agitated mind, I went straight back to contemplating civil war and deluges of unlikely items. They seemed the least unpleasant options.

We reached Great Queen Street, and I stuck my whole head boldly out the coach window to see Matthew waiting for me at the academy doors. The horses were still stamping when I stripped off my mask. With that article dangling from its chain at my waist, I ran up the steps to meet him. The smile that spread across my face as he made his bow might best be described as entirely silly, but I cared not one jot.

"Is it here?" I cried. "Do you have it?"

"Come see." Matthew pushed the doors open with a great flourish.

When Matthew first moved himself and his belongings

to the academy, we endured some disagreement over which entrance I should use when visiting. He wanted me to enter from around the back. I declared I would not. Unlike other court ladies, I did not care to be thought of as sneaking about when I called on my beau. Matthew, rather cautiously, indicated that a number of the front rooms were taken up with classes "drawing from life." By this he meant there were naked women posing for the students. I pointed out I had seen more naked women than he—at least, it was to be hoped I had. He mentioned that the quality of woman who might be induced to pose naked in front of a room full of men was not of the best. I inquired as to whether he was worried that I would see these women or that I would see him staring at naked women of dubious quality. And what exactly would be the reason behind that worry?

With this, I carried the argument. I could now enter through the front door, along with anyone who could pay the guinea fee to study the elements of drawing, painting, engraving, and sculpting. As a result, the dim and narrow halls were crowded, and our progress slow. It was slowed further yet because most of the inhabitants had some word or jest for Matthew as he passed.

"There you are, Reade!" cried one plump young wit. "Going to teach Miss Fitzroy to hold your pencil?"

"At least he has one of his own," I answered sunnily.

"Mind your tongue, Wake, or I'll have it out for you," Matthew growled as he hustled me past. I rolled my eyes at this show of protectiveness, but could not help being a little pleased by it.

"Hullo, Reade!" called a slouching fellow I remembered was named Torrent. "Your servant, Miss Fitzroy. Have you seen that thing Holburn's creating? It's . . . astounding."

"That'd be one word for it." Matthew grinned.

Torrent was elbowed out of the way by August Heathe, a stout, bristling youth who had in his ham-hands, Matthew assured me, the makings of the finest drapery painter in England. "Reade. Miss Fitzroy. Come about the book? In the library, isn't it, Reade? Curious to see how it turned out myself." He rubbed his great, meaty hands together and looked at us expectantly.

"Then come you shall, Mr. Heathe," I said. "The more the merrier, surely."

"Capital girl of yours, Reade." Heathe gave a single, thunderous clap. "I'd take great care of her, if I were you."

"You may be very sure," said Matthew darkly, but he added a quick smile. Heathe and Torrent at once formed up behind me as my honor guard, and we all together trooped toward the library. The truth of the matter was, I loved this place nearly as much as Matthew did. After the confines of court, it was a breath of madness that revived the spirit.

The library had only four other students at the desks when we got there. Every one of them leapt to his feet as Matthew opened the door for me, and all shouted their individual variations of greeting or promises of servitude. This was accompanied by a series of envious looks at Matthew, which caused him to puff up proudly—a fact I would be teasing him about later, you may be sure.

"Well, are you going to stand there with your chest thrust out, or are you going to open the d—blasted thing?" demanded Mr. Heathe.

"Open it! Open it!" roared the students. In a single mass that reminded me strongly of the royal lap dogs, they surged forward and grabbed Matthew by the arms.

A wooden box lay on one of the chipped and paint-stained tables. Someone had already untied the cordage and loosened its nails. The other young men all crowded around Matthew's back as he bowed me forward to do the honors and lift the lid.

I stripped off my gloves so they would not be marred by the splintering wood. Inside, packed in straw and wrapped in cloth, lay a book. Its leather cover was trimmed with red and stamped with gilt letters:

The Game Beasts and Birds of Greater Britain
Illustrated by the Members of the Academy
for the Improvement of Art and Artists
in Honor of His Royal Highness,
George Augustus, Prince of Wales

It was a slim volume, but deeply beautiful, composed of a dozen ink and watercolor pages. Each illustrated a different creature, whether furred or feathered, considered suitable for the chase, and the dinner table. The accompanying text was written in a flowing copperplate hand, detailing the finer points of the animal, where it might be most frequently found, and the time of year and even day when it was best hunted.

The Prince of Wales's birthday was to be celebrated in barely three weeks, on the thirtieth of the month. A masked ball and all other manner of grand celebrations were planned. Of course, the natal day of our prince and future sovereign meant that we courtiers must present gifts. This was an even more daunting task than procuring a suitable wedding gift for a puppy. The prince was a man who, rather more literally than most, had everything. But he was also an avid hunter. When I proposed the project of a survey of the game beasts of his future kingdom to my mistress, she had been charmed by the idea. She even contributed to the cost. Enough, Matthew sheepishly confessed, to buy all the students who had helped him with the drawing and writing several very good dinners, and perhaps rather too much wine, with enough left to pay the stationer, the printer, and the bookbinder.

As I turned the pages, I realized that not one of the young men behind me had drawn breath since I'd lifted the box lid.

"His Royal Highness will love it," I declared.

The cheer that went up from them fairly shook the shelves. I grinned at Matthew, and he laughed out loud and threw up his own fist in triumph, which only made me laugh and clap my own hands in answer.

Now the students crowded around, each fighting to be

the first to tell me which bit he had drawn, or colored, and to discuss point by point the work of his fellows, with due comparisons to the leading journeyman artists of the day. This, I could tell, would take hours, if hours were allowed. I leaned close to Matthew.

"We need to talk," I told him as seriously as I could manage.

"As my lady commands." Matthew firmly elbowed the students back, closed the book, laid it in its box, and turned around to make a great shooing motion, as if he were dealing with a flock of outsize, tobacco-scented chickens. "Out, you ruffians! You heard Miss Fitzroy. She needs to talk sensibly, and that can't be done with you hogs in the room! Out!"

There was much complaining, and many elbows dug into ribs and eyes rolled. I swatted and poked at a few of the slower ruffians myself with my fan, which hung on its chain next to my mask. In the end, the students obeyed, even bristly Mr. Heathe, and Matthew was able to shut the doors behind them.

He turned and pulled out a chair, gesturing for me to sit. I did. Once I was settled, Matthew leaned back against the nearest table. He folded his arms, cocked his head, and waited. He was in his workaday clothes—a plain smock and nankeen breeches. His stockings were black, where they weren't stained with paints, and his shoes matched them exactly. Yet Matthew Reade took my breath away as no man in silks and lace ever could.

"What is it, Peggy Mostly?" he asked.

I looked up into his fond, patient gray eyes and found I had no idea where to begin.

When his use of my pet name did nothing to start the words flowing, Matthew moved closer and took my hand. I could never get enough of being near him. Matthew's presence had worked its way deep inside me. Even with just our hands touching like this, I flushed, and my heart beat frantically. I knew many ladies swore they would die without the object of their love, but in that moment, I felt I actually might. Panic descended. I trusted Matthew, but our feelings —our love, if I dared whisper the word to myself—it was all too new. Such revelations as I meant to make could easily crush it, at least in him. Surely it was better to remain silent than to take the risk. My marriage to Sebastian would never happen, so why did Matthew need to hear about the threat of it?

I took a deep breath. I willed my heart to cease its trembling.

I watched the color drain slowly from Matthew's face.

"Peggy," he breathed, "are you come to tell me goodbye?"

CHAPTER TEN

IN WHICH OUR HEROINE MAKES HER
FULL AND FREE CONFESSION AND MUST
ACCEPT THE CONSEQUENCES.

Lord, no!" I cried. "How could you think that?"

Matthew's sigh of relief slumped the whole of his lean frame. He reached up one shaking hand and pushed his dark red hair back from his face. "Because you're staring at me like you're about to burst into tears. I thought it must be goodbye, or imminent disaster."

"No, no!" I said hastily. "Well, no, and yes, and . . ."

"Peggy." Patience strained the edges of Matthew's voice. "Yes?"

Matthew straightened up. He stepped closer to me once more and took my hands. "You stopped making sense half a dozen syllables ago."

"I know. I'm sorry."

"What is it? You know that you can tell me anything."

He shook my hands for gentle emphasis. "I swear by all that's holy, I won't be angry. Or dramatic."

A certain native skepticism rose in my maiden's breast. "You're an artist, and you expect me to believe there will be no drama?"

"And here's to seal my pledge." Matthew lifted up my right hand and kissed it. Then, while I dealt with the fact that various internal organs were melting like ice in the sun, Matthew hooked a stool out from under the table and sat down. All without letting go of my hands. He truly was most talented.

"Now," he said, assuming a businesslike air, "tell me everything."

"You'll remember your promise?"

Matthew nodded solemnly. "I'll remember."

I liked the feel of his hands closed around mine. I liked the way his palms were slightly rough against my skin. I liked that he held my fingers delicately, and yet I could still feel the raw strength of him. No man at court had hands to match his. I did not want to lose this. I did not want to even risk the least possibility of losing it.

"I'm betrothed."

"*What!*" The force of the exclamation jerked Matthew to his feet and finally pulled his hands from mine.

I said nothing. I just looked at him. Matthew retreated several feet and turned to stare. He approached me again, and stopped, and retreated. I wanted to ask if he was demonstrating some new form of the minuet, but caught myself before I initiated that fresh disaster. This proves the age of miracles is not behind us.

"When did this happen?" demanded Matthew loudly enough that I prayed without much hope that no one was listening at the doors. "Was it at the dinner? Your uncle . . . he can't do such a thing! I thought your father was still living!"

"My father abandoned me eight years ago and has not been seen nor heard from since," I reminded him, striving for patience. I was not angry with him, truly I was not. I was angry with my circumstances, with my uncle, and very much with my absent father. "He may be dead anywhere between Paris and Moscow, and I am a female and underage. Unless I can produce a living male relative who is closer kin to me than Sir Oliver, I remain wholly at his mercy. And no, this didn't happen at the dinner," I added. "This happened before I came to court."

Those words sank in, and I saw the disbelief in Matthew's expression make way for the first flash of genuine anger. "And in the several months of our acquaintance, you could not find time to mention it?"

"I'd forgotten," I said helplessly.

Matthew folded his arms, letting me see exactly how much belief he was willing to wager on the truth of that statement. It was not a great deal. A feeling of uncomfortable and unfamiliar meekness stole over me, but I rallied against it and met my paramour's stern gaze.

"Very well, not forgotten entirely, but I swear to you, Matthew, if I thought on it at all, I had no idea anyone meant to try to enforce the agreement. I'd assaulted Sebastian

Sandford with a fan. Then I called him names before a witness and was thrown into the street because of it."

Matthew was staring at me. I gave my declaration a moment to sort itself out in his mind.

"You assaulted your betrothed with a fan?" said Matthew.

I did not know why I should feel shame at this. What
shame was there? I had defended myself when no one else
would. And yet I was now watching my hands fidget with my
skirt rather than looking proudly and defiantly at Matthew.

"It was necessary. He was trying to . . . He meant to . . ."
I couldn't say it. My halting tongue simply refused to shape
the words. In the end it didn't matter. Matthew had already
guessed.

"Peggy," he whispered harshly, "did the blackguard
touch you?"

Matthew Reade was a slender man with a manner that
was both mild and engaging. Having seen him actually wield
a sword, however, I knew him to be more dangerous than
he looked. In that moment, every bit of danger he carried
inside rose to the surface. It showed clearly in the careful
way he held himself just then, in the tightness of his jaw
and the clear, cold, and terribly steady gaze he turned on the
empty air, as if seeing Sebastian standing in front of him now.
This gaze could break down a complex figure into its simplest
components, or break a human body down into its most vulnerable parts. I maintain that Sebastian was fortunate in the
extreme that he was not there in that moment.

"Yes." I gripped the chair arm so my hand would not

shake. I hated the fact that something over and done with months ago could still set me shaking. "Hence the fan. In his Adam's apple."

It was only slowly that Matthew brought his attention back into the room where we stood.

"Adam's apple," he echoed my words harshly. "Not the apples I would have chosen."

"Nor I, but those others were sadly out of reach at the time."

Matthew barked out a single bitter laugh, and I watched the danger subside a bit further. His eyes turned kind once more, and he lost that careful, alert stance. I felt myself begin to breathe more easily.

"I take it this is what you couldn't tell me before you dined with your family?"

I nodded. "There was no time. Sebastian had showed his face only moments before. I was still too stunned to know what to think."

I'm not entirely sure Matthew believed this, but he seemed willing to let it pass without extra examination. "He didn't . . . importune you again, did he?"

"No. If anything, he seemed afraid. He asked me to write him so we could arrange to meet."

A muscle twitched in Matthew's jaw, and I saw the knuckles on his hand turn white where he clenched the table edge. Despite this, his voice remained perfectly calm and disinterested. "Have you?"

"Not yet, but I must." I dragged in a deep breath and

rallied my nerve. It was time to begin behaving like the independent woman I was. This silly little girl would accomplish nothing. "Matthew, I don't want this betrothal. I never wanted it, but my uncle's insisting on my carrying through. I've got to find out why so that I can stop it."

"Can't you just go to the princess? If she can order Thornhill to take me back after everything that happened, surely she can order your uncle to rip up an unwelcome marriage contract."

I sighed, somewhat impatiently. "These are not the old days, Matthew. Even the king must obey the law as written. I don't think my going in front of Parliament to argue for a girl's right to overrule her guardian on the grounds that she does not care to marry a baron's son would go down well in the Commons."

"Perhaps not." Matthew hung his head. "But I don't like it."

"Neither do I, you may be sure."

We stayed like that for a moment, with me twisting my fingers together, and him examining the stained and splintered floorboards.

"Are you worried my feelings for you are going to change over this?" he asked finally.

The palest ghost of a smile formed on my mouth. "*Worried* is not the word I'd choose. I think perhaps *terrified* touches closer to the mark."

Matthew lifted his head so that I could see the light had returned to his gray eyes. "Flatterer."

"That is my profession, after all," I replied, with all the grave dignity at my command.

Matthew laughed, and I knew we were friends again, even before he perched once more on the stool and pressed his palms together, an attitude he assumed when he was thinking. "What is it you plan to do?" he asked.

"I will write to Sebastian and ask him to come to the drawing room next Tuesday. No one is likely to notice my talking to him in the crush." Except Mary Bellenden, of course, but that couldn't be helped. Trying to meet with Sebastian outside of an ordinary court function would arouse far more suspicion than meeting him apparently by accident at a drawing room.

"You're sure there's no other way?"

"I wish there were. I will be enlisting Olivia's help, of course . . ." From the way his face twisted, I could tell this statement did not reassure Matthew. "How else am I to find out my uncle's side of the story? I can't ask him."

"I know, I know, but, you've said it yourself, your cousin loves drama too much for her own good, or yours."

"That's when the drama's at a distance," I said, mostly because I felt I should defend Olivia, even if that meant defending her from Matthew. "When it's real and involves her own family, she'll prove steady."

"I'm sure you're right," replied Matthew and we both chose to believe him. "But if this Sebastian Sandford is to be at the next drawing room, then I shall be there as well."

I had anticipated this declaration, and I took one of his

hands between both of mine. Then I had to allow for a minute for the inevitable little flutters to calm themselves. Maiden's first love is a wonderful thing, but its side effects can become both awkward and time-consuming. "There is no good way to say this, Matthew," I told him when I was once more sure of my voice. "But I have to get Sebastian to talk. He doesn't think much of me, but if you're there . . ."

"Assuming a stern and manly demeanor, he might take umbrage and resolve to keep his secrets to himself."

I pulled a face. "I told you there was no good way to say it. You have only proven my point."

"What if I promised I would not interfere? Took my oath there would be no challenges or other imposition of my masculinity on the conversation while you are exercising your feminine wiles?"

"Then why be there?"

Matthew looked at me as if I'd begun to speak Arabic. "You just told me Sandford attacked you, and you still ask that question? I will be there because I could not stand to be anywhere else."

I kissed him. It was the only answer available to me. And he returned that kiss with the warmth and gladness that so delighted me. In this moment, resolve formed in my soul as unyielding as London's paving stones. I would break this betrothal to Sebastian. I would use whatever means were necessary to that end, and any man who got in my way would find out just how far those means reached.

CHAPTER ELEVEN

IN WHICH OUR HEROINE ATTEMPTS
SOME ACTUAL SPYING,
WITH FRUSTRATINGLY LIMITED RESULTS.

Was that all, miss?" inquired Libby, pointedly covering her yawn as I climbed back into the coach.

I deposited the box containing the gift for His Royal Highness in Libby's lap and lifted up my mask. I didn't put it on, I just stared at it. Until a moment ago, I had truly meant to return to the palace. This was not, after all, one of my days off. Tonight, the Prince of Wales and his family dined "in public," as they did weekly. I needed to be in attendance at table, which meant I needed to allow time for yet another change of clothing. Olivia would also be at the palace with her basket to fetch Guinevere. If I tarried, I'd miss a chance to speak with her, and it was almost as important that I speak to Olivia as it was that I speak with Matthew.

But my silent resolve in Matthew's arms left me restless.

I was frantic to know what turning of my uncle's mind made him so insistent on my marriage. I had to discover the means that would allow me to smash his plan to pieces. Surely it was to do with business. Business and his bank were the driving factors in my uncle's life.

Now I did replace my mask and lean out the coach window.

"The House of Pierpont, in Threadneedle Street," I called up to the driver.

I pulled my head back in. Libby huffed, set the box to one side, and picked up her mending, which she resumed peevishly. I tried not to be concerned that one or more of those seams might be designed to fail at a critical moment and instead spent the jouncing, creaking journey telling myself that this was a good idea. It was just the sort of thing a confidential agent should do.

As it transpired, the House of Pierpont was just that —a house. It was one in a row of newish red brick buildings. A sign swinging on chains above the black door showed a gilded cup and plate, still gleaming despite the generous coating of the black soot that attached itself to all things hung out in the London air.

Like many private bankers, my uncle's family had once upon a time been goldsmiths. Men looking for a secure place to store coin, plate, and other valuables came to them and rented out a share of their strong room. Such worthies were then able to withdraw their coinage as needed for their expenses or write letters authorizing deputies to withdraw it on their behalf. Eventually, these enterprising gentlemen concocted a scheme whereby one smith would agree to lend another money against the value of the gold in their vaults. Over time, this engendered the mystical alchemy of debts, promises, interest, and alliances that had become the life-blood of the city.

This knowledge had largely come to me as I stood unnoticed and listening while various men who wanted the flow of those promises controlled (or expedited) explained things earnestly to Her Royal Highness. But I still had next to no idea what Uncle Pierpont actually did with himself within the confines of his bank. He had never encouraged visits there from the distaff members of his family. Perhaps I could go in now. I amused myself for a short moment by picturing the goggle-eyed look on my uncle's face if I skipped in Bellenden-style and asked to deposit my money and jewels with the House of Pierpont or, even better, asked for a loan against them.

Clearly the house did not lack for custom. In the time I sat trying the patience of both coachmen and maid, I saw three gentlemen enter the door. All were dressed in clothes of good quality, with plenty of gilt embroidery edging their hats and lace flowing from their coat sleeves. I tried to memorize their walks and faces while peeking out from the corner of the curtained window, as I imagined a first-rate spy should be able to do. This attempt failed. I would not know any of those men if they walked up and made their bow, with the possible exception of one heavy-jowled gentleman, but that was mainly because he wore a plain black coat of the sort favored by Quakers and certain foreign dignitaries, along with an exceedingly full and old-fashioned three-part wig.

At one point, a monstrous, heavy coach bearing no fewer than six rough-looking men creaked up to the bank. Once the great shire horses pulling their conveyance had been halted, these grim, hairy, and bedraggled individuals ranged themselves around the coach with stout staffs ready in their hands. A withered man in good, plain clothes, with a black walking stick in hand, climbed down from the coach and paused to speak with the driver before he entered the bank. The driver, who remained in his seat and held the reins, looked as if he had never seen a barber in all his born days. Despite the cold, he wore no coat, so I could see the pistol roughly the length of my forearm that hung at his side.

Whatever their master was taking away from my uncle's vaults, he clearly meant to keep hold of it. Unfortunately, the bulk of their coach blocked my view of the bank entirely. In my frustration over this point, I uttered several (soft and entirely ladylike) curses.

Eventually, the ruffians clambered back onto the coach, to sit on the roof or to cling to the rails behind. The driver touched up the horses, and the coach lumbered away. After it was gone, the man I'd seen in full wig and black coat came out carrying a leather-wrapped package bound with red ribbons and sealed with red wax. This startled and annoyed me, because I realized I hadn't even noticed he must still be inside the bank. This, I told myself sternly, was an unpardonable lapse.

Libby yawned, and I ignored her. She snapped off her sewing thread in her teeth, and I ignored her again. She coughed hard, just before the church bells rang over the cries of the clothing sellers and scissor grinders who passed us in the street. Privately I was beginning to understand this exercise was not only dull, it was futile. How on earth was I to make anything of these comings and goings? What did I honestly think I'd learn during this narrow window of time? If something mysterious was happening within the confines of the House of Pierpont, I'd have to watch day and night to catch a glimpse of it, or worse, I'd have to get inside the bank itself without being recognized.

It was then my uncle emerged. I ducked back behind the coach's curtains before I remembered I was masked. When I looked again, I noted he had under his arm a leather envelope similar to the one the Quakerish gentleman had carried. I also noted, somewhat to my surprise, that Uncle Pierpont had been spending some of the money he usually counted out with great reluctance. A new ebony walking stick with a silver tip swung in his free hand.

I found myself wondering if there could be any significance to those matching envelopes. Was my uncle in some illicit trade with the Quaker dissenters? They were supposedly great ones for banking, as well as heavily involved in this new business of trading "shares" in business enterprises, something that I confess I did not at all understand. I did know the broadsheets and pamphlets hawked on the streets regularly decried their predations on honest Church of England members.

"Miss," said Libby severely, "my feet's cold, and you're going to be later than usual if we don't shift. If you please."

Unfortunately, she was right again. Whatever I imagined my uncle might be doing, I could hardly be directing my coachmen to follow him through the teeming streets. I nodded to Libby so she in turn could shout the direction to the palace up to the coachmen. In the meantime, I slumped back in my seat and pretended not to hear the cursing as the men attempted to get the traffic to make way, or the cursing as they were ordered to stop cursing, or the cursing in response to the orders about cursing.

"I suppose there's a reason for this," remarked Libby as she moved on to another section of stitching.

"You may ask, if you choose," I answered absently. "But before you do, no, I will not say what it is."

"As you please," Libby replied to her mending. "My feet's still cold."

I was not, however, going to be able to maintain my silence with Libby. If I continued to sneak out and to spy on my relatives, she would notice, and if I didn't give her some kind of convincing argument to the contrary, she would talk. She might talk anyway, so at the very least I should concoct a covering story. This fact rankled me, even more than the note

Olivia had left on my desk. It had obviously been written in a fit of pique and demanded to know where in the *world* I had taken myself. This rankling continued all the while, as I carried dishes back and forth during the public dining.

The public dining is one of the oddest of all royal affairs. It has its origins in the idea of the play, or perhaps the tableau vivant. Once every se'en night, a high table is set up on its dais in the largest hall the current royal residence offered. The table is laid with tapestry, plate, and crystal of the finest quality. All the royal family are decked out in silk, lace, velvet, and golden trim. Then the doors are thrown open to admit whosoever can cram themselves into the galleries, be they gentlefolk or simple citizen. While all these worthies gaze upon them, the royal family and their attendants process in, sit in the designated chairs, and eat dinner.

For the length of this performance, we maids must wait on the princess, carrying dishes and bobbing curtsies as we serve, dressed in our most unwieldy court clothes. For once, our male counterparts have the worst of it, because they must kneel to the prince with each dish they present.

I didn't mind being on display. What I minded was the witty citizens in the galleries who did not confine themselves to shouts and jeers. These merry "cits" amused themselves by spitting pips and tobacco, sometimes making target practice of us. Fortunately, they were usually so full of cider and bad wine, their aim tended to be very poor.

Eventually, our performance came to its natural close, and we were all able to leave the stage for the dim and blessedly quiet confines of the palace. Princess Caroline declared herself too tired to attend the evening's private gathering and card playing, and I could not believe my luck, for this meant that if we chose, we maids could also retire early. I fully intended to do so. I had letters to write and arrangements to make, and more seemed to be suggesting themselves to me with each moment. But as I started up the corridor toward the stairs, the most unwelcome voice of Sophy Howe stopped me dead.

"Do you think we'll be seeing our Peggy anymore tonight, Mary?" Sophy asked, loudly, just in case there was anyone about to hear. She and Mary Bellenden posed together at the foot of the grand staircase. Or rather, Sophy was posed; Mary Bellenden was just leaning her forearms on the banister and grinning. The light from the flambeaux on the walls sparkled on the bracelet I had lent her.

"Oh, I hope we will see her," replied Mary cheerfully. "I'm dying to know what new developments her *business* has brought about."

I can't say I stared in disbelief. I believed what I saw far too easily. Sophy would have arranged this little scene in the hopes of drawing blood and scoring some sort of victory. Mary, on the other hand, was simply enjoying herself, like a spectator at a bearbaiting. At that moment, I truly didn't know which was worse.

"She was gone for so long today, it was surely on *business*, don't you think?" mused Sophy.

This remark sent Mary into a fit of giggles. "Oh, most

definitely *business*. I begin to wonder whether she'll ever be back among us. After all, so much *business* must be done behind closed doors." Mary laughed as if this were the veriest soul of wit. Sophy smiled wanly. Neither one of them looked at me.

"And what is Sophy on about this time?"

I jumped. Molly Lepell had glided up behind me. She was not looking her best. She was clearly tired. In addition, an unusually well-aimed and fairly rotted apple had caught her gown during the public dining and left a huge smear across her skirts. She saw me taking note of this, and we both grimaced.

"Truly, there has to be a better means for the royalty to display themselves to the public," I said. "As soon as I think of it, I will apply for a patent on the method, make myself a fortune, and never be put on show again."

I was talking nonsense, and I knew it, but I wanted to keep Molly here. While she was talking to me, she wasn't off deciding to hate me, after all.

Molly sighed, as if guessing what my babble meant. "Sophy was trying to cozen me today. She thinks to form an alliance with me against you, with Mary too, if she can be brought to pay attention for more than ten minutes altogether."

I bit my lip. "Did you . . . what did you answer her?"

Molly waved in weary dismissal. "Sophy will ever be Sophy. She worries at anything she gets between her teeth. You just happen to be on hand."

"How do you advise I deal with this latest? Shall I go down to cards tonight and draw her out, or stay away?"

Molly paused. The look she turned to me was long, and not entirely comfortable. I watched her struggle with feeling and knowledge, all of it heavy, and much of it pinned up from beneath by matters I didn't know anything about, yet. I remembered Mary Bellenden's little aside about Molly having fallen in love. I wondered if it could possibly be true, and if so, whether the gentleman returned the sentiment. Unrequited love could explain the weariness in Molly's attitude, but so could the endless necessity of dealing with Sophy Howe.

"Go to bed, if you want to." Molly gave the tiniest shrug. "I'll let you know if Sophy does anything truly outrageous."

I meant to ask if she was sure, but I saw this offer to watch out for my interests for one evening as what it was: an olive branch.

"Thank you, Molly," I said, but she had already turned to walk briskly across the larger chamber, making sure she brushed close to Mary and Sophy as she mounted the stairs. Sophy made a great show of ignoring her. Mary rolled her eyes and laughed, to all appearances enjoying the show. I hesitated. I did not like this new intimacy between Mary and Sophy, especially after Mary had seen Sebastian in my room. Careless Mary had no more control over her own tongue than I did over the revolutions of the Earth. But I had more important things to attend to than one night of trading barbs with Sophy Howe.

I could make up a hand for that game at any time.

CHAPTER TWELVE

IN WHICH OUR HEROINE RECEIVES A
HIGHLY UNUSUAL DANCING LESSON.

Fortunately, one thing I did not have to concern myself with was Olivia's pique. It so happened that the perfect way to soothe her ruffled feelings was at my fingertips.

Saturday morning, in the brief period between Libby dragging me from my bed and then dragging me from my morning correspondence, I dashed off a note to my cousin letting her know that at three of the clock, I would be taking my dancing lesson with one Monsieur Janvier. I begged her in the strongest possible language to forgive me for my absence and to please join me for the lesson and to share supper afterward.

I did not set down any details as to where I'd been or what I'd been doing that had caused me to be so late. I had perfect faith in Olivia's discretion, but etiquette and prudence dictate that if one must inform one's cousin one has spied on her father, it is best done in person. I sealed the missive and trusted it to Libby's tender care, reminding her to put the letter into the maid's hands and on no account to be seen by Uncle Pierpont.

Neither Libby nor Olivia disappointed. When I returned from waiting at the princess's nuncheon, it was to find Olivia sitting primly in my chair, with Guinevere in her lap. Both of them wore remarkably similar expressions of frosty indignation.

"You've brought the young princess's favorite for a visit, I see, cousin," I said by way of greeting. Guinevere, aware she was being talked about, gave an imperious yip, for which feat her doting guardian immediately patted her head.

"It was reasonably warm today, and I felt the danger but slight," replied Olivia. The studied distance of her tone was meant to inform me that her displeasure was as yet undiminished. "Now, I am here as you insisted. But, good heavens, Peggy, you know how much I loathe dancing."

I smiled at this, because at least Olivia sounded like herself again. "Ah! But this is an entirely new form of dancing come but lately to the court. You must trust me when I say you will enjoy it extremely."

This, of course, gave rise to a barrage of questions, none of which I answered. Enjoying my cousin's mystification more than a properly meek and charitable soul should, I led Olivia down several corridors and up several staircases to meet my dancing master.

It had been difficult to find a suitable location in St.

James's narrow confines for my particular variety of lessons. We had at last settled into a chamber on the second floor overlooking the Chair Court. The long room was entirely without carpet or furnishings, except for a table and a stool too old to be used in any other part of the palace, but this was perfect for our purposes.

Monsieur Janvier was already inside when Olivia and I arrived. His violinist, whom I knew only as Felix, stood by the window, tuning his instrument. The table was decorated with two unlit candles and a brown-paper package tied with string.

"There you are, Miss Fitzroy!" Monsieur Janvier executed a perfect bow as we entered. Naturally, he spoke in French. "And who is this you bring me today?"

I introduced Olivia. While her curtsy was scrupulously polite, my cousin did not bother to hide how she used the moment to closely inspect my instructor. Monsieur Janvier was not tall, topping my own height by a scant two inches. He had a square face whose only refinement lay in a pair of large black eyes with a curious tilt that rendered them positively arresting. To go with these, he possessed a strong frame, with thick arms and dramatically curved calves earned in the practice of his particular arts. His hands too were broad and callused, and his wrists rawboned. He wore no wig, but pulled his black hair back in a curling queue.

Her Royal Highness, being an educated woman herself, believed that ladies should spend their time in improving activities. Therefore, she had been more than ready to agree to Mr. Tinderflint's plan to engage me a private tutor so that I might refine my skills at dancing and several related activities. What I do not know is whether Mr. Tinderflint ever told her the exact nature of the steps Monsieur Janvier taught.

"You must be a formidable instructor, Monsieur Janvier," said Olivia, in her excellent French. "My cousin has never shown such enthusiasm for the dance."

"It is all to do with the style of presentation, Olivia, I assure you." I winked at Monsieur Janvier. "I think Miss Pierpont will be very much interested in learning some of your newer steps, monsieur."

"Will she?" Monsieur Janvier smiled in the face of Olivia's open skepticism. "Well, we shall soon see if your cousin has something like your facility with my particular lessons."

This, apparently, was a step too far. Olivia turned on me with all the air and expression of a thwarted governess. "Margaret Fitzroy, what are you up to?"

Before I could answer, Monsieur Janvier clapped his hand to his forehead. "Ah! But I forget. I have the commission you sent Madame Rosalind." He untied the package and held up a stomacher, beautifully embroidered with a complex pattern of gray, green, and silver.

"It is perfect!" I clapped my hands. "What do you think, Olivia? I'm to be an autumn willow for the prince's birthday masque. This will go over my dress."

The sound Olivia made was something between a snort

and a wordless bellow. "I think it is the first time I've seen you excited about a stomacher, of all things. You usually refer to them as bars on your cage."

"But this one is special, is it not, Miss Fitzroy?" Monsieur Janvier laid the stomacher on the table and deftly slipped two fingers into the concealed pocket. With a gentle tug, he removed a slender silver blade about three inches long.

I had the indescribable satisfaction of seeing Olivia's jaw drop.

"It will be most useful in case I lose this one." I put my hand to the front of the pink and gold stomacher I wore currently and pulled free the jeweled pin Mr. Tinderflint had given me. With a flourish, I revealed its gilded blade made in imitation of a tiny rapier, which also happened to serve nicely as a straight pin.

Olivia goggled. She gaped. I clapped my hand over my mouth, a gesture that did little to cover the laugh.

"Peggy Fitzroy, I'm going to *murder* you!" cried Olivia. "What is going on here?"

"Monsieur Janvier is an actor at the Drury Lane Theatre," I said, and Monsieur Janvier bowed once more in acknowledgment of this fact. "He teaches dancing to the other actors, as well as card tricks. And fighting," I added.

"*Fighting?*" Olivia whispered in tones young women normally reserve for speaking of their latest infatuation.

"Shall we demonstrate, Miss Fitzroy?" Monsieur Janvier doffed his sky-blue jacket to stand before us in a plain buff waistcoat and spotless white shirt.

"I am entirely ready, Monsieur Janvier." I curtsied. My instructor signaled to Felix to draw the drapes and motioned for Olivia to stand back. For once, my cousin obeyed without question. When both Olivia and the candles were safely out of the way, the fiddler struck up a sprightly country tune.

Monsieur Janvier advanced and bowed. I curtsied and retreated, careful to take note of the distance between myself and the door. Monsieur Janvier straightened—and charged. In an eyeblink, he had hold of both my wrists. He did not pretend during our lessons. The grip that captured me was both tight and painful. The first time he'd done this, I all but panicked. This time, I twisted both wrists hard and yanked down. As soon as I felt his grip give, I danced sideways. My skirts swayed around me so I felt like a clapper in a bell, and my high heels rendered my balance precarious, but I was getting used to them. With each lesson, I learned a little better how they felt when I moved quickly, so that I could slip myself in any direction without losing breath or balance, even as I once more yanked my jeweled straight pin free of my stomacher. I held the little blade down at my side as I'd been taught. A knife brandished at the eyes will keep an opponent at bay, but it can be more easily taken away.

Monsieur Janvier feinted left and right. Olivia gasped. I backed away, and backed again, angling for the door. My blood was up, and my heart beat hard. I took small dancing steps, so my feet would not tangle in my skirts and my breath would not be shortened by my corsets. I was frightened, I was thrilled. I felt daring and dangerous and deadly earnest all at once. No one, *no one*, would ever render me helpless again. No one would be able to hold me down, or hold me at bay because I did not know what to do.

My tutor charged again. I dodged, but was not quick enough. This time, Monsieur Janvier grabbed my free hand and twisted my arm up tight behind me. In response, I let my knees buckle sharply, using the whole of my weight (and incidentally the weight of my hoop and skirts) to drag him off balance before I swung about. The swift and violent motion sent him stumbling, and I was able to pull free. I ran for the door again, but he was there before me, blocking the exit. Now my blade came up, and without permitting myself an instant's hesitation, I drove the tip right into his waistcoat.

Olivia screamed. Felix's playing halted abruptly.

"*Sacre bleu!*" Monsieur Janvier laughed. "You did not warn her!"

I hastily stowed away my blade and hurried to my cousin's side. "I'm sorry, Olivia, truly. He's padded. I can't touch him with that little thing."

I laid my hand on her shoulder, but Olivia shook me off. Without casting a single glance in my direction, she advanced on my tutor, slowly, as if she were now the one intending violence. Monsieur Janvier held his ground, quite unperturbed, and let Olivia poke her fingers into the fresh slash in his buff waistcoat. The waistcoat itself, as well as the vest beneath the white linen shirt, were both padded with horsehair, which kept him safe from any blow of mine and also accounted for at least some of the perspiration dotting his brow.

Olivia pulled some of that horsehair out now. She looked from the tangle in her fingers to my instructor's square, laughing visage. Then she rounded on me, her hair all but standing on end with the force of her own individual variant of righteous indignation.

"Peggy Fitzroy, I am never going to forgive you for not telling me about this! And *you!*" She jabbed a finger at Monsieur Janvier. "You fraud! You . . . you . . . you're a WOMAN!"

Monsieur Janvier laughed and clapped "his" broad hands heavily together. "Bravo! You have a quickness of perception, Miss Pierpont. Trust it well. Most will not believe what they see is an illusion, even after such close inspection."

"After everything that happened this summer, Mr. Tinderflint thought I should learn how to defend myself properly," I told Olivia. "He engaged Monsieur Janvier for me."

Olivia flushed, and if the intensity of her color had borne any relation to the length of the scolding she intended to deliver, we would have been there until well past the dinner hour. Fortunately, Monsieur Janvier gave her one of his showiest bows and held out a hand. "Would you care to try my dance, Miss Pierpont?" he inquired.

"Could I?" Olivia clasped her hands together. "Do you have a spare knife?"

Monsieur Janvier laughed. "I appreciate your enthusiasm,

but we must begin with something more basic. Now, if you are attacked, Miss Pierpont, it is most likely to be by a man, and he is unlikely to expect serious resistance, so he will grab hastily. Here, for example." Monsieur Janvier took Olivia's wrist and held it up for her. "They do this, however, without realizing they have brought their weakest point, that is, their thumb, into easy reach . . ."

Within a half hour, Olivia was doing a creditable job of breaking some of the basic "brute grabs," as Monsieur Janvier called them. By the time Felix packed his violin away, Olivia was gasping for breath, her hair was disordered, and perspiration traced streaks down her powdered face. I had never seen her so happy.

"You are a quick study, Miss Pierpont," said Monsieur Janvier as he reclaimed his coat. "You are welcome at my lessons anytime you choose to come."

"Oh, thank you!" Olivia squeezed my hand. "Peggy, you are entirely forgiven. Although . . ."

I rolled my eyes at her feigned hesitation. "Although what, Olivia?"

"I've always wished I could dress as a man." She peeped shyly at Monsieur Janvier. "Could you teach me that?"

Monsieur Janvier smiled. "Wearing the clothing is not the difficulty, as your cousin could tell you. As with all impersonations, it is how the body moves, and how one talks that completes the illusion. The clothes are only the finishing touch." Olivia listened to this like someone who had been hungry all her life and had just been invited to a banquet.

If the truth be told, the intensity in her face made me a bit uncomfortable.

"What about swordplay?" Olivia breathed.

Monsieur Janvier looked Olivia carefully up and down. "I could, and I think you could learn. But what would your parents say to such instruction?"

"My mother would faint," Olivia answered. "My father—"

My tutor held up his hand. "No more need be said. Normally, I would not consider it. But I have been told a little of your recent adventures. I think you are not a girl who will stay out of trouble, and if you are going to enter into trouble, it is better you go in with some skill and science."

Olivia beamed and curtsied. "Thank you, Monsieur Janvier."

"He" laughed again and made his bow to us both. As he straightened, we shared a serious look, Monsieur Janvier and I. I knew we both hoped this was not the beginning of something rash. Unfortunately, we also both knew there was no way to tell.

❦✦❦

CHAPTER THIRTEEN

IN WHICH A SECOND AND MUCH MORE
COMFORTABLE SUPPER IS GIVEN, AND PIE
IS CONSUMED BY ALL CONCERNED.

Oh, Peggy, how marvelous!" Olivia cried as we hurried down the corridors to my room, and the supper I hoped was waiting for us. Monsieur Janvier's lessons always left me ravenous. "I still can't believe you never told me. What else have you been concealing, you horrid thing?"

"Cards, mostly." I patted my new stomacher, which I carried wrapped once more in its brown paper. "I've become quite adept at it. But, Olivia, you do know this is serious, don't you? What Monsieur Janvier is teaching me, us, it's not for fun and games."

"Of course I know, but it's still marvelous." Her eyes took on that misty quality that meant she was already seeing past the confines of this dull moment and into her dreams of the future. "I can't believe I'm going to learn to use a sword! And to dress like a man! Do you think Monsieur Janvier might let me go backstage at the theater? I've always wanted to!"

I rolled my eyes. "You will run short of exclamation marks if you keep on like this. What do you intend to do with all this knowledge? Take to the highways and hold up carriages with sword and pistol?"

"Now, there's a thought!" cried Olivia cheerfully. "And would it not make an excellent play?"

It was at this point, I fear, my sense of humor wavered. "Don't give me cause to regret this, cousin."

Olivia snorted. "I'd ask when I have given you cause to regret anything, but I suspect you'll just make faces at me."

"Exactly," I agreed as I pushed open the door to my rooms.

Guinevere greeted us immediately, with a high-pitched tale, full of sound and fury. The withering look Libby gave me as she left to see about our dinner told me this was not the first complaint Guinevere had made during the past hour. Olivia, of course, noticed none of this. She just scooped up her dog and rubbed its nose with her own, making the most amazing series of cooing noises. How was it possible that a girl bloodthirsty enough to want to learn how to stab people with assorted sharp objects could be so besotted by a tiny nuisance of a dog?

"Thank you for getting her back for me, at least for a while," said Olivia, her words slightly muffled by fluff as she kissed the top of Guinevere's head before setting her down on the floor to patrol the room at a wobbly trot that reminded me rather too much of myself in my court mantua. "I'll say this, Peggy," Olivia went on. "The world had better take care. When Princess Anne grows up, she will be a formidable woman."

"You noticed that, did you?" One of my duties as maid of honor, and godmother to the royal white hounds, was regular attendance at the nursery to help supervise walks and other activities congenial to dogs and their small princesses. I had, as a result, experienced the full measure of that young royal's headstrong and too-clever ways.

"And if I were you, I wouldn't turn my back on that governess," Olivia went on. "I think she'd do you an injury given the opportunity."

"Oh, she's made that perfectly plain. Fortunately, open murder of one's social inferiors is frowned on at court. Most of the time, anyway." It was scarcely a matter of months since someone had tried to do exactly that to Olivia herself. "Frankly, I wouldn't blame you if you decided to have nothing more to do with any of us."

"Don't be ridiculous, Peggy. As if I would ever desert you, especially now. You're learning to fight. You've become a confidential agent for Her Royal Highness. I could expire with envy."

"I'd change places with you if I could." I attempted to speak lightly, but failed. "Maybe your father would be less eager to remove you into a hateful marriage."

"That won't happen, Peggy." Olivia spoke firmly, but I would have been more willing to believe her if she'd been looking at me instead of at Guinevere, who was in turn yip-ping at a loose hearth tile. "He's just angry now. He'll soon see it's better for us all that you remain here."

"I can't be sure of that, Olivia." I plumped down on my footstool. "There's something more going on."

"With my father?" she replied incredulously "Peggy, I'm supposed to be the dramatic one. Father's a banker. He wouldn't know an intrigue if it bit him."

"Yes, well, it's never too late to learn something new." I watched pensively as Guinevere waddled back and forth in front of the hearth, looking for more wayward tiling. "Has anything changed at your house since I've been away?"

"Aside from the fact that the days are screamingly dull and Mother keeps to her bed most of the time, no, not a thing."

"No new visitors? No unusual meetings? My uncle hasn't left for somewhere and refused to say what it was about?"

"You must be joking."

"No, I'm not." I lifted my face so she could see there was not a trace of amusement here. "There must be some reason why your father is set on me marrying Sebastian Sandford."

Olivia appeared ready to give a heated answer, but that would have to wait. Just then, Libby made her entrance at the head of several servers with trestle and board to set us up a table for dinner, lay the cloth, and present the trays. The jostling, sidestepping, and strained beggings-of-pardon this invasion set off made further conversation not only unwise, but next to impossible. I noted that two of these servers were spotty Norris and young Cavey. Norris, at least, was giving Libby a whole series of grins and winks when he passed close by her, which was frequently. More winks were exchanged as I distributed tips for their service and for the bottle of wine that I was fairly sure was more costly than my allowance strictly admitted. I felt confident some of what I gave Norris would wind up in Libby's pocket. They clearly had an understanding, and given the sheer number of darting glances between them, I suspected it extended beyond the purely financial.

I dismissed all and sundry, saying we would serve ourselves. "You may go as well, Libby," I added.

For a moment I thought she was going to rebel. She knew full well we were about to say all sorts of interesting things, some of which might lead to profit, or at least fame below-stairs. But it seemed my maid was not prepared quite yet for open and public defiance. Either that, or she succumbed to the temptation of a few leisure moments with her Norris.

Once the door closed behind them all, Olivia and I settled ourselves at the table. It was a light supper, with a breast of mutton with collops and greens, fricassee of kidney beans, a purée of salsify, and a boat of sauce to pass, as well as roast potatoes and fresh bread. We were so occupied with passing, pouring, portioning, and tucking in, I nearly forgot our earlier topic. Olivia, however, did not.

"Peggy, I don't want to hurt your feelings, but you know there's really only one reason Father wants you married."

"That would be to get me off his hands," I said. "I'd believe it, except I'm already off his hands. There is something else." I scowled at my plate, pushing the greens about as if looking for the answer underneath the boiled stems.

Olivia fell silent for a long moment, which was unusual. What was even more unusual was the serious expression that overtook her. While I was pushing greens about, she occupied herself with slowly mashing the fricasseed beans into a pale paste. I wished I knew something comforting to say. It was one thing to imagine strangers involved in dubious, even criminal, activities. But one's own flesh and blood? That was quite another matter. She must feel it extremely.

Yet as I watched fresh light blossom in the depth of her gentle blue eyes, I was abruptly reminded that this was Olivia seated before me. She felt all manner of things extremely, but hers weren't the feelings of a normal person.

"What if you're right?" she breathed, much more to herself than to me. "What if Father is involved in nefarious dealings?"

"Olivia, I never said—"

"You did!" She pointed her fork at me. "Or near enough. You're trying to spare my feelings, I know, and you're a dear. But think about it." That fresh light brightened to a veritable sparkle. "He could be anybody. I could be anybody, just like you."

I nearly choked on my bite and had to grab for my wineglass before I could sputter, "Oh, Olivia, don't wish for that."

But she wasn't paying any attention. She was too lost in turning her world upside down, reordering it in terms of hoped-for adventure. "He owns a banking house. He could be holding money, or anything, for anyone! Everyone says that King James threw the Stuart crown overboard when he crossed the channel. What if he didn't? What if it's in Father's vault? He could be a secret Jacobite, gathering treasure from the Highland lairds and passing it to the court in exile—"

"That is about as likely as your mother being a deadly assassin." Olivia opened her mouth and leaned forward eagerly, and I could only groan. "Forget I said that, please!"

"But he could be conspiring with Jacobites. It's not impossible. I've heard that some of those lairds signed over their estates and inheritances to other family members before the uprising so they wouldn't be seized if things went wrong. That sort of thing takes a lawyer, and a bank."

I stared at my lovely English rose of a cousin. "Only you could make such leap seem even vaguely possible."

Olivia laid her hand over her heart and gave a seated bow. Then she noticed the expression my face had screwed itself into and laughed. "Of course you're right. He probably isn't harboring any sort of dread secret, more's the pity." She said this to the remains of her mutton. Guinevere yipped hopefully from near her hems, and Olivia picked a bone out and laid it down for Guinevere to happily, and noisily, gnaw. She watched the little savage pensively. I found myself wishing I hadn't brought the subject up. I loved Olivia. She was true, and she was brave. But while I'd not forgotten her love of drama, it seemed my belief that she would come back down to earth with the rest of us once the dramas all became real had been hopelessly naive.

There was a black currant caudle pie for dessert and, with only some misgiving, I set about brewing a pot of Sebastian's tea for us to share.

Olivia stared at the steam swirling from her cup. She barely blinked when I cut her a slice of pie. For my part, my appetite had grown muted. I left my pie alone and sipped the steaming beverage. Soon I began to feel somewhat calmer. Perhaps there was something to the stuff after all.

I was not the only one who thought my cousin looked far too solemn. Guinevere grabbed a bit of Olivia's skirt in her teeth and tugged. Olivia tossed the little creature a scrap of pie crust to gobble down.

"We're not asking the right question," she said suddenly.

"We're not?"

"No." Olivia spoke slowly, as if the words had not quite finished forming themselves in her mind. "Remember the very end of your argument with Father? He went from ordering you to marry to trying to find out what you've been doing since you came to court. Why was that?" She paused, her attention focused inward. She was watching that argument in her thoughts, turning it over with her dramatist's sensibilities, looking for the thread of story and character. "What did he say? Someone placed you here, deliberately, to do his bidding. He wanted very much for you to hand him a name."

Her eyes narrowed. "If Father just wanted to get you away from court or honor his agreement with Lord Lynnfield, why would it matter to him how you got here in the first place?"

"Your mother might know."

Olivia froze with a fresh bite of pie halfway to her mouth. "Mother?" she cried, setting her portion gingerly down. "Peggy, Mother's a dear, loving woman, but she's not exactly clever. Besides, Father doesn't speak to her of business any more than he does to me."

"But she's still his wife, and she knows something's happening, Olivia." I remembered Aunt Pierpont's face as she spoke her parting words to me. *Peggy, you must stop this game. If he gets truly angry, it will not go well for anyone.* "You need to talk to her. Try to draw her out. She likes me. She tried to warn me against being foolish." We shared an appreciative pause at the irony of this. "She might be coaxed into saying something."

Olivia took a stab at her pie before she answered. "I could try, I suppose."

"Only if it's not too much trouble."

"Forgive me if I appear surprised," she answered in a tone equally arid. "I did not anticipate that my first commission as an aide to my cousin the spy would be to have a cozy chat with my mother."

"Or look after a breeding dog."

Olivia smiled a little at my quip. "Do you know," she began thoughtfully, "I think I might see some merit to your scheme after all, cousin."

A distinct feeling of unease stole over me. "Oh?"

"Yes. In fact, it's quite perfect, because when I am occu-pied drawing my mother out about Father's business, you can be occupied searching his book room."

This suggestion was delivered with such unparalleled delight, it was a full minute before I could gather breath and wit enough to answer. But when I did, I answered firmly.

"Olivia, that is a *dreadful* idea."

This simple declaration of unvarnished fact failed to dim my cousin's excitement, which circumstance, sadly, I could have predicted. "It's perfect," she repeated slowly, as if I'd misheard her the first time. "You can come during the day when we know he's away at the bank."

"It is not perfect. If we need to risk our necks searching anywhere, it should be the bank itself."

"Don't be ridiculous." Olivia waved her fork. "He won't keep anything important there. Anyone might walk in and find it."

"As opposed to keeping it at his house, where you might be nosing about at any hour of the day?"

"I never nose!" Olivia was able to meet my gaze for all of five seconds before she slumped back as far as her corsets per-mitted. "Oh, very well, have it your own way. Let us agree we'll search the book room. Then, should there perhaps be anything else we need to find, we will search the bank."

"Olivia, I am not going into the house." There was noth-ing to prevent my uncle from having me arrested for theft and housebreaking. I had no interest in being transported to the colonies for a fool's errand. The climate of Virginia would not suit me in the least.

"You won't come into the house when Father's not there, but you'll go into the bank when he is? And you accuse me of being witless!"

I will admit that when she laid the situation out in those terms, it looked less promising. "Obviously, I would not be the one to go into the bank."

"Then who would be? I'm afraid I'd be rather easily recognized."

"I hadn't formed the entire plan yet," I confessed. "But that is not the point. The point is that a man with something to hide is not going to keep it in his home."

"Nonsense. A man with something to hide will keep it with his most private and valuable possessions. That indicates his home."

This was a ridiculous argument. Neither one of us had any direct experience with men's secret papers. Pointing this out, however, would do nothing to convince Olivia to drop the subject. I could tell as much by the set of her jaw and that dark light her inner obstinacy kindled in her eyes. I would have to find another way to get round her.

It does not speak well to my character at all that another way came quite quickly to hand.

"We'll draw cards for it," I told her.

"I beg your pardon?"

"We'll draw cards." With only a little difficulty, I squeezed myself into the space between the table and my writing desk and pulled an ivory box from one of the lower drawers. Guinevere, of course, shoved her way around my ankles to bark at the drawer, and I had to hand her to Olivia so she wouldn't accidentally be shut inside. When I returned to the table, I slipped back the box lid to reveal my personal deck of pasteboards.

"Whoever chooses the winning card decides where we search first."

Olivia petted Guinevere as she eyed my pack of cards with their diamond-patterned backs and gilded edges. Her expression was shrewd enough to cause me to shift my weight uneasily, even though it was just directed at the cards. When she turned that expression toward me, I became very afraid I might lose my countenance altogether.

"You recently informed me you have learned new methods of cheating, and now you expect me to draw cards with you?"

"Do you believe I'd cheat you?" I replied, as calmly as I could manage.

This question did nothing to lighten the scrutiny my cousin leveled against me. "Peggy, if you thought it was to keep me from doing something you considered dangerous, you'd cheat the king himself."

I was not sure whether to be flattered or insulted by this statement. Fortunately, I was also not entirely surprised by it. "Very well. I won't even touch the cards." I pushed the box toward her. "You shall shuffle and cut them yourself."

Slowly, with her gaze fixed on me, Olivia set Guinevere

back down. She lifted the pack from its box. Still watching me, she shuffled them, not once but again, and again. Then she cut them, twice. And shuffled them again. I waited. Patience is essential whenever a card pack is involved. Neither did I drop my gaze from hers.

"High card to win?" I asked her.

"Low card." Olivia continued to watch me with great care and attention. Let me state for the record, I was in no way enjoying this. I had no doubt as to what I was doing, but the fact that I was playing such a game with Olivia, even for the best of reasons, was digging into my skin as sharply as any pin.

Olivia turned over the top card from the pack and laid it down. It was the ten of diamonds.

I nodded. "You will draw for me as well. Shuffle the cards."

This was the tricky bit. This was where luck might actually come into play, and as Monsieur Janvier had told me a thousand times, luck could sink any enterprise at the table. I was grateful to all my practice in the glare of court, because without it, I would not have been able to keep from biting my lip.

Olivia shuffled the cards, once, twice, and three times, just as she had before. She cut them once, shuffled them three times, and cut them twice more. When circumstances allowed, I would have to warn her against such patterns. They made one predictable.

Olivia lifted the top card.

"Are you sure?" I asked her.

"Yes," she answered.

"Very well."

Olivia turned the card over. It was the five of clubs.

"And there it is," I said to her. "We go to the bank first."

For a long moment, Olivia did not move. Then she picked up the cards. She sorted through them, looking at the backs and then the fronts. I let her look. Unless she thought to run her fingers across the edges, there was nothing for her to find.

"You did something," Olivia said, as she set the card pack down.

I did not answer.

"You did something, and you're not even going to have the decency to tell me what it is."

Again, I said nothing. On the list of things I had learned from my eclectic assortment of tutors was that when one is queried about actions that might contain some hint of dishonesty, it is better to remain silent. I did not want to provide Olivia with any excuse to cry off our bargain. Therefore, I did not tell her that I had previously marked those cards using a discreet methodology taught to me by a Mr. Peele and refined by Monsieur Janvier. Thanks to those marks, I could tell by looking that the first card Olivia agreed to having turned was of relatively high value. Therefore, I declared high card would win. This prompted my justly suspicious cousin to counter that it would be the low card. Although she thought she was further complicating any chance of deception, she was giving me an advantage. In a full pack, the majority of the cards are worth less than a ten. When she finished her shuffling, my marks allowed me to see that such a card rested on top, so I had no need to urge her to cut or shuffle one more time.

This was, of course, a sneaking and deceitful practice, especially when used against my beloved cousin. There were times, however, when Olivia needed to be saved from her own dramatic instincts. This, I felt quite certain, was such a time.

"Are you going to cry off?" I asked her.

Olivia shook her head. "No. I said I would do this thing, and I will, just as soon—my dear and entirely too clever cousin—as you work out how we are to lay siege to a stout English bank without being seen."

I felt myself smile. "I was hoping you'd help me with that. I've been to look at the banking house, but I confess, I am stumped."

Olivia shut her mouth hard. For a moment, her face tightened in disapproval and the awareness she had just been manipulated into a corner. But Olivia, being Olivia, could not resist a challenge. She leaned forward, resting her elbows on the table.

"Tell me everything."

CHAPTER FOURTEEN

In which Our Heroine

AVOIDS A CARD GAME, INITIATES A BUSINESS

TRANSACTION, AND RISES TO A CHALLENGE.

Most evenings saw a gathering of some sort in Her Royal Highness's apartments. Large, formal parties such as the drawing room occurred at regular intervals, but Princess Caroline liked to intersperse these obligations with relatively intimate occasions with particular friends or people whose friendship she particularly wished to cultivate. Ceremony and protocol eased at these parties. Of course, cards were played. Her Royal Highness also made sure a great deal of very good wine was served. In combination with the lightening of the ceremony, this encouraged people to speak their minds freely, and Princess Caroline had very sharp ears.

During such gatherings, we maids were not only allowed, but encouraged, to circulate and enter into conversation with as many people as possible. This would give me the perfect chance to find Molly's Mrs. Egan.

Only heroic efforts on Libby's part allowed me to make my entrance before the clock touched the hour of Unforgivably Late. It had taken longer than I expected to convince Olivia that I had given her all the details I had regarding her father's bank, that I really did need to get dressed, and that I was not going to change my mind and decide to break into the book room instead of the bank. I made my curtsy to the princess, had it accepted, and was then allowed the freedom of the room.

Perhaps two dozen persons had gathered, all of them dressed in a shining array of colored silks and velvets, and most of them strolling about the room to take one another's measure. The effect was a little like the arena at the start of a cockfight, only the birds were more finely plumed and the spurs less immediately obvious.

Eventually, I located Mrs. Dorothea Egan. Standing alone by the windows, she watched the currents of the gathering with a serious demeanor. There are levels of courtiers. Some on the lower tiers manage to maintain a decent income by providing services of various sorts to those of us farther up the twisted Jacob's ladder that is aristocratic society. Not all of these are services anyone will admit to needing.

"Mrs. Egan?" I pasted on my blandest and most pleasant courtier's smile as I reached the lady's side. "I beg your pardon, but I hoped I might be allowed to introduce myself.

Margaret Fitzroy." I dropped a shallow but still respectful curtsy.

"Oh, there is no need to beg pardon, I assure you." Mrs. Egan bobbed her own curtsy. She had a deep and raspy voice, the sort that made your throat itch as you listened. "I've been hoping to make your acquaintance, Miss Fitzroy."

Mrs. Egan was an inch or two shorter than myself. She still wore the fontange, as well as a black lace veil indicating her widowed state. Her round-skirted gown was mostly dark green velvet, instead of the lighter silks that were in vogue. The effect was of a confirmed dowdy, but her faded blue eyes were very much of the calculating kind.

I flipped open my sandalwood fan. "There was a matter I was hoping to consult you about."

"I am extremely flattered, Miss Fitzroy. How may I be of assistance?"

"It is my understanding that ladies of the court sometimes have duplicates of select jewels created, in order that the genuine might be stored away securely. To deter theft," I added. My patience strained at having to go about this in such a circuitous fashion. But I was a maid of honor and therefore a Delicate Lady. A Delicate Lady could no more discuss business transactions directly than she could be seen in public without her corset secured, especially if that business involved her jewelry.

Fortunately, Circuitous proved to be Mrs. Egan's native language. She would have gotten on well with Mr.

Tinderflint. "Why, yes. Acquiring a paste or glass copy of the original to have when traveling, or for more everyday occasions, is common practice among many of our best ladies."

I nodded in languid agreement. One did not appear too enthusiastic in public. "That's exactly the sort of thing I was thinking. Do you know of any workmen who could take on such a task?"

Mrs. Egan looked me in the eye. The dowdy receded, and the business woman peeped out.

"There are several reputable houses who can be relied upon to make the copy and value the original," she said. This last was important because a house that could assess the value of a piece of jewelry could also be relied on to purchase that same item, should the lady wish to sell the original and keep only the duplicate. "It would be my pleasure to contact any of their principals on your behalf, if that would be of use to you."

"Thank you, Mrs. Egan. That is most kind."

We said our polite goodbyes, and I promised that I would write soon. Already, I was enumerating which of my various pieces I could safely copy and sell. I did not wear many jewels at one time, so the temporary absence of this bracelet or that pin would not be much remarked upon. I fingered the jeweled brooch with its long, straight pin that decorated my stomacher. That one I would keep, come fire or flood.

My personal business concluded, it was time to set about my public duty of Being Charming. I circled the room, greeting the other guests, laughing and trading repartee and commonplaces with the gentlemen. It would not be long before I was drawn to one of the many card tables that had been set up. The men at court adored cards, and they loved, for a variety of reasons, to play with the maids and the ladies. They also, it happened, liked to cheat when they thought they could get away with it. They cheated in a positively gleeful and outrageous fashion if the stakes being played for included a kiss, or a lock of maiden's hair, or a similar "love token."

One could not complain about this. Men might invite one another out to a duel, but we fair maids were expected to laugh and lose. Some of these same gentlemen, however, were not safe. At all. Therefore, it was important not to lose to them during those games. The pockets that the Drury Lane wardrobe mistress Madame Rosalind had cunningly stitched into my stomacher and the folds of my skirt were my answer to this social difficulty. Subtly adding or subtracting cards from the pack is among the most popular weapons in the sharper's arsenal. It is also, as far as I can tell, the only practical use for the acres of fabric with which the court lady is required to clothe herself.

Of course, I would never encourage anyone to study cheating, let alone to attempt to become adept at it. I simply wish to caution all delicately bred ladies that such schemes do exist. Forewarned, we are most correctly taught, is forearmed.

It was not only the gentlemen one had to be careful of at

these royal card parties. The ladies could be as deadly, play for stakes as ruinous, and cheat with as much alacrity and ingenuity. I saw the Mistresses T-bourne & C-bourne taking up positions on either side of the already obviously drunken Lords of Addingford and Allendale. I hoped those men had brought full purses with them. Sophy Howe, I noted, was engaged in a game of ombre with Mary Bellenden and a pair of gentlemen I did not know. They were all laughing about something. Sophy gave me a maliciously merry look as I passed her table, and I felt a sudden tremor of nerves.

But it was when I saw Molly Lepell seated at the piquet table with Lady Bristol that I halted in my tracks.

In daily life, Lady Bristol was a broad, tall woman with a handsome face. But there was nothing handsome about her when she took up a hand of cards. Her head thrust forward on her long neck as if she were a vulture who sought to devour the cards, and her brow furrowed tight with concentration as she stared at each pasteboard revealed.

When it came to the gaming tables, Molly Lepell played because play was required as part of the persona of maid of honor. Like all things Molly did at court, she proceeded carefully. I had seen her cry off from games with the bedchamber ladies, who played in earnest for very high stakes, and I had never once known her to accept an invitation from Lady Bristol. Yet, there she sat, calmly attentive to their game of piquet. Molly had a bare handful of coins in front of her, while Lady Bristol had an entire palisade of gold and silver stacked on her side of the table. The pile of wagers in the middle was all gold and silver coins. There was even a garnet ring among the coins, and I found myself wondering with a certain amount of alarm which of them it belonged to.

"Well, Peggy." Mary Bellenden sidled up to me, hiding her coy smile behind her silver lace fan. I'd been so intent on watching Molly, I hadn't even noticed Mary and Sophy had finished their own game. "What do you think of Molly's new taste in card partners?"

"I think she generally chooses better, but who am I to say?" I tried to speak lightly, but I was worried. I remembered again our conversation in the garden. When Molly thought I had suggested she might be in need of money, she had grown positively outraged. Now, her brow furrowed, she allowed her hand to hover uncertainly over first one card and then the other.

"Who are any of us to say?" Mary giggled as the doors opened to admit a cluster of new arrivals. "Ah, now!" Her eyes lit up with a keen amusement that did not bode well for anybody. "Here comes the sun himself. Let us watch and see where it sets."

I followed Mary's gaze to one particular guest who advanced with the others to make his bow to Her Royal Highness. He was a young man, probably only a little older than myself. His bearing was strong and straight, and he moved with a pleasing confidence. While his dark coat was rather plain, it did sport gilt buttons, and his waistcoat was fairly crusted with silver thread. He also wore a long and full wig, very much in the older style, but this served to emphasize the width of his pale brow while elegantly framing the outline of his oval face. Humor filled his dark eyes, and a smile played about his mouth, as if he'd just heard some excellent joke. Looking at him, I felt a jolt under my ribs, uncomfortably like the one that came when I looked on Matthew.

While I scolded my fickle self for this most inappropriate reaction, Mary, who had no such qualms, stared hungrily over the edge of her fan. The object of her attention threaded his way across the room, nodding to various acquaintances. He paused at the table where Molly Lepell played, but not at Molly's side. Rather, he laid a hand on Lady Bristol's shoulder. I noted the similarity in their faces. It was too great to miss. This young man must be Lady Bristol's son, which meant he was the Honorable John Hervey.

Lady Bristol patted Mr. Hervey's hand without looking up from her cards. While noting this display of maternal affection, I might have missed the other bit of the show, had Mary not helpfully elbowed me. For a single eyeblink, I saw Molly glance at the handsome Mr. Hervey. In that instant, the most remarkable change overtook her. The polished courtier faded away and it was only a simple, shy, pretty girl who looked up at John Hervey.

"You cannot be serious," I murmured, only partly aware I spoke at all.

"When have I ever been serious, Peggy?" Mary giggled in answer. "But I am right. I'll wager you a guinea our Molly has fallen in love with the divine Mr. Hervey."

Molly's eyes had already dropped back to her cards, but John Hervey's gaze was still fixed on her with an intensity that sent goose bumps crawling up my arms. It did not last. John Hervey moved away, taking the moment and its intensity away with him. But like Mary, I knew that moment for what it was.

"Have you said anything to anyone else?" I asked more sharply than I meant to.

"You mean to Sophy?" Mary tossed her head. "Sophy isn't listening to me at present. If she wants gossip, she can find her own."

"Well, this is news," I murmured. "Especially since you were just her card partner." I waited for an explanation, but Mary merely let her gaze wander about the room, looking for less inquisitive company. I decided not to be deterred. "What has Sophy done to you?"

"Not a thing that I'm aware of." Mary's shrug was eloquent and yet vacant. It was an astounding accomplishment. "But she seems to think I've done something to her. Perhaps she takes it ill that I would not back her in your latest quarrel."

I would have been more grateful if I had not known this would change the moment Mary decided it would be more fun to quiz me than Sophy. Still, any reprieve was to be cherished. "Mary—"

"You're about to tell me to beware the Howe, aren't you? Oh, *lud*, Peggy, how dull."

"Courting trouble is never a good idea."

"Better you give that warning to our Molly. Or take it for yourself. A little bird . . ."

But I was not to hear what information that little bird might have to impart, because a gentleman in a coat of a truly amazing shade of blushing rose silk raised his glass toward us.

"Oh, there's Lord Blakeney!" As easy as that, Mary slipped away to greet her current favorite, all but skipping up to his side—quite a sight when the girl in question was wearing a heavy court mantua, with train.

"Ha!"

This exclamation came from the piquet table. Lady Bristol laid her cards down with a flourish. Despite her heavy powder and paint, I could see the bright color that triumph brought to her sagging cheeks. Molly smiled wanly as Lady Bristol raked in the pile of coins and the garnet ring.

Molly, what are you doing? I found myself looking for Mr. Hervey. There he stood by the fireplace, ostensibly listening to the gentleman beside him, but his gaze was fixed on the piquet table, and his mother, and Molly.

"Not joining in the games tonight, Miss Fitzroy?" inquired a voice very close to my ear.

I bit my lip to muffle my startled squeak, and turned. Really, this was too much. As both maid and agent, I could not have people sneaking up behind me.

This time, my sneaking inquisitor was a man who stepped up close enough that my hems were in grave danger of being trod upon. I recognized him as Mr. Robert Walpole.

Mr. Walpole was a frequent guest at Her Royal Highness's gatherings, but he did not flirt (too much), or play cards. His were deeper games. Rumor said that Mr. Walpole was all but taking control of the House of Commons and, by exten-sion, the Parliament. Some suspected that had birth permit-ted, he would have played for the crown itself.

I allowed myself a mental sigh. I had in the space of half an hour gone from arranging to sell my jewels, to uncovering a secret love affair, to gaining the attention of a man who sought to run the kingdom.

Another simple, informal card party for Peggy Fitzroy.

"Indeed I will be joining in, Mr. Walpole." I fluttered my fan and turned a flirtatious shoulder toward him. With the same motion, I gave myself and my hems a few inches more of breathing space. "But it is important to pick one's game and partner with care, as I am sure a man of your experi-ence knows."

Mr. Walpole chuckled. "So it is, Miss Fitzroy. I hope you will not be put out if I watch with you awhile." His eyes measured the increased distance between us, but he stayed where he was.

"I could never be put out in your company, sir," I lied with a smile from behind my fan.

Mr. Walpole's nod said he understood exactly. What-ever else he was, this man was a veteran of the little drawing room skirmishes that occurred daily.

"Do you hear much from Lord Tierney since he left us?" Mr. Walpole inquired.

"A little," I said. "He was rather delayed by the weather in the channel." Mr. Walpole nodded, and I decided to take a risk and pose my own question. "I expect you, sir, hear of him nearly as often as I."

"I hear some. I hear some." This time the nod was judicious. "As you may imagine, Mr. Townshend and I take a particular interest in his business."

Mr. Townshend's name was tightly linked to Mr. Walpole's. In fact, the pair were supposed to have entered into a partnership of sorts—uniting behind the Prince of Wales as part of Mr. Walpole's bid to consolidate power in Parliament while King George was away in Hanover. It occurred to me Walpole and Townshend were probably the Misters W and T whom Mr. Tinderflint named in his letter as "reckless beaus." My gaze darted to where Princess Caroline sat laughing with a tiny group of ladies and gentlemen.

Mr. Walpole followed my glance. He smiled, just a little, and he leaned in, also just a little. "If there is anything you need while your patron is away, Miss Fitzroy, you may speak to me on any subject," he said in a tone meant to be both confidential and comfortable. "You know that I am a great friend of Her Royal Highness."

I did know that, and it rendered me distinctly queasy. What was I to make of a man who was a friend to Princess Caroline, but not to Mr. Tinderflint?

"Friendship is a scarce commodity in our circles," I said, striving for neutrality.

"Well put." Mr. Walpole snickered. It was not a nice

sound. I reminded myself to avoid eliciting it again, ever. "But should you care to inquire of the Princess of Wales, she will certainly vouch for me."

"But why is it you choose to form an acquaintance with me now?" If Mr. Walpole cared to engage in a game of Hint and Innuendo, he could not object to my taking a turn. "Lord Tierney has been away from court for some weeks. You could have addressed me at any time."

"I was informed you were observant, especially for so young a girl." Mr. Walpole's eyes flickered up and down my person once more, and I made ready to move another few inches away. "In the past few days . . . there have been certain . . . stirrings. Certain matters of business, I'm sure you understand."

"Northern business?" Olivia would have been proud of me, speaking spy's cant like I'd been born to it.

"Just so," agreed Mr. Walpole pleasantly. "I thought a word to the wise might be in order, especially as these stirrings coincide with your patron's departure."

That was disconcerting, but the emotion I felt most strongly at that moment was annoyance. Couldn't the Jacobites keep themselves amused elsewhere while I sorted out my own life? As it was, I stood in need of a confidential secretary to keep track of my various suspicions and troubles. I might have to tell Olivia there was no time left for housebreaking.

"Thank you for your notice, Mr. Walpole." I smiled as if he'd just said something remarkably flirtatious, and curtsied.

This effectively signaled the end of our conversation. Mr. Walpole bowed over my hand. He had warm and clammy palms.

I watched Mr. Walpole flow effortlessly between the clusters of people, card tables, and servants. He was circling slowly, casually, ever closer to Her Royal Highness — the center of the gathering and the center of power.

At another time, I would have indulged in a strangled sigh and some muffled cursing. But the lioness ladies of the bedchamber, Mistresses T-bourne & C-bourne, were both watching me with narrowed eyes from their card table. I did not want them whispering to Her Royal Highness about me later. So I shook myself, took as deep a breath as my stays allowed, and prepared to get back to being charming.

I was, however, frustrated in this plan, because the footmen opened the doors again, and this time it was Sebastian Sandford who sashayed through.

CHAPTER FIFTEEN

IN WHICH THERE ARE FAVORS PROPOSED,
CONFESSIONS OFFERED, AND MORE THAN
A FEW WORDS SPOKEN IN HASTE.

It was not possible that Sebastian should be here. I had not written him. I did not have Matthew near to watch over me. This was not a drawing room or public dining, or any other event into which the second son of a country baron could simply saunter on the strength of his family name. Besides, I already had far too many deeply problematic individuals to pay attention to. I simply didn't have *time* for Sebastian Sandford.

It was then that I got my second, and worse, shock. Sophy Howe excused herself from her companions and sailed across the room. She timed her steps exactly. The very moment Sebastian finished making his bow to the princess and backed away far enough that he might politely turn around, Sophy stood in his path, poised and smiling. Sebastian repeated his elegant bow, to which Sophy returned her, admittedly pretty, curtsy. Miss Howe waved her fan, indicating the room in general. Sebastian glanced about more casually and said something. Sophy's reply was clearly an offer to keep him company, because Sebastian held out his arm.

I could not be seeing this. It was not possible that Sebastian had somehow become not just acquainted with the Howe but was on open flirting terms with her.

"Why, Peggy, what is the matter?"

It was Molly Lepell, speaking softly and looking rather paler than she had at the card table with Lady Bristol. I'd entirely lost track of Molly. Indeed, I had all but forgotten the existence of everyone in the room, except Sebastian strolling past the hearth with Sophy Howe holding on to his arm.

Then I did recall one other person. My gaze shot across the room to find Mary Bellenden. She, surely, was the explanation for Sebastian's presence. Mary had either decided it would be a good joke to invite him here, or in her utterly careless fashion, she had told Sophy about how they'd met in my room.

"Peggy, people are going to stare," murmured Molly. I realized my hand was hurting. I looked down to see my fingers clenched tight about the staves of my fan. "Who is that young man with Sophy?"

"No one," I lied through gritted teeth.

"Well, pull yourself together, because No One and the Howe are coming this way."

I had no opportunity to respond. Sophy and Sebastian had already arrived, and Sophy gestured toward me with a flourish of her gilded fan.

"And here she is, as I promised!" Sophy announced. "Hello, Molly, are you here as well? Molly Lepell, I present Mr. Sebastian Sandford. He knew our Peggy before she came to us! Isn't that exciting?"

"Miss Lepell." Sebastian bowed. "And Miss Fitzroy. I must say, when you asked me to come meet you, I didn't expect it to be in such grand style." His eyes were on my gown, specifically my bodice.

"Oh, this?" I said loftily as I smoothed down my skirts. "Just my workaday clothes, I do assure you." My flirtatious response was purely reflexive. What did he mean, I had asked him to meet me? I hadn't even begun my letter to him. "For my part, Mr. Sandford, I had no idea you were friends with our Sophy."

"Alas!" Sophy sighed, making her own bosom heave enough to divert Sebastian's fickle attention. "I cannot claim friendship. It was only that I could not bear to see such a gentleman wander without a guide through our little gathering." She smiled up at him and blinked her great, green eyes. "But now that Mr. Sandford is among friends, I will not intrude further."

"Oh, but you must stay," said Sebastian, and I ground my teeth. I could not tell whether he knew he'd just been trapped or not. "Perhaps if we talk a little, we may yet become friends. Not," he added, with the sheen in his blue eyes that he seemed to be able to summon at will, "that a lady such as you requires the humble friendship of such as I."

"I think I should be very pleased to count you as one of my dear friends," murmured Sophy. I'd not seen her powers of flirtation at such close range. It was a subtle and deeply impressive performance. Judging from the way he stared, Sebastian thought so too.

"And since you and Peggy are friends, we must be too. Here's my hand on it." Sebastian held his hand out, and Sophy, hesitantly, delicately, gave him her fingertips, while with her other hand, she held her fan in front of her face to hide her blush. Sebastian bowed. Sophy curtsied. Molly breathed out something that sounded like a plea for help.

For my part, I swallowed a growl. But I also saw the next look that passed between Sebastian and Sophy. It was the acknowledgment of one master of the craft to another. These two knew exactly what they were doing. The only question was, why were they doing it at all?

I turned to Molly, letting her see the desperation in my eyes. I hated to involve her, but there was no one else nearby I could petition for help. Certainly not Mary. In fact, it was probably better for Mary Bellenden's continued good health that she stay on the other side of the room.

Molly might be tired, but she was always quick to take a hint. "Oh, look, Sophy, there's le comte de Troisheur. Her Royal Highness asked us particularly to look after him this evening." Still talking, Molly scooped up Sophy's arm and led her firmly toward that foreign gentleman.

I faced Sebastian. "Oh, dear. I do hope that wasn't too awkward." Then I quite deliberately snapped open my sandalwood fan.

Sebastian clearly recognized it. He swallowed, as if his Adam's apple recognized my chosen weapon as well.

"How did you even get here?" I asked. "These evenings are by direct invitation only."

I spoke *sotto voce*. Fortunately, we had our backs to the wall and a good view of the room, so no one could come up behind us or listen without being observed. We received some curious glances from the ladies of the company, and I noticed not a few of the gentlemen sizing Sebastian up, looking for some indication of his level of wealth and my level of interest.

"But you did invite me." Sebastian pulled a folded letter from his pocket. "I received it today. I assumed you were ready to talk."

I took it from him and did not bother to hide the gesture. There would be questions and quips about this later, but I opened it anyway.

The note inside was short and to the point.

Consider this your invitation to the gathering at St. James's Palace this evening. I am looking forward to seeing you there,

Margaret Fitzroy

It was also in Sophy Howe's writing. I recognized her hand perfectly. I had seen it before, on another letter also intended to deceive.

Anger robbed me of speech, but I couldn't tell where to direct my fury first—at Sophy for luring Sebastian here, or at Mary Bellenden for telling Sophy about him. Oh, yes, there was no reason I should tell Mary to beware the Howe, as they were clearly close bedfellows.

"Oh, I must have forgotten," I said through clenched teeth as I handed the note back to Sebastian.

Sebastian narrowed his eyes at me, and I saw there an uncomfortable glimmer of intelligence.

"Perhaps we should go somewhere we can be private?" he inquired.

"Certainly not. It would be remarked on."

"And bring yet more scandal to your name?" There was a certain malicious satisfaction behind the remark.

"Which might find its way into the papers. Do you see that man?" I flicked my fan toward a rotund individual in short-queue wig and saffron coat. "He regularly feeds information to the various broadsheets. I would have no problem making sure your name was attached as well, which ought to please your father."

That remark seemed to strike home. "All right, all right. I shall be meek as a lamb. But if it's not to renew our acquaintance, exactly why am I here?"

"You were the one who said we needed to talk," I countered.

"I did, didn't I? It seemed like a good idea at the time."
He paused, considering. "I suppose you realize by now, we're
still . . . as we were?"

I had to give him a point for discretion. The word *betrothed* would be heard by every ear in this place, no matter
how softly whispered. "Yes. I suppose you realize I have no
intention of *staying* as we are."

"There are those ready to force the issue."

"Are you one of them?"

Sebastian did not answer for a very long time. When he
did, I barely heard him above the general babble and laughter
of the room.

"No."

This was not a safe conversation. People had begun to
notice I was being monopolized. Sophy was not the only one
casting ever more frequent glances in our direction.

"Your new friend takes quite an interest," I said.

"Jealous?"

"Do you intend to attack her as well? How do you fit us
all into your busy day?"

Sebastian made a low and thoroughly aggravated noise.
"Miss Fitzroy, let us end this. I was wrong. I was more than
wrong. I am sorry I did it, and upon my honor, I will not do
it again. Are we quits?"

"I wish we could be. Why in Heaven's name does your
father, who is a baron and owner of massive sugar plantations
in Barbados, want to marry even his second son to such a penniless, friendless creature?"

"I rather expect it's because he doesn't like me." Sebastian was trying to speak humorously, but there was a genuine bitterness in those words. "That and, well, Miss Fitzroy, it would seem my family is in trouble."

I frowned. "What sort of trouble?"

For one of the few times since I'd come to know him, Sebastian looked abashed. "Those plantations turn out to have been a bad idea. According to my brother, Julius, we've lost them."

"How?"

He shrugged. "There was a hurricane that took the ships, and there was a plague that killed most of the slaves. The foreman decided that the gold would do more good in his pockets than in my father's. So the acres were sold, my brother came home, and here we are."

"When did this all happen?"

"Early last year. I found out about it shortly before I was told about my . . . our . . . situation."

This news was going to take some time getting used to. Sebastian surveyed the room vaguely. Clearly his attention was still focused on his run of troubles. I noted his coat was not a new one, and the lace was beginning to fray around the edges. At the same time, I thought on the jar of tea in my room. I could not believe Sebastian would spend a small fortune on a bribe for me when his clothing needed mending.

"But wouldn't that indicate you were destined for a rich bride?" In fact, it would have made more sense to betroth him to Olivia, who actually had a dowry. "If your family needs—"

"Oh, we need," said Sebastian quickly before I could say the word *money*. "And yes, I would have thought so. Unless you've a secret fortune of some sort?"

"Not unless my uncle's hiding something. Which, I grant, is not out of the question."

The truth was, I'd never considered this. Then I wondered why I had not. The one thing I knew for certain about my father was that he'd spent some years adventuring for the crown. Such adventuring could be a profitable affair. Was it possible that my father, living or dead, had money and had intended that I should as well? Was it further possible that my uncle and my would-be father-in-law were in collusion to get their hands on it?

But that would mean that Uncle Pierpont had some idea where my father was and whether he still lived. It would also mean my uncle had known about any potential fortune since my mother died. I was only an eight-year-old child at that time. No one would have thought to tell me directly of any inheritance of money or property. They would, however, have told my guardian.

Was it possible? Could I be an *heiress* and not know it?

The possibility rendered me speechless, a fact that Sebastian failed to notice. "And thus, Miss Fitzroy, absent any fortune on your part, I find myself forced to ask for a favor." Sebastian spoke without looking at me. He was engrossed in watching Sophy Howe, who stood laughing with a Mr. Beresford. To all appearances, she had forgotten poor Sebastian, but then she turned her head, as if suddenly feeling the touch of his gaze.

It was an astounding spectacle, and I was tempted to laugh out loud. Here they were, a pair of fortune hunters sizing up each other, neither knowing the other was penniless. They were lucky I was not the malicious sort; otherwise I might have considered throwing them together, just to watch the show.

"You want to ask *me* a favor?" I said, more loudly than necessary, but it did make Sebastian turn his attention from the fascinating and flirtatious Howe.

"Yes." Somewhere between gazing at Sophy and gazing at me, Sebastian's suavity had dimmed perceptibly. In fact, he now appeared positively sulky. "I'll make a bargain with you. I'll do everything in my power to get my brother to break off things—"

I blinked at him. "Your brother? You mean your father, surely."

"Of course, of course, I meant Father." Sebastian waved his hand impatiently. "You, in return, will get me a post at court."

Sebastian's brother was becoming quite the figure in this conversation. It occurred to me I'd never met the baron's heir apparent. Which set me wondering about another member of Sebastian's family.

"What does your mother have to say to all this?" I asked.

"My mother's opinion is neither here nor there," answered Sebastian sharply. "What do you say to the post? It has to be a good one, no assistant clerk to an assistant clerk. It must be something worthy of a baron's son, with a salary."

"Those don't grow on trees."

"That's my price."

"Why? You don't want this either."

Sebastian smiled as if he'd just scored a palpable hit. "But you want it a great deal less." His eyes roved the room, and he nodded coolly, even in friendly fashion to the assorted gentlemen watching us together. "For myself, I don't particularly care. I'm to be married off someday, and you'll do as well as any other."

If my palm pressed flat over my little pin-knife just then, it was purely coincidence.

"Why do I suspect that your father and your brother know nothing about this conversation?"

Sebastian shrugged. "First I was packed off to Barbados and then I was packed off to Cambridge. Now they can't meet the price of keeping me out of the way and so are determined to make use of me. Well, I won't have it."

He wasn't talking to me. He was speaking to figments in his mind. I'd never caught Sebastian unguarded before. It changed his face entirely. He looked younger, and he lost his rogue's charm. This Sebastian knew hatred, and seeing him thus exposed made me shiver.

"Do not mistake me, Miss Fitzroy." Sebastian leaned sideways to whisper into my ear. His breath smelled sour and felt damp and warm against my cheek. "I can hurry our matters rather than stall them, or I could tell that gentleman with the newspaper connections you so helpfully pointed out a few interesting tidbits about the behavior of Her Royal Highness's most recent and most dubious maid of honor, and you might find yourself thrown out of this house as well."

I wanted to cringe, but I dared not let him see weakness. I pressed my hand more tightly against my jeweled pin. If he touched me, I would use it in front of Her Royal Highness and all the world.

Sebastian smiled and pulled away, every inch the smooth and charming son of the aristocracy. "Well, Miss Fitzroy?"

I had to wait until I was certain my voice would hold steady. "I'll look into matters."

"I can give you until the next drawing room for the task. After that, I may be forced to make other arrangements." Sebastian's gaze drifted once more to seek out Sophy. She was just settling down at a card table with three other gentlemen.

Merciful Heaven, I thought. *He really is smitten.*

"A word to the wise, Mr. Sandford. The lovely, friendly Miss Howe is also penniless."

Without hesitation, I turned and walked away. But any satisfaction for this small triumph was swallowed up by an inescapable fact. As fanciful as the notion seemed, an inheritance could explain the matter of my betrothal. But to discover the truth of this possibility, I'd have to do what Olivia wanted. I'd have to search my uncle's house.

CHAPTER SIXTEEN

IN WHICH OUR HEROINE MUST
ACCOUNT FOR HER ACTIONS.

I did not sleep much that night. My thoughts lurched from the possibility that an inheritance from my father might be hidden somewhere to wondering how in the name of Heaven I was going to find Sebastian a post by the next drawing room. It was six days away. That was barely enough time to find out to whom I might apply. But I had to be able to tell him something by then. I had to stall him long enough to make some effective use of his family's ruin, or break into my uncle's bank so I could make effective use of whatever ruin he might face.

Or break into his book room to find out what truths he'd been hiding from me about the state of my family and my finances.

Eventually, I did fall into a doze, but my ghost returned

almost as soon as my eyes closed. His boot heels drummed against the floor, and his eyes glowed blue and gray in the dark as he circled the bed. I saw the blood spattered on his hollow cheeks, across his withered hands, and over his sunken chest. I felt certain this time he would speak. He would finally tell me what he wanted. But he merely backed away, fading into darkness and leaving only the sound of footsteps. I cried out and woke with tears streaming down my cheeks.

When at last Libby came in bearing a tray with my roll and chocolate and, thankfully, a lit candle, she found me awake in bed with my knees drawn up to my chin and Flossie clutched in my arms. I had no idea how long I'd been sitting in the dark, but it had left me stiff, and with a headache. A flicker of actual concern crossed my maid's face as she poured my cup of chocolate. I drank it down like it was the draft of life itself.

Libby, for a wonder, did not ask any questions. She just brought me my blue silk wrapper to put over my nightdress, and a fresh cap for my head, then went to the closet to lay out my clothes for Sunday services.

Left alone, I devoured the warm roll and poured myself a second cup of chocolate. But even that was not enough to clear the cobwebs from my mind. I had heard too much, seen too much, and gathered too many new questions. I wanted to know why Molly lost at cards to Lady Bristol. I wanted to know what "stirrings" Mr. Walpole heard, and why he made sure to point out that they had begun since Mr. Tinderflint left. I wanted to know how much truth there was in what Sebastian had told me. I wanted to find Mary Bellenden and tell her exactly what I thought of her willingness to betray my private business to Sophy Howe.

I wanted to know why this absurd notion that I might be an heiress still clung to me.

I feared, however, this was the one answer I already possessed. If my father really had left me money — even a shilling, even a sixpence — it was a sign that he had cared. He had not deliberately abandoned me and my mother. It would not be his fault if I had been deceived and imposed upon by my uncle. In the secret chambers of my soul, there lived a little girl who wanted to know her father loved her. She was willing to take any risk for that proof, even if it meant getting arrested by that same uncle for housebreaking and theft, or having to swallow her pride in front of her cousin.

I was contemplating this, and the bottom of my chocolate cup, when a knock sounded on the door. I frowned and waited for Libby to emerge from the closet, but either she did not hear or did not choose to respond. With a sigh, I set down my cup and stood to answer for myself.

There, in the gloomy corridor, stood Mrs. Titchbourne.

"Her Royal Highness is asking for you, Miss Fitzroy."

I swallowed, although my mouth was quite empty. "Yes of course. Just let me . . . Libby!"

Libby appeared, took in the situation at a glance, and proceeded to hustle me into the closet so she could wrestle me into stays, a relatively modest hoop with a cream lace petticoat, and ice blue sacque gown, then pin back my hair into some semblance of order.

For her part, Mrs. Titchbourne walked uninvited into my room. She looked about like one who already carried her disapproval and was just searching for a place to lay it down.

"Mrs. Claybourne and I have been hoping for a chance to speak with you, Miss Fitzroy."

We'd left the closet door open. I could see Mrs. Titchbourne pick up my mother's fan from the table. My temper tried to rear its head, but I swatted it down and limited myself to the reply I was certain I could make polite.

"Oh?"

"Perhaps you could see your way to joining us for a dish of tea some afternoon." Mrs. T-bourne turned the jar on the mantel so she could inspect its painted sides. "I see you are yourself a tea drinker. So much finer than chocolate, don't you agree?"

She also surely saw the chocolate pot on the tray. This was a test. She was waiting to see if I would try to flatter her by agreeing.

"Actually, I myself prefer chocolate. That tea was a gift."

"Well. A very fine gift. Whoever gave it must admire you greatly."

I decided it would be better for us both if I declined to be drawn out on that subject. Libby stepped back, indicating I was at least presentable, and I gathered my skirts.

"Shouldn't we be going, Mrs. Titchbourne? I would hate to keep Her Royal Highness waiting any longer."

"Of course. If you're quite ready." She was looking at my hair. I did not wince, at least not visibly.

Mrs. Titchbourne set a brisk pace through the St. James's maze. If those we passed were of a rank to be noticed, she nodded to them without breaking stride.

"Did the princess say what she wished to speak about?" I asked.

"That is for Her Royal Highness to tell you," replied Mrs. Titchbourne.

This was all the conversation I had from her until we reached the doors to Princess Caroline's apartments.

All royal apartments follow the same basic pattern. There is an antechamber where those seeking an audience can wait. This is followed by a larger drawing room for social gatherings. After this comes a series of private rooms, each open to fewer and fewer people, until one reaches the "closet," which is to say, the royal bedroom.

At this hour, and because it was Sunday, the antechamber was empty. The drawing room likewise. Mrs. Titchbourne's slippers padded neatly across its bare floorboards while mine shuffled and skipped. Monsieur Janvier would have scolded me sharply for not managing my movements better. The footman on duty opened the door to the parlor, releasing a wave of coal-scented warmth. This room was shrouded in tapestry, its floor piled deep with Turkey carpets, and there was a fire of a size that reminded one that the princess did not have to worry about her allowance. It was also most decidedly not empty.

I had in my life been stared at by cits, royals, puppies, and my uncle. All these were as nothing when compared to walking into that room and being stared at by these most senior of Her Royal Highness's waiting women.

Not one of them stood, much less offered a curtsy. Lady Cowper looked dyspeptic. Lady Bristol looked as if my coming this close meant she would need to wash her hands. Mrs. Claybourne exchanged a narrowed and knowing glance with her sister lioness, Mrs. Titchbourne. The closest to a friendly glance I got came from Mrs. Howard, who looked up from the prayer book she was reading as Mrs. Titchbourne swept past to knock softly at the next door.

"Good morning, Margaret." As we entered, the princess waved me to a stool beside her. I made my curtsy and sat where indicated, back straight, hands folded. From this position of appropriate modesty before royalty, I both waited for her to speak and attempted not to panic.

Her Royal Highness reclined in an armchair. The spindly table at her elbow held a teapot and cup, and a maid hovered in the background to refresh pot or cup as required. If the Princess of Wales was taking to tea, everyone would soon be doing it, and hang the expense. Would I have to bid farewell to my beloved chocolate?

"You may all go," Her Royal Highness said to the other

maids who moved about the room. "Mrs. Titchbourne, you will close the door."

Mrs. Titchbourne did as instructed. I noted she stayed on this side of it, however. She took a stool beside the great four-poster bed, picked up a bit of embroidery, and set about pretending not to listen.

"You were keeping some very interesting company last night, Margaret." The princess had switched to German. "You and Mr. Walpole held some conversation, I believe?"

"We did, Your Highness." I pressed my lips together. "Ma'am, do you trust him?"

My mistress smiled at the question. "One does not trust men such as Mr. Walpole. One may make use of them, however."

This, I suspect, was not the ringing endorsement Mr. Walpole had been expecting. "I imagine Mr. Walpole thinks he's making use of you."

"I would be most shocked if he did not," the princess replied. Then she winced.

"Ma'am?" I started to my feet, with my hands out but no idea what I actually meant to do. "Are you all right?"

"Perfectly, perfectly." She rubbed her rounded belly. "I am sure this is a prince in here. He certainly kicks like one."

"Perhaps I should . . ." I looked toward Mrs. Titchbourne for assistance, but she remained apparently engrossed in her embroidery.

Her Royal Highness rolled her eyes to Heaven for

patience. "Margaret, I have given birth to four living children. Should something be wrong, you may trust I will be the first to know it." She winced again. "But come, you look grave. Surely that is an unusual attitude for a young woman who was so very much in the company of a single swain all evening."

So, Sebastian's would-be rivals were not the only ones who took note of us. "It was not company I sought, Your Highness, I do assure you."

"But it was company you kept," she said evenly. "I am interested in the source of this contradiction."

My fingers were twisting. I glowered at them, willing them to stop. They took a long time to obey. "His name's Sebastian Sandford, ma'am. He's a son of Lord Lynnfield's, and . . ." I bit my lip, but it was already too late. Princess Caroline had the patience of a stone. If she thought she had not heard the whole of a story, she could wait for the rest until the palace fell apart around her.

"We're betrothed," I said.

Her Royal Highness reached across for her tea. She took one long, slow sip, and then another. She set the delicate cup down silently on its saucer, laid the silver strainer across its rim, and carefully refilled it from the pot. Watching all this slow, precise motion tightened every fiber in my body until I thought my bones would snap.

When my mistress had filled her cup as she liked it, she took it up in both hands. "You will tell me the whole story," she said.

I did. By that point, I'd been wound to such a pitch that talking was a relief, which was certainly the royal plan. My words came out in a muddle of confused German and French with a syllable or two of English thrown in to bob along in the flood. Princess Caroline glowered at me, and I could not tell whether this was for my confessions or for mangling her native tongue.

When I at last ran out of breath, all Her Royal Highness did was sigh.

"Do you know, Margaret, I understand what it is for someone to attempt to browbeat you into marriage." I must have looked surprised, because Princess Caroline smiled over the rim of her teacup. "You have not heard that story? I am surprised. I was supposed to be married to Frederick, the Holy Roman Emperor. I would have had to become a Roman Catholic, of course, but I was not to mind that. The question of my preferred religion was as nothing. Marriage to an emperor was the most desirable match to be imagined." She shook her head. "Sadly, it does not matter how highly we women are born. When it comes to marriage, we are all the pawns of family ambition."

"But you married His Royal Highness."

"He visited me in disguise and was smitten. It was most romantic." She ran her hand fondly across the swell of her belly. I thought of Mrs. Howard out in the parlor and kept my mouth shut. "At the time, he was only the son of the future Elector of Hanover. This was a rank not to be disdained, but certainly nothing so very special. Not one of us truly believed we would ever be here in London." She sighed again. "Margaret, if you discover a way in which my word may be of assistance in this matter of your betrothal, I will speak for you. But we both have our names in the papers enough, you understand?"

"Yes, ma'am." Then I realized there was something. It was impudent, to say the least. It also wasn't anything close to what Sebastian wanted, which lent the idea definite charm. It also might mean I wouldn't have to engage in another round of housebreaking, or at least I could put it off. I marshaled my finest German.

"Ma'am, this betrothal was arranged by my uncle. My father, he was an agent for Her Late Majesty Queen Anne and vanished while in her service. If you could say with confidence that my father is still alive, my uncle could not force me to marry."

Even though it was rude, I looked directly at Her Royal Highness. She saw what I asked. I asked her to lie for me. I also saw that for a long moment, she considered doing so.

But, however long it was, that moment did not last. "I am sorry, Margaret. I have been given no information on this subject. I believe, however, that Lord Tierney is looking into the matter on your behalf?"

"Yes, ma'am," I whispered, trying to sweep my disappointment quickly aside. "But, well, it is that, you said . . . you said men like Mr. Walpole were not to be trusted. What about Lord Tierney?" I spoke Mr. Tinderflint's real name in a rush, afraid to be considering the question at all, let alone asking it aloud. He swore he was looking for my father, but at this point, I was beginning to doubt whether my own shadow was really following me.

"Men like Lord Tierney become a fixed point," she replied slowly. "When they have thrown in their lot, they will not change their side, only their approach. The trick, then, is to discover what side they are truly on." She held me full in the gaze of her clear, intelligent eyes. "It is up to you, Margaret, to discover which side that may be, for everyone's sake. I would so hate to lose you, my little friend." She reached out then and squeezed my hand. "You, Margaret, I do trust."

Tears were forming. It was ridiculous, but trust was not something I had been given much of. Impulsively, I kissed her hand. "Thank you, Your Highness."

Her smile was genuine, and it reached her eyes as she sat back, dismissing all our serious conversation with a single wave of her hand. "Now I trust you to let me get properly dressed," she said, switching to French. "It is Sunday, and we are commanded to rest, but I think God will comprehend that there are many preparations yet to be completed for my husband's birthday celebrations, and I am over my knees in lists. Then tomorrow, we have the theater, yes? Yes. Mrs. Titchbourne, you will open the doors."

Dismissed, I made my curtsy and backed away until I reached the parlor. All the women and ladies were still in their former positions, as if they were statues who came to life only when there was someone to see them. I picked my way between them as quickly as I could and then retreated through the empty drawing room. I had wasted my best chance to ask a favor of the princess. Now it would have to be the bank, or the house, or some kind of stalling maneuver, and just then, they all looked equally hopeless.

I was most of the way across the room before I realized I was not alone.

"Miss Fitzroy," said a soft, deep voice behind me, "may I walk with you for a space?"

It was Mrs. Howard.

I suppressed a mighty urge to squirm, or stare, or at the very least cry, "Now what?" I could not see any way a conversation with the Prince of Wales's mistress—his married mistress, no less—could simplify my overly complex situation. I didn't even know what to think, or to feel, about this woman. We were told such women were to be scorned, and that they habitually ended up dead in gutters, probably of unspeakable diseases. They did not sit in a princess's parlor, or wait at table during the public dining. This was the modern age, after all, not the shameful, scandalous court of Henry VIII. Or James I. Or Charles I, Charles II, or James II.

Then again, King George had taken his mistress to Hanover with him, as well as his three illegitimate daughters. His former wife was not our queen, because she had been locked up under house arrest in a German palace somewhere, a state of affairs that occurred after her lover had been murdered on his way to their assignation.

In my mind, I threw up my hands.

"I should be glad of your company, Mrs. Howard."

"That is kind of you to say." *And you don't mean it.* I saw this last pass behind her gray eyes. I looked for signs of the malice or petty intrigue that hardened the visage of those like Sophy Howe, but saw none. There was only her peculiar resignation.

The footmen pushed open the door to the hallway. Sunlight fell in bright bars across the corridor, and the diamond-paned windows showed the sky was bright autumn blue.

"You are, I think, friends with Molly Lepell?" Mrs. Howard asked, but not, I noticed, until we were out of earshot of the footmen attending the princess's door.

It was odd to hear someone infer, however obliquely, that we maids of honor might not all be loving sisters. "I hope we are friends."

"You know then about her . . ." Mrs. Howard's eyes flickered this way and that. But we were still alone. "Affection for Mr. Hervey?"

"Something of it," I admitted, remembering how Molly had looked at the handsome John Hervey, and how in that moment the polished, perfect Molly Lepell had become nothing more than a besotted girl.

"I do not have much time," breathed Mrs. Howard. "I am going to speak plainly. As Miss Lepell's friend, Miss Fitzroy, I urge you, most strongly, to counsel her against forming any lasting attachment in that quarter. Mr. Hervey is not a safe man."

"You say that very decidedly."

She'd stopped in one of the sunbeams. I had a clear view of her face. If she was lying or acted from some selfish motive, it did not show. Not that this meant anything. I could name any of a dozen courtiers who could lie without batting an eyelash. I was on my way to becoming one of them.

"I have some familiarity with the type, and the man himself," she said. "His motive force is money, and need of money will drive him harder and farther than love ever could. If Miss Lepell attaches herself to him, she will be likewise driven."

Money again, always money. My mind's eye showed me Lady Bristol—her neck and chin thrust forward, her eyes cold and stern as she clutched her cards. Such a prisoner of the gaming tables would be much in need of money to feed her habit of play.

But I could not separate the words from the messenger. This was not a good woman in front of me. She was deceitful. How could she be anything else? She might even desire the handsome—and much younger—Mr. Hervey for herself.

This time Mrs. Howard's wry, tight smile was notably lacking in sympathy. "I have done what I have done, and for my own reasons." She did not look away from me as she said it, not once. "Nevertheless, I mean none of you any harm and would help you if allowed." She drew herself up, all calm and resigned dignity. "Please consider what I've said, Miss Fitzroy, for the sake of your friend."

As I watched Mrs. Howard take her leave, I could not escape the sensation that some opportunity had been missed. I tried to tell myself that was not possible. I could not be loyal to the princess and make friends with her deceiver at the same time. Except it was impossible that the princess should be deceived on a point that was common gossip. Except she could not be *allowing* this alliance between Mrs. Howard and her husband.

Except she clearly was. I pressed both hands against my scalp as if to keep my hair from flying off. I did not need a confidential secretary to keep track of what was happening around me. I needed my own Royal Bureau of Plots, Gossip, and Conspiracy. Perhaps I could apply to Mr. Walpole for the funding.

CHAPTER SEVENTEEN

IN WHICH OUR HEROINE ENGAGES
IN A PAIR OF ENTIRELY
UNSATISFACTORY CONFRONTATIONS.

One of the great frustrations of a maid of honor's life is that her time is not her own. That frustration is multiplied when the maid is supposed to be engaged in conspiracies and robbery.

I had planned on asking Molly to take my afternoon waiting. I could send Norris for Olivia and Matthew, and we could find a way to assay the bank. But I arrived at the pavilions Monday morning to find Mary Bellenden was not in waiting. Her maid—an ancient dame with a hunched back and a knowing gleam in her eyes—came to tell us that Mary had a terrible cold and did not wish to expose Her Royal Highness to the contagion. This meant there was no maid to spare, and I had no escape for the rest of the day.

During that entire morning's gathering, I was conscious of the most unusual hope that Sophy's witty quips would turn in my direction. I was angry and restless and far too aware I was wasting a whole day. This all left me itching for some sort of fight. But Sophy remained serene. Worse, when I took my leave to rest and change clothes for supper and that evening's excursion to the theater, she smiled at me.

The disquiet bred by that smile was profound. Sophy was not a complex personage. The list of things that made her happy was short—a new lover with money, a new scheme that met with success, or a new verse in the paper complimenting her charms. In an effort to mitigate my growing reputation for indulging in the extremes of tardiness, I had not paused to read the papers that morning, so I might have missed a new verse. I did not believe even Sophy could have tumbled Sebastian so quickly as to consider him her lover; besides, he said he had no money. That left only a new scheme, and one she thought was working.

Contemplation of this unpleasant possibility may have caused my footsteps to lag a trifle as I returned to my rooms. Libby was waiting for me, of course.

"About time," she said as she got to her feet. There was also something about "strapping a clock to your back to give you some notion of time." I ignored that. "I was asked to give you this, miss."

She held out a folded paper. I took it, puzzled. It wasn't ordinary letter paper, but heavier and rougher. I felt somehow

I should recognize it. I undid the black ribbon to find a raggedly torn piece of newspaper and my answer to the riddle of What Made Sophy Smile.

The article was titled *Fashionable Observations,* and it did not take long to discover why this had been sent to me.

What are we to make of Miss F——, this mysterious miss who so recently tripped into the most exclusive of court circles? This ever-elusive Fair One is not noted for allowing herself to be fascinated. Yet recently, a young swain whom Our Observer names as the Honorable Mr. S——, one son of the Baron of L——, seems to have scaled that parapet. The Observer reports that they spoke in low tones and on the terms of greatest intimacy for some considerable length of time.

Alas! We must hope that Miss F—— has not yet entirely lost her heart, for she has a rival for Mr. S——'s affections. Despite her repeated efforts and the best use of all her considerable charms, Miss F—— was not able to keep Mr. S—— from leaving her side to join her sister maid, Miss H——, at a game of cards. There, according to the knowing eye of Our Observer, Mr. S—— proceeded to charm all at the table with his wit and gallantry. Miss F——, on the other hand, was seen to leave the room in a state of considerable pique.

One would not look to see a vow of vengeance upon so lovely a face, but it is well known that a young lady who has been crossed in so deep and obvious an affection may act in a rash manner—

"That's not what happened!" I cried. "That's not even remotely what happened!" But it might not matter, because on the heavy paper that wrapped the article was a single line written in Matthew's clear hand.

Was this your Sebastian?

I felt the blood drain from my cheeks. "Did Matthew bring this?"

Libby glanced aside. "I was not to say."

The sentence had barely left her lips before I ran into the corridor, in some vain hope of seeing Matthew step out from a nearby room. But there was no one. Even the sunbeams had deserted the dim hallway.

"I tried to keep him, miss," said Libby behind me. "But he wouldn't wait."

Neither did I. I flung the paper in Libby's direction and snatched up my hems to run down the hallway. If my maid tried to follow me, she gave it up as a bad job, because I was alone by the time I reached Mary Bellenden's door and pushed my way through.

"Wad on eard?" she cried. "Peggy! Wad are you doing here?"

Mary was in bed, propped up on bolsters and clutching

a massive handkerchief. Her nose was an extraordinary shade of red, and her eyes were streaming and shadowed. At the hearthside, her ancient maid poured boiling water into a basin full of something that smelled remarkably foul.

"You stupid, poisonous, careless, mindless . . . creature!" I shouted at Mary. "Did she pay you to tell her my secrets, or did you just decide it would be fun?"

Mary stared at me. She stared at her maid, who stood frozen in place with the kettle in her hand. "She'd lodt her wits," declared Mary.

"Oh, yes, I've lost my wits, and that's why Sophy knew to write to Sebastian and invite him to the party!" And give him a chance to issue his demands and his deadlines —

"Sophy wrod to your beau?" Mary sneezed and honked into her kerchief. "Ad you care? I tought you didn't like him."

"That's not the point!" I shouted. "The point is that you told her, and now, now, it's all over the papers and people think . . ."

Oh, God in Heaven, people would think I actually cared about Sebastian! Matthew would think I didn't tell him about the betrothal because I harbored some affection for that arrogant monstrosity! That had to be why he wrote so tersely.

"Lud, Peggy," groaned Mary. "Do go away. I'b doo tired to keeb ub wid your delirium."

"I'll tell you who's delirious!" I snapped back. "You are, if you think it's not plain as paint who told Sophy about Sebastian, you snake!"

The next thing I knew, a damp towel hit me in the face. I snatched at it, to see Mary reared up on the bolsters, her face flushed with far more than fever.

"Because of course it could'd possibly hab been dat sneaking liddle maid you pay to spy for you," snapped Mary. "Oh, do! Peggy de Mystery Girl can't possibly be mistagen aboud adybody! Eberybody loves Peggy, from da princess on down. It's just mean old Sophy and stubid, careless Mary Bellenden who don'd!"

She flopped back on the pillows and gave me a glower of professional sharpness spoiled only by a fresh sneeze. "Ged away frob be until you cad talk sense."

I did "ged away." Slowly and reluctantly, carrying the far-too-heavy possibility that Careless Mary—bedridden and most thoroughly provoked—had just spoken the truth.

I sat miserable and sulky through the play that night. This was probably a shame. The comedy was *The Wanton Wife*, and it had the rest of the party in stitches, including Her Royal Highness. But I could not get past Mary's assessment of my judgment. I truly might have been mistaken about who had talked to Sophy about Sebastian. It could easily have been Libby.

The fact that I'd had no time to write to Matthew, let alone Olivia, did not help my mood. Among the unpleasant possibilities that had squeezed into the royal theater box with me was that Matthew must believe I had flirted with Sebastian. The strength of our feelings had never really been tested before, and I realized, bleakly, that I had no idea what I would do if it failed.

With such pleasant thoughts as these for bedfellows that night, my readers will not be surprised to learn that once again sleep proved elusive. This meant my ghost could not make an appearance, but that seemed poor compensation for the aching head and burning eyes caused by hours of staring into darkness.

When dawn, and Libby, at last arrived, I sat in bed for a long time, watching her. I don't know what I expected to see as she moved about the room. Perhaps I thought that if she really was the one who had talked to Sophy, I could disconcert her guilty conscience with the strength of my weary gaze.

"Will you be getting up today, miss?" Libby inquired mildly as she handed over my chocolate.

"Yes, yes." I gulped my drink and was rewarded with a scalded mouth. Even chocolate was conspiring against me.

"And when might this grand event be occurring?" asked Libby.

This was quite enough. She was not the only one with the right to be snippy this morning.

"Libby?" I said. She folded her hands, and Waited at me. "Someone told Sophy Howe that Sebastian Sandford came to see me, and . . ." I stopped. I did not need to elaborate for Libby what other people might think. She probably knew better than I did. "Was it you?"

I waited for her to deny it, energetically. But Libby just

snorted. "It didn't have to be me. That one's got plenty of her own spies."

I had nothing at all to say to this. Libby apparently took my silence and my codfish stare as evidence of a certain weakness in my powers of reason. "You must know you're not well liked below-stairs, miss." She enunciated each word carefully. "It doesn't take a great deal for some people to start telling what they think they know."

"I'm not well liked? What have I done?" *Except pay out more than I could afford to every single servant in the whole of St. James's Palace,* I added silently and perhaps a trifle irritably.

"You've forgotten?" Libby rolled her eyes. "Well, he was only a footman, and was not much to remember, I expect."

Oh. No. "How could anybody blame me for Robert Ballantyne's ruin?" I meant to shout, but I could barely manage a croak. "He acted alone. I had nothing to do with it." Although I had to admit, it wasn't for lack of trying. "Besides, he was the Jacobite."

"I'm sorry to inform you, miss, but it don't matter. He was below-stairs, and his family was below-stairs, and for some, blood is not only thicker, but . . ." Libby stopped and shrugged.

"Robert still has relatives in service?" I knew his father had been, but I hadn't stopped to consider that there might be others. I'd been too busy trying to sort out my life above-stairs.

"Not anymore. They were all dismissed for the crime of

being his relatives, and for maybe wishing they were cleaning up after the King Over the Water instead of German George."

And there it was. If I'd lost someone his position, I instantly became the enemy of all those who remained behind.

"Not that it matters to me who's in the bed I'm making as long as I've got a roof, dry feet, and a full belly at the end of it," Libby went on. "But it's amazing what some people will let get in the way of what's important."

Yes it is, I agreed silently. None of this, however, answered my original question.

"But was it you who told Sophy about Sebastian?" I asked.

"No," said Libby flatly. "Neither was it Norris or Cavey —that I would have known. I can name you plenty who might have done it, if you want to hear."

I found I had no answer to give to this bald declaration, and Libby returned to the closet without waiting to be dismissed. I stayed as I was for a long moment after that, clutching my cup of chocolate as if I feared it might be planning its escape.

I had honestly not thought about it. I prided myself on understanding the workings of the world below-stairs and its inhabitants, but I hadn't thought about loyalty and family, and that there might be a whole group of people somewhere in this palace who did not like me for what I had done. Aside from Sophy Howe and any of her friends, that is.

The worst part of it was that I was dependent on these

people. The life of a maid of honor is essentially that of a permanent houseguest. I had very little power over those who served, aside from some slight ability to make their days uncomfortable if I chose to turn shrewish. But these unknowns could do far worse to me.

I tried to tell myself that hand had been dealt and I must play it out as best I could. This effort met with limited success. Seeking distraction, I took up the first of the letters that lay on the tray beside the plate. It was from Mr. Tinderflint. I broke the seal, hoping it might provide me some sort of guidance. But as I scanned the lines of Latin, French, and Greek, that hope plummeted with breathtaking rapidity.

My Dear,

I write this from the city, where your letter has just found me. I hope Jane continues in her quiet and peaceful life there, untroubled by any suitors importuning her.

"You know Mr. Walpole's talking to me," I murmured. "If you were that worried, you might have said something before you left."

As to your inquiry about the Family S——, they are, as you know, not townsfolk, preferring to keep to their own neighborhood on the skirts of the Great Romney marsh. It is not my ideal of country. The air in that district, I'm convinced, is bad for one's health. Neither is the company there of the most wholesome sort, as the marsh is a notable haunt of thieves, smugglers, Jacobites,

and men of similar ilk. I fear the family may have made a ques-
tionable exchange when they decided to quit Barbados to return
to that country. I do wonder at it myself. I would council Jane to
avoid them as much as possible. If necessary, I think you may ap-
ply to your good friend Mrs. PG for assistance in advising Jane
regarding the family.

I tossed the letter down, my teeth grinding in frustration. What was the point of a spy master if he could not supply his spies with important information? Here my great, schem- ing, mysterious patron could only tell me that Sebastian was a conniving no-good from a family of conniving no-goods who associated themselves with other conniving no-goods from a county well populated by members of that species.

"Will you take another cup of obscurity with your roll, Miss Fitzroy?" Then a highly unwelcome thought flitted about the back of my mind. What if Mr. Tinderflint did have important information? What if he was withholding it?

Impatience and a sudden chilly unease impelled me to action. I put the tray aside and kicked my way out from under the covers. Grabbing my keys from my dressing table, I un- locked my desk.

Libby popped out from the closet like she'd been launched on a spring.

"Miss!"

I stopped her with a glance. That was a new thing, and I admit it pleased me.

"I am writing two letters," I said. "I will be quick, and

I will put them and my keys in your hands afterward. You will see that the letters get where they need to go. Get Norris to help, and make sure he's paid for his trouble. That is your work for today. Do you understand?"

Libby raised her brows in surprise that was not entirely devoid of disapproval. "Yes, miss. Very clear."

My first letter was to Matthew. It was brief.

Yes, that was Sebastian. It was also most emphatically not my idea, and not at all what happened. Come at five o'clock tonight, and I will tell you everything.

P. Mostly

I was in the process of pressing my seal into the wax when a knock sounded and the door opened. Molly Lepell stepped into the room in an unusually hesitant fashion.

"Oh. Hello, Peggy. I was thinking . . . that is . . . if you were ready, we might walk down together."

Oh, no, Molly. I haven't time for your troubles. Just go away, just for a little while—let me sort out Sebastian and the Jacobites and Mr. Tinderflint and my uncle and my criminal acts and then I'll be right with you.

This, of course, was not what I said. I set my quill back in its stand and from somewhere mustered a smile for this girl who was, after all, my friend. "Come and talk while Libby dresses me. It will help me hold still."

"I doubt anything could manage that," said Molly, but she smiled and followed me to stand in the doorway of my tiny closet while I assumed the Dressing Position—standing still with my arms straight out while Libby removed inappropriate garments and substituted more proper ones. All the while, Molly looked about her. She even sidled over to my table and adjusted the pots and bottles there, clearly searching for some way to begin a conversation. I decided to take a leaf from Her Royal Highness's book and say nothing. It might kill me, but I would hold my tongue and let Molly speak when she was ready. I would. Truly I would.

"I think I saw you with Mrs. Egan the other night?"

"Yes. Thank you for giving me her name." I said this as casually as possible, which was difficult because Libby now pushed me into the vanity chair and gripped my chin to square it up so she could start wielding her paintbrushes. "She seems most discreet."

"I am glad to hear it."

There was that uncharacteristic hesitancy again. I cocked an eye at Molly, only to have Libby grab my head in both her hands and firmly square it up again. "I'm sure she'd be more than willing to help you with any of your business as well," I said, ignoring Libby's threatening glower and the meaningful gesture with the powder box.

"No!" Molly blushed. "Well, that is, I was hoping you might speak to her on my behalf."

"Without mentioning that it is on your behalf?" I am not actually as slow to take a hint as Libby might believe.

"Yes." Molly looked down at her hands as she spoke. "I mean, she doesn't know your jewels, does she? One or two extra pieces would not rouse her suspicions in any way."

I bit my lip. Then I pushed Libby's hands away and stood to take Molly's arm instead, walking us toward my bedchamber. "Libby, we need a moment."

Libby scowled. "At least you'll be late together!" For emphasis, she slammed the closet door behind us.

Unusually docile, Molly let me steer her toward my chair and sit her down.

"Molly, what's the matter?" I sat on the stool at her feet and took her hands. "Are you in trouble?" She didn't answer. This time I was not inclined to wait. "I saw you playing cards with Lady Bristol."

Now she did raise her eyes to mine, and I saw they were swimming with tears.

"I have to do something. For John . . . Mr. Hervey."

"Oh, Molly." I squeezed her fingers gently.

Molly shook her head. "I'm a fool, I know it. But there's nothing to be done about that. His mother, Lady Bristol, she plays so deeply, and she loses so badly. It's draining them dry." She stopped, and her mouth twisted up. "I thought if she lost to me, then she'd have enough money, at least for a little while."

As far as it went, it was a good idea. There was one problem: for a player such as Lady Bristol, there was no such thing as enough money, not even for a little while.

"Molly, does he love you?"

"I don't know." A tear trickled down one cheek, and she wiped at it with the heel of her hand. "I only know I love him."

"I understand." In my mind's eye, I saw Matthew and his smiling face and his clear gaze. Would I sell my jewels if he needed the money? I wouldn't even hesitate.

What Molly saw in my face, I do not know, but it was enough to pull her back into something like her old humor. "To be honest, I never thought to find myself in love."

"Neither did I."

"It is . . . awkward," she ventured.

"So the poets tell us. I believe the word *painful* is also frequently mentioned."

"*Inconvenient*," Molly suggested.

"Conducive to a gross disordering of the faculties."

"It makes one wonder why we persist in it."

"I have heard it is because we are weak and frail female creatures."

"Ah, yes, of course."

Our gazes met. It was Molly who laughed first, but I joined her readily.

When our mirth had spent itself, I hesitated. I feared she would take offense at my next question, but I had to ask. "Molly . . . Mr. Hervey hasn't *asked* you to sell your jewels, has he?"

"No!" she exclaimed. "I did try . . . His mother's debts . . . You can't begin to imagine . . ." If I'd needed proof of the reality of Molly's distress, I had it now. Never in my time at court had I heard her fail to finish so many sentences. "But when I suggested it, he scolded and told me to never mention such a thing again. So, the best help I can give is to play with her and lose. But the money, well, it must come from somewhere."

I was beginning not to like the sound of this Mr. Hervey. "You should not have to deceive him to help him. If he cares, you should be able to speak openly to him."

"And you always speak openly to your beau?" countered Molly. She meant the remark as a barb, but it quite failed to stick.

"I try to. If nothing else, it keeps things simpler, given that my most innocent transgressions might well turn up in the papers."

"Then perhaps you are a better person than I am," said Molly. "Or perhaps your beau has less pride to injure." My first impulse was to leap to Matthew's defense, but I held myself admirably in check. "I know only that John is in straits and I can help him." She looked at me, and I saw all her familiar strength had returned. "But I can't go to Mrs. Egan myself. Someone might see. Will you help me, Peggy?"

"You know that I will." Hope and guilt warred in me, because my friend's cry for help meant I might impose upon her for my own business. "But I need your help as well. I may need to get away from the palace for a few hours tomorrow."

Molly pulled back. "Tomorrow? To do what?"

"It's a private family matter." Molly nodded as if she understood. Exactly what she thought she understood, I could not say and did not ask. "Mary's planning to be back tomorrow, isn't she? You can tell Her Royal Highness I've caught Mary's cold and am lying down."

"Very well, if Mary's back, and if you're in place by evening. Any more untoward gossip, and Her Royal Highness might decide to make some changes in her household."

"I know it. Now, we can be going just as soon as I write this one last letter."

There was a groan from my closet that made it sound suspiciously as if Libby had overheard these words. I ignored it as I hurried to my desk and pulled out another sheet of paper.

This time, I wrote to Olivia.

Be at my rooms tonight at half past six. It's time for our plan.

P.

CHAPTER EIGHTEEN

IN WHICH OUR HEROINE MAKES

ONE MORE BOLD ATTEMPT

AT BOTH RECONCILIATION AND ARTIFICE.

S o it was that I found myself hurrying away from the
Tuesday afternoon party of coffee and cards to meet Matthew.
I could not decide whether I should be ready with apologies,
insouciant explanations, or arguments. None of these options
felt right, and I was left with the understanding that I simply
wanted to see him. I felt at my wits' end. Precious days had
passed. I'd found no way to stall Sebastian and his ridiculous
deadline, and no way out of the risks of delving into whatever secrets my uncle held. I needed Matthew's warmth, his
solid intelligence, his embrace. I had then to find some way
to achieve that meeting of hearts in tender reconciliation as
was appropriate between lovers who have quarreled. This
all must be done before Olivia arrived at half six to help plot
our infiltration of her father's innermost secrets.

My life, it seemed, was not destined to become any simpler.

When I opened the door to my rooms, however, it was not Matthew who was waiting for me.

"Hello, Peggy," said Olivia from where she sat beside the hearth. "I'm a bit early, I know. Princess Anne has caught cold, and I had to submit my report on Guinevere's progress by written note."

My response to this friendly greeting and explanation did not rise to the heights of affection I normally reserved for my beloved cousin. "Olivia! You can't be here yet!"

"Why on earth not?"

"Hello, Peggy," said Matthew from the corridor behind me. "And hello, Olivia." That both unease and suspicion entered into his voice at this moment can perhaps be readily understood. It also probably should not have been the cause of as much exasperation as I then felt.

"One moment, please, Matthew. Olivia was just leaving."

"Why was I?" inquired Olivia without so much as lifting her feet from my stool. "Hello, Matthew. Peggy's told you what's happening, then?"

"No." Matthew was looking at me. I could feel it. "She hasn't told me anything."

"Go away, Olivia. You're not needed yet. Matthew, close the door," I added. "And, I promise, I did not ask Sebastian to Her Royal Highness's card party."

"Oh!" The light had clearly dawned within Olivia, but it did not seem to be causing her to move one inch closer to the door. "This is about that bit in the paper? *Lud*, Matthew, you cannot possibly be upset over that!"

"Go away, Olivia," said Matthew as he stepped through the doorway. "I need to speak with Peggy."

"I am not going anywhere," my beloved cousin replied, with a calm as unreasonable and unwarranted as it was unshakeable. "The two of you won't speak a word of sense if I'm not here. Libby, make us some of that tea, would you?"

Libby looked at me. I looked at Matthew. "She's not going," I said to him.

"I see that," he replied.

"I wasn't the one who brought Sebastian to the princess's party," I said again. "And you can't really think I flirted all night with him . . . can you?"

Matthew frowned, and my heart dropped into my slippers as if its strings had been cut. "I can't believe you're even asking that question. I thought you had a better opinion of me."

"She does—that's why she's so worried," said Olivia, with every intention of being helpful. My response at that moment, however, may have appeared somewhat less than grateful.

"Will you for once keep quiet!"

I would like to believe it was deep sympathy for my current plight that caused Olivia to fall silent. I suspect, however, it had more to do with the fact that I hadn't shouted at her since we were both nine and she'd gotten us lost during a wholly unauthorized expedition to the market.

When I turned back to Matthew, it was to see that he had grown grave. This threatened to cause me severe internal disarray, and, worst of all, a humiliating burst of tears.

"It was an awful risk, Peggy," he said. "And you'd agreed I should be there when he came near you. I wasn't jealous. I was frightened."

"And angry that without you there, she might do something foolish," prompted Olivia.

"Olivia wants to be a playwright," I reminded Matthew. "She tends to practice at inconvenient moments."

"Am I mistaken in some particular?" asked my cousin.

What could I do but sigh? "You are not." I said this for Olivia, but I was looking at Matthew. After an anxious moment, one corner of his mouth turned up in a soft smile, and all the breath rushed out of me.

"Well, there we are, then," Olivia announced loftily. "Now you, Peggy, can forgive Matthew for being worried about your being reported as swanning about the room with Sebastian Sandford. And you, Matthew, can forgive Peggy for said swanning, as it was not really her idea."

"I was not swanning!"

"Of course not," she said in those soothing tones that never actually impart any soothing feelings. "You only swan in a strictly professional capacity."

Matthew and I both glared at her. In response to this dread admonishment, Olivia rolled her eyes. "You may not believe it, but I do know I'm a nuisance and unwanted. You, however, must realize that we simply do not have *time* for a lovers' quarrel."

"She could be right," said Matthew to me.

I sighed. "It has happened before."

"We will talk more about this."

"I know it." I pressed Matthew's hand. "I'm sorry. It was Sophy again, being Sophy."

"Which makes far more sense than anything written in that article."

"*Now* are we friends?" asked Olivia in a tone indicating the extremes to which we had driven her patience.

Matthew did not look away from me, even for an instant. "I will always be your friend."

My heart tipped over, and it took all my discipline not to kiss him there and then. I could only hope Matthew saw in my eyes that I meant to remedy this neglect as soon as we had a single instant alone.

"The tea's ready," announced Libby.

"Thank you, Libby. And you might go and see if Norris was able to deliver that other letter."

Libby hesitated, clearly torn between the desire to hear what might be said next and the desire to snatch a few moments alone with her Norris. In the end, personal desire won out, and she curtsied and left us.

I poured the tea, and we all took a cup. Matthew sniffed, and sipped, and looked startled and took a larger sip. I rolled my eyes. Another convert.

While we drank, I narrated for Matthew and Olivia the gist of my conversation with Sebastian. I made sure to include his promise of assistance in return for my finding him a post at court, and the deadline he gave.

"This would be so much easier if Sebastian were actually stupid," muttered Olivia.

"He's stupid enough to think threatening Peggy will get him what he wants." There was a darkness under Matthew's words that reminded me murder had already been done in my name, and I wished I had not heard it.

"But he's smart enough to get Sophy Howe on his side," she countered. "How neatly it all works out. Now if Peggy can't get Sebastian what he wants, the Howe will, if only to spite Peggy."

Which was not something I'd considered. I'd been too busy watching the pair of them be professionally charming at each other. Admiration for Sebastian's cleverness left a strong and terrible taste in my mouth, and I needed a large gulp of tea to wash it away.

"Which may be clever, but doesn't give her any way to get free of him," said Matthew.

I opened my mouth. I was going to have to say it. I was going to have to tell Olivia I might be an heiress. I was going to have to go back into my uncle's house, to risk arrest, shame, and the loss of the life I'd only just gained.

"What I want to know is, how does a man afford forty pounds' worth of tea in a gilded jar when his family has lost its last penny?" asked Olivia blandly. "Someone is lying through his teeth about something, and it's probably Sebastian. Probably this whole business of needing a post to make his own way in the world is made up entirely."

I looked at the pale brown liquid in my cup, grateful that she had not decided I was the liar. At the same time, an absurdly mathematical part of my brain was attempting to calculate the cost per cup of the gift. "I can't see how he thought lying about his family's circumstances would get me to help him."

"Perhaps he thought you'd feel sorry for him." In response, I choked on nothing but air. "I didn't say it was a good thought, did I?" Olivia waved her cup. "Just that it was Sebastian's."

"You will make an excellent playwright," said Matthew.

Olivia blushed and made a great show of dropping her gaze. "You flatter me, Mr. Reade."

"Unfortunately, my uncle is hardly likely to care that Sebastian's a liar and an opportunist."

Neither of them attempted to challenge this assertion.

"I'm not sure it matters anyway," Matthew went on. "As long as he's your guardian, Sir Oliver can still come for you at any time. He can even arrange another marriage if this one doesn't take."

I had been trying very hard not to think of that. "But

it will delay him." I took Matthew's hand. "Remember, my father might still be alive. Mr. Tinderflint's looking for him now."

"Oh, yes, Mr. Tinderflint." Matthew did not bother to hide his bitterness. "Because he's always been so concerned for your welfare, he's left you in a nest of snakes without bothering to tell you which ones are the actual vipers."

"He saved Peggy's life," retorted Olivia.

They bantered back and forth, debating my patron's merits and detractions. I stared at my tea. There was another possibility, one I had not considered until this moment. It was genuine, it was sound, and it would save me from having to confess to Olivia any hint of a chance I might be an heiress until I had some kind of proof in my hands.

"This is about money," I said. "The only question is *whose* money?"

"What are you talking about?" asked Olivia.

"You asked the question, Olivia. If Uncle Pierpont truly wants this marriage to happen, why hasn't he simply published the banns and packed me up?"

Matthew looked at Olivia, and Olivia looked at Matthew.

"We've been assuming it's the Sandfords who are in straits financially. But what if Uncle Pierpont is in trouble?" I met Olivia's gaze apologetically.

"If you get married, and Father can't live up to whatever settlement is in the contract, it will raise questions," said Olivia slowly. "People will start to wonder if the bank's on a sound footing. If he just calls it off, people will wonder anyway."

I watched the light begin to dawn in Matthew's gray eyes. "So he's got to come up with some reason to break the betrothal that doesn't have anything to do with money. Something to do with the Sandfords, or with Peggy herself."

"Or convince the Sandfords to call it all off for some reason other than money," I added.

Matthew nodded. "At the very least he needs to stall matters until he can get the capital together to pay off whatever he's promised to the Sandfords."

Olivia was quiet for a long time, her hands wrapped tightly around her cup. I understood. Smugglers, highwaymen, illicit marriage, treachery and treason, these were all fine dramas. But bankruptcy and arrest presented a far different picture.

"I'll ask him," she said. "I'll demand an answer."

"Olivia, do you really think he'd tell you the truth?"

She set her cup down. "Then what? We've been sitting here talking round and round. It might be this, it might be that, but we don't *know* anything."

I felt as though we'd switched places, my dramatic cousin and I. At that moment, it was not a feeling I relished.

"We stay with our first plan," I told Olivia, and Matthew frowned in silent inquiry. I took a deep breath. As firmly as I could manage, I said, "If there's any record of Uncle's doings, he'll keep it at the bank." *And if that record holds bad news about the stability of the House of Pierpont, I can use it against*

my uncle to break the betrothal, and just maybe to force him to tell me about
any inheritance, and never have to break into the book room at all. "I have
to find a way into the bank."

"And *we* do have a way," said Olivia, sounding piqued
that I'd gotten the pronoun wrong. "We have you, Matthew."

Carefully, Matthew set his cup down. "I may be an in-
sufferable coward, but I do not like the sound of this."

"You could go in disguise," Olivia informed him, and I
know I did not imagine the envy in her voice. "We could get
you a coat and some velvet breeches. You could pretend to be
a lord with gold to deposit—"

"No," Matthew cut her off. "There's not a coat in the city
that's going to allow me to pass as an aristocrat." He held up
his callused, paint-stained hands. "This isn't the court we're
talking about. It's a banking house. They'll be looking more
closely at anyone who goes in, and they'll be sober."

"There you have a point," I said. "But what are we to
do?" I thought for a moment about asking Monsieur Janvier
to undertake the task. "He" could most certainly pass himself
off as a gentleman. But that would involve taking yet another
person into our confidence. To be sure, my dancing master
was good at keeping secrets, but I already had too many people who knew my particular business.

Olivia, however, was smiling, and she lifted her cup to
us both in salute. "We might not be able to pass you off for a
gentleman, Matthew, but what about a clerk?"

CHAPTER NINETEEN

IN WHICH THE FORTRESS IS BREACHED.

We decided our venture would be the next day.
There were three reasons for this. The first was that I'd already arranged for Molly Lepell to cover for me with Her
Royal Highness. For a wonder, Mary had this time not disappointed any of us. She might be sneezing after every other
word, but she was on her feet and back in her place. The
second was that it would give us the maximum number of
days before Sebastian's ultimatum played out to make good
use of anything we learned. The third, as Matthew himself
pointed out, was that it meant he would have less time to
change his mind.

There was no problem in making Matthew look the part.
His best coat was a sober and surprisingly un-paint-stained

blue. With Libby's help, we were able to procure a better waistcoat than the one he owned. His good shoes had brass buckles, and although he seldom wore it, he did own a short-queue wig. His place at the academy allowed him considerable freedom of movement, so choosing a time when we could all meet near the bank was limited only by how quickly I could leave the palace after the Wednesday nuncheon.

But watching from behind the curtains of the hired coach as Matthew walked briskly down the street and strode up the stairs to vanish into my uncle's bank—that was agony.

"He'll be fine," said Olivia confidently. Like me, she had donned a mask for the occasion. In contrast to my white and gray creation, hers was a black silk affair meant to call to mind highwaymen and other such ne'er-do-wells. I would have to convince Monsieur Janvier to give my cousin lessons in the art of subtlety. "Honestly, Peggy, you can't think Father keeps footpads in there for the purpose of knocking young men over the head."

"Of course not. And if you have any other similarly pleasant ideas, Olivia, you might keep them to yourself."

"Although wouldn't it be marvelous if he did?" she went on, apparently unaware that I had even spoken. "Perhaps he's not working for the Jacobites after all. Perhaps he's working for the press gangs and—"

I reached out and grabbed my cousin's chin, turning her face toward me in a manner I'd learned from Libby and assorted governesses. "Olivia. Be quiet."

"I'm sorry. I promise you, Peggy, Matthew will be out

in a moment. Then we'll be done with this little exercise and can get on with what we should be doing, which is searching the book room."

I never would have believed it possible, but I wanted to agree with her. I wanted Matthew to fail. If he couldn't convince anyone to speak with him, if he emerged from the bank this very minute, then he would be out of the danger I had sent him into.

Because that was the worst of this: I was blatantly, self-ishly using Matthew for my own ends. That he had agreed to it meant nothing. If Matthew was caught—if he was ar-rested or worse—it would be entirely my fault. Because I was a coward and a fool and a selfish thing. I had not wanted to risk returning to my uncle's house, where everyone knew me and anyone might report me, if not to the thief takers or the militia, then to the palace or the papers. I had decided to risk Matthew instead.

"There he is!" cried Olivia.

"Matthew?" I yelped.

"Wake up, Peggy! It's that foreign-looking parson you told me about. That is the same man, isn't it?" My cousin lifted her curtain back a little so I could look. Reluctantly, I shifted my attention from the doorway to the figure in the black coat and old-fashioned wig walking down the street, carrying his black and silver stick and an air of intense pur-pose.

"Yes. That's the man."

"I've seen him at the house. I'm sure of it." Olivia craned

her neck, trying to get a better look without actually poking her head out into the street.

I could see him from my side of the coach now. He mounted the steps to the bank and walked inside. I pressed my nose directly against the window glass, praying for a glimpse of Matthew. But the door shut at once, and I collapsed back.

"Did you hear?" Olivia rapped my hand with her fan. "I've seen that man at the house!"

"That can't be unusual," I said, if only to avoid another swat from Olivia's fan. "Doesn't your father do business from his book room as well?"

"Only with people he knows personally. And that man's never been introduced to Mother, or to me. I shall make a note of it." Olivia pulled her sketchbook and charcoal pencil out of her work basket to set about writing down time, place, personage, and speculations.

"I don't know . . ." I said.

"Honestly, Peggy, how is it you came to get a post as a spy? You don't suspect anyone of anything."

"I suspect you lack understanding of anything resembling the real world."

Olivia just went on with her notes. I found myself wishing I'd brought such a book. It would give me something to do with my hands. Although my notes would consist of nothing but *Four o'clock, Matthew still inside. Four and a quarter, Matthew still inside. Four and a half, Matthew still inside.*

The day was growing chill, and a breeze that smelled of

London and lowering winter whipped through the carriage, yet I was scarcely aware of it. All I felt was that a moment passed, and another, and another, and Matthew still did not come out. Another five long moments passed. Another ten. The church bells rang the hour, and Matthew did not come out. The hawkers and the porters and secondhand clothes men with their wares held high on poles came and went past our coach, and Matthew did not come out. Olivia tried several times to engage me in conversation or speculation. I didn't bother to answer her. My world had narrowed to the dark doorway of the House of Pierpont.

I pushed my mask up and knuckled my eyes. Not only did they ache from staring, but my legs were beginning to cramp from stillness and cold. The foot warmers with which Libby had supplied us had gone stone cold long since.

But then something happened that made me sit up, and lean forward, and dare to ease the curtain open another fraction of an inch. A great black carriage loaded down with hairy, ragged ruffians and their armaments creaked slowly up the street. This unmistakable conveyance stopped directly in front of the House of Pierpont.

"Again?" I murmured.

"What is it?" Olivia peeked out from her side, and together we watched as, once again, the withered man climbed out of the coach, and the ruffians ranged themselves about it. Again, the fellow with the pistol in his belt stayed up top. He must have been freezing, but he waited without visible uneasiness, his hat pulled low over his brow.

"This is just what happened before, isn't it?" asked Olivia eagerly.

"But what is it?" I asked, speaking more to myself than to her.

Just then, the driver atop the coach turned his head slowly. I ducked back from the window, dragging Olivia with me. The man looked lazily up the street, and down again, seeming to scan the passing crowds like one who is idle and bored, but my scalp had begun prickling with goose pimples.

"We have to move," I croaked.

"We can't move. Matthew's still in there!"

"You think I don't know that?" I demanded hoarsely. "But we've been seen, Olivia. We have to move!"

I have hated myself for many things, but never was that self-loathing so complete as the moment when I thumped on the ceiling of the coach, the signal to drive on and leave Matthew alone in my uncle's banking house. And our driver did.

"Where to?" he hollered down.

"Around the corner, and stop there!" I gripped Olivia's hand. I will be eternally grateful that she chose this moment to be sensible.

"It's all right," she told me. "Matthew's steady. If we're not there when he comes out, he'll just start back for the academy. That's all there is to it."

"Of course," I said. "Of course."

But I couldn't make myself believe it. I did not like that black coach, or its withered owner. I most especially did not like its driver, with his pistol and his searching eyes. Visions of press gangs and worse rose up before me. Matthew might be locked inside the bank with that coach come to take him away, and I was not there. I was lurking around the corner, like a coward and a fool.

I was going to begin crying any moment. I was going to burst from the carriage and run screaming up the steps of the House of Pierpont demanding to know what they'd done with Matthew Reade. I was going to beat Olivia to death with my fan if she didn't stop that idiotic scribbling and help me work out how we were going to storm the transport jails, where Matthew had surely been taken.

The carriage rocked. I screamed and grabbed at my straight pin as the door on the far side was snatched open. A dark figure scrambled in, losing its hat and wig in the process.

"Stand back, brigand!" cried my cousin, waving the tiny scissors from her work basket.

"Hello, Olivia." Matthew plumped himself down on the seat beside me. "Hello, Peggy. I'm back. Let's go."

I screeched again and threw my arms about him, only to recoil instantly.

"Where have you been? You smell like a tavern!"

"So now you know where I've been." He coughed hard, and the sickly sweet smell of beer that hung so heavily about him grew that much stronger. "Olivia, your father's clerk smokes like a chimney. Lord knows how he can stomach the stuff. I thought I was going to be sick!"

"I've been going mad here waiting for you!" I informed him, in quite a reasonable fashion, I do assure my reader.

"And it looks very well on you. Or it would if it weren't for that silly mask." With a grin, Matthew reached out and pulled it off. "Much better. Have you a kiss for your hero?"

I swatted him and turned my face away. Matthew after too much beer and tobacco was clearly not someone I wanted to know.

He fell back against the seat, breathing rather heavily.

"I think we'd better get back to the academy. I'm not sure I haven't had too much smoke." He burped. "An' drink."

With that pleasing and gentlemanly statement, so in keeping with the elevated character of my gallant swain, I hollered up to the driver to return us all to Great Queen Street.

The sight of Matthew Reade walking through the academy accompanied by not one, but two, masked women was the cause of much comment among the other students, not to mention applause and whistles. Especially as Matthew kept waving and doffing his cap, and was clearly not walking very steadily.

I managed to catch Mr. Torrent by the ear and order him to find us some strong coffee and a basin of plain water.

"What are those for?" inquired Matthew as I deposited both on the library table.

"You are to drink one and soak your head in the other. I do not care which," I informed him.

"Now, Peggy, you are not being fair," said Olivia. "Matthew has done us a great good service. It is not his fault there was nothing to find."

"He left us sitting in that freezing coach and went carousing!" I shouted. "I thought he'd been taken away! I thought I'd condemned him to the gallows! I thought . . ." I couldn't finish.

Matthew was staring at me, as was Olivia. I plumped myself down on the nearest stool, folded my arms, and turned away. Behind me, I heard splashing, and then the hesitant sort of gulping that comes when a person tries to drink a hot liquid too quickly.

Matthew walked into my field of vision. His face was red, and his damp hair was slicked back from his forehead. "I'm sorry, Peggy. I had too much to drink. I'm better now."

I glowered up at him. Olivia came to join him. So that things would be fair, I glowered at her as well. "Is she right?" I growled. "Was all this for nothing?"

"As a matter of fact, I did learn something very interesting." I had the satisfaction of watching Olivia's face fall at this. "And the tavern turned out to have a part in it." Matthew pulled up a stool and perched on it, much more steadily than he had walked down the hall.

Olivia, reluctantly, also found a seat.

"On the other side of that bank door is a lobby," he said. "Very well set up, with tiles on the floor, candle sconces on the walls, the main office on one side, and a waiting room on the other. There's a high desk guarding the entrance to the office. A sort of chief clerk sits on duty there, with a great ring of keys at his waist. Behind him are the apprentices at their desks, doing what I suppose is the copying and ciphering." Matthew frowned, concentrating on his inner vision to make sure he'd gotten all the details right.

"As I was going in, I was trying to decide who would be most likely to talk to me," he said. "Not that I've much experience with banks, you understand, but I do know about being a 'prentice. The newest always has the worst time of it, because he hasn't just got his master's work to do. Usually, he ends up carrying half the load for the others as well. So as I gave my name and story to the senior clerk fellow at the front, I kept an eye on that line of copy desks behind him, until I was sure I had picked out the youngest man there.

"I told the senior fellow—his name was Kerridge—that my gentleman had a great deal of business overseas, particularly in Paris and Amsterdam. It was not just any house that could manage these sorts of affairs. 'Oh,' he says, 'you may assure your gentleman that Pierpont's routinely handles letters of credit and bills of exchange from France, the Germanys, and the Netherlands.' I hemmed and hawed some more, and the fellow starts naming names. I start taking notes"—he indicated his book on the table—"and wondering what on earth I was going to do next. Then I had a stroke of luck. You won't believe it, but in walks—"

"A foreign-looking parson sort in a wig about ten years out of fashion?" said Olivia.

"That's what I thought. But Senior Clerk Kerridge tells

me the apparent parson's name is Herr Pietersen. He's a banker from Sweden, and he's doing business on behalf of the Swedish ambassador. Someone with an odd long name, sounded like Gillyflower, but wasn't."

"Gyllenborg," I said, and they both stared at me. I shrugged. "He came to a drawing room. He didn't drink, at all. It made him memorable."

"That was lucky," admitted Olivia.

"Ah!" Matthew held up his hand significantly. "But it wasn't all luck."

My annoyance, which had begun to ebb, returned in its full force and compass. "I swear, Olivia, I'm not letting you near him anymore. You've infected him with the Madness Dramatic."

Matthew, sensing perhaps an unwanted diversion of our previously rapt attention, went on. "Well, because this Herr Pietersen works for His Excellency the Swedish Ambassador Gyllenborg, Herr Pietersen is important. Kerridge has to conduct him up to the partners' offices right away. He asks me to step into the sitting room, and he'll have someone bring me coffee. And sure enough, the fellow who gets this unenviable job is the same fellow I picked out as being the youngest apprentice.

"So, while this new fellow's setting out the coffee, I start making friendly conversation. You know the sort of thing—must be nice for thems as can do as they please and hobnob all day drinking brandy while the likes of us freeze in the basement because they can't be bothered to pay for coals.

He's chuckling and agreeing, and pretty soon I'm saying how this coffee's all very well, but I'd rather nick out for some honest English beer instead of waiting around here for the mucky-mucks to finish up, and the 'prentice asks am I buying? And I say I am, and he shows me out the back door and across the alley, where there's a public house. There, I stand him to a jug of beer and a pipe of tobacco. Or three." Matthew rubbed the corner of his mouth.

"But what did you learn?" demanded Olivia.

"I learned that his name's Weeks. I also learned that with Mr. Weeks, Sir Oliver has taken to 'prentice one of the most foulmouthed men I've ever met. First came the complaints about the work, how it's run, run, run all day, fetching this and carrying that, and finding oatmeal—"

"Oatmeal?" cried Olivia, and I repressed the urge to slap my hand over her mouth so Matthew might be able to finish his story. "Is Father banking for horses?"

"That I don't know. I asked, and Weeks shrugs and says, 'His . . . nibs is paid to find seven thousand barrels of oatmeal, so we finds him seven thousand, it's all the same to me.'"

"Seven *thousand* barrels of oatmeal?" I exclaimed. "Is that sort of thing normal for a bank? I thought they just handled gold. Coin. Made drafts and letters of exchange."

Matthew shrugged. "Apparently the House of Pierpont has been branching out into other businesses."

"But oatmeal?" The face Olivia pulled would have had her mother in fits. "It's so dull!"

Now it was my turn to smirk, and I did so. "What came after the complaints and the oatmeal?" I asked Matthew.

"The bragging about the ladies, naturally. It seems the House of Pierpont holds the jewels and plate for some of the most high and mighty of the realm, many of whom Mr. Weeks believes are giving him the eye and he could swive any time by crooking his little finger . . ."

"I don't think that's how swiving is accomplished," said my cousin sweetly.

"*Olivia.*" I tried the glower again. Olivia shrugged. Matthew was grinning, and I paused to spare him a glower as well. It had no more effect on him than it did on Olivia. I made a note to myself to apply to Monsieur Janvier for lessons in the more advanced forms of glowering. Clearly, my skills needed to be sharpened.

"Did you see anything of an old man who arrived in a great black coach?" I asked Matthew. "Possibly accompanied by a pack of ruffians with staffs and pistols?"

"No," said Matthew. "And I'm glad of it. So will you be, once you hear the rest. While Mr. Weeks is warming to his theme of willing women, I'm considering how to get myself out of there. Just then, a new fellow walks in. He has a bright blue jacket on his back and blue hat on his head. He calls for a barrel of wine and one of water."

"A barrel of water?" I frowned, and Matthew nodded. "He himself taps the wine cask and serves out the wine to the other patrons, making sure all the glasses are handed across over the top of the water barrel." He waited, clearly expecting me to understand why on earth a man would do such an extraordinary thing. Olivia clapped her hand over her mouth.

"Then he invited us all to toast the king," said Matthew. "And everybody did, loudly and repeatedly."

"Don't you see, Peggy?" said Olivia. "The glasses passed *over the water*."

I did see, and I blushed for having been so slow. "It was a Jacobite tavern?" I said incredulously. "My uncle has a Jacobite in his employ?" Mr. Walpole had said there were "stirrings." It was beginning to look as if he was right.

"And a noisy one, too," said Matthew. "The wine had them all up making speeches about how this time they'd show German Georgie his place and how the new Regent of France would honor the old king's promises, and the silver would soon be flowing up north for guns and men." He paused. "That's why I drank so much, Peggy. I didn't dare stop while they were talking and toasting."

Of course. They'd have set on him in a mob if it had looked like he wasn't keeping up with the rest. Revolution was like a court masque. Nothing truly innovative could happen if the participants stayed sober.

"I see that, and I'm sorry," I told him. "Were they serious, do you think?"

"I don't know," said Matthew. "Drunken men in taverns say all kinds of things. In fact, in the middle of all this speech making, Mr. Weeks is back on about the ladies, and wouldn't the German princeling love it if he knew some of his wife's associates were taking such fine care of their persons and their property as some he could name."

"Did he name any?" I asked.

"Oh, yes. He went on, and at length, about one masked individual in particular who had just hired out a box in the strong room for her most precious jewels. You can imagine where he went with that—"

Olivia waved this away. "Out with it! Who is she?"

"Sophy Howe."

CHAPTER TWENTY

IN WHICH OUR HEROINE SUFFERS
AN INFURIATING DELAY.

Shortly after Olivia and I left the academy, I formed a plan of how I should deal with all of Matthew's news. It was a good plan, subtle yet practical and effective. It had every chance of succeeding in all its aims, I'm certain of it.

Unfortunately, I cannot remember one single bit of it, because by the time the coach pulled up in front of the gate-house at St. James's Palace, my head was aching, and I fell prey to a fit of violent sneezes.

I had, in short, caught cold.

It was a horrid and complete cold, accompanied by fever and chills, a nose that dripped constantly, and a head that felt like a swollen bladder on a stick. Libby dosed me with rhubarb and brandy and made me sit with my feet in a hot mustard bath. I lay in bed for nine days, wretched to the bone. I was by turns frantic to be up and doing, and bored beyond endurance. The physician prescribed regular bleeding and a black purge. I must have been delirious with fever and rhubarb at that point, because I believe I told that learned gentleman to go stuff his purge somewhere most unsuitable.

Matthew sent me a dreadful-smelling concoction to rub on my chest. This, he said, was an infallible remedy from his father the apothecary. He also promised he'd sneak in on the public dining day, when everyone would be busy and no one would notice a gentleman entering my rooms.

To add to all these diverting pleasantries, I received another letter from Mr. Tinderflint. I had been writing him regularly with my news, and the inquiry from the princess about the growing rumors of King George staying permanently in Hanover. This was the first reply I'd received, however, and it was filled with his usual level of clear reasoning and steady reassurance.

My Dear,

As much as I miss London, I will admit there are many fine advantages to be had here and I am certain to be quite comfortable for the duration of my stay. I have a most excellent cook and can assure you I am well looked after and entertained.

I read your last letter with great attention. I cannot understand how the news that the elder Mr. G was remaining at his country house came to you. I know of no such plans on his part.

Indeed, his business there being successfully concluded and the hunting finished for the season, I expect him to be returning to London shortly after the new year.

As to that other business which I was sent here to pursue, I have not been idle. Early inquiries have produced definite results. Alas! They were not the results I hoped for. I had hoped to find that particular jewel we seek in this city, or at the very least nearby. But from what my friends now tell me, its ownership has been transferred, and I must seek its likeness in a much different location from the one I expected. I understand this will be disappointing news for you, but please believe I am pursuing every line of investigation open to me. I hope to have more news by next week at the latest.

Write to me soon, my dear. I find myself thinking of you a great deal, and naturally, I am anxious to hear how you and Jane do.

Yr. Obedient,

Mr. T

Bored and out of sorts as I was, my reply was short, to the point, and not entirely in the best humor.

Mr. T:

Jane and I both suffer from the same wretched cold. I'll pass on your message to Mrs. PG as soon as I'm better, whenever that happy day should occur.

I know you will be interested to hear of Jane and her

would-be suitors. I'm afraid we are too late. She has rather more about her than she can conveniently manage at this time, including Mr. W. And Mr. S has joined the throng, although he is likewise occupied with S.H. Jane tries to go about her business in a calm and straightforward manner, but these gentlemen are making that exceedingly difficult. There is also some indication that her former interest, Jacob Waters, might be about to make a reappearance.

Should you be in possession of any useful advice, I shall be sure to pass it on to her.

Yrs.,

P. Mostly

I found myself rather proud of my new cant name for the Jacobites. Of course, I'd been drinking brandy and rhubarb again, which might have accounted for it.

Mr. Tinderflint's was not the only letter I received during that endless succession of bedridden days. Olivia wrote with regularity, urging me to rest so I could recoup my health more quickly. Having taken my hints about the inadvisability of committing too much to paper, she ended these notes with the simple reminder that we had "much left to do before winter sets in." Meaning that since Matthew's foray into the bank had yielded more questions than answers, it was her opinion that we now needed to search Uncle Pierpont's book room.

The letter that wounded, though, was from Sebastian.

I'd had no choice but to write him. I had to grit my teeth and grip my pen and beg him to understand that I was truly sick and could not make any progress with his request. The answer I got back was nothing short of infuriating.

My Dear Miss F,

I have confirmed your story from certain reliable persons. You have my sympathy in your affliction but are not to spare a thought for me. I am well looked after and comfortably situated. I do, however, look forward to your return and the successful conclusion of our business. Otherwise we must allow that business to take its natural course.

Yrs.,

S.

With this in hand, I had no real need for Molly's court gossip. For Molly also came to sit with me—and bring me a terrible-tasting tisane she swore was an infallible remedy from her grandmother. Why cannot a remedy be infallible and pleasant at the same time?

She only meant to be of use with her updates on the doings in the court. Unfortunately, these were at least as unpleasant as any cold remedy. Sophy and Sebastian had become inseparable. Sebastian had been making himself present at just about every public event, and not a few of the private ones. Always, he was seen on Sophy Howe's arm or as her partner at the card tables. The two of them were rapidly becoming notorious for the size of their winnings. I wasn't surprised. If Sebastian hadn't been a card sharper before he sat down with Sophy, he would be one now.

But that was not what left me frightened and raging against my unforgivably weak constitution. I was afraid because I understood what Sophy was really doing. She was fishing for information about me. Sophy wanted me gone from court, preferably after I'd been thoroughly humiliated. She would be more than ready to use extortion, her poisonous pen, and all Sebastian's cunning to accomplish this goal. She wasn't even bothering to hide her scheme. Not only did she write me her own little notes every day inquiring after my health, but she actually sent me a present. Molly Lepell was in my room on Invalid Watch when Libby brought it in.

When I saw what my maid carried, I gaped. Even Molly looked consternated, except she didn't sneeze at the same time. It was a fresh jar of tea, not only as large and expensive as Sebastian's, but in a jar that was an exact match for the first. There was a label on the ribbon, written in very large block letters, as if intended for someone who was barely literate.

FOR YOUR HEALTH, SOPHY H.

Libby, prudently, put the jar on my mantel, out of my immediate reach.

"Dat's id," I growled, kicking at my counterpane, trying desperately to find a way out from under the smothering layers of wool and eiderdown. "I'b habig dis oud wid her."

"She's only taunting you," Molly reminded me.

"Dat mush id obvious." I finally got the blankets thrown back. "An' I'b goig to trow id in her fire." Or possibly her face. But I felt Molly might balk at this and so did not mention it. While I was struggling to find my balance on my unusually unsteady feet, Molly got between me and the door.

"Don't, Peggy. It's exactly what she wants."

"Den what?" I demanded, closer to tears than my pride was comfortable with. "What do I do?"

Molly didn't answer immediately. She looked at my twin jars of tea—those precious, thoughtful, mocking gifts from two people who wanted more than anything to see me ruined.

"Triumph," she murmured. "Find some way to orchestrate a public triumph. Something that will cause a seven-days' wonder and seal your consequence. She won't be able to touch you then."

"Yes, thank you." I plumped back down on the edge of the bed. "Because dat's so easy."

"I know, believe me." Molly sighed. "But it's your best chance."

I nodded. She was right. The flaw in Molly's advice came not from her approach, but from the fact that she didn't know what the real danger was, and I couldn't tell her. If Sophy and Sebastian sniffed out the truth about me and mine before I did, the consequences would be disastrous. That Sophy had hired a box at my uncle's bank told me they were already interested in the House of Pierpont. They might very well discover that my uncle's bank was not on a sound footing or, worse, that my uncle had employed at least one Jacobite. After all, we had found out as much, and it hadn't been so very difficult. Sophy and Sebastian would not hesitate to use what they found, whether it was a matter of money or high treason. They would certainly not spare Olivia the ravages of whatever scandal they exposed, or Matthew either.

My ghost was very busy walking the halls on those long, dark nights.

All this combined to pull me from my bed the moment I could walk across the room without breaking into a sweat. I could not wait for Sophy and Sebastian to finish their work. I must find out the truth before they could threaten those I cared for.

To this end, I shamelessly begged Molly for yet another favor. By rights, now that I was upright and not dripping like a drainpipe, I should have returned to waiting. But if I did, it would be several more days until my next afternoon off. That was not acceptable. I had to get to Olivia and my uncle's house at once.

To avoid giving my nemesis any further aid, when Molly came to visit and drink yet more of Sebastian's tea, I explained that my family business had taken a turn for the worse, and I now had an extremely delicate matter to broker. I also took two jewel boxes from her with the promise that I would put these into Mrs. Egan's hands at the first opportunity. In return, Molly promised to help me delay my return to waiting by just one day.

She proved true to her word. Molly told Her Royal Highness that in my zeal to resume my place, I had overtaxed myself. Molly had personally put me back into bed and admonished me to stay there. For verisimilitude, I sent along a shakily written note assuring my mistress I would be better by tomorrow.

I tried not to picture the cool taint of suspicion coming over Her Royal Highness's face as she read my missive or the narrow-eyed scrutiny I would receive from the Mistresses T-bourne & C-bourne when I next made my entrance. I failed in both these aims, rather miserably.

Fortunately, once the matter of my turn in waiting was settled, making my escape from the palace itself was relatively easy. There was no need for me to try to arrange coach or sedan chair. The fashionable St. James's Square where Uncle Pierpont lived took its name from its proximity to the palace. Even a lady unescorted and on foot could be fairly sure of her safety while hurrying down the few well-appointed streets that separated the square from the royal residence. It was also one of the few times I felt entirely grateful for the vicissitudes of fashion. The deep-hooded cape and half mask hid my face from passersby in the neighborhood, who might all too easily recognize me.

My uncle's home was one of a new row of gabled brick houses—prosperous and respectable, but nothing grand. Considering the nature of my errand, Olivia and I had decided it would be a mistake for me to enter by the front door.

Instead, I circled around to the east, begrudging each extra inch. The rain had turned the streets into a swamp of well-chilled mud, and it was a struggle to avoid sinking in over the tops of my shoes, or possibly up to my neck.

Eventually, however, my wandering, mincing, and occasionally hopping footsteps brought me up to the brick wall and iron gate that fenced in Uncle Pierpont's back garden. Olivia waited on the other side of the bars, trying to peer nonchalantly through them as if waiting for the post or the fishmonger, and making a pretty poor job of it. Especially as she squealed happily when she saw me.

"There you are!" Olivia pulled me through the gate. Naturally, Guinevere was with her, and naturally, she left off digging around the roses to bark at my muddy shoes. "I was beginning to think you wouldn't come!"

"I'm sorry. I had to make sure Her Royal Highness would accept my excuse." I removed my mask so I could see my cousin better. "Olivia, we have to hurry. If anyone besides Molly Lepell takes it into her head to check on me, I could lose my place." Sophy Howe's smiling visage still loomed large in my imagination.

"Don't worry, Peggy. I've arranged everything!" My cousin peered beneath my hood, rather obviously looking for signs of joy and relief at this news. I'm afraid the best I could manage was a weak smile.

Olivia shrugged, grabbed my hand, and proceeded to drag me up the garden path. "Bromley's gone to see about a new delivery of wine. He's taken Lewis with him. I told Cook the fish for supper was completely unacceptable and sent her to the market, and said that I would take Mother's tray up to her myself. That's almost half the house accounted for, and of course Templeton's completely on our side." Templeton was Olivia's personal maid. I didn't know her well, but what I did know bore out my cousin's confidence in her. "She'll watch the corridor, and she's already been in to open the window."

Olivia delivered this pronouncement as we reached the back of the house. Just as she said, one window sash had indeed been raised a good foot. Olivia beamed with pride. Guinevere darted beneath the bushes, barking furiously. "Since we know you can manage windows, I thought it would be the surest way to keep you from being seen. Now, I must go take Mother her tray and keep her occupied. Good luck!" She squeezed my hand and hurried away before I could point out that the last time I had "managed" a window, I'd been dressed as a boy, I'd had Matthew's help, and I had been in good health, rather than recovering from more than a week in my sickbed.

I faced the window. The window faced me. The lower sill was level with my shoulders. I paused to be thankful that Guinevere had gone with her mistress. The last thing I needed now was that dog yipping out her complaints while I engaged in this latest bit of housebreaking.

I stood on my tiptoes, tried not to wince as my shoes

sank into the garden loam, and pushed the sash up another inch. The soft grating sound made me freeze in place.

It took a moment, but I rallied my nerve. I reminded myself sternly that I was a veteran housebreaker and should act like it. I kicked a decorative stone a bit closer so I could clamber atop it and grip the sill with both hands. I also prayed for luck.

I believe I can safely say that what followed was as graceless a moment of heaving, scrabbling, puffing, coughing, wriggling, and frantic, muffled cursing as any known in the history of sneak-thievery. This magnificent living display of the manifold reasons why one should never attempt to burgle a home in skirts culminated in my falling to the floor of the book room in a great, silken heap.

I huddled where I landed behind the draperies, heart hammering, waiting for the door to fly open. Surely the whole house had heard that hideous, humiliating entry.

The door did not open. Nothing in that dim room stirred.

As my doom failed to arrive, I pushed myself to my feet and stepped out from behind the curtains to face the book room. The chamber was cold and dark, with neither fire nor candles lit. I ventured a few timid steps forward. The chill air smelled of dust, leather, and old paper. Silence pressed against my ears. Now that the curtains had fallen closed behind me, I could not even hear the ticking of the great case clock in the hall, much less the traffic on the square.

It all felt immensely strange. I had never been in this

room when it was empty. Indeed, I'd never come into it voluntarily at all. If I was here, it was because I'd been summoned. What followed was usually an icy scolding from my uncle regarding my conduct, my expense, my heritage, and my very existence.

The memory of those encounters set my jaw and moved me forward. I had no idea what I was looking for, but there had to be something. It could not be simply spite that made Uncle Pierpont behave so oddly regarding this betrothal and my post at court. Neither could it simply be Olivia's dramatics or my own vain and silly hopes. There was the Swedish banker, the Jacobite 'prentice, the black coach and its withered owner. Something real was happening, and I had no choice but to find out what.

If Uncle Pierpont loved anything in this world, it was order. His correspondence had been stacked neatly on his massive desk, with the piles separated according to the recipient or sender. Each pile was flanked with any official documents related to the letters. It was the work of but a few moments to find correspondence bearing the name of Augustus Sandford, Baron of Lynnfield.

From the sheer height of the stack, it appeared that Lord Lynnfield did a great deal of business with my uncle. It also became quickly apparent that business was as dull as the gray October skies. Many of the documents in the stack were not even proper letters. Rather, they were bills of exchange for goods or for currency. There was certainly no mention of any grand conspiracy to defraud me of my inheritance. The most exciting thing I found was one large elaborate document that it took me longer than it should have to understand was the deed to a warehouse Uncle Pierpont and Lord Lynnfield had purchased jointly.

"Because of course one would need someplace to store seven thousand barrels of oatmeal," I muttered as I stowed the deed back in its place.

Disappointment wrapped itself around my thoughts. It was beginning to look as if I had been wrong. Not only was there no unusual reason for my betrothal, there was nothing here from my father. No inheritance, no property, no token of care and love held back by my wicked uncle. That had all been the manufacture of the lost child inside my soul telling fairy stories. My eyes prickled, and I squeezed them shut. The fact that I was standing there in the shadows of my uncle's deserted book room, on the brink of bursting into tears, felt unbearably ridiculous. As ridiculous as my shocked stammering had been the day I was told of my betrothal. I'd been on the edge of tears then, too. In fact, I'd been in such a state of agitation that I hadn't even picked up the contract spelling out my future. I'd left it here and retreated to cry about the unfairness of life.

I'd left it here.

My eyes opened themselves, and I turned in place, staring at the whole of the paper-filled room. What if it was still here? What if I found *that*? That contract was a real document, not an imagined will or incriminating letter. If I found my betrothal contract, if I took it . . . A moment alone with that one paper and a hot fire could end this whole affair. If Uncle Pierpont couldn't produce the contract, he couldn't prove the betrothal had ever been arranged.

I glanced at the door. I strained my ears to hear any sound. How long had I stood here? I had no way to tell. I bit my lip and recommenced my search in earnest. That I had no fire nor the immediate means to make one could prove problematic when it came to swiftly burning the thing, but I was confident I could sort that out.

How much paper could one room hold? There were boxes within drawers within cabinets. There were folios within bound ledgers and whole legions of scrolls tucked into pigeonholes in other cabinets. So many were bound and sealed in blue and black and red, I imagined the ribbon makers of London rubbing their hands together in delight over the thought of gaining my uncle's extensive custom. My heart was hammering. My mouth had gone dry. The betrothal contract had to be here. It was clear my uncle never discarded anything. If I could but lay my hands on it, this would all be over. I would be free.

I suppose in the back of my mind I knew there would be a copy somewhere, probably with Lord Lynnfield, but that seemed a trivial matter. In the rush of the search, in the hope and the fear of my circumstance, and the disappointment at failing to find any sign of concern from my father, that contract had taken on the strength of a talisman. If I could but hold it, its power would be mine—not Uncle Pierpont's, not Lord Lynnfield's. Mine.

It was then I heard the patter of footfalls. I jumped and clapped my hand over my mouth to stifle the scream. Keys rattled outside the room, and I had just time enough to duck behind the curtains before the door flew open.

⟿⟾

CHAPTER TWENTY-ONE

IN WHICH A NUMBER OF MOST
UNWELCOME DISCOVERIES ARE MADE.

As it happens, several distinct disadvantages await any person seeking to conceal herself behind draperies, especially when she is recovering from nine days' worth of cold. The first is that any person so concealed is enveloped in both darkness and the pervasive smell of dust and polish. Second come the united problems of motion and sound. The slightest stirring of fabric will alert any personage on the other side to one's presence, likewise the faintest of noises. Therefore the persistent tickling of velveteen and dust against one's already aggravated nose becomes actively dangerous. Finally, the concealed person quickly finds she has no way to see just who has come to discover her. The result is a long, heart-pounding period during which said Concealed Person has no idea of exactly how much danger she might be in.

To my surprise, it was Olivia who put an end to this final danger.

"I told you, Mother." My cousin's muffled but desperately annoyed voice sounded from beyond the drapes. "There is no one here."

Mother?

I heard movement. I shrank back a fraction of an inch, groping for the window behind me. But before I could get a decent grip on the sash, the velveteen flew back and I found myself face-to-face with nervous, foolish Aunt Pierpont.

I looked at her, and she looked at me, appreciating, no doubt, the full dramatic effect of my being frozen in shock with my mouth hanging open. Her lip quivered, and I could not in truth blame her. Finding that one's permanently exiled niece had clandestinely returned by means of an open window might reasonably induce quivering. Unfortunately, Aunt Pierpont did not confine herself to a quiver. As I searched for an appropriate explanation, my aunt burst into tears and ran from the room.

I turned on Olivia, who put up both her hands as if she might need to defend herself, which, I confess, was not outside the realm of possibility.

"I said nothing, I swear. She guessed."

"Well, now she's going to raise the house." I hiked up my skirts and pushed past her. Fortunately, I knew exactly where my sobbing aunt had gone. With Olivia on my heels, I hurried up the steep stairs. By the time I reached the second floor, I was puffing, coughing, and seeing stars from shortness of breath. The sound of weeping drifted from the doorway at the end of the hall. Together, we ran toward it.

My aunt's rooms perfectly reflected her personality. Every item of furniture was adorned with quantities of enameled panels, painted flowers, or gilt curlicues. When Olivia and I pushed our way inside, it was to find Aunt Pierpont collapsed on the sofa, weeping noisily into her hands. Mortimer, my aunt's tired-eyed maid, was just emerging from the dressing room carrying a bottle of smelling salts and a pile of fresh handkerchiefs. I stepped into the woman's path and held out my hands for both. At the same time I jerked my chin toward the door, indicating she should leave. Mortimer's gaze shifted from me to Olivia. Olivia nodded, which caused the maid to shrug, hand me salts and kerchiefs, and take herself away. Olivia closed the door and shot home the bolt.

Aunt Pierpont saw none of this, as she was still covering her streaming eyes with one hand. But like her maid, she was clearly aware of the routine requirements for such a moment, because she held out her free hand and gestured impatiently. I pressed a handkerchief into her palm. She looked up in what I'm sure was meant to be a brief acknowledgment of her servant. When she saw me, her tears abruptly ceased to flow and her face twisted, wound tight by a new emotion so surprising, I took a step backwards.

"You *stupid* girls!" cried Aunt Pierpont. "How could you be so thoughtless!"

Olivia opened her mouth to protest, but I shot her

my best glower. For once, it hit its mark, and Olivia said nothing.

"You're right, ma'am," I told my aunt, and I meant it. "We have been very stupid, and it's entirely my fault. I thought if I could recover my betrothal contract, I could . . . put an end to things." Olivia looked impressed at this reasoning. I tried not to care. I was finding Aunt Pierpont's anger strangely difficult to bear. Perhaps it was because, unlike my uncle's fury, this was much newer, and far more justified.

"And *of course* you didn't think to come to me!" *Not even once,* I admitted silently as my aunt knotted her kerchief around her knuckles and dabbed furiously at her eyes. "I only spent eight years looking after you!"

"It's not at all her fault," said Olivia, attempting to rally us both. "I—"

"Oh, I know very well this was not her idea," Aunt Pierpont snapped. "This has all the hallmarks of one of your schemes, Olivia. I knew you to be reckless and cool, but I always believed you must have *some* kind of sense. He is your father, and if you cannot give him your love as a daughter should, you still owe him obedience!"

Olivia lifted her chin, the picture of stubborn defiance. "But no harm's been done, Mother. Nothing's been taken after all."

"Exactly how are you planning to keep the fact that the pair of you broke into his private room a secret? Would you have me let all the servants go at once?" The force of Aunt

Pierpont's words lifted her to her feet. "Do you honestly think *none* of them will talk?"

Neither my aunt nor my cousin was looking at me. I suspected they'd forgotten I was even there. Mother and daughter faced each other, unblinking.

"Of course he'll find out," Olivia told her. "And he'll be angry. What of it? He's been angry at me before."

"Olivia, you're so proud of your intelligence. Will you come out of the clouds and use it? Your father is a *banker*. You just helped someone get into his private room to *steal* from him. Do you honestly think this is going to end with him shutting you in your room for a week?"

Aunt Pierpont plopped back down on her sofa. I'd seen her in the many expressions of her nerves—from agitated, to uncertain, to fraught, to hysterical. I'd seen her merry, and I'd seen her worried. Until now, however, I'd never seen her defeated.

"I tried," Aunt Pierpont murmured. "After your mother died, Peggy, I wanted to raise you to be as good and true as she had always been . . . but I failed. I failed."

"You aren't to blame for this, Aunt."

"Then who?" Aunt Pierpont unwound the kerchief, seeking some dry spot she could ply against her streaming eyes. I handed her a fresh one from the pile I still held. "Oh, if you only knew how bitterly they quarreled, how difficult it was for me to convince him to take you in at all."

It was not much work to guess that "they" were my uncle and my mother. Impulse seized me, and I, in turn, knelt down to seize Aunt Pierpont's hand. "Tell me," I urged her. "Why did they quarrel? Why does he hate her so?"

Aunt Pierpont shook her head, her lips pressed tightly together to actively forbid her mouth from speaking.

"Mother, surely Peggy deserves to know," said Olivia quietly. "It concerns her most nearly, after all."

"After this exhibition, I don't see how either of you can claim to deserve anything," she announced bitterly. But then, because she was still Aunt Pierpont, she relented.

"We were friends, you know, Lizzie and I. That was why I was so glad to see you and Olivia become so close." My aunt smiled at her kerchief and her memories.

"I did not know." I certainly had never heard her refer to my mother, Elizabeth, as "Lizzie."

"Oh, yes. When I married your uncle, Lizzie was still at home and keeping his house. Once I moved in, we went everywhere together—all the best houses, and we were frequently at court. She sparkled at every gathering. It was so different then." Aunt Pierpont sighed and touched the corner of each eye. "Everything was gay and wonderful, even in that stuffy court when the old queen's health began to fail. Everyone was glad to welcome us wherever we went, even though Oliver was merely a banker. It became even better after he was knighted."

I sat back on my heels. My nervous aunt and my bold, beautiful mother had been the best of friends? It was too much effort to both picture this and keep myself balanced forward at the same time. Just as difficult was picturing Aunt and Uncle Pierpont being welcome in society or welcoming society into their home. I could count on one hand the number of times I'd seen them entertain at home. When Aunt Pierpont went out, it was mostly to chaperone Olivia. I had always assumed her habit of seclusion was another manifestation of her nerves. It seemed that, once again, I was utterly mistaken.

"We met Jonathan Fitzroy at Marlborough house," Aunt Pierpont was saying. "He was a great friend of the duke and duchess in those days. Oh, I remember your mother's face, Peggy, when she first saw him. It was like the sun had come out."

Olivia had moved behind me. She laid her hand on my shoulder in comfort and reassurance, and I was glad to have her there.

"What was he . . . my father . . . like?"

"He was very handsome." Aunt Pierpont gazed into the distance. "Not tall, but broad in the shoulder, with curling locks and a fine beard . . ." She smiled a little. "When we first saw him, we were sure he must be a Frenchman. He certainly looked the part. The truth of it is, I was in awe of him. We all were. He was so witty, so gallant. And older, of course. What girl wouldn't fall madly in love with him?"

She was talking about my father. My absent, hated, beloved father. My father was a gallant who could be taken for a Frenchman, and all the women had fallen madly in love with him. I tried to remember him. I tried until my head began to ache.

"Lizzie made a great show of being indifferent to him, but she was the one he always talked to. It wasn't long before they were spending hours together. I could barely follow half their conversation. I swear they spoke as much Latin and Greek as English and French.

"I knew it was going to be a match. There was nothing against it. Fitzroy's rank and fortune were as good as Lizzie's, if not better. He was extremely well placed. At first, Oliver was well pleased. Everything seemed to be going perfectly."

"But it did not end perfectly," I murmured. The bells of the timepiece on the mantel were chiming. It was four of the clock. Soon the princess would be dismissing her maids to dress for dinner. Sophy might take it into her head to stop at my room for a bit of personal taunting, or spying. Mrs. Titchbourne might stop in with another note from Her Royal Highness. Anyone at all might enter my door, and they would find me gone. I had to get back to the palace, immediately.

I did not move.

"The first I knew of the trouble was when the men came to our house," Aunt Pierpont said. "They stayed closeted with Oliver for hours and left with piles of papers. When Oliver finally came out . . . I had never seen him so shaken. He wouldn't tell me what had happened, but later that day, he and Lizzie had an absolute screaming fight. He . . . he struck her, across the face. He called her a whore. He called her a traitor. He . . ." She paused to blot her eyes again. "I think he would have killed her if Fitzroy hadn't arrived to take her away."

I was standing. I was turning away, moving away. Olivia caught me, holding me in place. She knew we were not done. There was more I had to hear, about how my father had rescued my mother from Uncle Pierpont, about why. But she also knew I had gone past speech. My uncle had hit my mother. He'd struck her across the face. For this, there was no understanding, and no forgiveness.

"But what caused it?" Olivia asked for me. "What did Aunt Fitzroy do?"

"I only heard bits and pieces of it," said Aunt Pierpont. "I was too frightened to go in the room when they were arguing. It was something to do with the business and its papers. Lizzie spoke of them to the wrong person or said the wrong thing.

"But whatever she did, it was serious. We lost all the money and the house. We had to move in with some distant cousins of mine." Her words drifted away into the current of memory, and for a long silent moment, my aunt looked old and exhausted. "You wouldn't remember this, Olivia. You were too young. But we were quite poor for several years. That was when I lost the twins. And little Michael. He was so ill for such a long time."

"I do remember," said Olivia. "I remember the coffin."

I did not remember, and I felt cold and hard and horrible for not being able to share this pain. I knew Olivia'd had brothers, of course, and that they'd all died young. There was nothing unusual about that. Most families lost one or more children in their cradles. It was the way of the world. But

I hadn't seen before how badly this way of the world could hurt.

"That was what broke him, you see," Aunt Pierpont whispered. "The loss of three children, three sons, in so short a time. Oliver blamed their deaths on our poverty, and he blamed our poverty on your mother, Peggy. Even though she'd offered to help. She did help, in fact. But, of course, I couldn't tell Oliver it was Lizzie who gave me money." She drew in a great, shuddering breath, seeking to pull herself out of those dark memories. "That time didn't last so very long. It felt that way, but it was only three or four years before Oliver reestablished the bank and began to make money again. But he never forgave Lizzie. When we received word she had died, he only said one word. Just one."

"What was it?"

Aunt Pierpont's lips moved for a moment, and then she whispered, "Good."

I should go now. I knew it. I should take what I'd learned and get out of the way. The sooner I left, the sooner Olivia and Aunt Pierpont could reconcile. If this wasn't motivation enough, then I had only to consider that I was not just in immediate danger of having my unauthorized absence discovered, but that my uncle must by now be on his way home. And then there was Matthew, who had promised to come to visit me tonight. If I wasn't there, he'd be very much worried.

But I couldn't go yet. I had a terrible, selfish curiosity that would not rest. I had not come here only to learn why I was hated. I meant to uncover the secrets lurking in my uncle's background, preferably before Sophy and Sebastian were able to find them. If Aunt Pierpont did not know exactly what her husband and my mother had quarreled over, she'd as much as told me there were others who did.

"Aunt, the men who came to take the papers when Uncle's business collapsed, who were they?"

"I don't know. I doubt I'd recognize any of them if I saw them again." She paused. "Except the one, of course. He was so fat, and so overdecorated . . ."

All the blood in me froze. Mind and thought were forced outside, and I had the unaccountable sensation of being a witness to my own actions as my body turned itself more fully toward my aunt. My mouth moved. I listened intently to the questions I asked.

"A short man? In a full-bottomed wig? He repeated himself constantly?"

"Why yes, Peggy. That's the man."

I nodded. Who else could it be—this fat, overdecorated man who had come to pick over the bones of my uncle's ruin years before he came to my rescue? He was my patron, Mr. Tinderflint.

CHAPTER TWENTY-TWO

IN WHICH A TIMELY AND HIGHLY DESIRABLE
ESCAPE IS, MOST UNFORTUNATELY, PREVENTED.

I was out the door before my aunt could make any reply. I was down all three flights of stairs before I realized Olivia had followed me. Indeed, I had no idea at all she was there until she grabbed my elbow and whirled me around.

"Have you lost your mind?" she inquired. "If you leave by the front door, you're sure to be noticed." She pushed me down the corridor, through the dining room, and then through the French doors that opened onto the garden. When we were halfway down the path to the back gate, she halted.

"Now, tell me quickly. What did you find?"

I found that Mr. Tinderflint had been concealing far more from me than even I had guessed. But of course that was not what Olivia meant. I forced my whirling thoughts to steady themselves. Fortunately, I'd had a good deal of practice at this of late.

"There was nothing in the book room, Olivia. A deed for a warehouse, some bills of exchange, but nothing else. I couldn't even find the betrothal contract."

This seemed to take Olivia aback, but not for long. "Well then, the proof must be in the Sandfords' house," she said. "That's going to be difficult, but we'll think of something."

Anger welled up in me. Had she heard nothing at all of what had passed in her mother's bedroom?

"Olivia, we can't continue with this," I said.

"We can't abandon it now."

Olivia's face had taken on her most serious expression, the one that indicated she was turning over her endless stock of stories and ideas to see which would best suit the current circumstances. If I gave her any more time, she would find something and cut it down to measure.

"Olivia, listen to me!" I grabbed both her hands. "This involves the king, and the Crown. I know Mr. Tinderflint looks odd and plays the fool, but he stands next to power, and Robert Walpole is watching over his shoulder, and mine." I had been a bit suspicious of my patron before. I had tried hard to be wary of him. Now I was afraid. "If Mr. Tinderflint learns I've been looking into Uncle Pierpont's affairs, he'll start looking too." And there was someone who could tell him all about it. Sophy Howe. I had absolutely no doubt that he could charm and deceive her, just as he had me.

I waited for Olivia to argue. I waited for her to remind me Mr. Tinderflint was still in Paris and couldn't possibly learn anything about my peregrinations around London. But given what I had just heard, Paris did not seem anything like far enough to keep Mr. Tinderflint from learning all he wanted to know.

Olivia folded her arms and faced me with an air of disappointment and patience stretched to the breaking point. "Is that all?"

"Isn't it enough?"

"I'll tell you what's enough. Your Mr. Tinderflint has been keeping secrets, from me and from you. And you're telling me to simply stand back and take no notice!"

I was unprepared for the full onslaught of her anger, or its source. I'd thought she would be annoyed with me for being so cautious and lily-livered a creature as to be unwilling to attempt an assault upon yet another house. But this was different.

"Secrets are hard things, Olivia," I told her. "Whole lives can be broken on them."

"Then let them break! I will not let that man pull *my* strings because it amuses him!"

Her words, and their implication, slapped me hard. I set it aside. I must. I had to douse the fury blazing in her, or it would burn her alive. She'd do something foolish, and she'd be caught out, and it might be by someone far more dangerous than her father.

"Olivia, you must let this go for now. Just until we

understand what's truly happening. He helped ruin your family before—he could do it again." Ruin came easily to bankers such as my uncle. I heard tales of such ruination gleefully bruited about over cards and wine cups. There might be pity for those broken by the lost investments, but seldom was any spared for the banker himself. If her father was ruined, if he was taken up under suspicion of treason, Olivia was done for.

"You go on, then, Peggy," said my cousin. "I'll see you later."

Fear stopped my breath. Surely she was already forming some new plan. There was no knowing what she'd do once I left, or where it would lead.

Inspiration struck, and it struck with such force that it knocked the next words out of me before my mind had any chance to properly consider them. "Come stay with me."

"At the palace?"

"Yes. It can be for as long as you like," I said, my confidence growing with each word. "We can sort through this mess together. I can ask the favor of Her Royal Highness. You're already friends with Princess Anne. She'd love to have you as a companion for her and her puppies. You know she gets whatever she wants."

Olivia did not answer; she just kept looking toward the house. *Why are you hesitating?* I wanted to shout at her. *Don't you see this is perfection?* But even as I considered the scope of its perfection, I involuntarily found myself counting coins in my head. If she came to stay, I'd have to manage Olivia's keep along with my own. I told myself it didn't matter. I would find a way, even if I had to sell every single thing I owned.

"You're inviting me to come to the palace now?" Olivia held her blue eyes wide open in an expression of entirely feigned wonder. "So you can stop me from going where you do not want me? Or from asking too much about my father, or yours, or your precious Mr. Tinderflint?"

Now it was my turn to be angry. This was about her and her life and whether she could be saved from a descent into chaos and misery. In short, whether Olivia's life could be saved from Olivia's intervention.

However, since she'd brought up my family to illustrate her particular point, hers was entirely fair game for mine. "You can't really want to hurt your mother, can you?"

My cousin paused, and for a moment I thought I'd carried the day. But when Olivia spoke again, it was with a terrible politeness I'd never heard from her before.

"If you do not want to know how you came to be as you are, Peggy, that is your decision. I will respect it. You can go back to the palace and your Mr. Tinderflint, and we will simply never speak of this again."

"That's monstrously unfair, Olivia."

"Is it?" she replied, raising a single perfectly arched brow. "Then I apologize."

This cool, distant declaration struck deep in my heart and lodged there. I do not think Olivia knew in that moment how close I came to turning around and walking away.

But I was facing the house, and a motion caught my eye. The curtains in the book room window were still open. Aunt Pierpont had drawn them back to discover me, and none of us had bothered to close them. None of us had stopped to think that when my uncle came home, he would have a clear view of the garden—and Olivia and me.

My uncle now stood at his open window, taking in that particular view.

"What on earth . . ." began Olivia, but she turned as she spoke, and so there was no need for her to finish. She saw exactly what on earth had transfixed me and sent all the color rushing from my cheeks.

While we both watched in wide-eyed disbelief, a second man—older, with a weathered face and good clothes —came to join my uncle at the window. His mouth moved, and my uncle made some reply. Whatever the stranger said in response did not please my uncle. Uncle Pierpont raised his long hand, crooked his finger, and slowly, deliberately gestured for me to return to the house.

Olivia's cool distance fell away at once. "Leave," she urged, pushing on my shoulder for added emphasis. "Quickly. He can't stop you."

But I couldn't. Because it wasn't my uncle who wanted my return. It was the weathered man next to him. Whatever he'd said had caused Uncle Pierpont to summon me. The combination of the dim room and the reflections on the glass of the partially raised window obscured the details of his face, but I knew that withered frame and those slouching shoulders. This was the man who'd twice emerged from the great black coach in front of the House of Pierpont.

The old man wasn't the only stranger in the book room. Yet another man moved into my field of view, so that the window framed the group to make a formal portrait of them — *Three Men Spotting Trouble in the Garden*. This third, younger man also spoke. My uncle shrugged and gestured again to me.

I should have ignored them all and left at once. I was at the very least jeopardizing my post and risking hurting Matthew's feelings yet again. But I had come here for answers.

"I'll go in," I told Olivia. "It will be all right."

"And you think I'm the one who's lost her wits," breathed Olivia.

Nevertheless, she gathered her hems and we started up the garden path. We walked so close together our skirts and shoulders brushed each other constantly. We stepped through the French doors to find Guinevere flopped down by the threshold. She heaved herself to her feet with an affronted growl for her errant mistress and waddled after us, still complaining. Olivia paused just long enough to scoop the fluffy creature into her arms.

I wished that I had something, anything, to hold on to. The great case clock chimed solemnly as Olivia and I brushed past. The hour had gone on five of the clock. It was not possible my absence had been overlooked. Matthew was waiting in an empty room, and I was finished at court.

I'd dreamed of being back in this narrow hallway, of approaching the closed door and knowing my uncle was behind it. With each step, I shrank, becoming smaller and younger and more confused, and yet I could not stop walking. This was enough like those nightmares that for one wild moment, I actually believed I might wake up.

But I was not waking up. I was putting my hand on the cold metal knob of my uncle's door, and turning it, and walking once more into his book room.

CHAPTER TWENTY-THREE

_In_ which _Our_ _Heroine_ discovers
even previously identified problems
may contain unsuspected and
profoundly unwelcome depths.

The candles had been lit, so I could plainly see the two strange gentlemen who flanked Uncle Pierpont beside the great desk I had so recently rifled through.

The years had not been kind to the older of the two strangers. His face had been so battered by wind and burned by sun, it seemed less a human visage than the sculpted side of an ancient cliff. The skin of his hands, which he folded over the top of his silver-handled walking stick, was loose, leathery, and impressively spotted. His shoulders had taken on a permanent hunch, and his protruding belly looked decidedly at odds with his bony fingers and loose-jowled face.

I wondered if his black coach with its load of armed men waited in the street while he was in here.

The younger man had also been deeply bronzed by the

sun. His was a lean face with hollow cheeks, but his build was broad and square beneath his plain blue coat. The contrast was such as to make his head appear just a bit too small for the rest of him. Even as I thought this, it occurred to me I'd seen those blue eyes and that sharp face before, but I could not tell where.

For my uncle's part, he looked as he usually did—black and white and entirely disapproving.

"Well, miss, what is the meaning of this?" Uncle Pierpont growled to Olivia. "What is *she* doing here?"

Olivia moved to speak, but I touched her hand. Recent experience had taught me that being caught was a likely outcome to any of my confidential ventures. So, for once, I had made sure to have a story ready before I entered the house.

"I came to deliver Olivia a message from Princess Anne." I tried hard to keep my gaze directed toward Uncle Pierpont rather than letting it flicker to the as yet anonymous, but oddly familiar men. "Olivia had not been to deliver an update today, and the princess was anxious to know if her dog had given birth yet." Guinevere, apparently aware she was being talked about, whined and squirmed in Olivia's arms. My cousin shushed and patted her, bending over ostentatiously to set her down, in case any of the three men we faced had failed to take note of her existence.

"Well, well." The older man leaned forward and gave a smile that was supposed to be indulgent, but succeeded mostly in becoming a thin leer. "That would make you the famous Miss Fitzroy. Ain't you going to introduce us, Pierpont?"

But there was no need. The younger man was looking me over from head to toe, assessing me. All at once, I knew where those eyes and face belonged.

"Lord Lynnfield," I breathed, meaning the older man. "And you're . . ."

The younger of the strangers gave a perfunctory bow. "Mr. Julius Sandford, at your service."

Julius Sandford, Sebastian's elder brother, heir to the barony of Lynnfield, had kept hold of his walking stick, although custom and etiquette dictated that it should have been surrendered at the door. I noted Mr. Sandford's stick was a match for the one his father held. It could have, in fact, been a match for the one I'd seen Uncle Pierpont carrying when I'd spied on him in front of his banking house. My instincts as both courtier and agent rose up from the back of my thoughts.

"I, for one, am glad to find you here, Miss Fitzroy," Julius Sandford was saying. "We'd been meaning to come up to the palace to get a look at you, but instead you've come to us."

It was evident from this that Julius had none of his brother's easy charm. Still, I made my curtsy as if I'd been highly complimented. The gesture brought my line of sight closer to the silver handle of Mr. Sandford's walking stick. It was not just silver, I saw now, but silver-gilt, and heavily embossed with a design of islands rising out of a stormy sea.

"I'm only sorry, Lord Lynnfield, that it's taken so long to make the acquaintance of yourself and Mr. Sandford." I batted my eyes at Julius Sandford as I straightened. A great deal could be told about a gentleman from the way he reacted to the flutter of painted eyelids. But Mr. Sandford had no reaction. His sharp face did not so much as twitch. The cold finger of worry touched the back of my neck.

"I'm surprised Sebastian is not with you, Lord Lynnfield," I continued, using conversation to cover disquiet. "I hope he is well?"

"The only trouble my younger son has is what he's made for himself." Lord Lynnfield smiled at his own turn of phrase, revealing a mouth full of very black teeth. "And that includes some of your antics, I'll wager!" This, evidently, was the height of Lynnfield wit, and the withered baron laughed heartily at it, thumping his own walking stick on the floor in time with each guffaw. This angered Guinevere, who had to waddle over and yip imperiously at the cane, presumably commanding it to hold still.

I made myself smile. It was easier than it might have been, because that wheezing laugh told me something important. Lord Lynnfield liked the sound of his own voice. My uncle might be a closed book, and Julius Sandford a cold fish, but Lord Lynnfield could be encouraged to talk, and would probably talk a great deal.

"Unfortunately, Miss Fitzroy was on her way back to the palace," said Uncle Pierpont. "If you should wish to speak further with her, I understand she is easily had there."

Lord Lynnfield snorted loudly at this insulting double entendre. Fresh anger blossomed, which allowed me to meet my uncle's hard eyes and return my sunniest smile. "I would be happy to welcome Lord Lynnfield and Mr. Sandford. I'm sure we have a great deal to say to one another. What a pity, Uncle, you do not care for court. We could have so many cozy conversations, all of us together."

I thought I heard Olivia make a warning sound. I ignored her and kept my attention on my uncle. My statement was a direct challenge, and I knew Uncle Pierpont did not mistake it.

"Some men have business to conduct," he said. "They may not shirk their duties to their family, unlike maids of honor."

"And thus I am gently admonished," I said with a laugh to the Sandfords, both elder and younger. "But my uncle is of course right. I do have a duty to which I must attend." I swept into another curtsy, a deep and showy one, that caused Guinevere to yip indignantly and circle my impertinent skirts. "I am so sorry that I cannot stay and make your better acquaintance, Lord Lynnfield, Mr. Sandford," I told them, doing my best to achieve the appropriate levels of gentle regret and merry sparkle. "I will send you a card of invitation to the next drawing room. We can all have a long talk then. Forgive my dropping by unannounced, Uncle. I see that you are busy, and I will show myself out."

I turned away, the motion of my hems sending Guinevere into a fresh flurry of fluffy outrage. In a motion that was part waddle, part scamper, she hurried to bark at my freshly exposed and much embroidered heels.

"No," said Mr. Sandford quietly to my back. "You'll not go quite yet."

The calm certainty in those words sent goose flesh crawling across the nape of my neck. I had to grope for my indignation a moment before I could turn around with a properly cold expression. "I beg your pardon?"

Julius Sandford stepped toward me and planted his walking stick on the carpet between us. The abruptness of the gesture startled me and attracted Guinevere's attention. She left off scolding my hems to come to growl at Mr. Sandford's stick. For once I understood the impulse. Everything about Julius Sandford made me uncomfortable. The alertness of his blue gaze was made strange and cold by the straight line of his mouth. He neither approved nor condemned what he saw, but he saw it all, and perhaps saw through it. Just then, what he saw through was me.

"I understand you ladies of the court are great ones for cards," Mr. Sandford informed me. "I hope I can claim you for a game of piquet before all's said and done."

No! Every instinct in me screamed the word. *Do not sit at the table with this man. Do not bet against him.* Those same courtier's instincts, however, made me cast a glance toward my uncle. Uncle Pierpont was holding himself very still, but he'd not been able to properly school his expression. The disgust I read there was palpable, but for once it was not aimed at me. It was all for the smiling, chuckling Lord Lynnfield, with his hands folded on his black stick that exactly matched his son's, and my uncle's.

Something tiptoed closer in my mind; something about sticks and blue seals and the vision of Mr. Walpole and his "stirrings" was intruding, as was, for some reason, the smell of beer, but I couldn't make any sense of it. I was too discomfited by Julius Sandford.

"I take it you yourself are fond of cards, Mr. Sandford?"

"It is one of the chief pursuits of a man's life," he replied. "All one needs to know about another person may be learned at the gaming table."

I had heard such sentiments voiced before. They were generally spoken by people who believed themselves to be unusually expert at all forms of gambling. Mostly, they were wrong.

"I'd be delighted to play piquet with you, Mr. Sandford, should the opportunity present itself."

"Then I'll have to make certain it does, and soon."

I held my cheery smile in place, even as Mr. Sandford shoved Guinevere firmly aside with his cane. Unfortunately, she was not to be deterred and came right back, yipping.

"Olivia, control that creature," growled Uncle Pierpont.

"Of course. I'm sorry. Naughty thing." Olivia ducked down to pick her puppy up, but Guinevere had already darted back between us, barking at full force at the unwelcome cane tips and shoe tops. This time, the shove Mr. Sandford gave Guinevere was much closer to a smack against her skull. Olivia gasped, outraged.

And she was not the only one. Guinevere had never been anything but spoiled and indulged, and she found this indignity too much to bear. With a burst of speed I wouldn't have credited, the little dog lunged forward and sank her needle-sharp teeth into Julius Sandford's ankle.

Mr. Sandford lashed out with one foot, kicking Guinevere hard in her swollen belly. Guinevere flew back, howling in pain, and slammed against the wall. Julius Sandford raised his walking stick to deliver a fresh blow. Olivia screamed in anguish. She grabbed his arm and gave it a twist, just as Monsieur Janvier had taught her. But Julius was stronger than Olivia. He yanked his hand free and raised his cane high, his face absolutely stone still as he brought it down, not toward Guinevere, but toward Olivia.

It landed with a sharp smack against Uncle Pierpont's raised hand.

The two men stared at each other, with Uncle Pierpont gripping Julius Sandford's stick above Olivia's head. I grabbed Olivia and yanked her out from under that unlikely bridge.

"This is not your house, sir," said Uncle Pierpont, his voice as hard as iron and just as cold. "Neither is my daughter your property or concern. You will leave here, now."

He let the cane go, and Julius Sandford drew it back. Guinevere whimpered. It was as well she did so, because the sound distracted Olivia. A moment before she turned to rush toward her beloved dog, I had read murder in my cousin's eyes.

"Now, now, temper, temper, Julius," said Lord Lynn-field mildly. "You're upsettin' the little gels, ain't you?"

"You need to maintain better order among your beasts and women, Pierpont," said Mr. Sandford with an awful casualness. I backed away to stand beside Olivia as she knelt down to cradle Guinevere into her arms. All that while, I kept my eyes on Julius Sandford.

"I would never permit such displays." Julius Sandford looked right at me as he spoke these words.

Let him, I told myself. *Let him see I am not afraid.* But I was afraid. Not only did this Sandford have none of his brother's charm, he had none of Sebastian's hot blood. Julius's cruelty was winter cold. Now I knew why his brother wanted so badly to escape.

"All right, my boy." Lord Lynnfield patted his son's shoulder, an indulgent gesture that sent a wave of nausea sweeping through me. "You've made your point. Let's leave the little gels alone. We've more pressing business."

"We have no business at all," said Uncle Pierpont. "You will both leave here."

"Oh, now, there you're wrong, Sir Oliver. We've plenty of business left. And if you'll take a moment to think on it, you'll remember that." Sebastian's father smiled, and I saw every bit of Sebastian's malice in it, but aged, warmed, and strengthened. Lord Lynnfield was enjoying himself. The nausea returned and redoubled. I waited for my uncle to reply with scorn, to order them out again. But he subsided, slowly slouching and turning the anger inward so it showed only in his eyes.

"Get that dog out of here," he said to Olivia, and to me. "I'll not have it in this house."

Guinevere whimpered again. Olivia stood, holding the small creature. All the murder I had glimpsed before had returned to her pale face.

I put my arm around Olivia's shoulders and turned her away. "Keep quiet, keep quiet," I whispered urgently in her ear. "We can't fight this here. Let me get you out."

Taking her silence as assent, I led Olivia into the dim hallway. Aunt Pierpont had been waiting for us at the foot of the stairs, and she scurried up to us at once. She saw the dog lying listlessly in her daughter's arms and the look of anguish on Olivia's face, and pressed her kerchief to her mouth.

"Oh, my dear," Aunt Pierpont murmured, "I tried to warn you! I tried!"

"She's alive," I said. I did not take my arm from Olivia's shoulders. "But I think she's hurt."

Finally, Olivia spoke, her normally lilting voice made thick and rough by fury. "How could he permit this? *How?*"

I looked at Aunt Pierpont. I waited for her to ask what had happened. When she did not, I understood my earlier assessment had been wrong. She had not been waiting for us at the foot of the stairs. She had been listening at the door. She knew exactly what had happened in that room, and she'd done nothing. Nothing at all.

"Do you know, Aunt?" I asked her. "How could he?"

But she did not answer me, not directly, anyway. Instead, she lifted Guinevere out of Olivia's arms and deposited her in mine.

"You'd best take the dog, Peggy," said Aunt Pierpont. "Come, Olivia." She tried to grasp her daughter's elbow, but Olivia did not even look at her.

"You remember your plan in the garden?"

I nodded. She meant my plan for her to come and stay with me.

"I've changed my mind," said Olivia. "The answer is yes."

She turned and walked slow and straight-backed away from me and her mother, leaving us to face each other in mutual confusion and disappointment. Guinevere lifted her little head and gave a soft whine of regret. Olivia must not have heard, because she kept walking.

"I'll have your cloak brought," said Aunt Pierpont.

"Aunt," I said, "tell me what's going on. Whatever it is, I will do my best to help you and Olivia. I swear it."

"Just take the dog away," said Aunt Pierpont. "There's nothing else that can be done. Not now."

CHAPTER TWENTY-FOUR

IN WHICH OUR HEROINE BECOMES
THOROUGHLY TIRED OF UNEXPECTED
ENCOUNTERS IN DARK PLACES.

My velvet cloak was brought. I bundled it about myself and Guinevere and walked out the front door. I did not look back. I did not dare. I had just seen Uncle Oliver defend his daughter and then be quickly overwhelmed by a few brief words. Whatever business existed between him and Lord Lynnfield was not some mundane matter of trade and bills of exchange and a warehouse. Nothing so small could have defeated a man of such iron and unforgiving will as Uncle Pierpont.

I was so occupied with these thoughts that I was halfway down the steps before I noticed that I'd been right about one thing at least. The black coach was waiting in front of my uncle's home, as it had waited in front of the bank. As before, a half dozen ruffians waited with it, and every single one of those battered, tattered, armed men swiveled his eyes to look at me. This included the driver, who sat on his high board and held the horses' reins in his grimy hands.

I ducked my head and tried to hurry down the rest of the steps, but I needed both hands to hold Guinevere and so had none free to help manage my hems. I stumbled, hard, first down to the curb and then onto the cobbles.

Some man sniggered. Another pushed himself away from the coach and sauntered toward me, his cudgel cradled in his arms, much the way I cradled Guinevere. I was already turning away, goading my feet to hurry. I heard boot heels picking up their own pace behind me.

SNAP!

The explosion of sound froze me in place and jerked my head up. It had also frozen my would-be pursuer.

It took a moment to see that the coach's driver had moved. He now held the horsewhip in his right hand, pointed directly at his fellow ruffian. That sound had been him cracking the whip over that man's head. The implication in his face was plain, though he spoke not a word. I also could not fail to notice that his free hand rested on the pistol at his belt.

I had no idea why this man chose to come to my rescue, but I felt I should not waste this moment he'd bought me. Therefore, to demonstrate my grateful sensibility, I took to my heels and ran.

My mask still dangled from its chain beneath my cloak,

and anyone at all might recognize me. I did not dare reach for it, lest I drop Guinevere. I just made as straight a line as I could for the sanctuary of the palace. In time with my stumbling footsteps, Guinevere began an anxious, unsteady whining. I tried to convince myself this was a good sign. Surely, if she could make noise, she could not be too very hurt.

I crossed from the square to the Mall. As broad as that street was, it was full to the brim with all sorts of traffic. I'd completely forgotten it was Friday and therefore the night of the public dining. All manner of people had crammed themselves through the great arched gateway that led to the Color Court to try to gain a place to view their royalty while those august personages slurped soup and devoured roast fowls. The noise of massed humanity, horses, and conveyances was deafening. I could barely hear the bells ringing overhead, let alone tell what hour they signaled.

Not that it mattered. My absence had by now been discovered, and I would be dismissed from my post. Matthew would already be gone, and I faced the very real possibility that the beloved royal lap dog was expiring in my arms. I would have asked what more could possibly go wrong, but I feared that Heaven might answer the question.

I told myself I must not let what I had seen or all my fears get the better of me. I might not be able to save my post or the dog by hurrying, but perhaps I could get back inside before Matthew gave up on me entirely. If I hurried, if I kept my wits, I could reach my rooms and his arms. Then I could fall apart. Matthew would wrap me in his embrace. Matthew would listen to all that had happened. I had to see him, to be with him, to be reminded that there was a person who cared.

"Just a little farther," I said to the dog and myself, and made myself hurry with tiny, quick dancing steps, just like I'd been taught.

The gardens of St. James's Palace faced the Mall, and tonight those gardens were nearly as full as the streets with merrymakers. I ducked between crowds of gentry, cits, and women with their personal goods on sale and on full display. Once again my hooded cloak worked in my favor, since it prevented the crowd from noticing the presence of a maid of honor. Guinevere's unsteady whine had turned to unsteady panting, which worried me extremely. I told myself such rapid breathing might very well be normal for such a small dog. It was not as if I'd ever paid attention to her habits.

When I finally reached the doors, a yeoman lowered his long arm to bar the way. I tipped my face up and lifted Guinevere, who'd begun to wriggle uneasily, a little higher. I don't know whether the man recognized me or the dog, but he shoved the door open and stood aside, touching his cap to us.

For once, the dim, chill interior of the palace felt like a haven. I found the stairs and climbed them, not entirely sure of my way, but I kept moving nonetheless. I could see lights up ahead, which meant an inhabited corridor and a chance to get my bearings. I'd go to my room. I'd send a note to Molly for Her Royal Highness. I'd say that Guinevere had taken ill unexpectedly, and Olivia had gotten worried. I'd apologize profusely. Maybe I'd offer to resign. I'd ask Matthew what he thought. Because he was surely still here. He had not left me yet.

Unfortunately, it seemed Guinevere had become annoyed by my inexpert handling. Her uneasy wriggle became a sudden squirm, and I lost my hold. The dog plopped heavily to the floor, but heaved herself up again. She attempted to scamper away, but was hampered by her own belly, which she could not seem to quite lift off the floor. Considering that a moment ago I'd feared for her life, I should have been delighted. Instead, I said some things I would regret extremely later and lunged after her, but found myself as hampered by skirts, stomacher, and dim light as the pregnant dog was by her bloated belly. I missed and lunged again. So intent was I on the dog that I barely saw the pair of red shoes with gilded buckles. When I did, it was too late. I collided with their owner and bounced back.

The man I bounced off was, as it happened, the Prince of Wales.

"Now then, now then, what's this? What, eh?"

The curtsy I executed then was my fastest and my most clumsy. I wobbled so violently on the way down that His Royal Highness put out a hand and caught me by the elbow.

"I'm so sorry, Your Highness!" I gasped as he lifted me up. He had the strong and steady grip of a good horseman and held me smoothly, even as he peered uncertainly at my face.

"Miss Fitzroy, ain't it?" His Royal Highness said. "What're you doing out of bed, then, eh?"

"I'm sorry, Your Highness." An annoyed yip startled me back into my lost wits, almost. "I . . . it . . . the dog got away—"

"Ah, that would explain everything." Unhampered by corsets and skirts, Prince George reached down his surprisingly long arms and scooped Guinevere up. "Have you been leading your people in a dance, then, little one?"

Guinevere gave an angry yip, and I bit my knuckle. Images of blood flowing from the royal hand filled my mind. But the prince just chuckled and peered more closely at her. "Something wrong with you, eh?"

"She's not . . . well, sir," I said, thinking of broken bones, injured spines, a chill, a cold, and how on earth was I going to explain this to anyone at all?

"No, I think she's quite well." He tipped her into the crook of his arm and cupped one broad hand over her belly. "She is whelping, though."

Whelping? My cousin's beloved, the royal lap dog, was having her puppies *now*? It was too much. Wit, will, and all good sense fled screaming down the corridors of my soul and left me standing there to give out a single cry.

"OH!"

"Now, don't panic, Miss Fitzroy." His Royal Highness deposited Guinevere into my arms. "Take her to your rooms. She knows what she's about. I'll send the Master of the Hounds up, just to have a look, eh? Off with you." He gave me a gentle push to urge me along. I was so terrified, I forgot to curtsy. I also forgot to wonder why the Prince of Wales on the night of the public dining was wandering about the corridors of St. James's entirely unattended, which, like Guinevere giving birth in my arms, was not something that should have been allowed to happen.

I'm not certain how I found my way back to my room, but I did. Guinevere's distress was almost as great as my own by the time I shouldered the door open.

"Libby! Bring a blanket! Libby!"

"Peggy! What the holy hell's happened!"

Matthew! I swung around, still holding Guinevere at arm's length. This was not, I will admit, the best position in which to be carrying a dog about to drop her puppies, but I couldn't seem to make myself do anything else. Matthew had just leapt out from behind my writing desk. He'd been pacing, I thought. Pacing and waiting for me.

"You stayed—you're wonderful!" I told him before whirling myself and Guinevere back around to Libby, who threw open the closet door. "She's giving birth! We need a blanket!"

Libby screamed and retreated. Matthew stripped my cloak off my shoulders. I think he meant to lay it down, but then he caught sight of my disheveled dress.

"What have you been doing!" Just then he sounded far more like Uncle Pierpont than was good for any of us.

Guinevere lifted her head and howled. I ignored Matthew and hated both myself and the dog for doing so. Holding Guinevere in one hand, I grabbed the cloak from Matthew and tossed it to the ground. I dropped to my knees as if in desperate prayer. Just then, Libby emerged from the closet, a ragged length of cloth in her hands. She shrieked as she saw me holding Guinevere over the extraordinarily expensive velvet and dove forward to throw the towel down. Guinevere growled and tried to nip my fingers. I set her down hurriedly, and she whined and circled and flopped onto the towel. Libby hugged my gray velvet to her chest, shot me a glower that could have blistered paint, and retreated to the closet, banging the door shut behind her.

"Peggy . . ." Matthew loomed over me.

"I'm sorry," I gasped from my position at his feet. "I'm so, so sorry. I cannot tell you how sorry I am. I never meant . . . I didn't—"

Then Matthew was on his knees as well, gripping my shoulders tightly. "Peggy. Stop it," he commanded. "I need you to make sense."

"I want to! And if my life would make sense for ten seconds altogether, maybe I could! But I have just learned that Mr. Tinderflint helped ruin my uncle some ten years ago, Lord Lynnfield is somehow blackmailing my uncle, and now the royal lap dog is giving birth in my room and His Royal Highness is very kindly sending the Master of the Hounds to deal with it, and they've left me with no time to explain to my beau why he shouldn't be angry at me!"

Matthew lifted his hands off my shoulders and clapped

them to his head. Staring at me, blank faced and pale, he settled back onto his heels. I reached out. I had to find something to say, to erase that look on his face. His fear and distrust were too much to bear. I had to make them go away at once. Because if I didn't, I would lose Matthew, the one person I could not live without.

It was in this moment, a knock sounded at the door.

CHAPTER TWENTY-FIVE

I<small>N</small> WHICH IT BECOMES ABUNDANTLY CLEAR

THAT DRASTIC AND DECISIVE ACTION

IS REQUIRED.

I think I may have screamed. I certainly did stagger to my feet. Likewise, I stumbled across the floor and ripped open my door with such violence that Molly Lepell—who stood on the other side—jumped backwards.

"Oh, Peggy," said Molly, recovering from her surprise with professional speed. "I came to make sure you were all right—" Guinevere howled over the end of her sentence. "What is the matter with that dog?"

"She's whelping. I thought you were the Master of the Hounds."

From the way Molly furrowed her brow, this was evidently not explanation enough. At that moment, however, I did not particularly care.

"Oh," she said. "Perhaps I should come back later."

"Perhaps you should," I agreed.

Guinevere howled again. "You're certain you're all right?" Molly's glance traveled from the dog to Matthew. "I brought one more . . . for that matter we talked about." She held out a slim jewel case.

"Of course. I'll take care of it. Goodbye."

I closed the door in my friend's face. I told myself I would apologize later, that she really didn't want to know anything about the disaster that was currently occurring in this chamber, and that it had already been a very bad day.

I faced Matthew. His brow was puckered up even more tightly with consternation and confusion than Molly's had been.

"Dare I ask?"

"No."

I crossed to my closet door. I opened it to find Libby standing right at the threshold, as expected. It was, after all, the best place to hear what occurred in the outer room. I handed her Molly's jewel box and shut the door again. I looked at Guinevere. She was panting once more. How long did it take to give birth to puppies? Was there something I should be doing? Perhaps boiling water or writing announcements? I shouldn't just be standing here with my arms at my side and my beau watching me as I watched the panting dog, with my so-faithful maid listening at her door.

"What should I do?" asked Matthew, echoing my own thoughts.

"I don't know," I whispered without looking up from the fluffy white heap that was Guinevere. "Truly. I don't know."

I heard Matthew's shoes sound against the floorboards as he moved toward me. He put his hands on my shoulders and turned me around.

"Should I go?" he asked.

I looked up at him, struck absolutely dumb by the question. I heard myself answer yes. I heard myself weeping no. I heard myself laughing at the awful ludicrousness of our farcical quartet of maid of honor, swain, servant, and birthing dog. In the end, I asked the only question I could.

"What do you want to do?"

Matthew drew back, slowly, carefully, as if he feared one of us might break. I was breaking anyway. I could feel it. The slow fractures had begun deep inside, like river ice when spring finally comes.

"What do I want?" said Matthew. "I want you to be safe, Peggy. I want to keep you safe beside me, always." He was breathing hard now, so deep and ragged that his shoulders shook with it.

I was shaking as well. He could see that I was shaking, but he made no move to come close again. "You shouldn't be worried about me," I said. "You should be angry and jealous." It would be so much easier if he were. Then I could get angry back at him. I could endure the pure pettiness of my own anger, and his. But his concern, his deep care for me during what I knew was only the most recent disaster, how should

I endure that? "You should think me shameless for lying and scheming and flirting with a man you know I have reason to hate."

"It's not the men. You don't give a fig for any of those popinjays, much less . . . Sandford. But do you think I could forget for a moment what happened to us at Kensington Palace?" I'd never seen a man so close to weeping. Those fractures in my heart shuddered again. "You think I don't see it every night before I fall asleep — those men with their swords and you with blood on your hands and that mad desperation in your eyes? Every time I see you, I think how I almost lost you forever, and sometimes I want to rip out my own heart, because I can't stand the pain!"

There are moments when we are made aware of what is real. It is clear as glass and hard as flint, unmistakable and unclouded. I took a step toward Matthew. I took another. I raised my hand and laid it against his cheek. I felt the shape of his bones beneath the warm skin. I felt the stirring of my blood and the rasp of his fresh stubble against the softness of my palm. I felt the life of him and, yes, the love in him. He didn't have to speak the word. Not now. I was close enough to breathe in his breath, and I did breathe, deep and slow.

I did not dare make any other move. I wanted so much. I wanted to pull him close and fall into one of those wild, condemned embraces, giving him all and taking all he had to give. I wanted to hold perfectly still and spend the rest of my life standing in this place, touching Matthew and letting Matthew touch me.

"I'm trying," I said, aware that once again I was making no sense. "But there are too many problems and they keep piling up. I'm running from one to the next, hoping to get them sorted out, but no one will give me any answers, and everything I do seems to make things worse. I just . . . I just need more time," I said. "And you. If I know you are there, nothing else will really matter."

"Oh," he said softly. "Well, if you'd just said that in the first place, we could have avoided all this unpleasantness, couldn't we?"

I felt myself staring. I felt my jaw drop open. It was not my most attractive expression, and certainly not one I ever meant to show Matthew, but I couldn't seem to help myself. "Are you forgiving me?"

"Is there something to forgive?" he asked, and that wonderful cheeky, mischievous grin spread across his delightful, infuriating face.

I grabbed him. I kissed him. I would have wrapped my whole self around him if it weren't for the maddening and inescapable fact of my skirts and hoops.

"One day, Matthew Reade," I said when we were both gasping for breath, "I'm going to push you too far."

"But not today." He touched his fingertips to my swollen, tender lips. "And I suspect not tomorrow, either."

There was a great deal more kissing and holding to follow. There might even have been some tears. Definitely there was laughter, which confused Mr. Taylor—the bandy-legged, tobacco-chewing Master of the Hounds—when he at last stumped across my threshold.

In the end, Guinevere gave birth to six puppies, all living. This effectively doubled the population of fluffy white dogs at court. I decided that I would not think about what Lady Portland was going to do when she found out about the new additions. Princess Anne would, of course, be ecstatic.

I had intended to ask Master Taylor to take the puppies to Princess Anne, or at least to the kennels, but Guinevere had turned savage and snarled at anyone who came near her towel in a manner that was rather less amusing than it might have been, considering her size. Master Taylor assured me this was normal, and that the new mother's wishes should be respected. He then—and this was something I noted most particularly—made a hasty retreat.

Much to my regret, I had to ask Matthew to go away with him. It was bad enough that he had come to my rooms alone, but if anyone saw him also leaving alone, it would give rise to all sorts of speculation, and I needed no extra helpings of scandal. Matthew agreed with me, if only because he needed to be on hand to help open the academy in the morning. I promised to send him a letter by Norris to let him know how I did and was rewarded with another kiss.

It wasn't until I closed the door behind him that I realized it was near to midnight, and that I was not only exhausted and had a freshly dripping nose, but I was also famished past endurance. I sent Libby down to the kitchens to see what might still be had for dinner and then I sat in my chair by the hearth, watching Guinevere wash and organize her squirming puppies, any one of which could have fit into my teacup. All the while, I tried to sort out what I myself needed to do.

For one thing, I would have to find a way to explain my absence to Her Royal Highness. A way that could not lead to me being dismissed. In fact, it would have to buy me enough goodwill that my mistress would not be put out by the news that I intended to bring my cousin to live with me.

Then I would have to find the means to lodge Olivia and some way to convince her mother not to come and drag her back home. Given the fact that Aunt Pierpont knew all about what had occurred between Olivia, her father, and the Sandfords, this might not prove as difficult as it would have once.

Then there was my uncle. I remembered the way he had shrunk in on himself when he failed to order Lord Lynnfield from his house, as well as the disdain and disgust he'd showed for the baron and his son. There was something else, too. Something I had seen or had not seen. Possibly several somethings. I felt them in the back of my mind, like pebbles making ripples in the stream of my thoughts. If I could pluck out those pebbles, I'd know what to say to my uncle. I'd watched Lord Lynnfield bring him to heel. I could do the same.

The true problem there was that it was not only my uncle

who must be brought under control. It was merry, cruel Lord Lynnfield and calm, cruel Mr. Julius Sandford. I twisted my hands in my lap. Whatever I had expected of the Sandford family, it was not that Sebastian would be the best of them.

But what worried me most was the thing I'd pulled from the pile of letters Libby had laid out on my writing desk. Mr. Tinderflint had written again. He had also sent a cake of French chocolate with instructions on how it should be grated and mixed with my brandy as an infallible remedy for my cold.

My Dear,

I am sorry indeed to hear that you and Jane have not been well. These autumn days are treacherous, and you must take extra care of yourself.

Your last letter has left me most anxious. Word of the quarrels between Mr. G and his son has begun to spread. Not only that, but I'm afraid the elder Mr. G has received word that his son is having the town house redecorated and the staff reorganized to suit himself, and is growing increasingly angry. It is distressing to think that there are those, like Mr. W, who would seek to take advantage of this familial discord. I feel positive this is what the Mr. Waters you mentioned plans to do as well. He is a poor man and a fortune hunter. I have learned for a certainty that if JW was relying on his rich and well-connected uncle in this city to help him, those hopes are doomed to disappointment. Therefore, he will be seeking his fortune elsewhere.

"So the Regent of France means to break his promises," I muttered to the page. "Why should he be any different from the rest of you?"

As to Mr. S, the reports on that family remain mixed. They are much beloved in their own country, and the folk there are entirely loyal to them, but men do not always appear in the city the same as they do in the country. Has Jane spoken to Mrs. PG on that score? You did not mention it.

Regarding that other business I was sent here to pursue, I'm afraid I have bad news. It begins to appear that the jewel we seek has been sent overseas, and those merchants with whom I am familiar are being unusually closed about where it might be now.

Write to me soon, my dear. I find myself thinking of you a great deal, and I am anxious to hear how you and Jane do.

        Yr. Obedient,
        Mr. T

My obedient Mr. T. Before I realized what I was doing, I had crushed the letter into a ball. How he must have chuckled to himself when he wrote those words.

Until the disaster at my uncle's house, I had not only been on the cusp of trust with Mr. Tinderflint, but a fair way toward falling over into it. But now that was done. I could not allow this man to use me anymore, though I had no idea how to end our deceitful relationship. The truth of the matter was, I was trapped. I could not leave my court post in any sort of huff. I had nowhere to go, and there was the not inconsiderable fact that Her Royal Highness now counted on me. Mr. Tinderflint surely had realized that. He understood such things very well.

I tried to think, but nothing came. Thought and reason had fled; all that remained was my simmering anger. Mr. Tinderflint, Lord Tierney, had used me. He had used my mother, he had known my father. Now I got to add my uncle to the growing list of Tinderflint victims. I wondered in what way Uncle Pierpont had failed Mr. Tinderflint. It must have been quite serious to make that gentleman take a personal interest in his undoing.

I wondered if Mr. Tinderflint had been surprised when Uncle Pierpont rebuilt his bank. I wondered why it had been permitted. Perhaps he thought my uncle would be useful at some future date. I could not understand how, though. It was not as if Uncle Pierpont was much seen with the power players at court. Why would he come into this society where his formal disgrace would be constantly picked over? My uncle was no fool. He'd know that it was better to stay outside and work his will, and his business, from a distance. Possibly even through an intermediary.

Was that the tie that bound Uncle Pierpont to the Sandfords and the Sandfords to me? Did my uncle need someone who could move freely among the aristocracy to do his work?

I turned this over and looked at it from every side I could

find. Mr. Tinderflint had let me believe I was here because I was my mother's daughter. What if I was really here because I was Sir Oliver Pierpont's niece?

I raised my head. But in front of me I did not see the hearth with its fire or Guinevere with her puppies. I saw the pattern of waves and islands on the silver-gilt walking stick Mr. Sandford carried.

James Stuart was known as the King Over the Water. My uncle had a Jacobite clerk in his employ who openly toasted James the Would-Be King in a Jacobite tavern located quite near his bank. The Jacobite lords needed a sympathetic banker with whom to do business, to gather money and get it to the right persons, to hold their lands in trust so they could not be seized by the Crown. By, say, a prince who was looking to flex his power and gather his own friends about him in order to secure his eventual succession.

"Oh, Olivia," I breathed. "Oh, I'm sorry."

Because if this was true, Uncle Pierpont was guilty of high treason. This time ruin would be irrevocable. He would be hanged, and all his property would be seized—house, money, movables, all of it. Olivia and her mother would be left disgraced and destitute. I might not be allowed to bring them to stay with me, even if I could find a way to support us all.

I looked at the crumpled letter where I'd dropped it onto the floor, and all at once I hated Mr. Tinderflint. It was a pure, clean hatred. I had been lied to and led on; I'd had my heart's desire used against me. No more. This would end, and I would end it. I would not allow Olivia to be harmed by the actions of her parents. Not like I had been.

In a single moment of clarity, I knew what I would do, and I knew how it could be done. The solution lay not through my uncle, but through the Sandfords, all three of them. And, of course, through the duplicitous, overdecorated Mr. Tinderflint himself. The best part of it was, if it worked, I would be following Molly Lepell's calm and excellent advice. I was about to create a sensation.

I moved to my writing desk, uncapped the ink, and took up my quill. I made sure it was neatly trimmed. I laid out a fresh sheet of writing paper, and began.

My Dear Mr. T,

I am afraid I have no news for you. Things have been very dull here. Jane has gone to the country. I miss her terribly.

Yrs.,

Miss Mostly

—⁐⁌⁑⁍⁐—

CHAPTER TWENTY-SIX

Preparation.

T here was one absolute certainty regarding my plan: I was done trying to sneak about. What I did now, I would do in the open, or mostly so. Unfortunately, openness itself does not equal simplicity. My open actions would necessarily involve all the Sandfords, Sophy Howe, and the majority of the royal family with whom I had a personal acquaintance.

This, as one may expect, caused me some small concern. Enough, in fact, that sleep proved elusive for what was left of that night. I had at last managed an uneasy doze, when a massive thundering shook my room. I shot upright in bed in time to see the door slam open. A tiny, manic sunbeam of a girl with a candle clutched in her hand bolted through.

"Puppies!" cried Princess Anne. "They're here! They're here!"

The princess skidded to her knees beside her lap dog —somehow managing not to drop the candle or set the room on fire. For my part, I shrieked and kicked my way out from under the covers, trying to curtsy, push my hair out of my face, and sputter warnings all at the same time.

Fortunately, Guinevere, like all courtiers, proved to have an excellent understanding as to which side her bread was buttered on. While the princess squealed over the wriggly creatures, Guinevere simply lifted her head and assumed her most smug air.

Lady Portland, bearing her own candle, sailed in behind her little mistress.

"Good morning, Lady Portland." I ducked out of Libby's way as she stumbled about the room trying to get more candles and the fire lit.

"We have some new members of the household, I see," the governess replied, looking down at Princess Anne, who was cooing over each new pup.

"All healthy," I admitted.

"How fortunate. You must be very pleased."

"Lady Portland, you may believe me when I say I am every bit as pleased about these new dependents as you are."

"You will forgive me, Miss Fitzroy, if I say I very much doubt that." I searched her sour face to see if this remark was made in sympathy or challenge. I found I could not tell at all.

"Peggy?"

Princess Anne had lifted one of the puppies from its

improvised bed. "Peggy, you have been such a good friend to me and Guinevere, I want you to have her firstborn." She laid the tiny thing carefully in my cupped hands.

I stared at it. The initial comparisons that came to mind when I looked at the warm, bald, damp, and blind thing were not at all complimentary. But the creature stirred fretfully against my cold palms and gave a small whine. Something, reluctantly, began to thaw in me. Perhaps it was the natural sympathy we must have when encountering something else that is confused at finding itself in a strange place full of very strange noises.

"Your Highness . . . I don't know what to say."

Lady Portland smiled and folded her hands in a show of smug triumph that rivaled Guinevere's own.

"She's too little to be away from her mother, of course." The princess removed the pup from my hands with equal care and placed it among the others so its mother could nose it back into place. "And you will have to bring her to play with her brothers and sisters every day."

I was about to give my solemn promise that it would be so, but I was interrupted. There was a single knock at the door, but before Libby could react, the footman on the other side pushed it open to reveal the Prince of Wales in his stout morning coat and hunting breeches.

"Well, well. And how's the little mother?"

"Papa!" Princess Anne leaped to her feet while I was trying to drop an appropriate curtsy. "Come see!"

His Royal Highness chuckled and let himself be pulled along. He also let himself be sat on the floor and listened patiently while his daughter explained all that she had thus far divined about the nature, courage, and intelligence of each individual new puppy.

No one familiar with the habits of small children will be surprised to hear that this took a while. Eventually, however, the prince got himself to his feet and gave his daughter a nudge toward Lady Portland.

"Off you go, my dear, dressed and breakfasted. That's the thing." He kissed his daughter, patted her head, and shooed her and her governess gently away before turning to me. "A word, if I may, Miss Fitzroy."

"Of course, sir," I said. Not that there was any other answer I could make. Lady Portland shot me one more malicious glance before the door was closed behind her. Libby, thankfully, retreated to the closet.

His Royal Highness folded royal hands behind the royal back. "Been watching you, you know, Miss Fitzroy," he said. Somewhat to my surprise, he said it in English. "Wife's quite taken with you. Says we've got a good friend in you, but it might be prudent to speak a word or three. You've been gone from waiting rather a lot lately. It's been noticed."

The blood drained from my cheeks and took all possibility of intelligent reply with it.

"Now, now, no need to look that way. You're not being dismissed. It's not come to that, or anything like it quite yet.

So, buck up, eh?" He patted my shoulder. I think it was in a fatherly way. I was too busy wrapping my thoughts around the words "you're not being dismissed" and "quite yet" for more nuanced reasoning.

"But we're in an important time, Miss Fitzroy, and we must all keep up appearances." Prince George tapped the side of his nose. "It's all about appearances. My father, he appears to care more about Hanover than Britain. Doesn't improve his standing among the lords of the land, you begin to see?"

"Ermmm . . ." I confessed.

"Ha! That might be what I said to Her Royal Highness when she talked this way to me." He chuckled again, and I laughed, because it was what one did when royalty was amused. "Now, you understand how it is for us. There's the ones that pay us court, and we must pay court right back to them. It's our job to be open, bright, entertaining, you see? That's what your Englishmen like from their king. By showing them the glitter and the flash"—he waved one hand vaguely in the direction of the gardens beyond my blank walls—"we show how much we care for those same lords and the land they hold. Makes 'em more inclined to let things continue on as they are. D'ye see now?"

"Yes, sir. I think so." What he meant was that it made the aforementioned lords less inclined to attempt yet another change of royal horses.

"Quick on the uptake, just like she said. Good." The prince nodded vigorously. "All of us inmates here, we have to keep up our appearances, no matter how high or low. Not a woman living doesn't know all about that, eh? Now, appearances for a man, they're different, but must be kept up just the same, you know. There's things he's got to be seen to do, or there's persons—some of them very important persons—who'll think he's not so much of a man as he might be. And that's bad for a king, ain't it? And since there's no way out of it, it's best to do it in a way that don't disturb things too much. Now do you see?"

He was talking about Mrs. Howard. I was standing here with my eyes lowered, all dutiful attention, listening to my prince talk about the necessity of keeping a mistress so that he looked like a true man to the lords of the land.

The Prince of Wales was taking me into confidence. The heir to the throne wanted me to understand, to remain loyal to him and his wife, and not to make waves about Mrs. Howard. He did not want my naive young self put off by the convolutions of court sophistication.

He and his wife, for reasons of their own, wanted me here. I didn't know whether to cry out in triumph or expire on the spot from the weight of this understanding. At the same time, I couldn't help but notice that was the second time this man had referred to himself as king. Not prince. King.

"I do see, sir," I said. "And . . . if I may, sir . . . Mr. Walpole spoke to me recently of certain stirrings that might be happening, from the north, since Lord Tierney left for Paris—"

"Er? Eh?" The prince's face shifted, and for the first time, perhaps, I saw that I was looking not at a velvet aristocrat, but at a soldier.

"I think he is not mistaken, and I think I may be about to be able to put some names to the actors, as I have been requested to do by Her Royal Highness." I stopped. "But I will have to be making use of appearances before I can be sure."

The prince, my prince, nodded once. "It's good, it's good. Well, I'll leave you to it, then. Will be most interested to see what comes of it, Miss Fitzroy."

I made my curtsy. His Royal Highness patted my head, much as he had his daughter's, and took his leave. The footman closed the door, but not without a judicious glance at me.

At another time, I might have worried what rumors this private word between His Royal Highness and myself would give rise to. But I did not spare a thought for that now. Those rumors were nothing compared to the ones I was about to set in motion.

I had five days until Thursday and the next drawing room. It was barely enough time. I had to bring Monsieur Janvier in for extra lessons, not in fighting or dancing this time, but card playing. Julius Sandford had challenged me to a game, and he would not find me less than ready.

Naturally, there had to be a flurry of letters sent. I had to let Matthew know what I was planning, and when. I had to invite Sebastian to the next drawing room and pretend that I did not know Sophy would have already issued an invitation of her own. Finally, I had to make sure a separate, formal invitation reached Lord Lynnfield and the Honorable Mr. Julius Sandford.

I had to invite both Molly Lepell and Mrs. Howard to drink a private cup of tea and enlist their aid for the drawing room, and the plan.

But even more urgently, I had to retrieve the money for the jewels I had sold. My plan might be sound, but it was even more expensive than giving a private dinner. Fortunately, Mrs. Egan proved as good as her word and was able to fetch a respectable price for the four pieces of jewelry I gave her to copy, along with the three I passed on from Molly.

Molly was duly grateful to receive the purse containing her share of the spoils. So grateful, in fact, that she was willing to speak to the master of Leicester House on my behalf. Leicester House was a grand mansion on the same street as St. James's Palace that had the unusual function of being a sort of secondary palace when the royal family was in residence. Courtiers who could not afford, or had not been invited, to take rooms in the palace proper could find apartments there for themselves or their guests. Molly's good word, bolstered by my freshly acquired coin, reserved a modest suite of rooms there. That suite was, may I add, rather more spacious than my rooms at the palace and had not one but two windows.

What Olivia told her parents about where she was

going and what she was doing, I do not know. But she arrived at Leicester House with her maid, Templeton, and enough trunks to give even Norris, who was directing her fetching and carrying, pause.

"You don't intend to go back, do you?" I said, watching the footmen heave yet another box up the stairs.

"Not if I have to beg in the streets," Olivia replied.

This time I felt absolutely no guilt at all about counting coins in my mind. I might be in the confidence of royalty, but that confidence was fickle, and it tended to last only as long as success did—and it did not always bring monetary reward.

But I could not dwell on this. It would paralyze me with doubts I had no time for. I simply kept working and explaining. I explained part of my plan to Her Royal Highness in German, my command of which was improving rapidly. I explained rather more of it to Olivia, as she already knew most of the parts I did not dare explain to Her Royal Highness. I had ample proof that my mistress was a tolerant and practical woman, but one did not tell the Princess of Wales one had already turned thief, housebreaker, and cardsharp until it became absolutely necessary.

There was exactly one person to whom I told the whole plan. When I was finished, I looked up at Matthew with a single question in my mind.

"Have I gone mad?"

"I don't know," he answered me. We were in my room.

The supper had just finished, and I was supposedly here to change my mantua for the princess's usual private party.

"Do you have a better idea?" I asked.

"You could run away with me." To cement his argument in favor of this suggestion, Matthew kissed me—a long, slow, warm kiss of the sort he was particularly expert at.

"Yes," I agreed as soon as we were able to bear breaking away again. "That is a much better idea. I'll pack the dog, and we'll go at once."

Unfortunately, Guinevere was not inclined to let me or Matthew anywhere near her pups, so we had to abandon that excellent scheme. But Matthew did agree to act as Olivia's escort to the drawing room. In fact, he insisted upon it.

So it was that when the night of the drawing room arrived, the two people I loved most in the world were in my chamber when I emerged from my dressing closet.

"Peggy!" cried Olivia. "Is that really you?"

Matthew said not a single word. But the look on his face was that of a starving man presented with a banquet. I let myself smile and curtsied to them both.

The dress was new. It was sea green silk and figured silver satin over saffron petticoats. Pure white lace fell in four tiers to cover all but the tips of my fingers. The square neckline was cut to within a hair's breadth of propriety, and the expanse of skin and bosom it revealed was powdered with a blend of Libby's own creation that shimmered faintly in the candlelight. I wore my new stomacher as well, with my special jeweled pin in plain sight, and my little silver blade in its hidden pocket. I did not truly believe this evening would end in blows, but Sebastian was attending, so one could never be entirely sure.

I also wore my mother's sapphires at my throat and carried the all-important talisman of her fan in my hand. My hair was pinned with more sapphires and strings of gold beads that cascaded down my neck and shoulders to glitter among my dark curls. The patch by the right corner of my mouth was a blue heart. The patch beneath my left eye was a tiny black bird.

I'd intended this to be my costume for the prince's birthday celebration, but I was going into battle tonight. It made no sense to do so in anything but my best armor. Even Libby looked pleased as she hurried out to see to some final preparations.

Matthew left Olivia's side. He took my hand and pressed it to his mouth. He began to speak, but I rested my fingers over his lips.

"There's no time," I told him, not without a great deal of regret. "We're expecting company."

"Are you sure he'll come?" asked Olivia anxiously. "You didn't say if you got an answer—"

But my answer came there and then. A furious pounding began at the door. I made a flourishing gesture with my fan as Olivia moved to open it. On the other side stood Sebastian

Sandford—fist raised and face flushed. He was also breathing hard. Probably, he'd bolted up the stairs and down the corridor to come make this particular noise.

Displaying his usual understanding of propriety, Sebastian strode into the room without waiting for an invitation.

"What in God's name are you playing at!" he roared.

Matthew stepped forward. Sebastian was the taller of the two of them, but when he saw the expression on Matthew's face, he was the one who fell back.

"My brother's down there!" The menace in this statement was much reduced by the fact that Sebastian had to deliver it over Matthew's shoulder.

"Then he must have received my invitation," I replied. "Surely you heard we were introduced the other day at Sir Oliver's house."

At this, Guinevere lifted her head and growled.

"Quiet. Naughty thing," remarked Olivia.

"You have no idea what you're getting yourself into," Sebastian said, plainly expecting me to be shocked by this revelation. He, of course, was unaware that not knowing what I was getting myself into had become my most consistent modus operandi. "My brother will not forgive you if he thinks you're trifling with him."

"And, worse, he might think you put her up to this," remarked Olivia as she moved to stand beside me.

Sebastian blanched and stared at us all in disbelief. Whether this was because of what was said, or because he found himself thoroughly and unexpectedly outnumbered, I could not tell.

"Contrary to what you may think, Mr. Sandford, I do know at least some of what's happening," I told him, coolly. "And since you're here, I have an offer to make you."

"Oh, do you?" Sebastian snorted. "Miss Howe was sure you'd have something up your sleeve."

"I never keep my cards up my sleeve. They slip out far too easily." I made certain his gaze was on mine before I spoke my next words. I spoke them slowly and evenly. "I do not wish you to mistake me, Mr. Sandford, so I will be plain. I know your father and brother have Jacobite sympathies. What I do not have is proof. If you were willing to supply that proof, I could take it to certain persons who would make good use of it."

Sebastian was silent for a heartbeat, and another, and another.

"If I might even consider doing so ridiculous a thing," he murmured, as if he was afraid the walls themselves were listening, "what would it get me?"

"You would be free to go about your business, which is something I know you want as much as I do."

Again Sebastian fell silent. The moment stretched out. Olivia shifted her weight impatiently, and I silently pleaded with her to hold still. Sebastian was looking at me. He saw the richness of my dress and how well I occupied my room in the palace. He was thinking about power, and about freedom, and, I was sure, about Sophy Howe. If he agreed to this, there would be no need for either of us to face down his brother and father in the drawing room. I could send a note straight to Mr. Walpole, and all would be done.

"And the post?" he asked finally.

I was ready for this. I had spoken to Her Royal Highness about the matter. "The word I have been given is that your chances of securing a post would be greatly increased if you came forward publicly. It would exonerate you and clear your way to any available preferment."

"I can't do that. They'll kill me." He said this flatly and with certainty.

From what I had seen of his family's capacity for casual violence, I did not doubt him at all, but neither did I intend to let it change my position. Instead, I lifted one shoulder in the elegant shrug so much favored by the ladies of court, indicating that whatever he did, it was all the same to me.

"You little bitch," croaked Sebastian.

"I beg your pardon?" said Matthew, very, very softly.

Sebastian backed away another step. Then he smiled, and as he did, I saw his brother in his eyes.

"So, there it is. You've seen Julius. You think, 'There's the power in that family. What do I need Sebastian for? He's nothing at all next to his brother.'" The words were soaked in an old and sour bitterness. "Think again, my fine miss. You're not the only one with friends at court now. I will have that post, or I will have you. It's your choice."

No, I told him silently. *It's yours, and you've made it.* "Go back to your family, Sebastian. Or, if you prefer, go to Miss Howe. We are finished, you and I."

"Oh, no, we are not finished, Miss Fitzroy. And now we never will be."

I did not shiver as he turned on his heel, nor did I flinch as he slammed the door. In fact, I did not permit myself to so much as move until Matthew had closed the bolt and Olivia had wrapped her arms around me.

"You won't let him upset you, Peggy, will you?" she asked anxiously.

"Not anymore." I patted her arm and moved myself gently away. Then I took Matthew's hand, and I took Olivia's.

"Thank you," I said to them both. "I don't know what will happen tonight, but thank you for being here with me."

"Don't be ridiculous, Peggy," said Olivia as she squeezed my fingers. "It's a perfect scheme. I'm only surprised you thought of it first."

If my smile was a little weak, it was at least sincere. I turned my gaze to Matthew.

"I could not be anywhere else," he said, and kissed my hand.

If I had doubts, they fled. With Matthew and Olivia by my side, I could do anything, and I would dare the whole world to try to stop us.

I faced forward, flipped open my fan, and squared my shoulders. "Open the door. It's time."

CHAPTER TWENTY-SEVEN

The drawing room was already full by the time we reached it. For once, my late arrival was calculated. When the footmen pushed open the doors, every eye turned to us, just as I knew they would.

Let them look. I kept my own gaze straight ahead as I advanced. *For once, let everyone look.* Tonight, I would take center stage, and I meant to give the performance of my life.

Olivia and Matthew followed arm in arm, forming my personal entourage. The crush parted for us. Lords, ladies, and gentlemen drank in the details of our little procession as we made our way to where Her Royal Highness was seated among her other attendants. But it was not just Her Royal Highness. The Prince of Wales, resplendent in scarlet and gold, was also there, standing at his wife's side.

I made my deepest curtsy.

"Well, well, Miss Fitzroy," boomed the prince. "Mother and babies doing well, I trust?"

"Very well, sir, and I thank you," I answered.

"Excellent. Anne will be pleased to hear it, won't she, my dear?" I lifted my eyes just far enough to see him lay a hand on the princess's shoulder. "And this is your cousin, I think, ain't it, Miss Fitzroy?"

"Your Royal Highnesses, may I have leave to present Miss Olivia Amelia Pierpont?"

"Delighted." The prince smiled. "Glad to welcome our Miss Fitzroy's family at last."

Olivia dropped her curtsy a fraction of an inch in modest acknowledgment.

"And, sir, madame, this is Mr. Matthew Reade of the Royal Academy for the Improvement of Art and Artists."

"Ah, yes, yes, one of Thornhill's men." Prince George nodded sagely. "Heard of you, sir. My wife expects great things, you may be sure, as do I."

"I will endeavor not to disappoint, Your Highness," murmured Matthew.

I knew what was happening. It was known I had the princess's good opinion. Now the prince was publicly indicating his approval as well. Such an open sign of royal favor was protection, and it was power, and they were both handing it to me, even though Her Royal Highness knew that I planned on humiliating a peer of the realm if I at all could.

I thought about Mr. Tinderflint and how he was going

to be rather surprised at the strides I'd made once he returned from Paris. But that was a matter for later. If I had a later.

"And so I have done what I can, Margaret," said the princess in light and conversational German. "The rest is up to you."

I bent my knee that much farther in acknowledgment and gratitude. I also took the hint and backed away, with Matthew and Olivia following suit.

When I was able to turn around, the first thing I met was the fire in Sophy Howe's glare. This was yet one more thing I'd expected, as was the sight of Sebastian skulking at her elbow. He added his furious glower to hers, and I had a moment to wonder exactly what he'd told Sophy about our most recent conversation.

It was not a long moment, however, because Olivia, Matthew, and I were quickly overtaken by a wave of silk-clad individuals demanding introductions. The gentlemen, in particular, were pleased to see Olivia, and my cousin fell right into the part of court belle, flirting and flapping her fan with the finest of us. Mary Bellenden, in fact, looked quite green with envy at Olivia's easy demeanor as gentlemen, lords, and not one, but two, admirals kissed her hand in rapid succession. Not that I felt any satisfaction at seeing my sister maid of honor discomforted, of course. I had far weightier matters on my mind.

Because there at the edge of the crush waited Lord Lynnfield, and beside him stood Mr. Julius Sandford.

"I'm going," I murmured to Olivia.

"Good luck," she whispered back.

I felt the brush of callused fingers against mine. Of course it was Matthew, but I could not so much as glance back. I had to keep my gaze forward and a smile fixed on my face. I was not Peggy Mostly now. I was Miss Margaret Preston Fitzroy. I was the princess's favorite and her confidante, and I was in demand with every highborn person in that room. My company was a mark of honor that I would condescend to extend to a chosen few.

It was with this attitude that I glided up to the Baron of Lynnfield and his older son.

"Well, now, Miss Fitzroy," chuckled Lord Lynnfield as he straightened from his bow. "You're looking very well this evening." His eyes lingered a little on my sparkling bosom. I tried not to squirm.

"How do you do, Lord Lynnfield, Mr. Sandford? I am so very pleased that you could come."

"Hate court," said Lord Lynnfield. "Still. Must do the pretty every now and again."

"And you, Mr. Sandford?" I turned to his son. "What are your feelings toward the current court?"

Julius Sandford shrugged. He was dressed in a pale blue coat, white velvet breeches, and a minimally acceptable amount of gilt-edged lace. The only jewel he wore was a fat gold ring with a plain black stone. His gaze was not on my bosom. It was busy traveling from my jeweled pins, to my bracelets, to my necklace and up to the gold and sapphires decorating my curls. I found myself wondering uncomfortably if he was picking out which of them were genuine and which were paste.

"Court is a necessary evil," said Mr. Sandford quietly. "But I find of late it contains certain . . . surprises."

I was ready to go on making small talk, but I caught sight of movement from the corner of my eye. Norris and Cavey had entered the drawing room, quietly, as well-trained servants were supposed to. If I hadn't been waiting for them, I would probably not have even noticed. At almost the same moment, Libby slipped into place with the other ladies' maids who stood in a tidy, inconspicuous row by the far wall.

My prologue was over. The stage was ready for me.

"Mr. Sandford," I said cheerfully, "I believe you asked me for a game of piquet when we last met."

"I did. Unfortunately, I do not see the tables set up."

"Oh, we can play over there." I pointed with my fan. Norris and Cavey had taken a rectangular gilt and marble table from its place in a shadowed corner and were carrying it between them to the hearth. All this was being done under the watchful eye of no less a person than Mrs. Howard. She glanced up at me. Our gazes met. She nodded once and retired.

Mr. Sandford took note of all of this, as he was meant to. "Ah," he said. For the first time that evening, a genuine emotion colored his voice—curiosity. "I had no idea you were such a keen player, Miss Fitzroy."

"It all depends on the partner, Mr. Sandford, and the stakes."

Again, Mr. Sandford glanced over my shoulder. Norris and Cavey were putting the chairs in place now. Around us, the gathering became slowly but steadily aware that something unusual was being prepared. A murmur spread through the room. Lord Lynnfield chuckled, a nasty, wheezing noise that emanated from his nose as well as his mouth.

"What stakes do you envision for our particular game?" Mr. Sandford asked softly.

I did not speak softly. I pitched my voice to carry. "There exists a contract between my family and yours, Mr. Sandford. We will play for that."

I suspect that seldom in the history of the world has such a large gathering gone so silent so suddenly. The last sound was a smothered giggle. That was Mary Bellenden, I was sure of it, although I did not look to see. I kept my eyes on Mr. Sandford, and I smiled.

"Unless, of course," I went on, "you're afraid you might lose."

Mr. Sandford took three careful and deliberate steps toward me. Even though a distance of more than a yard separated me from my paramour, I still felt Matthew tense.

"It's a pity, you know," Julius Sandford drawled. His eyes once more traveled the length of my body, carefully picking out my valuables, both the genuine and the fake. "I might have had you for myself, but I declined the honor." He shrugged and turned away.

For a moment, I thought I'd already won. I thought he'd refuse. But in this I was disappointed.

"What do you say, Sebastian?" Mr. Sandford called across the room. Sebastian started badly. Now all eyes were on him, and on Sophy Howe. "She's your betrothed. Shall I win her back for you?"

Around us, the room erupted into laughter, applause, and loud speculation. That almost shook me out of my countenance. I'd hoped to fluster Julius Sandford, and I'd completely failed. He stood in the middle of the commotion and did nothing more than smile as Sebastian slipped off Sophy's arm and stalked over to confront him.

"You lousy bastard," Sebastian hissed. "Are you trying to humiliate us all?"

"Oh, heaven forbid, my brother bastard," Julius replied calmly. "But I will point out that you're helping Miss Fitzroy do the job quite admirably."

"A moment, if you please," called a single, clear, unmistakable voice.

The entire gathering turned around. Her Royal Highness had risen from her seat. All of us at once made our bows, including the Prince of Wales. My mistress moved gracefully forward to join my little conversational party. It was not to be missed that His Royal Highness fell into step behind her, and when she stopped, he remained at her side.

"This is most irregular, Lord Lynnfield," the princess remarked. "Don't you agree?"

"I'd have to say so . . . Your Highness." I'd never seen

anyone smirk at Princess Caroline before this. My estimation of Lord Lynnfield's nerve rose.

My mistress did not mistake his expression, or the hesitation before he pronounced her title. "And perhaps a little less than dignified?" she inquired.

"Well, these young persons, ma'am. You know how they get. Especially the gels, eh?" Lord Lynnfield chuckled, but only a little. Even he had a hard time keeping up his humor in a room gone as silent as a winter's grave.

The princess bent her mouth into a brief smile. "Matters of such importance are generally not settled over cards." The sneer she applied to that final word was a work of art.

"Naturally not, naturally not," agreed Lord Lynnfield. "But as I think Your Highness knows, all sorts of things may occasionally change hands under unusual circumstances."

The high, hissing sound of dozens of breaths all being sucked in at once rushed through the room.

But Her Royal Highness seemed inclined to ignore this remark. "Will you agree to follow through on these unusual circumstances, Lord Lynnfield?"

"Never walked out on a bet in me life," he replied curtly.

"And should your son lose?" inquired the prince.

For the first time, Lord Lynnfield seemed to notice His Royal Highness was there, and it startled him. "Ha! Not much chance of that. Sir."

"Then have we any objections to this game, sir?" Princess Caroline said to her husband.

"Actually, I think it would be quite amusing," said

Prince George. "Although, I will say, my money's going to be on Miss Fitzroy."

That sealed it. The thunder of more than a hundred voices erupted. All other topics of conversation were forgotten as speculation flew back and forth, right along with the wagers. Molly Lepell looked as if she might faint. Mary Bellenden was clutching Lord Blakeney's arm in her excitement.

Sophy and Sebastian stood side by side, watching, as I walked sedately toward the table.

Piquet is a two-handed game, and so the table was a narrow one. Matthew managed to keep himself as the first one in line to pull out my chair for me. I expected a number of gentlemen would have bruised feet and shins in the morning as the result of his efforts. I smiled at him and received in return his look of complete confidence. I could have flown to France and fought the Pretender one-handed after that.

Olivia took my fan. I needed her near me for this game, and like Matthew, she'd gotten herself into position admirably. Next, I gestured for Libby to come forward with the ivory box containing my cards. As I did, I noted that Mrs. Howard was standing right behind Sophy Howe. I saw her mouth move as she murmured something, and then I saw Sophy's head snap around like she'd heard a shot fired.

"Just a moment, if you please," called Sophy above the tidal rush of bets being orchestrated and paper being passed about.

This fresh interruption actually caused Julius Sandford

to raise his eyebrows. Sophy slipped neatly through the ring of courtiers. "I recognize that box, I think," she announced. "It's your *personal* pack of cards, is it not, Miss Fitzroy?"

I pulled myself up, assuming my best haughty air. "It is. What of it?"

Sophy smiled, and I could see that she smelled blood. "Well, I could not say, to be sure, but, perhaps—purely in the interests of impartiality, of course—this game should be played with a different pack?"

I let myself rise, slowly. I clenched my fists and did everything possible to make a blush rise to my cheeks as I faced her.

"Why, Miss Fitzroy," said Sophy. "What on earth is the matter?"

"Nothing," I replied, making sure my voice trembled. "Nothing at all."

I sat back down. I stared at the table. I heard Olivia clear her throat. She was right. I did not want to be seen as laying it on too thick. Mr. Sandford had very sharp eyes.

I lifted my gaze and made myself smile weakly.

There was an additional flutter from the gathered court-iers as a fresh pack of cards was found and laid in the center of the table. This was accompanied by the rustle of additional notes of all sorts being exchanged.

Mr. Sandford pulled a fat purse from his pocket. Of course there would be money involved. How else would we know when one of us had beaten the other, except by breaking him? With deliberate patience, he stacked its golden guineas on the table. Not pounds, guineas. In the end there were fifty coins making a small fortress in front of Mr. Sandford—my entire year's salary, and a little bit more.

Sebastian said his family was out of money, and yet he gave me expensive gifts, and now his brother brought out fifty guineas to stake to one game of cards. He looked me in the eye, waiting to see me blanch. I did not. I let my brows arch.

"And that's what I'm worth?"

"Oh, no, Miss Fitzroy," Mr. Sandford replied. "I believe you to be priceless. This is simply what I have with me."

This remark raised a chorus of "ooohs!" and a few sharp laughs from our audience. I smiled and dipped my eyes, as if flattered.

"Miss Pierpont, if you please?" I murmured.

Olivia stepped forward. She'd been holding my purse and gave it over now. Every coin I possessed—the whole of my salary, all my savings, and the money from the jewels I had thus far sold—I stacked it all in front of me. If I was mistaken about how this game would turn, if I had been wrong about Mr. Sandford's motives or means, I would lose every single penny I possessed in one grand stroke.

"Will you deal, Mr. Sandford?" I asked.

"As you wish." Mr. Sandford rubbed his hands together, the only nervous gesture I had so far seen him make. I could not help but notice that when he finished, his ring with its polished black stone had been turned toward his palm.

I felt myself relax, just a little.

Mr. Sandford cut the cards, stacking them neatly with his long, spidery fingers. I did nothing about it. I already knew he intended to cheat. His ring gave him away. A polished ring can be used to show the reflection of the cards as they are dealt. This, in combination with such techniques as stacking the deck or dealing from the bottom, can be most effective for controlling the flow of a game. But the mark of a true card sharper, as Monsieur Janvier had informed me, is how carefully the player uses the knowledge he gleans.

I believe I can state without fear of contradiction or exaggeration that in all the games I had participated in since I came to court, I had never sat across from a player so coldly and deliberately calculating as Julius Sandford.

Mr. Sandford cheated carefully, shrewdly, deliberately, and only as much as necessary. He never let himself win too much or too many hands in a row. Sometimes he'd arrange a strong run of luck for himself, taking me down to my last two coins, before reversing the play and letting me win, and then he'd double my winnings.

I had been prepared for someone like Lady Bristol—one of those prisoners of the tables who gambled obsessively. Such prisoners became careless during the course of a game. They got wrapped up in the play and forgot to pay attention to the details. Mr. Sandford showed no sign of doing any such thing. Quite the opposite, in fact. With each hand we played, his concentration sharpened.

For my part, I became nervous. I took up my kerchief

and dabbed my brow. I constantly rearranged my cards and tapped my fingers on the table edge. I scooted my chair forward. I scooted it backwards. I pressed my knuckle to my lips. I pressed my hand to my stomacher, and rearranged my cards again. Of course, I should have been nervous. I'd been denied my very-probably marked cards, hadn't I? I had to let Mr. Sandford see I was losing my nerve, so he wouldn't look for anything else. He did watch me, as closely and carefully as I watched him. That was all right. In fact, everything hinged on my keeping his attention fixed.

My head was aching, and my eyes were tired, but I kept up my fidgeting. The crowd pressed close around us. The smell of warm humanity, wine vapors, and perfume was dizzying. I heard the whispers and sometimes the guffaws. That was heartening. It meant I was putting on a pretty show, and I needed that. But I could not let it distract me, just as I could not let Mr. Sandford's orchestrated swings of fortune truly unnerve me. How much I won or lost did not matter yet. What mattered was the timing. Timing and keeping count of the cards. That was vital. If I lost count, if I blinked at the wrong moment, if I missed one deal from the bottom of the pack or mistook the results of one careful shuffle, I was done.

Did Mr. Sandford suspect the game I truly played? I couldn't tell. I had been trained by masters to read the faces and motivations of those I played against, but I had never seen a more perfectly inscrutable human being. Genuine worry crept into me. Mr. Sandford was giving himself a winning streak again, and I was down to three guineas. I met Julius's blue eyes, and for once, I could read them. His tiny smile told me he meant to play all night. He was in perfect control of himself and the cards. What he was doing now, with his runs and his stacked deck and his reflecting ring, was toy with me.

And that meant only one thing. I had him.

Time to finish this.

My skin prickled, hard and unpleasantly, as if I had just plunged my hand into icy water. Mr. Sandford did not bother to look at the pack he held. He watched me as his long hands shuffled, and shuffled again, and dealt the final hand. I watched each card carefully. I did not have to force the color to my cheeks now. I was too hot. I was exhausted. My head was throbbing, and I felt a runnel of sweat trickle down my temple.

I picked up my cards and fanned them out and looked at them. I ignored the crowd, ignored the whispers, ignored Julius Sandford's cool gaze. Was I right? Had I missed any pass? Had I counted correctly? I had. I must have.

I pushed all my coins into the center and smiled.

Julius Sandford looked at the coins. The corner of his mouth twitched. Then he matched my bet.

I patted my forehead with my kerchief again. "You'll take all I have," I whispered to Mr. Sandford.

"So I will," he answered, looking me right in the eye. "And keep all you are. How lucky for me."

There was a rustle about us as more notes changed hands. Matthew pushed himself to the edge of the crowd, making sure he stood right where I and all the Sandfords could see him plainly.

"Peggy," murmured Olivia, "be sure."

Sophy Howe smiled and stepped one inch closer to Sebastian. Sebastian was not smiling. He looked as openly frightened as I'd ever seen him.

"You will have no mercy?" I lifted my handkerchief to dab the corner of my eye, well aware that I was imitating Aunt Pierpont.

"Do you deserve mercy?"

"Oh, for God's sake, Julius, finish it," muttered Sebastian.

The older brother lifted his eyes to the younger. "Is there some hurry, Sebastian?"

Sebastian made no answer, and I wondered at that. I also wondered at the air of complacency emanating from Lord Lynnfield. He was quite content with this display from both his sons. I noticed a bulge in his coat pocket that had not been there before. The old snake had been collecting bets as the game went along.

I pursed my lips; I glanced over the edge of my cards with lowered lids and dabbed again at the corner of my eye with my kerchief. I rearranged my hand. I frowned at it. I pressed my hand against my bosom, and against my stomacher, and rearranged my cards again.

Dear God, please, I must have counted right.

Julius laid his cards down. Two queens stared up at us, accompanied by two jacks, and the ace of spades. "This hand is mine, I believe."

"But . . ." I stammered. "But . . ."

I laid down my hand. Two queens stared up at us, accompanied by two jacks, and the ten of spades.

The whole of the crowd gasped. There was applause. There was laughter. Mr. Sandford pushed his chair back. "And there it is, Miss Fitzroy. You're mine."

CHAPTER TWENTY-EIGHT

In which triumph proves to be
somewhat short-lived.

Sebastian cursed. Sophy laughed. Even over the rest of the exclamations, applause, shouts, and curses, that laugh was unmistakable. I did not move. I could not move. Nor could I take my eyes from Mr. Sandford.

"Oh! But wait a moment!" cried Olivia.

The din faded. Julius straightened up in his seat at the exact moment Olivia bent down and reached under the table.

"Mr. Sandford, you seem to have dropped one of your cards," she said, quite clearly despite the awkwardness of her position. "It's under your shoe, here."

My cousin stood up again and laid the two of clubs down on the tabletop, right next to Mr. Sandford's discarded hand.

"You must have dealt yourself an extra card by mistake,"

Olivia said with an air of perfect innocence. "Perhaps it was that ace?"

I met Julius Sandford's gaze. I dared him with my own. *Deny it, please deny it. Make the whole court suspect you had to cheat in order not to lose to a woman.*

A man might cheat at cards, but he could never be seen to do so. It was all about appearances. Sophy, I noted, had stopped laughing. Myself, I seemed to have stopped breathing.

Julius Sandford's cool gaze traveled from me, to Olivia, to his brother and father, and across the crowd of courtiers and royalty.

"She's right." He pushed his chair back. "It was my mistake. The game is yours, Miss Fitzroy."

Had the room been loud before? It was nothing compared to the roar that shook the walls now. People cried out, or laughed, or shouted, or began to challenge one another. I did the only thing I could think of. I rose from my seat and turned to face the direction of Their Royal Highnesses. In the manner of the leading lady in a drama, I gave them my grandest, most sweeping curtsy.

That was the last moment I had to myself for a very long time. The court descended from all sides, all of them talking at once and vying to praise, flatter, and congratulate me. I would have been hard-pressed to draw breath if Matthew and Olivia hadn't remained staunchly at my side, helping deflect at least some of the crush. I did catch a glimpse of Molly Lepell between the shoulders of the assorted grandees. My friend saluted me with her fan, and I saw she stood not just with Mary Bellenden, but Mrs. Howard.

I did not see Sophy or Sebastian in the crowd, but it didn't matter. They didn't matter, not now. I was giddy with relief. I'd done it. I'd actually done it! So great was my sense of triumph that I didn't bat an eye when I turned to take another hand and found it belonged to Julius Sandford.

"May I congratulate you on a game well played, Miss Fitzroy?" Mr. Sandford bowed. "That final hand was . . . inspired."

I nodded in acknowledgment of the compliment.

"I don't have your contract with me, of course," he went on. "I'll see that it's sent around tomorrow."

"I would have thought that would be your father's chore." The crowd had at last begun to thin. As I quickly scanned the shifting knots of people, I saw that Lord Lynnfield was nowhere in evidence. Neither was Sebastian.

Disquiet tapped lightly against my thoughts.

Julius shrugged. "I can't see that it would matter to you. You've gotten what you want."

He gave me no time to reply, neither did he bow. He simply turned and shouldered his way through the silken crowd, heading for the door. Disquiet tapped again, demanding attention. But Olivia's presence was more forceful than my internal feeling.

"You were magnificent!" My cousin seized my hands and crowed, "Simply magnificent! Wasn't she, Matthew?"

"She always is," he answered. "But I'm glad it's over."

I wished I could lean against him and bury my face against his shoulder and in general fall to pieces from relief. As it was, I had to settle for the smallest of smiles and the lightest of whispers. "Oh, so am I."

"You wish it were over," muttered Olivia. "But the Sandfords are still what they are, and that Sophy Howe is still after you."

I waved her assessment away. "Mr. Walpole can deal with the Sandfords as he sees fit," I said. Mr. Walpole had been the recipient of several of my recent letters. "What's important now is that the contract is broken, no matter where the paper is."

Despite this, I knew Olivia was right. She only mistook which players still had to be met. *Your father will be coming for you soon, cousin,* I thought, *and I'm going to have to blackmail him to save you all. And Mr. Tinderflint will be back any day now, and I must deal with him, and bid any hope of finding my own wayward father farewell in the process.*

A wave of weariness tumbled over me, washing away my triumphs and threatening the last of my strength. But I called on my training and kept smiling.

Gradually, the bids for my notice faded away. Her Royal Highness declared she was tired, and we were all permitted to depart. I knew from the glances that Molly and Mary gave me that I would be called upon to give a full account of exactly what I'd done to secure so public and thrilling a victory. I wondered what I would tell them.

But that, like the rest of my worries, was a matter for later. For the present, I would walk Olivia and Matthew to the gate. Afterward, I would take myself to bed as soon as humanly possible.

We three crossed the Color Court, with Olivia on Matthew's left arm and me on his right. The night was chill and smelled heavily of frost and more rain. We had the place nearly to ourselves. The rest of the court had packed themselves up almost an hour ago. That suited me well enough. I was done with being witty. The night had left me drained and empty. I wanted to see my friends on their way and find my bed. I would sleep for a week, waiting or no waiting.

Matthew looked insufferably pleased with himself as he escorted the two of us silken belles under the great arch of the palace gatehouse. I pressed a little closer to him, taking shelter against the cold and against an uncomfortable certainty growing in the back of my mind.

"I've forgotten something," I murmured. "I'm sure of it."

Olivia yawned until her jaw cracked. "You'll think of it in the morning," she said.

We emerged from the archway onto the cobblestones of the Mall. Matthew faced me and lifted up both my hands.

"Besides, whatever it is, it will all come out right," he told me. "We've gotten this far. We'll see it through the rest of the way."

I lifted my face to his. I did not care if Olivia and all the world could see. I craved Matthew's kiss with all the fibers of my being, and I meant to have it here and now.

Then Olivia screamed.

I whirled around and stumbled as Matthew shoved me to one side. Shadows rose up, seeming to walk straight out of the brick walls. I could not see faces, but in the instant before they rushed us, I could see the cudgels.

Now I knew what was wrong. There were no yeomen at the gate. There should have been. They were gone, and there were only these ruffians.

Lord Lynnfield's ruffians.

Olivia screamed again, and I added a scream of my own as one man swung his staff out to catch Matthew's brow and snap his head back. I didn't even see him fall. Two of the toughs blocked my view. I had my straight pin in my hand, but the third man, the one I didn't see, was behind me, grabbing my arms. I kicked and I screamed and I couldn't see Olivia, and I was hoisted high and they were all laughing. I felt my foot connect hard with a chin.

I felt the blow on my own head.

After that, there was nothing. Nothing at all.

CHAPTER TWENTY-NINE

IN WHICH OUR HEROINE RELUCTANTLY
FORMS SEVERAL NEW ACQUAINTANCES.

It is known, of course, that young ladies of a Certain Temperament are prone to episodes of unconsciousness in the form of the Faint. I cast no judgment on them now, but I will say that the variety of unconsciousness caused by a state of mental agitation cannot possibly hurt as much as that caused by a well-placed blow to the head. If it did, those young ladies would work much harder to avoid it.

My whole skull hurt abominably. The pain pulsed in time with my frantic heartbeat. After the pain, the next thing I became aware of was a stink. It was thick and vivid and carried a taste like copper and rot, and I wanted very much to get away from it. This base desire lent mind and body enough strength to attempt a more complete resumption of consciousness. As my eyelids hesitantly pried themselves open, I found only darkness. For a panicked moment, I feared I'd been somehow struck blind.

The next thing I became aware of was that I was being discussed.

"Why the f—'d you even bring 'er!" croaked a man. His voice was high, sharp, and brittle. "She was supposed to be at the bottom of the river by now."

My tongue was so dry, it stuck to the roof of my mouth. That was probably for the best, because it prevented me from making any startled sound at this casual proposal to dispose of my life and person. I turned toward the brittle voice. Now I could see a dim and flickering light several yards away and somewhat above the level of my head. I further became aware that I was lying on my side on a hard surface. The splinters poking against my cheek led me to conclude it was a wooden floor.

"What? An' waste all them good pickin's?" another man was saying. In contrast to his companion, his voice was plump and round. It lingered lovingly over each word. "She's wear-ing a f—kin' fortune."

"So strip 'er before you dump 'er!" snapped the first man. This practical advice was followed by a convoluted and dis-paraging assessment of the intelligence, ancestry, and sexual predilections of his companion.

There are, I would venture, few things in this world that will clear the mind like hearing strange men discuss one's impending murder in vulgar language. I was suddenly wide awake, and though I still hurt worse than I ever had in my life, I no longer cared. Wherever I was, I had to get away. Now.

There were, however, some barriers to this excellent scheme. To begin with, my wrists were tied. The hemp rope chafed painfully against my skin. My arms had been pulled so tightly in front of me that my shoulders ached. My legs and ankles had been left free. If I could get to my feet, I could at least walk.

I tried to take stock of every part of me that hurt. The answer appeared to be all parts, but none worse than my raw throat and sore head. I took some comfort in this. I was also clothed. That, too, was encouraging. If I could get out of this place, I would still have the resources I carried with me.

The men kept on talking.

"Ah!" said the plump-voiced man with the air of someone knowing he's about to lay down his ace. "But to the right buyer, a pretty little bit like her'll bring in at least as much as that dress she's wearing. Waste not, want not, is what I say."

This philosophy did not seem to carry much weight with his shrill companion. "You 'ad one job—*one*—and you 'ad to go an' get greedy."

Fortunately, the high-voiced man's tendency to allow his discourse to slip into long strings of insult bought me time. I kept my eyes slitted and carefully pulled my hands back toward my belly.

"'E's right, you know," said a new voice, this one slower

and deeper than the others. "She could be worth a pretty penny, especially alive and in one piece." This third man drawled these last words in a way that turned my blood to water. "We'd be cutting you in for your bit, o' course, Mr. Pym," he added with a deference that to my ears sounded rather hollow.

Mr. Pym, the high-voiced man, did not seem impressed either. "Johnny Leroy, you can take all your bits and—"

I was not entirely sure what followed, but I believe it contained several anatomical references to either the speaker or his mother.

I tried to arch my back. It was difficult to decide whether I still wore my stomacher. I knew I didn't have my straight pin. My hand remembered the pain of that weapon being ripped away. But what of the other blade? The little hidden blade? That was the question now, and the only question that mattered.

My vision had cleared somewhat. I could now make out that the light came from a single flickering lantern set on a table. Two of the men sat on barrels beside that table. The third leaned against the wall with his arms folded and ankles crossed. The lantern did not give me much help in making out their features. All wore hats. The man against the wall had a beard. The man showing me his right profile was all sharp angles and jutting chin. The man showing me his left profile had a round belly beneath his smock shirt.

"The job was to get rid of the girl." The sharp, right-profile man—Mr. Pym, I assumed—stabbed a finger toward me as he climbed to his feet. I could now see he had a hunched back and a long neck. "When I get back, I want 'er gone, or it'll be your corpse in the f—in' river right alongside 'ers, get me?"

Crooked though he might be, Mr. Pym was a spry man. I heard his boots clatter briskly against the floorboards as he vanished from my field of view. I had by this time gotten my wrists up against my torso. I could feel the rough embroidery of my stomacher and dragged my arms to the right, trying to find the seam of the hidden pocket. I strained and I wriggled, but I couldn't twist my hands around far enough to get my fingers to my pocket. I bit my cheek to keep down a desperate and undignified whimper.

"An' so we've our marchin' orders, Johnny." The round-bellied man in the smock shirt leaned his elbows on the table. "You doin' the deed, or is those 'ands too lily white for it?"

"Shut it, 'Orace Clay, you stupid sod," said Johnny Leroy, entirely without rancor. He pushed himself away from the wall. "My question is, do you know anybody who'd buy such goods as we got to sell?"

"I might," said Clay noncommittally.

"Well, move your lazy carcass and go wake 'em up! If Pym comes back, I'll 'old him off. Then, when you come back, well, there's two of us and one of 'im, ain't there?"

The sheer force of this argument was enough to give Clay pause. I strained, I twisted. The ropes bit into my skin. My dry and aching throat closed around my breath. I cursed myself for not having concealed my second blade in my skirts, or my bosom—anywhere but at my waist, where I could not reach it, no matter how I tried.

"Pym's right about one thing," Clay said thoughtfully. "'Is Lordship won't like it."

Leroy circled the table, putting his back between me and Clay as he leaned forward and planted both hands on the table. I blessed his name and strained harder, twisting my hands in the other direction. My little finger found the slit of the hidden pocket, and I pressed it in hard. The tip brushed the warm, smooth surface of the blade.

"'Is Lordship wants 'er gone," Johnny Leroy was saying. "Well, she'll be just as gone in the colonies or the 'orehouses as dead in the river, won't she?"

I jammed my little finger farther into the pocket and managed to hook it around the blade's handle. I began wriggling and pulling, worrying the slip of metal out of its embroidered sheath. It moved out one fraction of an inch. All my focus was on that tiny, rough bit of metal held by my smallest finger. I strained and I prayed, and I pulled and I prayed.

"Whatcher gonna tell Pym?" asked Clay.

"You leave that to me. You want the money or what?"

Clay evidently lived up to his name, at least in terms of speed of thought, because this question seemed to set off another bout of pondering.

The blade slipped free, and I scrabbled to turn it flat against my palm. My wrists were thoroughly raw by now, and I suspected they were bleeding. I didn't care. My fingers were going numb, but I had sensation enough to tuck the blade into my sleeve. It was not much of a hiding place, but at least I could reach it more easily now. I didn't dare try to cut the rope yet. That would take time, and I had no idea when one of these two might take it into his head to check on me.

"All right." Clay heaved himself to his feet so that he could poke Johnny Leroy in the chest. "But if I find out you've plucked our little chicken before I get back, I'll be takin' my share out of your sorry 'ide. Get me?"

"Yeah, yeah, an' I'm shakin' in me boots," said Leroy amiably. "Now, get goin'!"

Clay aimed a cuff at Leroy's ears, which Leroy ducked easily. Then Clay stumped across the boards and disappeared, apparently sinking into the floor. I realized we must be in an attic, and Clay was headed down through a hatchway.

Now there was only me and Johnny Leroy. Leroy stayed standing, his back toward me, as if waiting for something. There was the sound of movement below. There were some shouts outside the window. I tried desperately to remember everything Monsieur Janvier had ever taught me about fighting and escaping, but for those lessons, I'd had my hands free. Panic threatened again, and I pushed it aside. My hands were tied, but my feet were not. I inched them up under my skirts. Maybe I had strength enough now to get to my feet. Maybe I could run. At the very least, I could kick.

Leroy had moved to the edge of the space lit by the smoky lantern. He squatted down. I heard wood slam against wood and the slight rattle that comes when a bolt is shot home. He'd locked us in together. Fear bit down hot and hard, and my fingers scrabbled for my blade. Leroy turned around. Our eyes met, and I understood my mistake. In my desperate bid to get hold of my only weapon, I'd forgotten I was supposed to be unconscious.

"Well, well. Thought you might be awake." He walked over to me. Like his friend Mr. Pym, Johnny Leroy moved more quickly than I expected, but he was lighter on his feet than the other two. Despite his thick boots, his feet made barely any sound.

"Let's 'ave a look at you, then." He squatted down in front of me.

I shrank back. I tried to do as I'd been taught—that is, stay calm and keep my eyes open, looking for my openings and opportunities. But all I saw was a hard man, much bigger than I was, and one with his hands free. His beard was long, dark, and tangled, as was the hair under his battered, slouch-ing hat. He smelled of cider, onions, dirt, and the river.

"And what's this, then?" He touched my sleeve, right on the spot where I'd concealed my blade. My mind went ter-ribly clear and perfectly empty at the same time. I was com-pletely aware of every detail of that moment and unaware of any single thing I could do about it. "Not quite without a claw or two, eh?" Leroy chuckled. "Smart girl. Let's get you out of this."

With that, he pulled a far more impressive knife from

his own belt and set it to my ropes. With a grunt and a sharp jerk, Johnny Leroy sliced my bonds in two.

All at once, I knew him. This was the driver—the one who'd sat atop Lord Lynnfield's great black coach and used a warning crack of his whip to save me from the attentions of his fellows. He was saving me again.

In answer to this sudden realization, I believe I croaked out my gratitude in a single, elegant syllable. "Wha . . . !"

"I didn't sign on to kill me any girls," Leroy said simply. "Come on. I can 'andle Clay, but Pym's smarter an' stronger than he looks, more's the pity. An' 'e won't stay gone forever."

Johnny Leroy stood and held out his hand. I stared at it. Then I took it. It was hard as tanned leather, and he pulled me to my feet as if I weighed nothing at all. Without waiting to see if I'd gotten my balance, Mr. Leroy moved over to the hatchway in his unsettling, light-footed fashion, grabbing the lantern off the table as he passed. I drew out my little blade and followed him.

He held up his hand, signaling for me to stop. I did, instantly. Mr. Leroy went down on one knee beside the hatch and listened. I held my breath and strained my ears, but I could barely hear past the roar of my own blood. Men's shouts rose up faintly, but they were not the watch. There was also a rhythmic clunk of wood bumping against wood. I couldn't identify what might make that particular sound, but felt I should have been able to.

Leroy nodded, then softly drew the bolt and lifted the hatch. He lowered the lantern ahead of him to scan the space below. Whatever he saw seemed to satisfy him, because he started down what proved to be a broad ladder.

I gritted my teeth, grabbed up my hems, and followed as best I could.

When I joined Mr. Leroy on the ground floor, he was holding the lantern low. It was somewhat brighter down here, because firelight filtered through narrow windows set high in the wooden walls. Massive pyramid piles of casks, sacks, and chests filled a wooden chamber that was easily as large as the princess's drawing room.

I realized we must be in a warehouse on one of the many Thames docks. That rhythmic wooden thumping I'd heard was boats bumping against piles, and one another. The pervasive stench that hit me when I first came to consciousness was the river itself.

"If I tell you we're at the 'Owland docks of Rotherhithe, does that mean anything to you?" my rescuer asked. I shook my head, and he cursed. "Too much to ask for. Well, it's a boat for us, then. I 'ope you don't turn seasick."

"Try me," I said.

"Stout lass," Mr. Leroy murmured, and the sheer warmth in those words struck me as hard as anything that had happened yet.

There were two ways out of the warehouse that I could see. One was a small door I assumed led to the streets. The other was a large opening, like the great doors of a barn, that looked over the glittering expanse of the river. This was where Mr. Leroy headed. I clutched my hems close and followed with small, dancing steps. I could not become winded. I could not trip or become tangled. We must be quick. We must get away. That was all that mattered now.

But from behind us came the thud of running feet and the clink and creak of metal. I didn't need the shove Johnny Leroy planted against my shoulder. I was already diving behind the nearest pyramid of barrels. Leroy himself wasn't fast enough, and as the small door to the street burst open, he whirled about to face the three silhouettes who all trooped in together.

"Well, now. What's this, Mr. Leroy, what's this?"

I stuffed my fist in my mouth. Lord Lynnfield strode smartly into the warehouse, with Pym and Clay at his side.

CHAPTER THIRTY

IN WHICH CERTAIN DISCOVERIES ARE MADE,

AND THERE IS A SHORT

BUT EVENTFUL BOAT RIDE.

I see you've taken to playing the cat, Mr. Leroy," wheezed Lord Lynnfield. "Why else would I find you hunting rats among my stores?"

I held my breath. My fingers curled around the thick ropes that bound the heavy barrels in their pyramid, seeking something, anything, to hold on to. The whole of my concentration was occupied with trying to make myself silent and very, very small.

"'Eard a noise," Johnny Leroy answered. I could only just see his back from around the edge of my barrel palisade. Light and shadows swung as he gestured with the hand that held the lantern. "Wanted to make sure it wasn't soldiers. That girl up there's not some poor street kit. She'll 'ave someone out looking for 'er."

"Very conscientious of you. Just how I like my men to think," said Lord Lynnfield. "I was concerned about that very possibility myself. So was Mr. Pym, especially once he found Clay here taking a bit of a stroll on the dock."

This was bad. This was very bad. I eased myself and my treacherous shimmery skirts back into the shadows. I tried to think what I could possibly do. I glanced in the other direction, toward the little door to the street that Lord Lynnfield and his men had entered. Yards of open floor stretched between me and it, as they did between me and the great door that opened onto the waters.

"Now, Mr. Pym told me that not only had you failed to kill the girl, but you'd authorized an entire new program of entertainments for her." I heard the thump of Lord Lynnfield's walking stick being planted on the floor.

A cold breeze touched my back, and I glanced quickly behind in case some new danger was creeping up. What I saw instead made me stare. It was a dark and jagged hole in the wall. This warehouse was little more than board and timber, and one of those boards had rotted away, leaving an irregular gap for the cold, foul wind off the river to worm its way through.

Could I get through there? Maybe, if I was quick, if I didn't care about scrapes and tears.

If I didn't care about leaving Mr. Leroy to Lord Lynnfield and his creatures.

I looked at the pile of great, strong barrels in front of me that rose two or three times my own height. I saw how they were lashed together with stout hemp rope. I felt the pain in my bleeding wrists, which had been so recently freed by Johnny Leroy. I thought how those men out there wanted me dead, or worse than dead.

"Clay, you go make sure our gel's still safe asleep," said Lord Lynnfield.

"Very good, your lordship." Clay touched a knuckle to his forehead and stumped past the shadowed place where I crouched. I pulled out my slender blade. I prayed that Monsieur Janvier had gotten value for his money, set the edge to the nearest rope, and began to saw. I bit my lips hard enough to add a fresh item to my collection of pains. The hemp was dry and stretched tight, and might as well have been iron under my tiny knife. In my mind, I cursed and cried and screamed. But my hands kept working.

Johnny Leroy was out of my field of view, but he must have done something, because Lord Lynnfield said, "Whatever you're thinking, Mr. Leroy, don't."

Without ceasing my frantic sawing, I risked another glance around the edge of the barrels. I couldn't see Mr. Leroy now, but I could see Lord Lynnfield, and his pistol. "You think I don't know how to deal with bastards like you?" his lordship growled. "Even if that damn girl is all safe and sound, I'll still be giving you a proper lashing. It'll teach the others not to play loosey-goosey with my property."

The barrel rope parted a fraction of an inch. I almost forgot myself and cried aloud for triumph. But the rope was thick as my thumb, and my knife was in no way meant for this work. If the blade bent, if it broke, I was not the only one done for. I twisted it, trying to dig deeper into the rope's fibers. I sawed harder. The rope parted just a little bit more.

"Well, then," drawled Johnny Leroy. 'Ow about I save your lordship the trouble? You're too late. She's already gone."

"'S the truth." Clay came stumping down the ladder. "She's gone."

I'd cut almost halfway through the rope. Tears streamed hot and silent down my cheeks. The wind at my back tormented me. *There's a way out*, said the cold crawling across my skin. *All you have to do is leave him here. Go. Get away.*

The news of my disappearance did not seem to be discommoding his lordship in the least. I began to understand where Julius Sandford got his sangfroid.

"I thought she might be." I saw Lord Lynnfield straighten his arm. The rope parted just a bit further. "But how far has she gone? That's the question. She's a girl alone, in a rich dress out on the docks. I don't think our gallant knight here let her go wandering about without escort. Have a look round the warehouse, Mr. Pym, while I deal with this one."

I heard the long, slow sound of a pistol being cocked. My time was up.

With every ounce of strength in me, I hurled myself against the nearest barrel.

I also screamed.

I heard cursing. There may have been an order. I do not know for sure. I was too busy slamming my shoulder against the barrels again. It hurt, and I screamed some more, and threw all my weight against the barrel one last time.

The rope snapped. Someone shouted. The whole mountain of barrels thundered down like the wrath of God remade in wood and iron.

Men bellowed and cursed and scrambled away from the rolling, thundering mass. Clay wasn't fast enough. A barrel caught him hard at the knees and he went down, screaming. Another smashed against the wall and burst its staves, spilling a pale avalanche of grain across the floor. Lord Lynnfield I couldn't see. I was too busy pressing myself against the wall to avoid the tumult I'd set off, while still trying to scramble toward the door. Johnny Leroy leapt sideways, dragging Mr. Pym with him. They both fetched up against the wall, and Mr. Leroy dealt Pym a hard, precise blow to the head.

Clay was still screaming. I still couldn't see Lord Lynnfield. The barrels had mostly come to rest. I grabbed up my skirts in one hand and my tiny, blessed, wonderful knife in the other. I meant to run straight for the door, but a flash caught my eye and I skidded to a halt. Because in the middle of all that spilled grain, something metallic sparkled in the lantern light.

I turned, and I stared, and I stooped.

"Come on, girl!" shouted Mr. Leroy, who had, most sensibly, *not* stopped running for the door.

But with my shaking hand I plucked a silver coin out of the grain.

"Oatmeal," I said to Mr. Leroy, holding the coin up for

him to see. "He was supposed to find seven thousand pounds of oatmeal. Silver will flow into the coffers of the north."

"God's lousy beard, Peggy! Now's not the time!" Mr. Leroy changed direction and grabbed my wrist. My whole arm burned like fire as he jerked me into a run.

He'd also called me Peggy. He knew my familiar name. How did this man know my name?

Before I could further contemplate this tantalizing question, he'd pulled me into the street. I opened my mouth to ask where we were going. But I never did.

There was a flash of white fire and an explosion, quite loud and quite close. Something slammed into my stomach. I fell on my back with a scream. My head banged hard against the muddy ground, and I saw stars.

"PEGGY!" roared Mr. Leroy.

The next thing I knew, Johnny Leroy had caught me up in his arms. Still roaring, he bolted forward at a mad run, jolting and jarring me with every step. I couldn't breathe. I hurt, right in the middle of my ribs. I couldn't see anything but a blur of motion. I was dropped on my back again, and this time I landed with a splash. The world rocked hard, and the pain all but blinded me.

The world was moving again. I struggled to find some way past my pain, my lack of breath, and my more than usually confining stays in order to sit up. In this, I failed. My head spun badly as I collapsed back down into the water, but at least I now understood I was on a boat. Specifically, I was on my back in the bilge at the bottom of a rowboat. Mr. Leroy had hold of one of the oars and was using it to shove us away from the dock. Men were shouting. Mr. Leroy was cursing. I was cold and sopping wet.

The current caught us. The tide must have been on the turn, because the boat bounced up and smacked down hard as it lurched forward. There was another flash and another explosion, and I screamed and covered my head.

"Hold still!" Mr. Leroy crouched beside me. "God curse me. God forgive me. Say something, Peg! Where are you hurt?"

Johnny Leroy's voice had changed. The edge was gone from it. He had acquired a batch of *h*'s from somewhere, and even knew how to use them properly. He was also pawing me about the waist.

"What . . . what . . ." I gasped.

"You've been shot," he said. "But I can't see the blood. Christ and God and Devil take it! Why can't I see the blood!"

I laid my hand down against my stomacher, where he was groping. There was a hole there, right above the place the pain burned most strongly. Several points became perfectly clear, and I began to laugh. My rescuer jerked backwards. But my hand scrabbled at the hole and the pain underneath it.

Then I plucked the lead ball from where it had lodged against my corset stay and held it up for Mr. Leroy to see.

Johnny Leroy fell back onto his rump in the bilge, causing

the boat to rock sharply, and buried his head in his hands. "Christ. Christ, I thought . . ." He stopped. "Never mind that. Can you breathe? Can you see right?"

"Enough." This time I was able to push myself upright, shedding a quantity of stinking water as I did.

"Then keep down! We'll have trouble enough soon." Evidently forgetting he'd feared for my life a moment before, Mr. Leroy clambered past me to take the rower's bench in the middle of our tiny boat and seize both oars.

The sky had cleared, and the moon was out. The cold wind bit hard against all my pains and bruises. I could just make out the hulking shadows of London and Westminster that lined the banks. Larger boats with brightly shining lanterns passed us, all unconcerned as Johnny Leroy struggled to get ahead of the current so the rocking boat could be steered.

None of this mattered as I crept, shaking, into the stern. What mattered was the long, low boat gaining on us from the port side. A crooked silhouette stood in its bows and raised a lantern high. It was Lord Lynnfield. I was sure of it.

So, apparently, was Mr. Leroy. "What're they doing?" he cried.

"He's put the lantern down," I reported. "He . . ." He'd grabbed up something, and at first I couldn't tell what he'd done. Then, as he whirled the rope over his head, I did see. "He's got a hook!" He meant to grapple our boat, like a pirate on the high seas. I hoped I'd live long enough to tell Olivia this one.

"Get down!" cried Mr. Leroy. This time I obeyed,

throwing myself flat in the stern among the miscellaneous ropes and gear. My hand landed on a long pole meant for fishing. Lord Lynnfield let the rope with its grappling hook fly toward us. I rolled onto my back, swinging my pole up high, hard, and badly. The hook smacked against it and ripped the staff from my hands. The boat rocked again, and hook and pole together splashed into the rushing river. Thames water erupted over the gunwales. My skirts were soaked, and I couldn't breathe around my corsets. Lord Lynnfield was coiling his rope in fast. He'd try again, and I was out of countermeasures.

Mr. Leroy was cursing hard and throwing all his strength against the oars, trying for speed and distance. Lord Lynnfield had the hook in his hands again. But then something caught his eye, and he froze in the act of swinging the rope. I twisted to look, my heart in my mouth, hoping for rescue.

But it wasn't any form of rescue that rushed toward us as fast as the Thames current and strong oars could move. It was the great mass of London Bridge. The roaring I heard this time was not the blood in my ears. It was the thunder of the Thames boiling and crashing through the bridge's stone arches.

I'd heard about those arches. Certain young bloods thought it a great game to try to ride the roiling waters and shoot their boats through the narrow passages. They died with disconcerting frequency.

And Johnny Leroy was rowing straight toward those same arches.

"Turn!" I screamed. "We'll hit!"

"Not yet!" he cried, and I swear upon my life, I heard a note of exhilaration beneath his fury. "The bastards won't follow!"

But the bastards apparently would. Lord Lynnfield had turned to yell at his oarsmen. He swung the rope again and let his grappling hook fly. It hit our boat with a resounding THUNK! I scrabbled with both hands, but the hook had already bitten into the wood: Lord Lynnfield and one of his roughs hauled hand-over-hand on the rope to pull us toward them.

"Fools!" hollered Mr. Leroy. "Cut the line! You'll kill us all!"

The boats were dipping and rocking wildly. Waves splashed over the gunwales, and there was no way to tell whether they were getting higher or our boat was riding lower, but the water was up around my ankles and my hems were swimming. The roaring was louder, and Lord Lynnfield and his toughs were heaving on the rope.

"Peggy, get my knife!"

Scrabbling at the trouser belt of a strange man is never a pleasant activity, but needs must when the devil drives, and I soon had a long, blessedly stout knife in my hands. I stabbed ineffectually at the sodden rope that tied us to Lord Lynnfield's boat, gasping out my own curses. The ruffians hauled. The boat bobbed and tipped. The gunwale went under the Thames, came up, and went down again. Kneeling, the water halfway up my thighs, I hacked desperately at this new rope. We were sinking. Only a few feet separated us from Lord Lynnfield's boat. The river tossed us harder.

I hated ropes. All of them. I would order them banned as soon as I could have a word with Her Royal Highness. Except I'd never have a word with her. We were going to drown. We were going to die.

"Duck!" bellowed Mr. Leroy.

I ducked. The boat listed sideways and something heavy whistled over my head, followed by a shout and the crunch of bone being shattered. I got my face up just in time to see Lord Lynnfield topple into the rushing river and disappear. For a single moment, Mr. Leroy towered over me, one oar hefted in both hands.

In the next heartbeat, he charged, and I ducked again, all the way under the water. The boat rocked, listed, and righted only reluctantly. I couldn't hold my breath anymore, and I shot up, gasping and shoving the filthy stinging water from my eyes.

Mr. Leroy was in the other boat, wrestling with whoever still manned it. The current had us all now, and we pitched and rolled, helplessly tangled together by the grappling rope. I clung to the gunwales, struggling to find a way to clamber across to where the men fought in that other rocking, sinking boat, seemingly oblivious to the oncoming bridge, only seeking to throw each other into the maelstrom and be the last standing.

I grabbed hold of the grappling hook where it dug into our stern and heaved with what remained of my strength. It came free with a sodden splintering of wood. I'd just torn a hole in the boat and did not care. I reached out with that rough iron hook to the other craft, crying and praying to God, who surely could not hear over the roar of the waters. I reached to the ends of my strength and fingertips, but at last caught the gunwale of Lord Lynnfield's boat. The hook's tip bit into the bow, and it held. I wrapped both numb hands around the shaft, and I hauled myself over the rail.

I couldn't have done it without my corset. That hated cage shielded my body as I dragged myself—chest, belly, leaden skirts, bruised feet—into that other boat. I tumbled into the new bilge, limp, cold, without strength, and halfway convinced I had already died. Overhead, the men were cursing and swearing. One fell to his knees. The other hefted an oar. I could not tell one from the other. A wave splashed over the gunwale, and I coughed and cried out, evidently not yet dead after all. The boat listed to port, then starboard, and I curled in on myself as far as my stays would allow. Then I heard Mr. Leroy holler, and my head jerked up. Pym was bearing Mr. Leroy back, down toward the Thames's raging waters. Any minute now, Johnny Leroy would slip, he would fall, he would be gone.

I screamed with what felt like it must be my last breath. I grabbed Pym's boot and I twisted and I heaved.

As he fell into the boiling Thames, I dizzily thought how proud Monsieur Janvier would be.

Mr. Leroy was on his knees in the water beside me, gathering me to him. "I'm sorry, Peg," he gasped.

I made no answer. I am ashamed to say, I cowered against him.

In the next heartbeat, we were at the bridge. The bows slammed against a wall of water, and our boat tipped up, and the waves came down, and the force of it all washed away the remainder of the world, and it seemed there was nothing to be done at all.

Except drown.

CHAPTER THIRTY-ONE

IN WHICH THERE PROVE TO BE MULTIPLE
ENDINGS, PLUS ONE BEGINNING.

My assessment that there was nothing left to do
was made under great duress. Like most such assessments, it
eventually proved incorrect.

Across an unknown space of time, I found there were
several items left to be accomplished. There was a significant
amount of pain to be felt, along with cold like the end of the
world. There was a buffeting from all directions to be with-
stood, and the memory of a pair of arms strong as bronze and
leather holding on to me.

This was followed by a space of darkness when I sincerely believed that not breathing was the most peaceful feeling in the world and that I should never bother with such
nonsense again. It is entirely possible that if I had not seen

my old nightmare ghost waiting for me at the end of that darkness, I might have given up my own.

Then the air hit with all the force of a storm wind, and I was gasping and crying and vomiting up Thames water onto an expanse of stinking mud. I will never in my life forget the indescribably foul taste.

But I was alive. Each painful breath against what felt like a great, granite stone under my chest told me I was alive, as did my corset stays, which seemed to have become deformed and were digging into my aching ribs.

But I was alive.

I rolled onto my back and stared at the sky for a time, doing nothing but breathing. It was cold—colder than I have ever been and it is to be hoped colder than I ever will be again. The first gray hints of dawn glimmered above the great sleeping bulk of London town. Despite cold and pain, I laughed for the delight and wonder of it all.

There was a groan beside me. Johnny Leroy rolled weakly onto his side. He was black with mud and Thames water, but his eyes opened, and they were clear and focused as he looked at me.

"Stout lass," he croaked, and coughed. I suspect that had there not been so much waterlogged beard concealing it, I might have seen a smile. "Stout lass, Peggy."

"Why?" My throat was so dreadfully raw, even that one word hurt, but I couldn't remain silent. "Why did you . . ."

He did not speak in reply. He just fumbled at his shirt

collar until his trembling fingers got hold of a chain and pulled it out. On the chain hung a ring. How the bauble had stayed about his neck, I will never know. I could barely feel my own fingers, but I lifted that ring to my eyes.

It was a signet ring. The gold surface was carved with two letters, twinned tightly together: J and E. My heart stopped. Because I knew this ring. I had played with it as a child.

This man—this wild-haired, greasy ruffian turned river pirate, lying in the mud, perhaps coughing his last breath away—this was my father, Jonathan Fitzroy. That was why he called me Peggy. That was why when he grew so agitated, his voice and diction changed. That was why he had risked himself to save me not once, but over and again.

I thought about him being in the warehouse owned by my uncle and the Jacobite Lord Lynnfield, with a load of silver coin hidden in barrels of oatmeal. I thought how Mr. Tinderflint wrote me that the jewel he sought had been sent from Paris overseas.

My father was a spy, and the natural haunt of a spy was a nest of Jacobites and traitors, of course, and the nearest destination overseas from Paris was England's own shore.

I thought of impossibilities and coincidences, and why had no one told me? But this made my head hurt even worse, so I tried not to think about it anymore. There did remain the question of what I should say now. How did a fond and tender maiden properly greet her father upon his grand reentrance into her life?

"I promised myself I'd slap your face if ever I found you."

My father received these words of esteem and affection with a grave demeanor. "I'll endeavor to stay alive long enough to give you the chance."

"Mother is dead," I told him.

"Yes, I know." He spoke these words so softly, I could barely distinguish them from the lapping of the Thames nearby.

"I was eight. They sent me to live with Uncle Pierpont."

"I do know, Peggy, and I'm sorry."

"But you didn't come back."

"I'm here now." He gestured weakly. "Such as I am."

It was a statement I could not argue with. I had, however, a thousand other things I intended to say to this man, a thousand questions to ask him, and a thousand curses to level against him. I wanted to yell and cry and explain to him in exacting detail what his absence had cost me and my mother. But I had no strength, and in the end, I just lay there and stared at the signet ring.

Slowly, my father, Jonathan Fitzroy, sat up. He took the ring from me and tucked it back beneath his shirt.

"We need to go, Peggy." He looked behind us. "There'll be those combing the docks who would be glad to find such fresh pickings as you and I."

This sober and believable statement rallied my spirits enough that I found myself able to sit up, broken stays and all.

"We are not done," I told him.

"I hope that's true." My father took hold of my forearms and heaved me once more to my feet.

My readers will, I hope, forgive me if I pass lightly over what followed—how, shivering and mud coated, we stumbled through the meanest, filthiest streets London had to offer. How we fetched up in one blind court after another, trying to find our way. How a gang of drunks almost dragged me from my father's side, on the assumption I must be a whore. How we discovered that I still had one gold pin tangled in my hair, and with that treasure clutched in my fingertips, we all but toppled into a tavern that smelled roughly as foul as the Thames. How it was my begging and my father's threatening that got the tavern keeper to send a boy running with a message to Great Queen Street.

That was my choice. Wherever in the depths of London we might be, Matthew was still my closest and surest friend. Also, I wanted him to know I was alive. More than that, though, I wanted to know *he* was alive. I wanted above all things to fall into Matthew's arms and know that I had not escaped a river a thousand times worse than the Styx only to find myself alone in the world.

I could barely stand to think what might have happened to Olivia.

After the boy took to his heels, there was only waiting. We did this slumped on the bench before the fire. Eventually, it occurred to the tavern keeper that there was something out of the ordinary wrong with us. With a grunt, he stuffed wooden mugs of a hot, strong drink I could not even begin to identify into our hands. I drank this murky, anonymous beverage as quickly as I could swallow it, grateful beyond measure for the warmth and the taste of something besides Thames in my mouth.

I cannot say for certain if I slept, but time did seem to proceed in fits and starts. Despite this, when the battered coach came lurching over the rutted dirt street, I came instantly and fully awake. In fact, I was on my feet and halfway out the door without memory of how I got there.

But it was not Matthew who leapt down from the postilion's perch. It was his friends from the academy, Heathe and Torrent, and both of them reeled back as I ran to them.

"Where is he!" I shouted. "Where's Matthew! Where's Olivia!"

"My God, Miss Fitzroy!" cried Heathe, covering mouth and nose with one great ham-hand. "It is you! The world's been searching for you! Soldiers in the streets and all of it! There's a reward."

"And you can claim it if you live long enough!" I told him. "Where're Matthew and Olivia!"

"Miss Pierpont's at Leicester House writing advertisements and offering more rewards. Matthew's abed with a broken skull and a foul temper. We didn't dare tell him about your message for fear he'd try to get up—"

"Take me to him! Now! No! Wait!" I staggered back into the tavern and shook my dozing father. "We're leaving."

"I can't be seen at the palace," he said groggily.

"Good, because we are not going there." I tossed my gold pin to the tavern keeper and hurried out, leaving it to my father to decide whether he would follow.

I will say this for the students of art. They are an easy-going lot, and those vibrant imaginations let them accept all manner of possibilities that would drive the strongest man of the court to distraction. As my wild man of a parent followed me out, Heathe and Torrent initially attempted to spring to my defense. But as soon as I told them to never mind him, they shrugged and did not mind. There may have been some extra odd glances shot between them, but for this, I cannot blame them.

The ride that followed was long. The poorly sprung coach pitched and rolled as badly as our boat had when caught in the flood of the Thames. All my bruises and pains were doubled and tripled with each rattle and jounce as we crawled through the warren of narrow streets and alleys. But eventually, we did reach Great Queen Street and the academy. This time I made no protest at being led in the back way. Neither did I refuse the arm Heathe offered to help me up the stairs to the low, dim dormitory room where Matthew lay in bed.

He was pale as the sheet that covered him and with a bandage around his skull. My knees gave way. It was fortunate Heathe had shoved a stool underneath me.

"Matthew." I laid my filth-encrusted hand over his pale one.

His eyes flew open.

"Oh, lord, don't look at me," I said. "I'm a horror."

"You're here," he said. "You're alive."

Without ceremony, Matthew pulled me down to him and kissed me. If I had not loved this man before, in that moment, I loved him more than life itself.

Shortly after this reunion, the entire school moved itself to his—our—assistance. I remain uncertain whether this was a measure of the esteem in which Matthew Reade was held or a measure of the artistic love for drama of all sorts. Water was heated, and screens were raised around great copper kettles that could be used as hip baths. The models who let themselves be drawn from life proved kind and practical women. They lent me enough articles of clothing—a shift, a plain woolen dress, stockings, slippers, a cap—to make me minimally decent. A collection was taken up so that bread, cheese, mutton, and pease pottage could be procured from the public house in the next street. A maid was persuaded to give up her room for at least a few hours so that I could sleep, although I left Matthew's side only when he told me that my presence was interfering with his own ability to rest.

That I slept like the dead goes without saying.

When I woke, it was to darkness, panic, and no memory of how I came to be in this room. Then I saw the candle burning on its pewter dish and Matthew sprawled in the battered chair at my bedside. His bandaged head lolled back, and a snore of remarkable length and volume rumbled from his open mouth.

I smiled and turned over and went back to sleep.

When I woke the second time, it was to the press of a callused hand holding mine. I opened my eyes to see Matthew smiling softly down at me.

I think I meant to speak his name, but I had no chance, for he was kissing me with infinite gentleness. All memory of pain and fear and fury fled as I gave myself over to this moment and the simple, joyful act of kissing my paramour. It was not until we parted that I realized there were voices in the room. Over the curve of Matthew's shoulder, I saw my father standing in the corner, talking softly.

The person he was talking to, as it happened, was Mr. Tinderflint.

I'm afraid the next words that came out of my mouth would have done Mr. Pym proud.

"Rest easy, Peggy Mostly," said Matthew as he gripped my shoulders. I was attempting to kick back the covers and scramble to my feet. "Easy!"

"I am not a horse, and you will let go of me, Mr. Reade!" I snapped or, rather, croaked. My throat still seemed to be suffering from its prolonged contact with the Thames. Regardless, I had no intention of telling my patron what I thought of him and all his doings while flat on my back like an invalid. I was going to look him right in his watery eyes.

This mildly admonishing discourse caught the attention of both men, and they turned toward me.

"It's all right, Peg," said my father.

"Why on earth should I listen to you, sirrah!" I swatted at Matthew's hands, but he didn't let go. I was forced to remain in the bed unless I wished to apply some of Monsieur Janvier's teachings, which, I will say, was not entirely out of the question. Matthew did at least permit me to sit up.

"You're a lying blackguard, and you're standing there talking with another!"

My father sighed and cast a sidelong glance at Mr. Tinderflint. "She has a point."

"You will find, my friend, that she generally does, and a good one at that. A very good one."

"Just like her mother."

Mr. Tinderflint nodded until all his chins flopped.

I looked at Matthew. "Let go of me," I ordered. "I'm going to murder them both."

"No, you're not," Matthew answered with infuriating calm. "You're going to trust me when I say that if murder were called for, I would have already done it."

I had no immediate answer for that.

"My dear—" began Mr. Tinderflint.

"Don't you *dare!*" I cut him off. "You've done nothing but lie to me! You ruined my uncle once before. You put me up to this business of maid of honor and spy and the rest of it to ruin him again, *and* my cousin! You led me on with all those stories about my mother, and you knew all the time where my father was, and you have the gall to call me "dear"! And you!" I turned to my father. "You let him! You let him! I could have died right along with Mother for all you cared!"

"You know that's not true," said my father.

I fell back against the pillows and folded my arms tight across my chest. My cheeks were hot, and my eyes burned, but no tears fell. Matthew squeezed my shoulder. He said nothing, only made sure I knew he was there.

"Mr. Reade, if you would give us a moment?" inquired Mr. Tinderflint.

"No," said Matthew.

Mr. Tinderflint looked at my father. "Let him stay," said Father.

Mr. Tinderflint shrugged. "Very well." Someone had moved a battered wingback chair into the room, and Mr. Tinderflint lowered himself into it. "Now, Peggy, I'll tell you. Yes, I will."

I did my utmost to make sure he saw that this story had better be a good one. I was gratified to see him blanch, just a little. A thorough rinse in the Thames evidently did wonders for a person's powers of glaring.

"Our late Queen Anne's death was a slow, sad time coming," said Mr. Tinderflint. "There was, as you must understand, a great deal of jockeying for position and power while it was happening. There was also much going back and forth over whether Hanover or Stuart would take the throne. The power games were deep and complex. They played out for money and patriotism and religion and a thousand other reasons. Then, as now, some plots were true threats to the nation and the throne, some were nothing but air and the dreams of drunken men.

"Those of us who were ready to declare for Hanover knew it would be vital to tell the difference between the two. We had to put in place our best men to learn the differences and report back. One of these men was your father, Mr. Jonathan Fitzroy."

"Johnny Leroy," I said. Father bowed his head in acknowledgment. His hair had been combed and pulled back into a respectable queue. His beard was also trimmed, and he now wore it in a neat point that made him look worldly, French, or devilish. Possibly all three. I turned my eyes away.

"Your mother stayed behind, of course," Mr. Tinderflint went on. "To look after you and to do what she could for our cause in the drawing rooms of London. It was a great shock to us all when she died."

"I thought I'd die myself when I got the news," Father said softly.

"Die, but not come back," I reminded him.

"I couldn't, Peggy." His eyes pleaded with me to understand. Unfortunately for him, I felt my sympathies had been much overtaxed of late.

"Are you going to blame duty or loyalty?"

To my surprise, a small smile formed on my father's face. "Actually, I'm going to blame old Louis XIV. He had me in the Bastille at the time."

"Which was where I had initially sought him," said Mr. Tinderflint. "I was somewhat surprised to find my information rather dated."

"Not by as much as I would have liked. I was five years getting out," Father said. "And no, Peg, the process is not something I care to share with you. But by the time I made my way back to the Royal Embassy in Paris, there was a new crisis, and a serious one. Some of the lords in the southeast of England were making a determined play to get money to the Scots rebels. Someone had to go in and find out how this was being done. I received my orders, and I went.

"My only defense, Peggy, is that I thought you were safe. I never, ever thought for a moment that your uncle would risk his neck and his family by getting involved with the Jacobites again."

"Maybe he couldn't make his fortune any other way," said Matthew. "Who would deal with a ruined man but other men risking ruin?"

Mr. Tinderflint looked startled. "That might be true, Mr. Reade. It very well might."

"So Uncle Pierpont really was funneling money to the Jacobites?" Olivia would be pleased. Olivia would be shattered.

"And taking a healthy percentage of every exchange for

himself," said my father. "It worked well, until the Sandfords and the baron came into it. Lord Lynnfield, it seemed, had his own ideas about how things should be run and was ruthless enough to enforce them."

I did not want to think about Lord Lynnfield. I did not want to hear the scream and the splash of his dying. I did not want to think there might be two ghosts coming around the next time I closed my eyes. Three, for there was Mr. Pym as well.

"Was it money that Uncle Pierpont and Mother quarreled about all those years ago?" I asked.

"No," said Mr. Tinderflint. "They quarreled because she tried to warn him that he was suspected of moving moneys about for the conspirators in the earlier uprising. One of the earlier uprisings, I suppose I should say. For his part, Sir Oliver thought a sister should shield her brother, no matter what, and blamed her for setting the interests of the Crown over those of family." Mr. Tinderflint leaned forward. "Peggy, I did not know where your father was when I came to you. I did not even know for certain if he still lived. I sought you out because I had a great need and I hoped to find your mother's spark and talent in you."

"And that you surely did, sir," said Father.

"Oh, yes. I did indeed."

I took my aching head in both hands and pushed my hair back from my face. What was I to say? What was I to think? I looked at the two men, the lean and the plump, the plain and the glittering. I wanted to hate them. I wanted to love them. I wanted to trust them, and I wanted to throw them out of my room and never see either of them again. In truth, I wanted too many things to be encompassed by my poor wounded heart.

"Why did the Sandfords insist on my being married into their family?" I asked.

"That is not yet entirely clear. My best guess is that they wanted a hostage." Mr. Tinderflint said this with remarkable calm. "Unlike my poor self, they seem to have known that Fitzroy was active and in pursuit of their confederates. If you, Peggy, were in their house, they would have a final ace to play should he turn up." Mr. Tinderflint paused. "Speaking of cards and turning up aces, I heard about your little game with Mr. Julius Sandford. Remarkable. Wholly and entirely remarkable."

Against all judgment and good sense, his praise sent a flicker of warmth through me.

"So all that business with the sugar plantations being lost, what was that?" asked Matthew. "A distraction?"

"Yes, to cover the whole family's return to England and their entrenchment in their home county," said Father.

Mr. Tinderflint favored Matthew with his most careful look of appraisal. I found I did not like this at all. I did not want Matthew to come to Mr. Tinderflint's attention. Those of us who did tended to fare rather badly.

"The Swedish ambassador, Gyllenborg, had been reaching out to the Jacobites. King Charles XII of that nation is in need of money to fund his own wars, and, incidentally, to keep Hanover and Hanover's allies in check. King Charles knew the Jacobites would pay for arms."

"So it was silver to the Swedes, arms to the Scots, death to George, and long live King James III," my father finished for him.

"What will happen to Uncle Pierpont?" I asked.

My father was silent for a moment. "It's already happened, I'm afraid. He's dead."

"Dead?" I echoed. The word made no sense. How could Uncle Pierpont be dead?

"There was a fire," said my father gravely. "It began, they think, in his book room."

A fire. In the book room, with all that paper. All that incriminating paper, which could, I now knew, prove him to be a traitor. Fragile, flammable paper that could send him to the tower and his widow and orphan daughter to the streets. I pictured him in the darkened room with a single candle in his hand, making up his mind. Hadn't I stood in that room myself and thought of burning? No one was going to say the words, I knew that. They didn't have to. I could see him carefully and methodically locking the door and then setting the candle's flame against one pile of paper after another.

A tear trickled cold and slow down my cheek. "And Olivia?"

"With her mother at Leicester House," said Mr. Tinderflint. "They are in the very capable hands of Molly Lepell and

Mrs. Howard until you can return to them. There will be scandal, and grieving, but that is all."

Because my cold, unerringly practical, hardhearted uncle had done the last service he could for his only surviving child and destroyed the evidence. All of it.

"What of the Sandfords?" asked Matthew. I suspected he did this so I would not have to.

Mr. Tinderflint gave a gusty sigh. "Mr. Julius Sandford is now, technically and possibly temporarily, Baron of Lynnfield. He is at this moment speaking with certain ministers and other important personages about this scheme of silver, arms, and oatmeal. In some ways, he is most fortunate indeed."

"In what ways?"

My patron's expression was a wry one. "His father is dead and so may easily be blamed for a great many things. And since this whole enterprise looks to have been the king of Sweden making a deliberate move against the king of Greater Britain, the new Lord Lynnfield becomes a very small fish indeed. If he tells enough truths, and swears to enough ignorance, he himself may be let off with his title and lands intact."

"He knew all of it, from beginning to end," I said. "I would swear on the Bible to that."

"As would I," replied my father. "Unfortunately, I cannot prove it, and Mr. Julius—the new Lord Lynnfield, I suppose we must say—is making a great show of surprise and sincerity. He was, after all, in Barbados while the foundations of the scheme were being laid."

"And he's a peer of the realm," added Matthew. "The rules are different for them."

"But surely they'll listen to what you say about the brothers," I protested to Mr. Tinderflint. "You're Earl Tierney, after all."

My patron bowed. "Unfortunately, I am Earl Tierney who is not at all trusted." He smiled modestly at my expression. "No, Peggy, it is not just you. I have made myself the object of suspicion in a great many circles."

"You sound almost proud of that," I said. "What of Sebastian?"

My father shook his head. "Unless he is willing to bear tales against his elder brother, no one particularly cares what becomes of the younger Mr. Sandford."

"I'd be surprised if Sophy Howe wasn't trying to talk him into doing just that," I muttered. "She'd like a collaborator with a title and some money."

"Ah! That reminds me. It reminds me." Mr. Tinderflint patted his coat pockets. "A note for you, Peggy."

He handed the letter across to me. For a single alarmed moment, I thought it must be from Sophy. But then I saw the seal and realized it was much worse. It was from Her Royal Highness.

Matthew squeezed my shoulder again as I broke the seal.

Miss Fitzroy (I read): *I look forward to your returning safe and resuming your position. At that point, I shall expect a full account of your most recent adventures.*

All the breath rushed out of me, pushed by the force of my relief. But on the heels of this came the question. Did I wish to return? To return would be to plunge myself right back into those same intrigues that had come so close to killing me, not once but twice.

I looked up mutely at Matthew. He read the question in me, and I watched a wish pass behind his eyes. He wished I would refuse, that I would answer this note by tendering my resignation and retiring to some country spot.

"It's up to you," he said. "I am with you, no matter what."

I thought of the princess. I thought of Olivia. I thought of barrels of silver and oatmeal and yet another scheme to bring down a war upon us. Did I care whether Stuart or Hanover held the throne? I liked my mistress, and her daughters, and even the puppies. I suspected I was a fair way to being charmed by the prince. Did they hold the throne by right, though? How was I to tell?

What I could tell was that I did not want war. I did not want to play into the hands of men—like the Sandfords, like my uncle—who would use rebellion to line their own pockets and increase their own power. And it happened I was in a position to do something about this.

That notion, I found I liked very much.

"I'll go back," I announced. "After all, I have family to care for now. Olivia and Aunt Pierpont need me."

I said this directly to my father. I waited for him to bluster and insist he would and could care for us all. He did neither of these things. Instead, he just turned to Mr. Tinderflint and Matthew. "May I have a moment with my daughter?"

Both these worthies looked to me, and I nodded, although seeing Mr. Tinderflint patting Matthew on the back as they left the room awoke fresh qualms in me.

The door closed, and I was once more alone with my father. I might be rather cleaner and more comfortable this time, but I was only a little less confused.

"The next months will be difficult, Peggy," he told me. "I cannot say for certain what will happen or how it will end. I ask only one question of you." He paused, and I think we both were waiting to see what he decided to say. "Do you think you might be able to forgive me?"

I looked at him, my hated, beloved, long-absent father. This was the man I had blamed for ruining my life, and who had so recently returned to save it. I thought on all I had been through, and all that was yet to come that I could not see. There would be Olivia's troubles added to mine now. And mine already included small details, like the fact that Sophy and Sebastian were still at St. James's Palace and that Julius Sandford might very well escape punishment. All of this had been set in motion by the choices this man had made — he and my mother together.

"I don't know if I can forgive," I said. Then I reached out and took his hard, stained hand. "But I know . . . I would like to try."